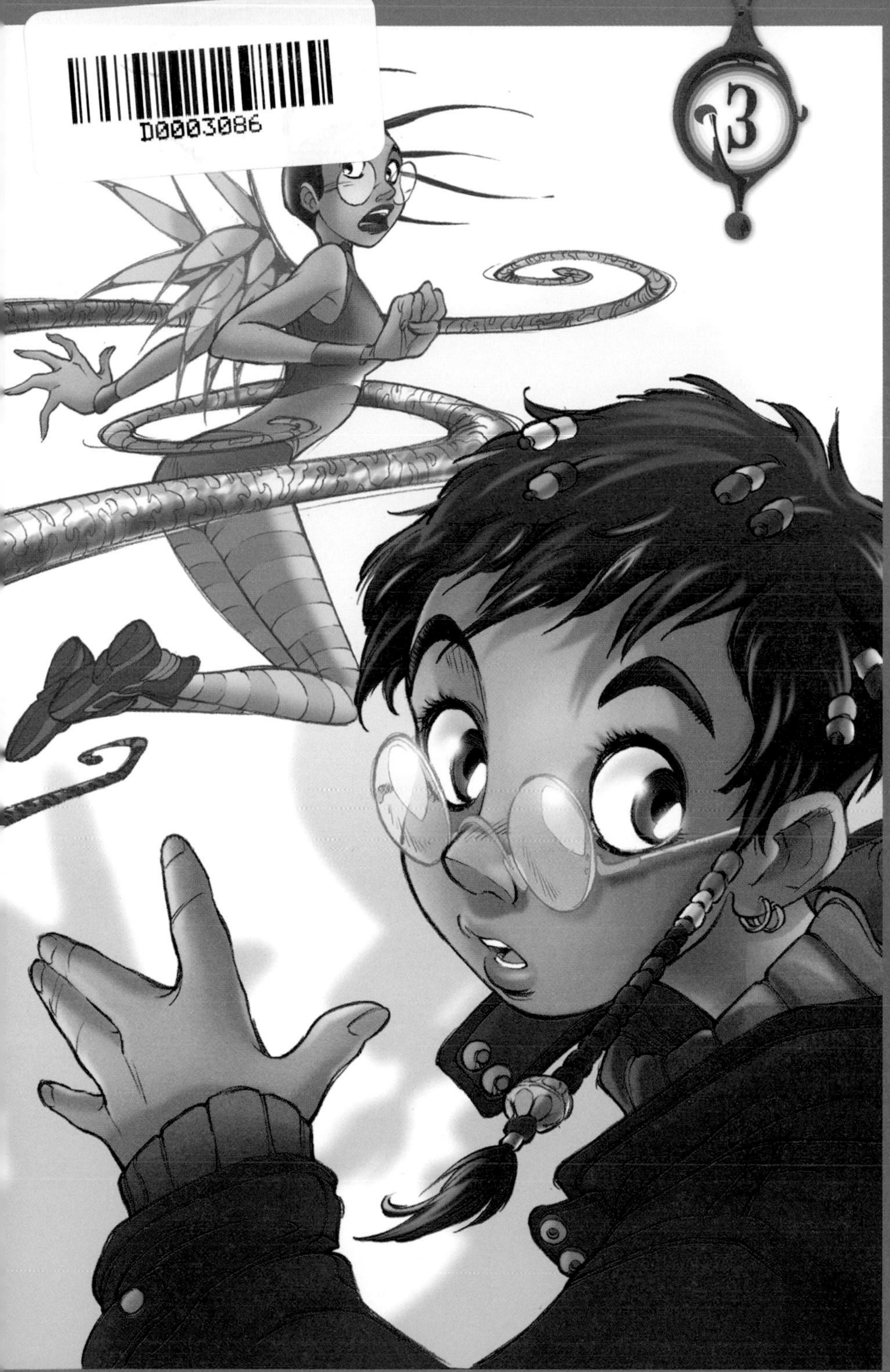
13

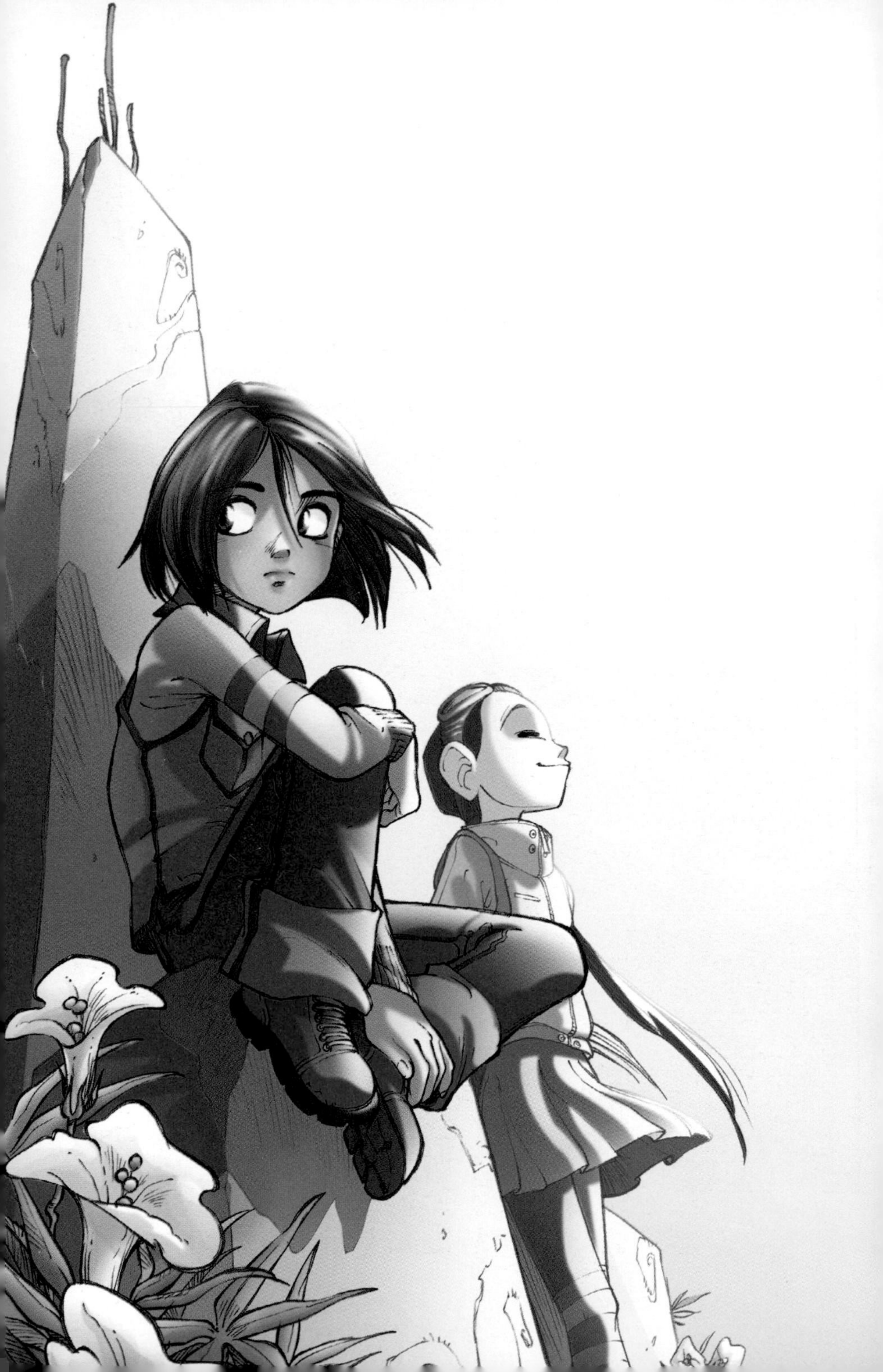

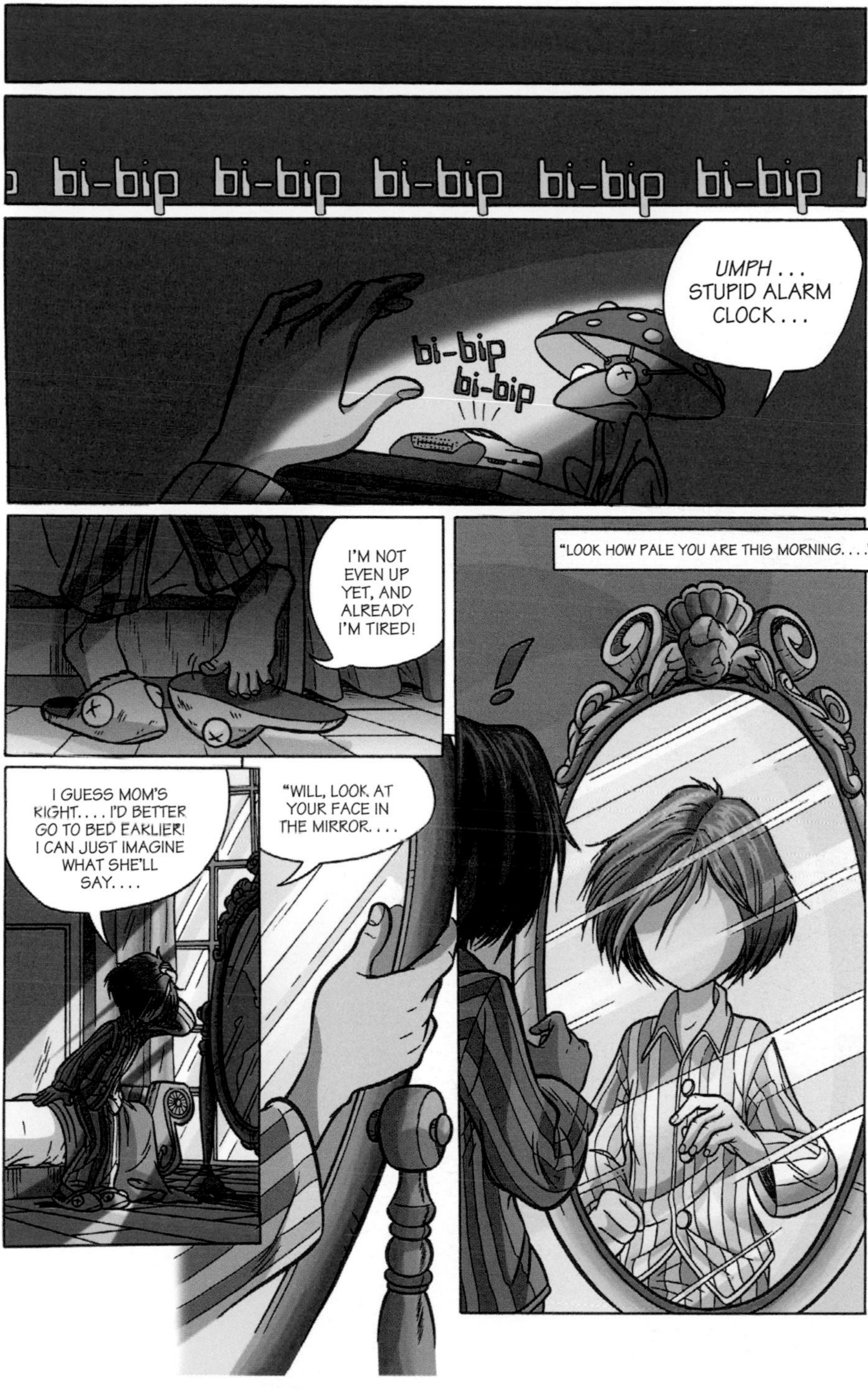
bi-bip bi-bip bi-bip bi-bip bi-bip
UMPH . . . STUPID ALARM CLOCK . . .
bi-bip bi-bip
I'M NOT EVEN UP YET, AND ALREADY I'M TIRED!
"LOOK HOW PALE YOU ARE THIS MORNING. . . ."
!
I GUESS MOM'S RIGHT. . . . I'D BETTER GO TO BED EARLIER! I CAN JUST IMAGINE WHAT SHE'LL SAY. . . .
"WILL, LOOK AT YOUR FACE IN THE MIRROR. . . .

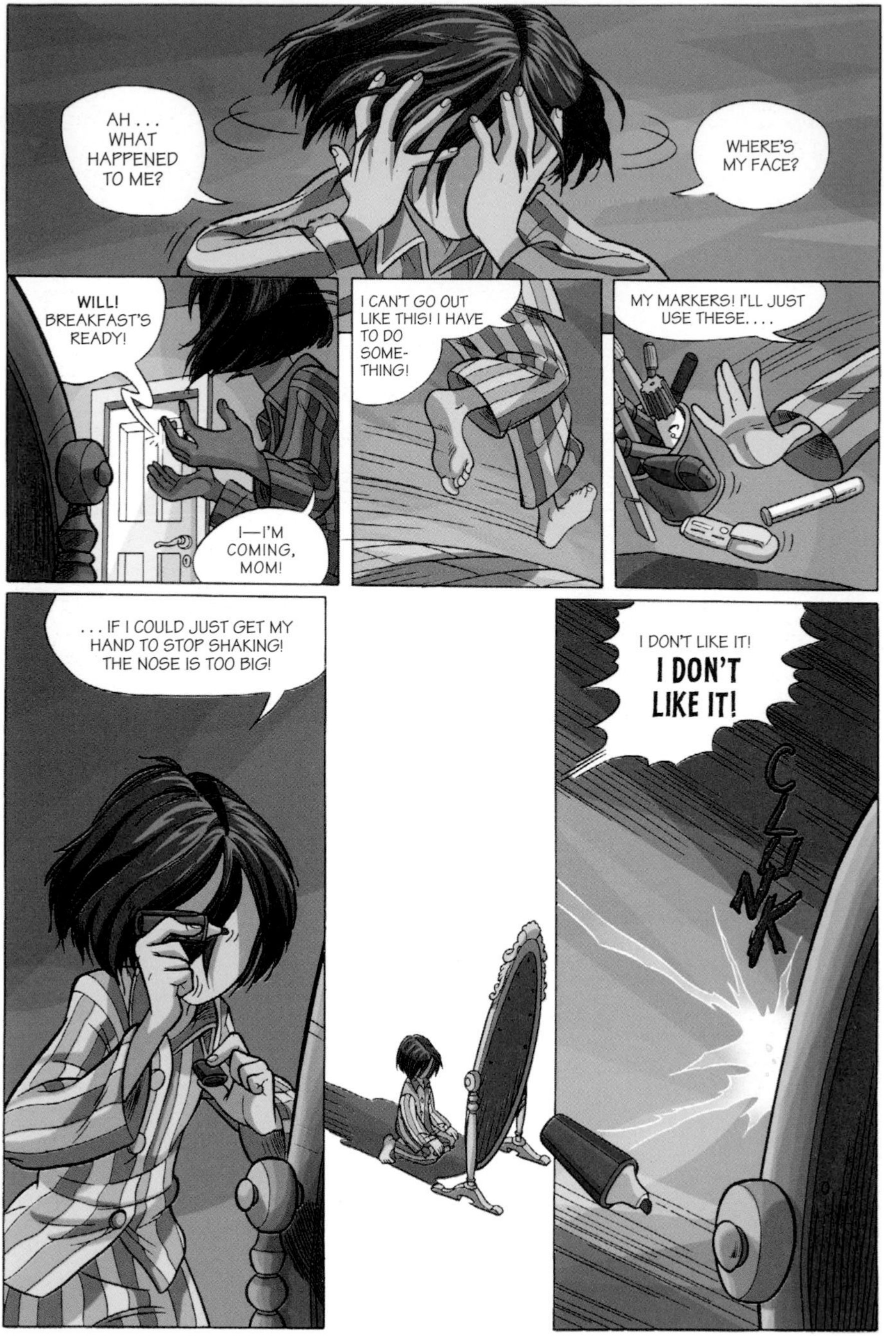
AH . . . WHAT HAPPENED TO ME?
WHERE'S MY FACE?
WILL! BREAKFAST'S READY!
I—I'M COMING, MOM!
I CAN'T GO OUT LIKE THIS! I HAVE TO DO SOME-THING!
MY MARKERS! I'LL JUST USE THESE. . . .
. . . IF I COULD JUST GET MY HAND TO STOP SHAKING! THE NOSE IS TOO BIG!
I DON'T LIKE IT!
I DON'T LIKE IT!
CLUNK

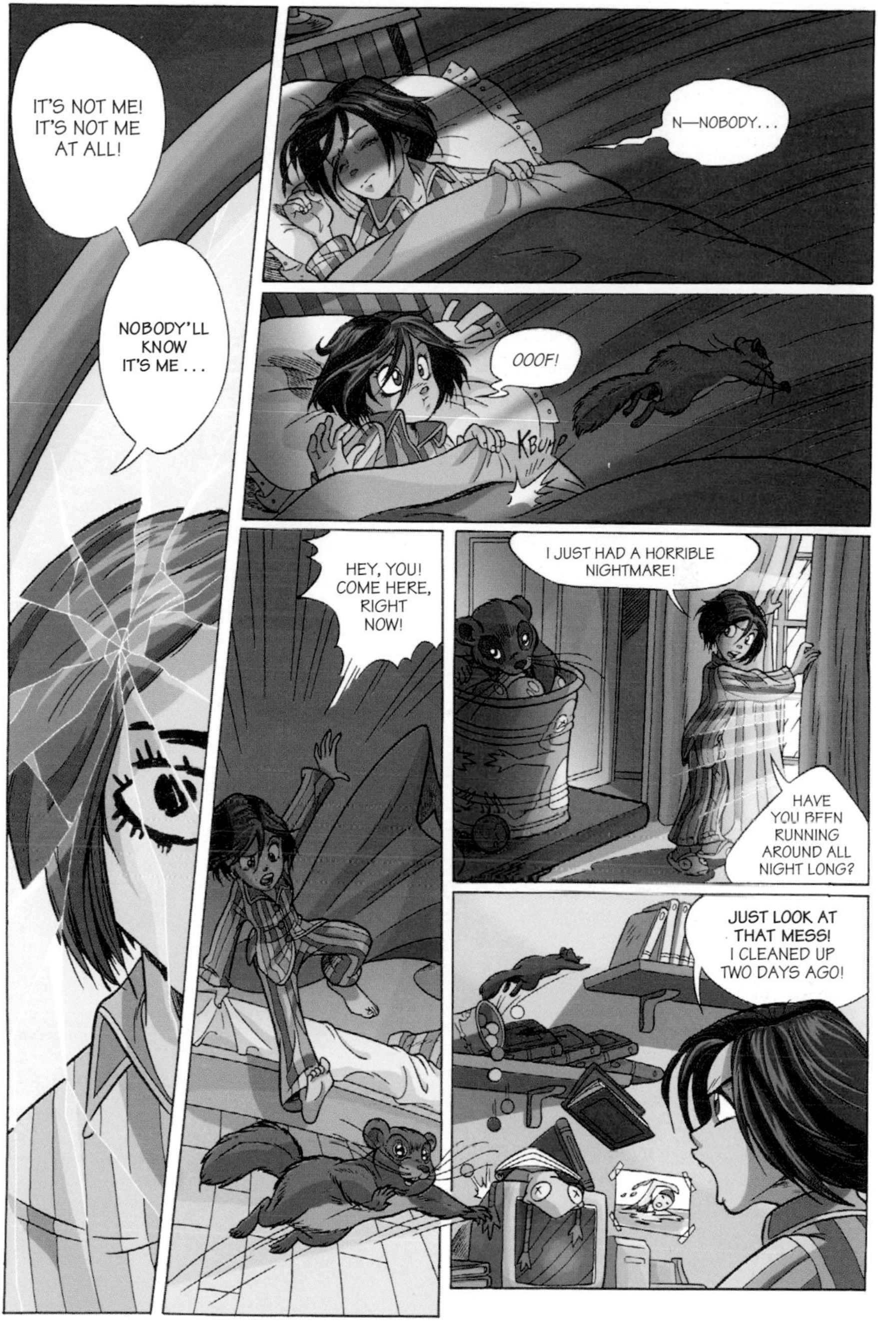
IT'S NOT ME!
IT'S NOT ME
AT ALL!
NOBODY'LL
KNOW
IT'S ME . . .
N—NOBODY. . .
OOOF!
KBUMP
HEY, YOU!
COME HERE,
RIGHT
NOW!
I JUST HAD A HORRIBLE
NIGHTMARE!
HAVE
YOU BEEN
RUNNING
AROUND ALL
NIGHT LONG?
JUST LOOK AT
THAT MESS!
I CLEANED UP
TWO DAYS AGO!

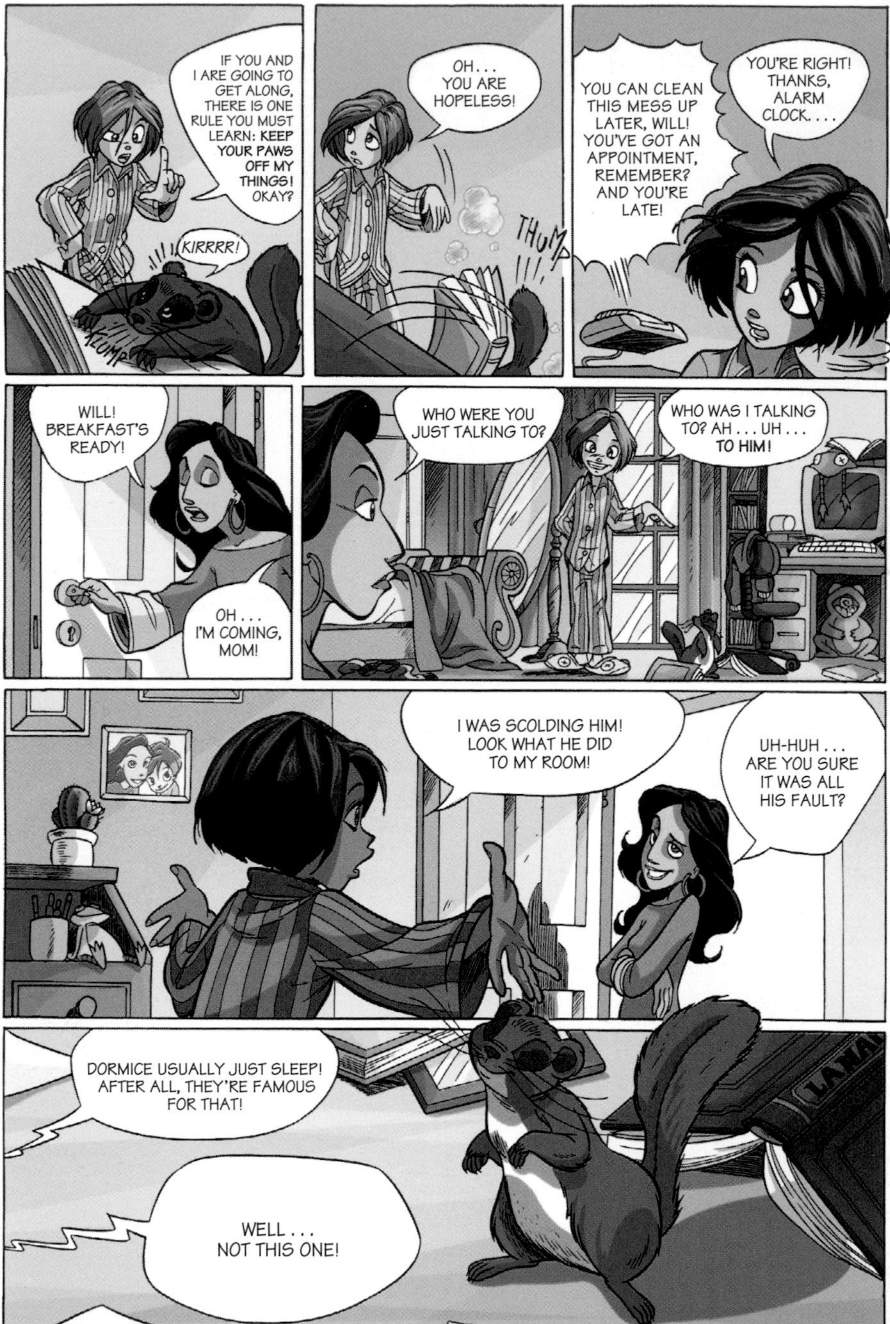
IF YOU AND I ARE GOING TO GET ALONG, THERE IS ONE RULE YOU MUST LEARN: **KEEP YOUR PAWS OFF MY THINGS!** OKAY?
KIRRRR!
OH . . . YOU ARE HOPELESS!
THUMP
YOU CAN CLEAN THIS MESS UP LATER, WILL! YOU'VE GOT AN APPOINTMENT, REMEMBER? AND YOU'RE LATE!
YOU'RE RIGHT! THANKS, ALARM CLOCK. . . .
WILL! BREAKFAST'S READY!
OH . . . I'M COMING, MOM!
WHO WERE YOU JUST TALKING TO?
WHO WAS I TALKING TO? AH . . . UH . . . **TO HIM!**
I WAS SCOLDING HIM! LOOK WHAT HE DID TO MY ROOM!
UH-HUH . . . ARE YOU SURE IT WAS ALL HIS FAULT?
DORMICE USUALLY JUST SLEEP! AFTER ALL, THEY'RE FAMOUS FOR THAT!
WELL . . . NOT THIS ONE!

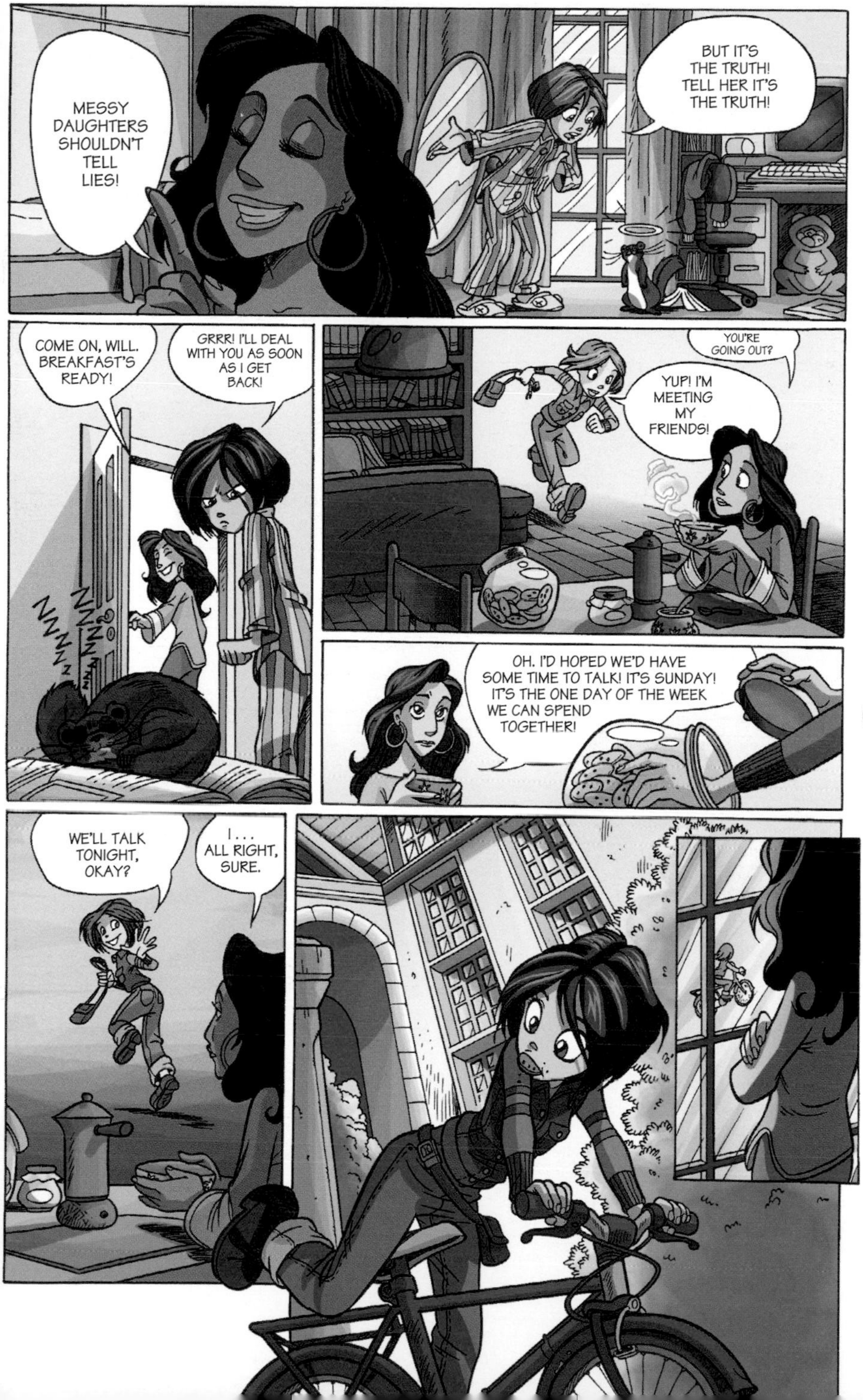
MESSY DAUGHTERS SHOULDN'T TELL LIES!
BUT IT'S THE TRUTH! TELL HER IT'S THE TRUTH!
COME ON, WILL. BREAKFAST'S READY!
GRRR! I'LL DEAL WITH YOU AS SOON AS I GET BACK!
ZZZZZZ
YOU'RE GOING OUT?
YUP! I'M MEETING MY FRIENDS!
OH. I'D HOPED WE'D HAVE SOME TIME TO TALK! IT'S SUNDAY! IT'S THE ONE DAY OF THE WEEK WE CAN SPEND TOGETHER!
WE'LL TALK TONIGHT, OKAY?
I . . . ALL RIGHT, SURE.

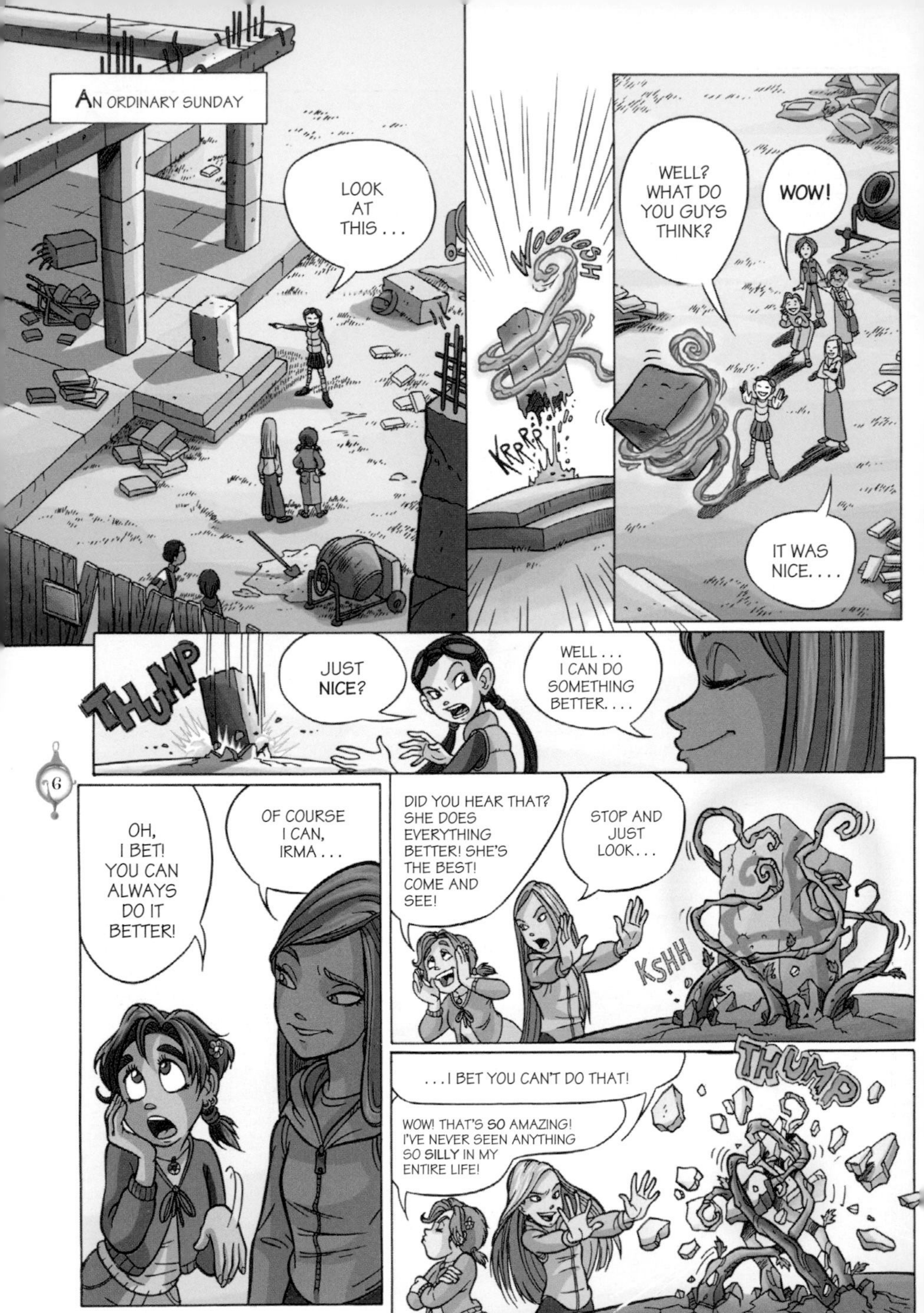
AN ORDINARY SUNDAY
LOOK AT THIS . . .
WOOOOSH
KRRRR
WELL? WHAT DO YOU GUYS THINK?
WOW!
IT WAS NICE. . . .
THUMP
JUST NICE?
WELL . . . I CAN DO SOMETHING BETTER. . . .
OH, I BET! YOU CAN ALWAYS DO IT BETTER!
OF COURSE I CAN, IRMA . . .
DID YOU HEAR THAT? SHE DOES EVERYTHING BETTER! SHE'S THE BEST! COME AND SEE!
STOP AND JUST LOOK . . .
KSHH
THUMP
. . . I BET YOU CAN'T DO THAT!
WOW! THAT'S SO AMAZING! I'VE NEVER SEEN ANYTHING SO SILLY IN MY ENTIRE LIFE!

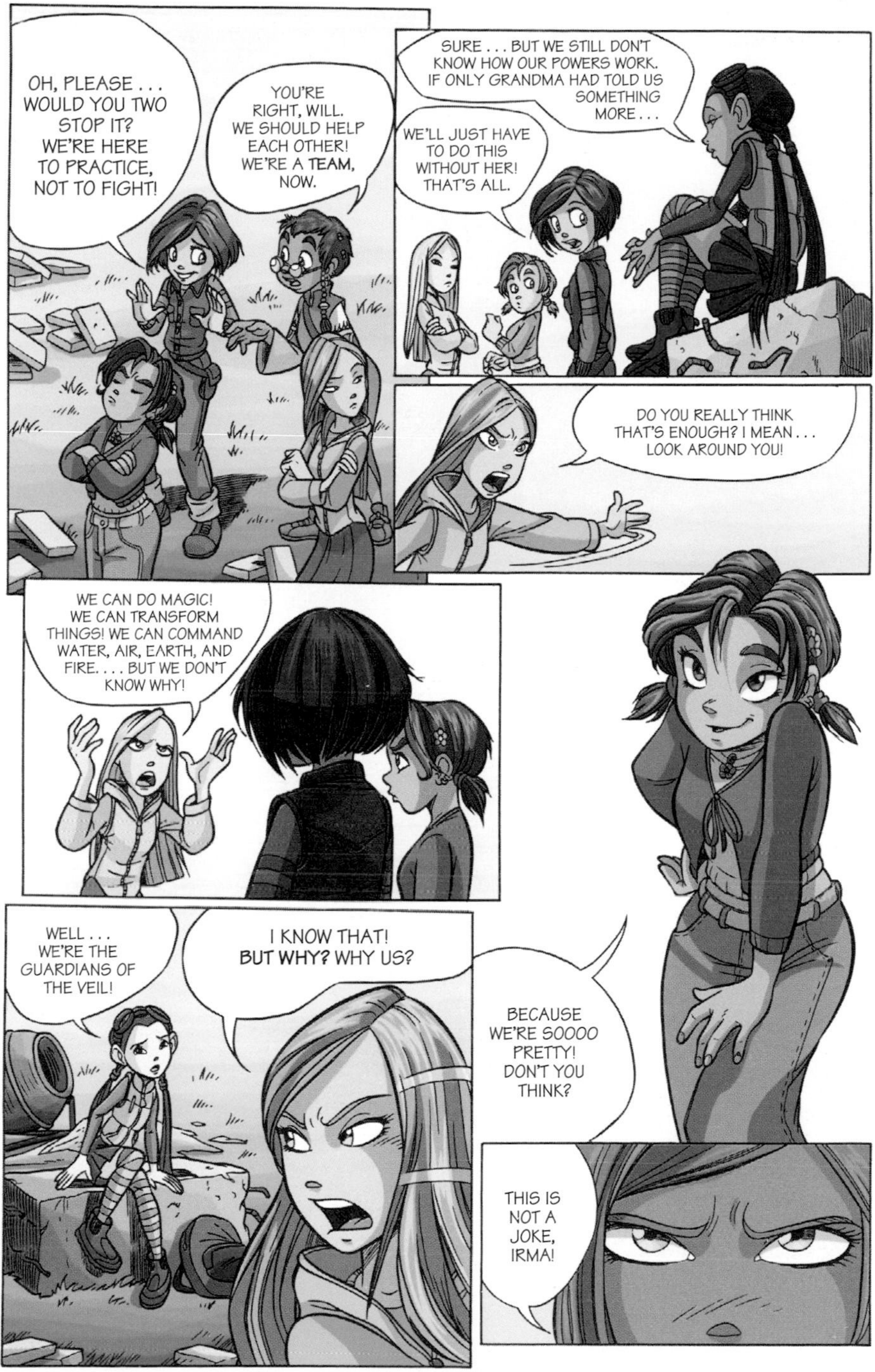

OH, PLEASE . . . WOULD YOU TWO STOP IT? WE'RE HERE TO PRACTICE, NOT TO FIGHT!
YOU'RE RIGHT, WILL. WE SHOULD HELP EACH OTHER! WE'RE A **TEAM**, NOW.
SURE . . . BUT WE STILL DON'T KNOW HOW OUR POWERS WORK. IF ONLY GRANDMA HAD TOLD US SOMETHING MORE . . .
WE'LL JUST HAVE TO DO THIS WITHOUT HER! THAT'S ALL.
DO YOU REALLY THINK THAT'S ENOUGH? I MEAN . . . LOOK AROUND YOU!
WE CAN DO MAGIC! WE CAN TRANSFORM THINGS! WE CAN COMMAND WATER, AIR, EARTH, AND FIRE. . . . BUT WE DON'T KNOW WHY!
WELL . . . WE'RE THE GUARDIANS OF THE VEIL!
I KNOW THAT! **BUT WHY?** WHY US?
BECAUSE WE'RE SOOOO PRETTY! DON'T YOU THINK?
THIS IS NOT A JOKE, IRMA!

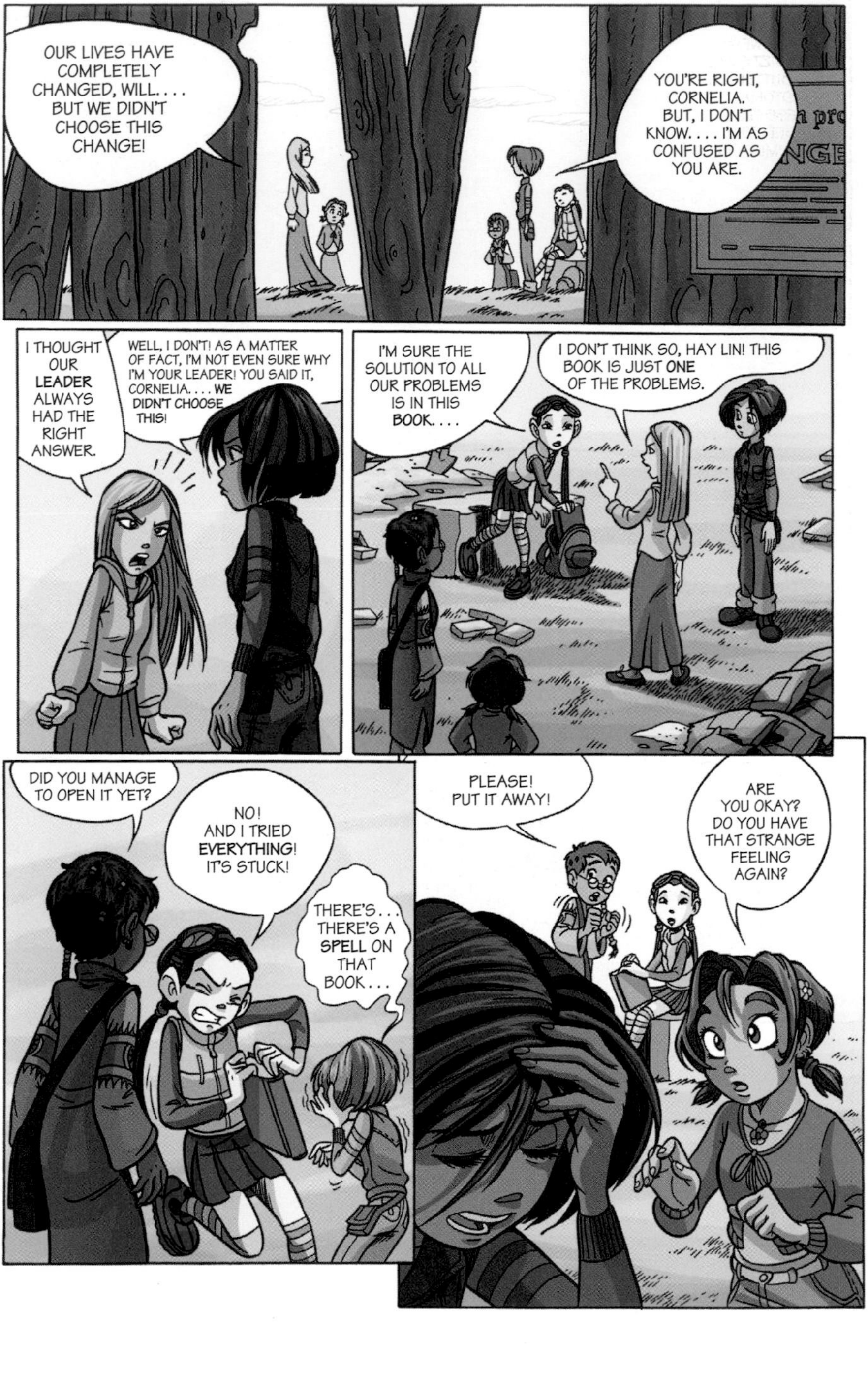
OUR LIVES HAVE COMPLETELY CHANGED, WILL. . . . BUT WE DIDN'T CHOOSE THIS CHANGE!
YOU'RE RIGHT, CORNELIA. BUT, I DON'T KNOW. . . . I'M AS CONFUSED AS YOU ARE.
I THOUGHT OUR LEADER ALWAYS HAD THE RIGHT ANSWER.
WELL, I DON'T! AS A MATTER OF FACT, I'M NOT EVEN SURE WHY I'M YOUR LEADER! YOU SAID IT, CORNELIA. . . . WE DIDN'T CHOOSE THIS!
I'M SURE THE SOLUTION TO ALL OUR PROBLEMS IS IN THIS BOOK. . . .
I DON'T THINK SO, HAY LIN! THIS BOOK IS JUST ONE OF THE PROBLEMS.
DID YOU MANAGE TO OPEN IT YET?
NO! AND I TRIED EVERYTHING! IT'S STUCK!
THERE'S. . . THERE'S A SPELL ON THAT BOOK. . .
PLEASE! PUT IT AWAY!
ARE YOU OKAY? DO YOU HAVE THAT STRANGE FEELING AGAIN?

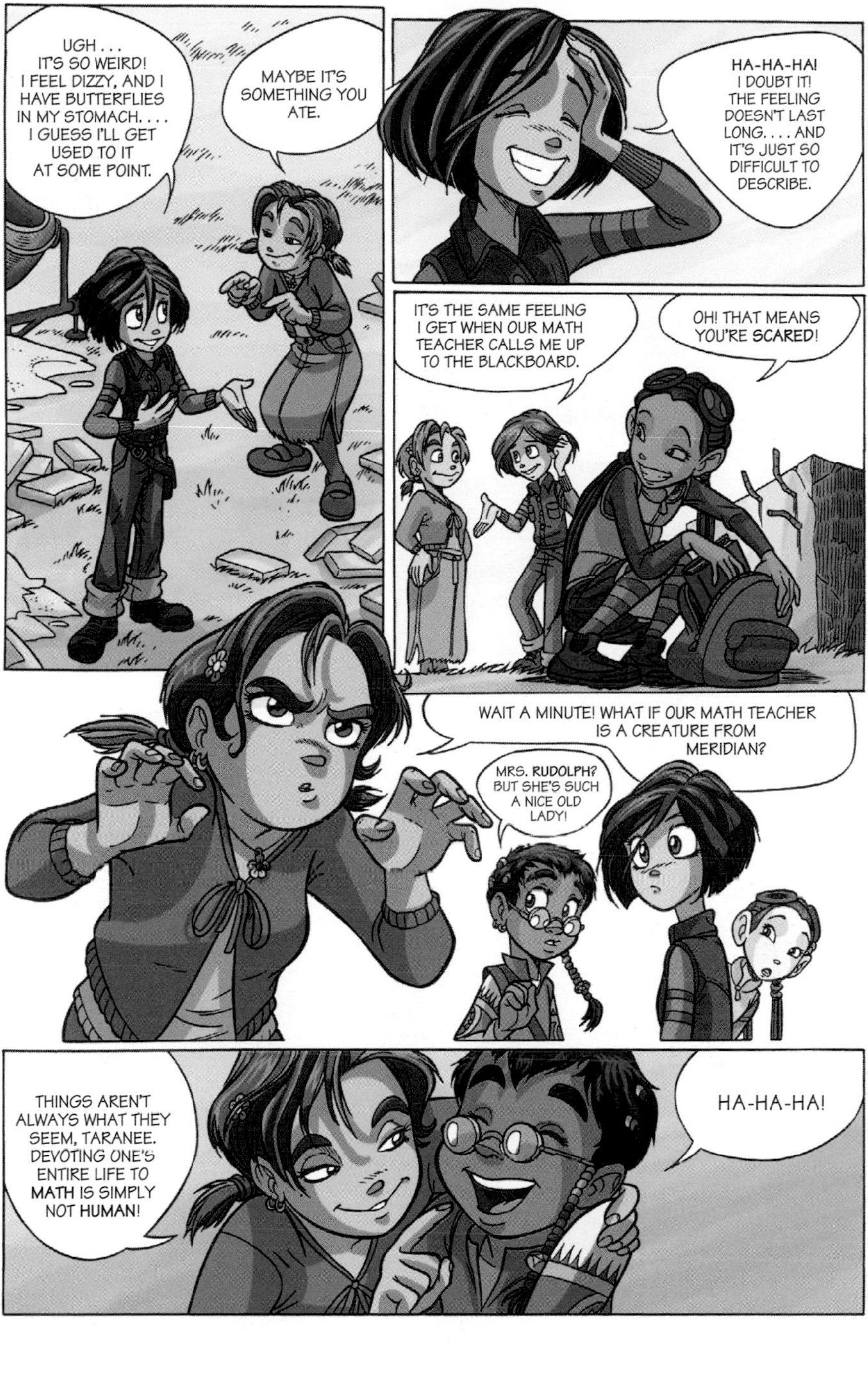

UGH . . . IT'S SO WEIRD! I FEEL DIZZY, AND I HAVE BUTTERFLIES IN MY STOMACH. . . . I GUESS I'LL GET USED TO IT AT SOME POINT.
MAYBE IT'S SOMETHING YOU ATE.
HA-HA-HA! I DOUBT IT! THE FEELING DOESN'T LAST LONG. . . . AND IT'S JUST SO DIFFICULT TO DESCRIBE.
IT'S THE SAME FEELING I GET WHEN OUR MATH TEACHER CALLS ME UP TO THE BLACKBOARD.
OH! THAT MEANS YOU'RE SCARED!
WAIT A MINUTE! WHAT IF OUR MATH TEACHER IS A CREATURE FROM MERIDIAN?
MRS. RUDOLPH? BUT SHE'S SUCH A NICE OLD LADY!
THINGS AREN'T ALWAYS WHAT THEY SEEM, TARANEE. DEVOTING ONE'S ENTIRE LIFE TO MATH IS SIMPLY NOT HUMAN!
HA-HA-HA!

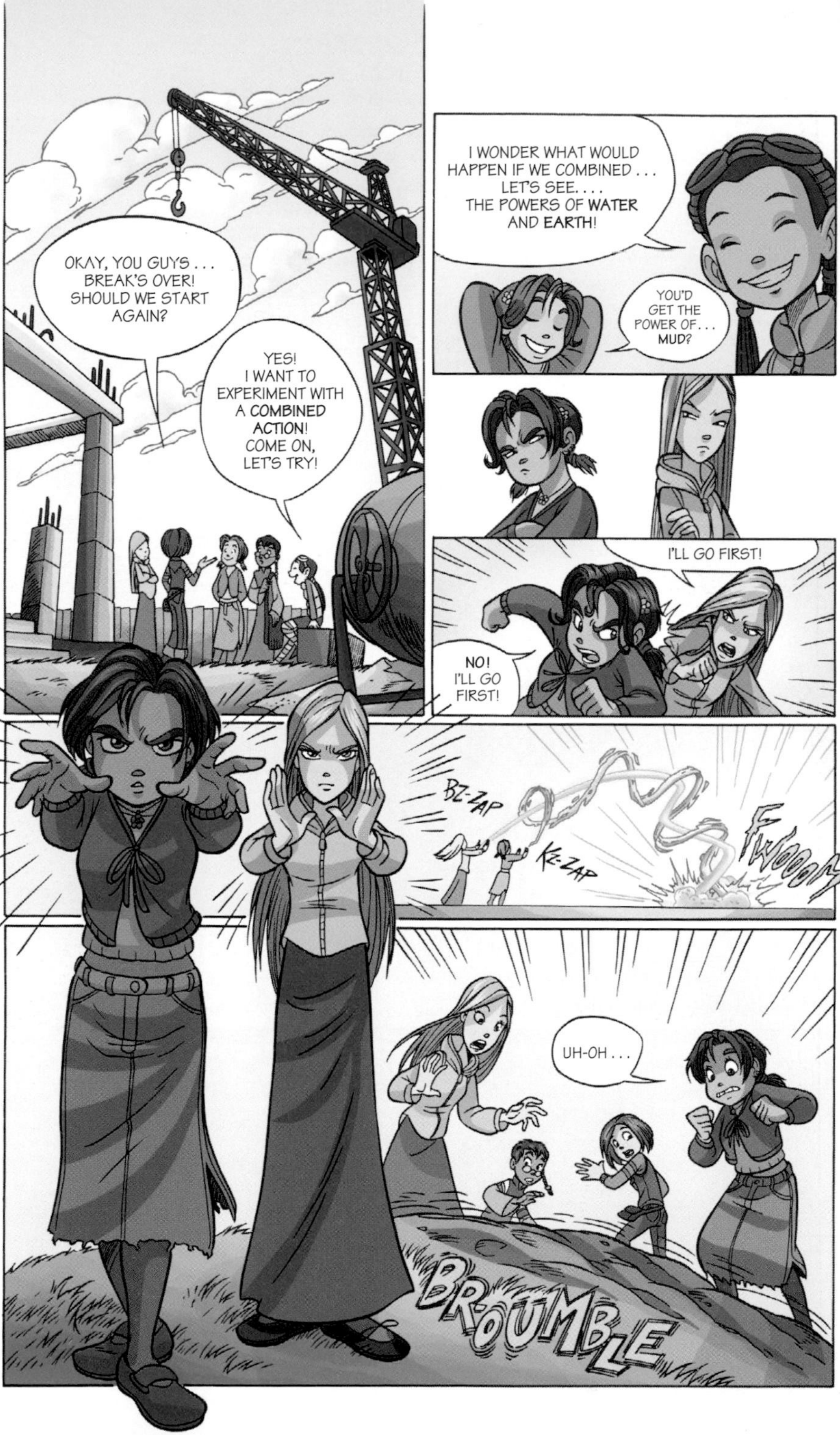
OKAY, YOU GUYS . . . BREAK'S OVER! SHOULD WE START AGAIN?
YES! I WANT TO EXPERIMENT WITH A COMBINED ACTION! COME ON, LET'S TRY!
I WONDER WHAT WOULD HAPPEN IF WE COMBINED . . . LET'S SEE. . . . THE POWERS OF WATER AND EARTH!
YOU'D GET THE POWER OF. . . MUD?
I'LL GO FIRST!
NO! I'LL GO FIRST!
BZ-ZAP
KZ-ZAP
FWOOOM
UH-OH . . .
BROUMBLE

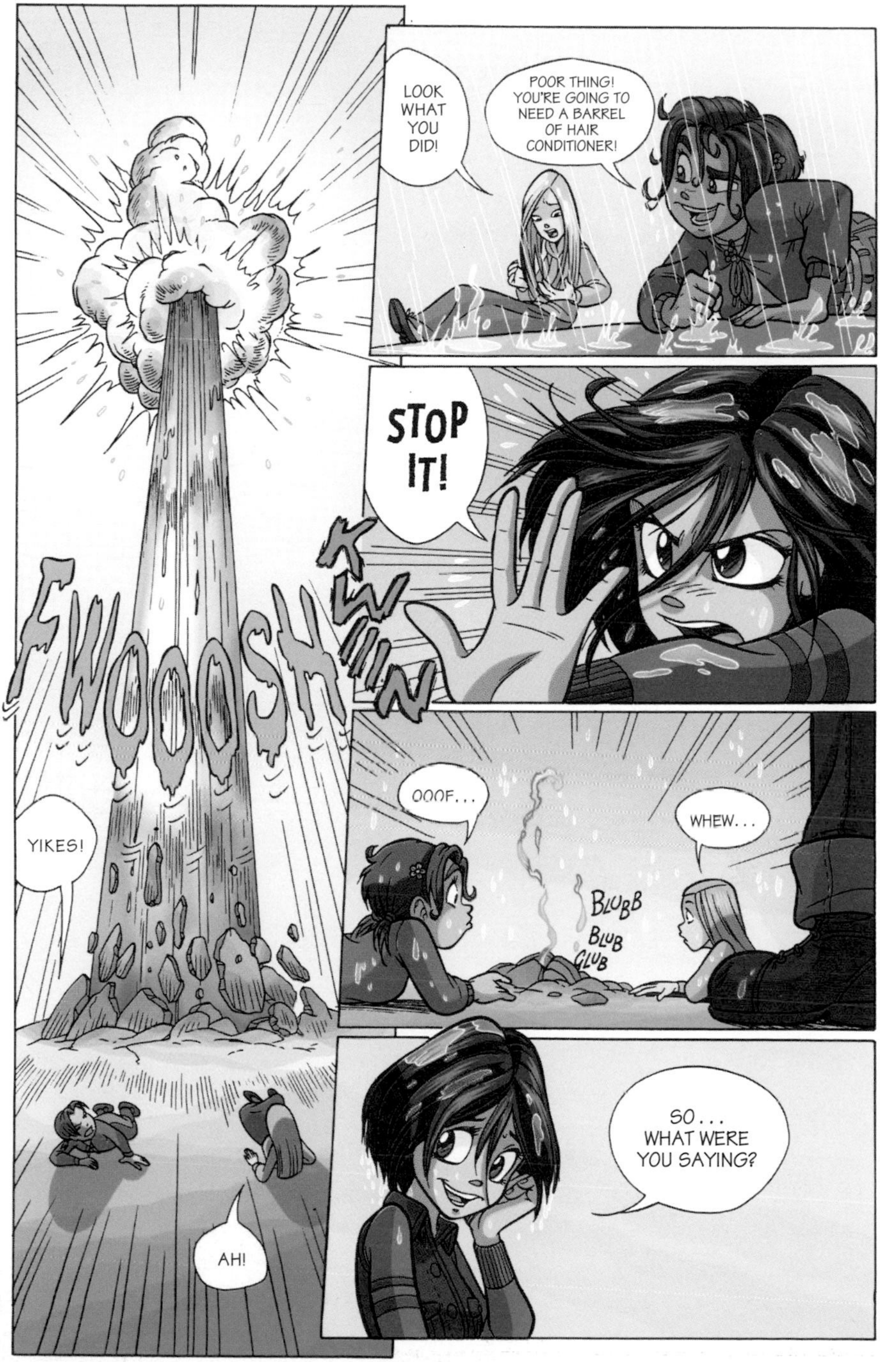
LOOK WHAT YOU DID!
POOR THING! YOU'RE GOING TO NEED A BARREL OF HAIR CONDITIONER!
FWOOOSH
STOP IT!
KWIIIN
YIKES!
AH!
OOOF...
WHEW...
BLUBB
BLUB
GLUB
SO... WHAT WERE YOU SAYING?

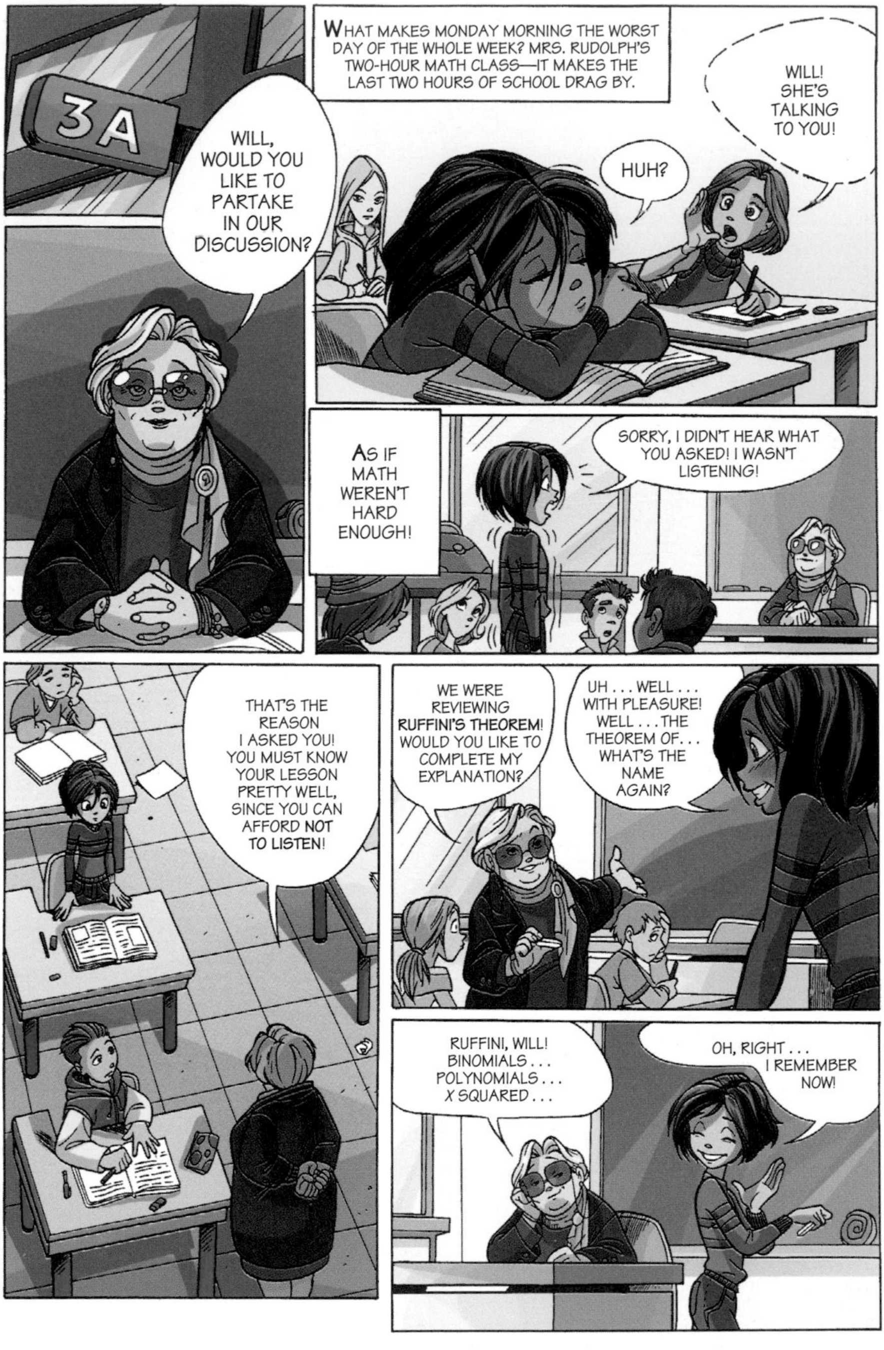
3A
WHAT MAKES MONDAY MORNING THE WORST DAY OF THE WHOLE WEEK? MRS. RUDOLPH'S TWO-HOUR MATH CLASS—IT MAKES THE LAST TWO HOURS OF SCHOOL DRAG BY.
WILL! SHE'S TALKING TO YOU!
HUH?
WILL, WOULD YOU LIKE TO PARTAKE IN OUR DISCUSSION?
AS IF MATH WEREN'T HARD ENOUGH!
SORRY, I DIDN'T HEAR WHAT YOU ASKED! I WASN'T LISTENING!
THAT'S THE REASON I ASKED YOU! YOU MUST KNOW YOUR LESSON PRETTY WELL, SINCE YOU CAN AFFORD **NOT TO LISTEN**!
WE WERE REVIEWING **RUFFINI'S THEOREM**! WOULD YOU LIKE TO COMPLETE MY EXPLANATION?
UH . . . WELL . . . WITH PLEASURE! WELL . . . THE THEOREM OF . . . WHAT'S THE NAME AGAIN?
RUFFINI, WILL! BINOMIALS . . . POLYNOMIALS . . . *X* SQUARED . . .
OH, RIGHT . . . I REMEMBER NOW!

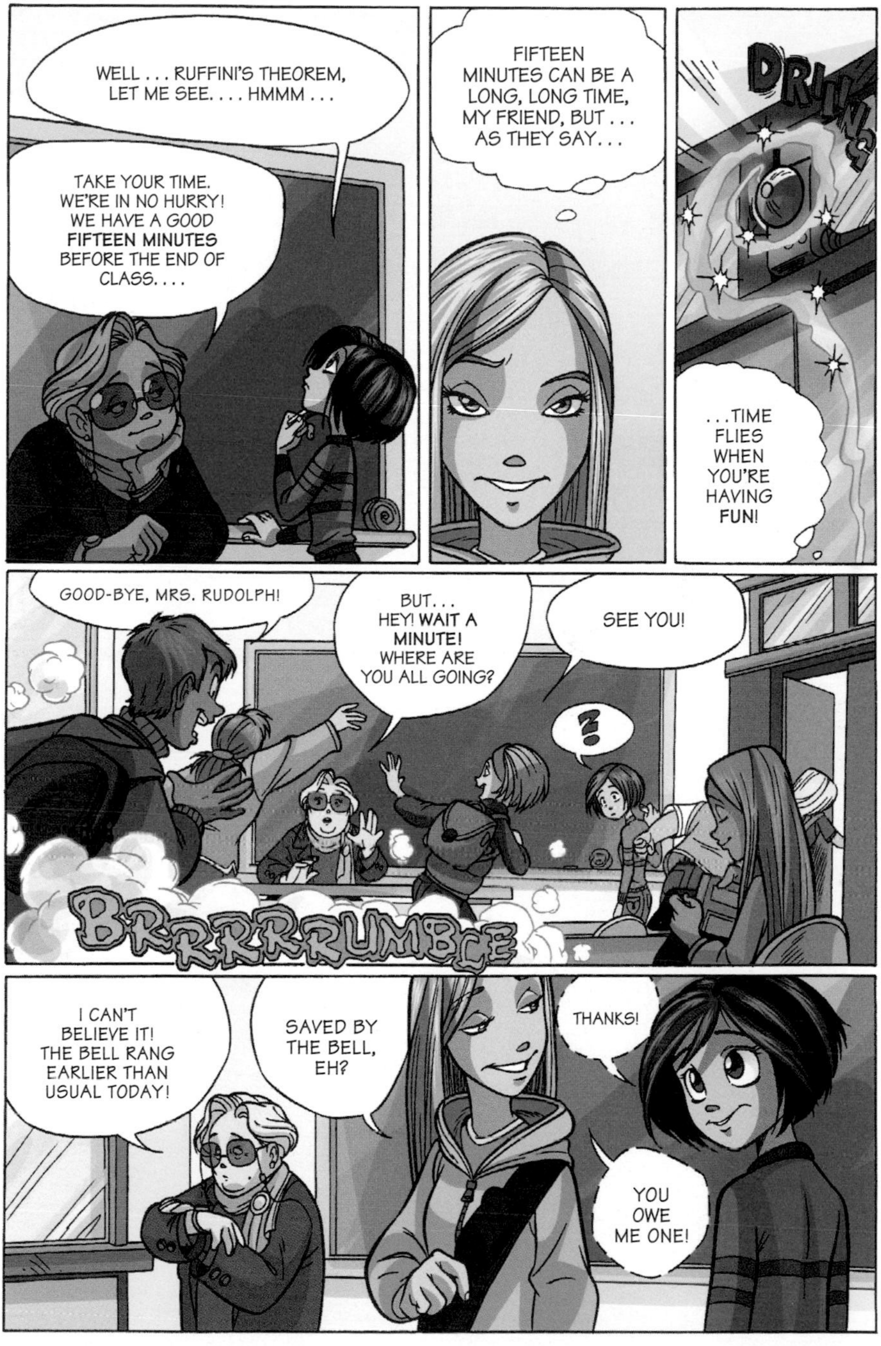
WELL . . . RUFFINI'S THEOREM, LET ME SEE. . . . HMMM . . .
TAKE YOUR TIME. WE'RE IN NO HURRY! WE HAVE A GOOD **FIFTEEN MINUTES** BEFORE THE END OF CLASS. . . .
FIFTEEN MINUTES CAN BE A LONG, LONG TIME, MY FRIEND, BUT . . . AS THEY SAY . . .
DRIIING
. . . TIME FLIES WHEN YOU'RE HAVING **FUN**!
GOOD-BYE, MRS. RUDOLPH!
BUT . . . HEY! **WAIT A MINUTE!** WHERE ARE YOU ALL GOING?
SEE YOU!
?
BRRRRRRUMBLE
I CAN'T BELIEVE IT! THE BELL RANG EARLIER THAN USUAL TODAY!
SAVED BY THE BELL, EH?
THANKS!
YOU OWE ME ONE!

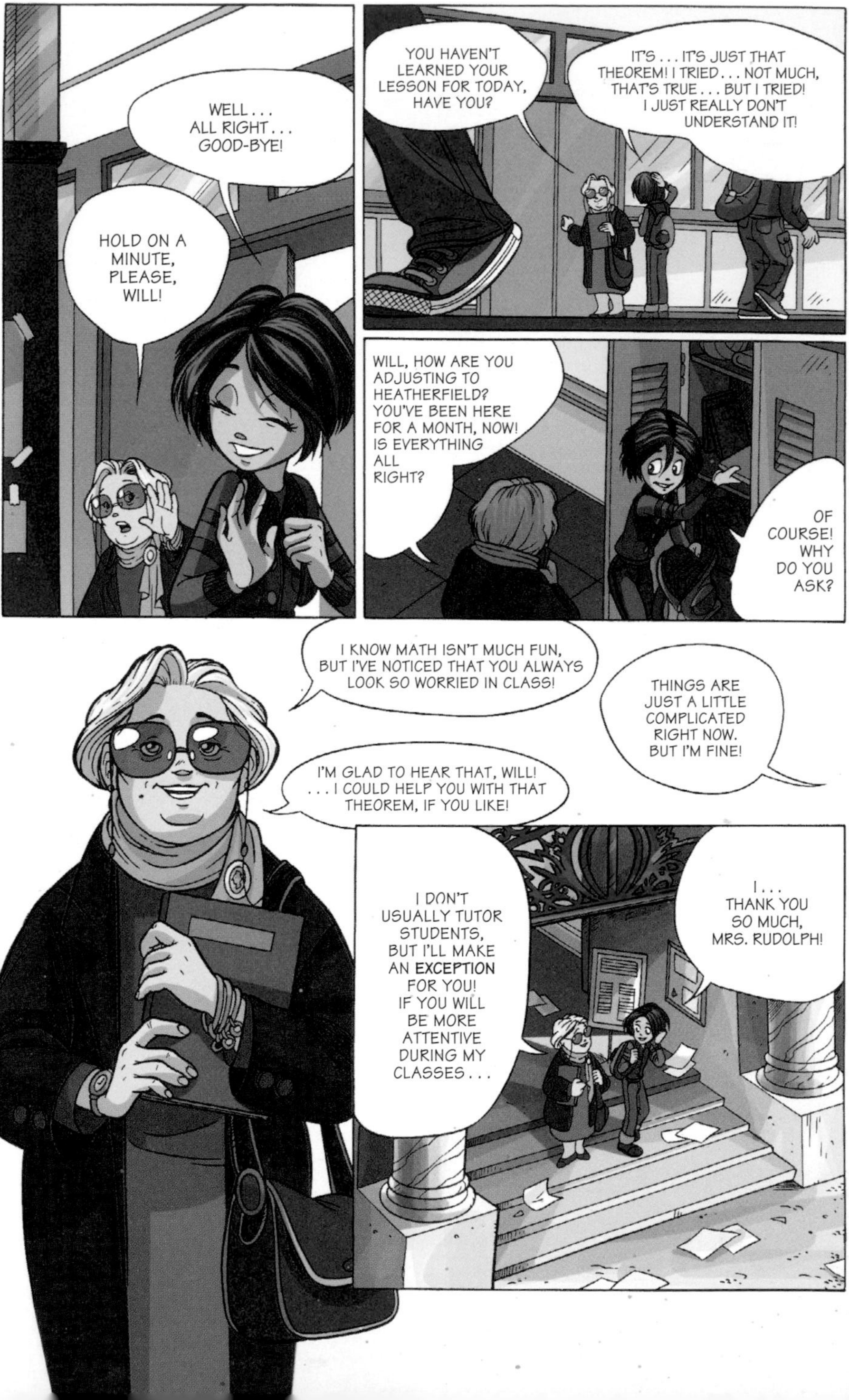

WELL . . . ALL RIGHT . . . GOOD-BYE!
HOLD ON A MINUTE, PLEASE, WILL!
YOU HAVEN'T LEARNED YOUR LESSON FOR TODAY, HAVE YOU?
IT'S . . . IT'S JUST THAT THEOREM! I TRIED . . . NOT MUCH, THAT'S TRUE . . . BUT I TRIED! I JUST REALLY DON'T UNDERSTAND IT!
WILL, HOW ARE YOU ADJUSTING TO HEATHERFIELD? YOU'VE BEEN HERE FOR A MONTH, NOW! IS EVERYTHING ALL RIGHT?
OF COURSE! WHY DO YOU ASK?
I KNOW MATH ISN'T MUCH FUN, BUT I'VE NOTICED THAT YOU ALWAYS LOOK SO WORRIED IN CLASS!
THINGS ARE JUST A LITTLE COMPLICATED RIGHT NOW. BUT I'M FINE!
I'M GLAD TO HEAR THAT, WILL! . . . I COULD HELP YOU WITH THAT THEOREM, IF YOU LIKE!
I DON'T USUALLY TUTOR STUDENTS, BUT I'LL MAKE AN **EXCEPTION** FOR YOU! IF YOU WILL BE MORE ATTENTIVE DURING MY CLASSES . . .
I . . . THANK YOU SO MUCH, MRS. RUDOLPH!

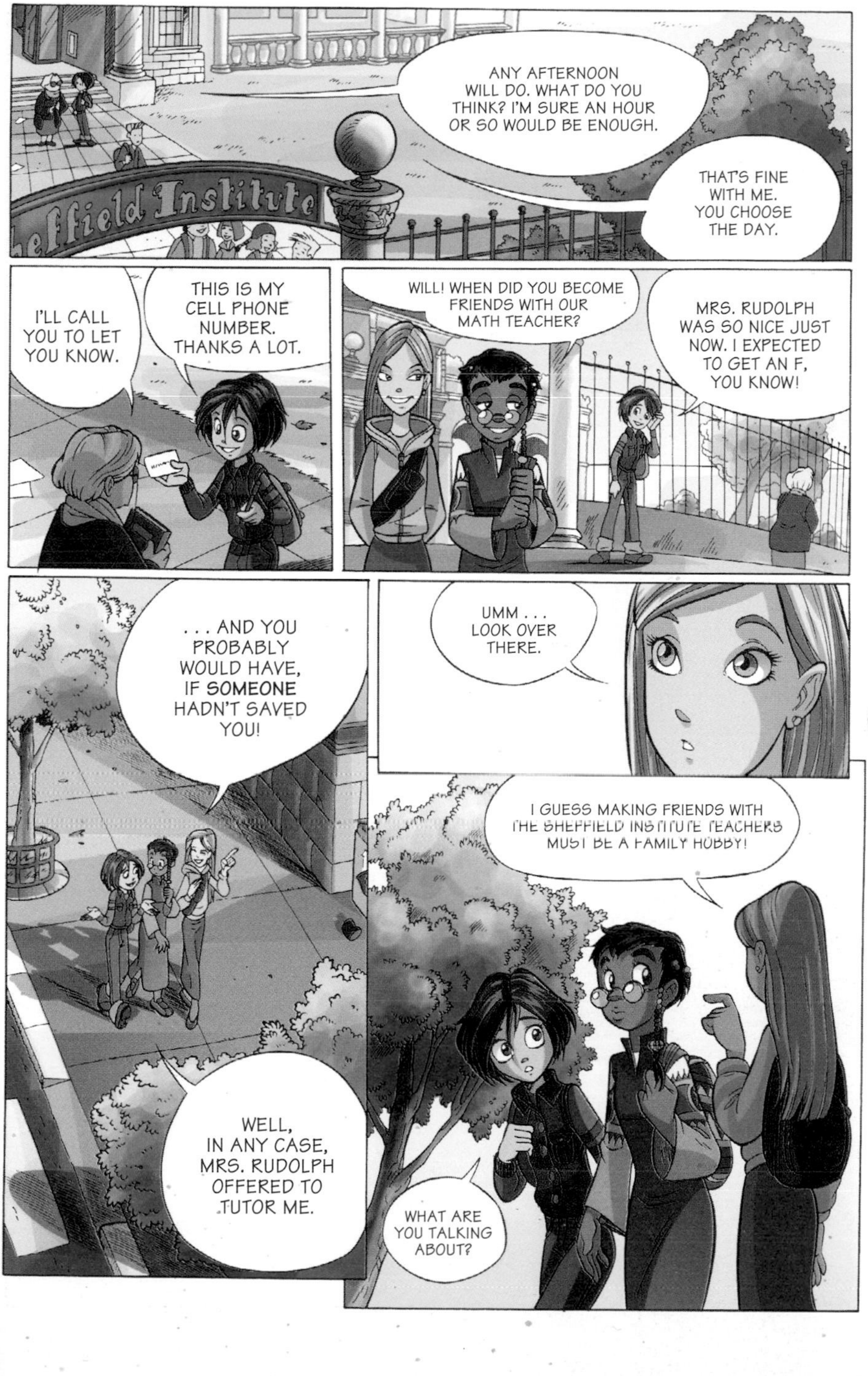
Sheffield Institute
ANY AFTERNOON WILL DO. WHAT DO YOU THINK? I'M SURE AN HOUR OR SO WOULD BE ENOUGH.
THAT'S FINE WITH ME. YOU CHOOSE THE DAY.
THIS IS MY CELL PHONE NUMBER. THANKS A LOT.
I'LL CALL YOU TO LET YOU KNOW.
WILL! WHEN DID YOU BECOME FRIENDS WITH OUR MATH TEACHER?
MRS. RUDOLPH WAS SO NICE JUST NOW. I EXPECTED TO GET AN F, YOU KNOW!
. . . AND YOU PROBABLY WOULD HAVE, IF **SOMEONE** HADN'T SAVED YOU!
WELL, IN ANY CASE, MRS. RUDOLPH OFFERED TO TUTOR ME.
UMM . . . LOOK OVER THERE.
I GUESS MAKING FRIENDS WITH THE SHEFFIELD INSTITUTE TEACHERS MUST BE A FAMILY HOBBY!
WHAT ARE YOU TALKING ABOUT?

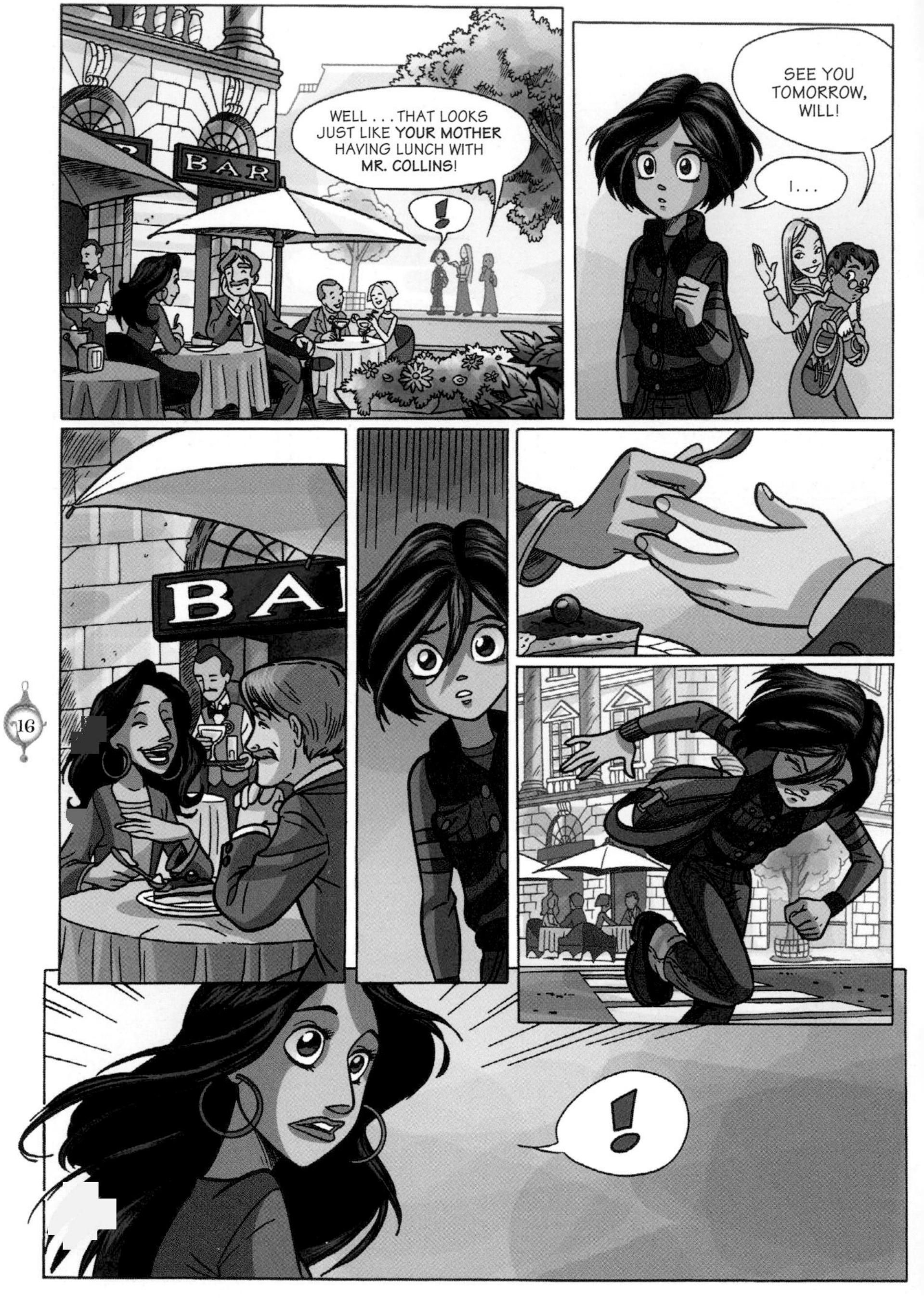
WELL . . . THAT LOOKS JUST LIKE YOUR MOTHER HAVING LUNCH WITH MR. COLLINS!
!
SEE YOU TOMORROW, WILL!
I . . .
BAR
BA
!

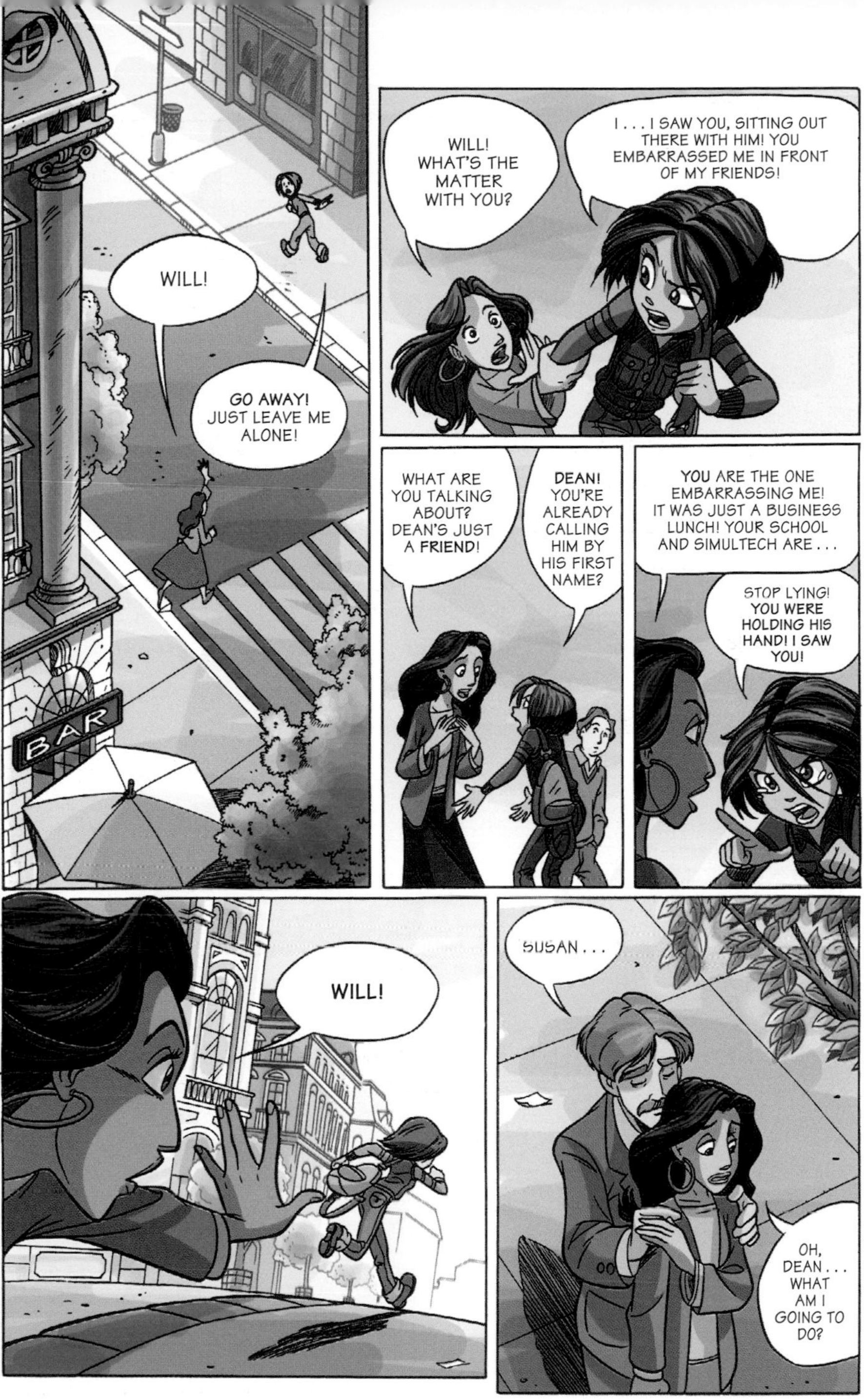
WILL!
GO AWAY! JUST LEAVE ME ALONE!
WILL! WHAT'S THE MATTER WITH YOU?
I . . . I SAW YOU, SITTING OUT THERE WITH HIM! YOU EMBARRASSED ME IN FRONT OF MY FRIENDS!
WHAT ARE YOU TALKING ABOUT? DEAN'S JUST A FRIEND!
DEAN! YOU'RE ALREADY CALLING HIM BY HIS FIRST NAME?
YOU ARE THE ONE EMBARRASSING ME! IT WAS JUST A BUSINESS LUNCH! YOUR SCHOOL AND SIMULTECH ARE . . .
STOP LYING! YOU WERE HOLDING HIS HAND! I SAW YOU!
BAR
WILL!
SUSAN . . .
OH, DEAN . . . WHAT AM I GOING TO DO?

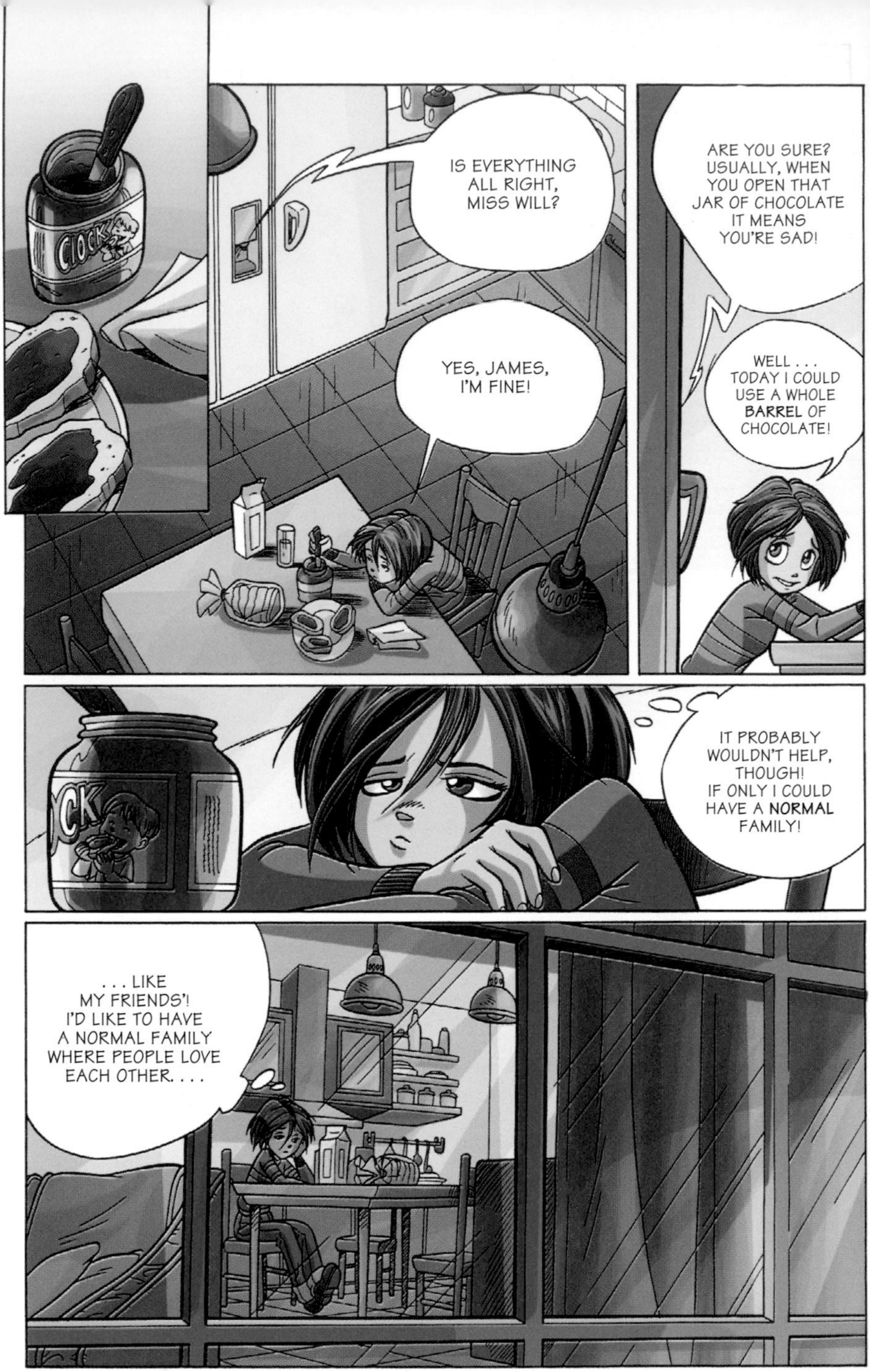
CLOCK
IS EVERYTHING ALL RIGHT, MISS WILL?
YES, JAMES, I'M FINE!
ARE YOU SURE? USUALLY, WHEN YOU OPEN THAT JAR OF CHOCOLATE IT MEANS YOU'RE SAD!
WELL . . . TODAY I COULD USE A WHOLE **BARREL** OF CHOCOLATE!
IT PROBABLY WOULDN'T HELP, THOUGH! IF ONLY I COULD HAVE A **NORMAL** FAMILY!
. . . LIKE MY FRIENDS'! I'D LIKE TO HAVE A NORMAL FAMILY WHERE PEOPLE LOVE EACH OTHER. . . .

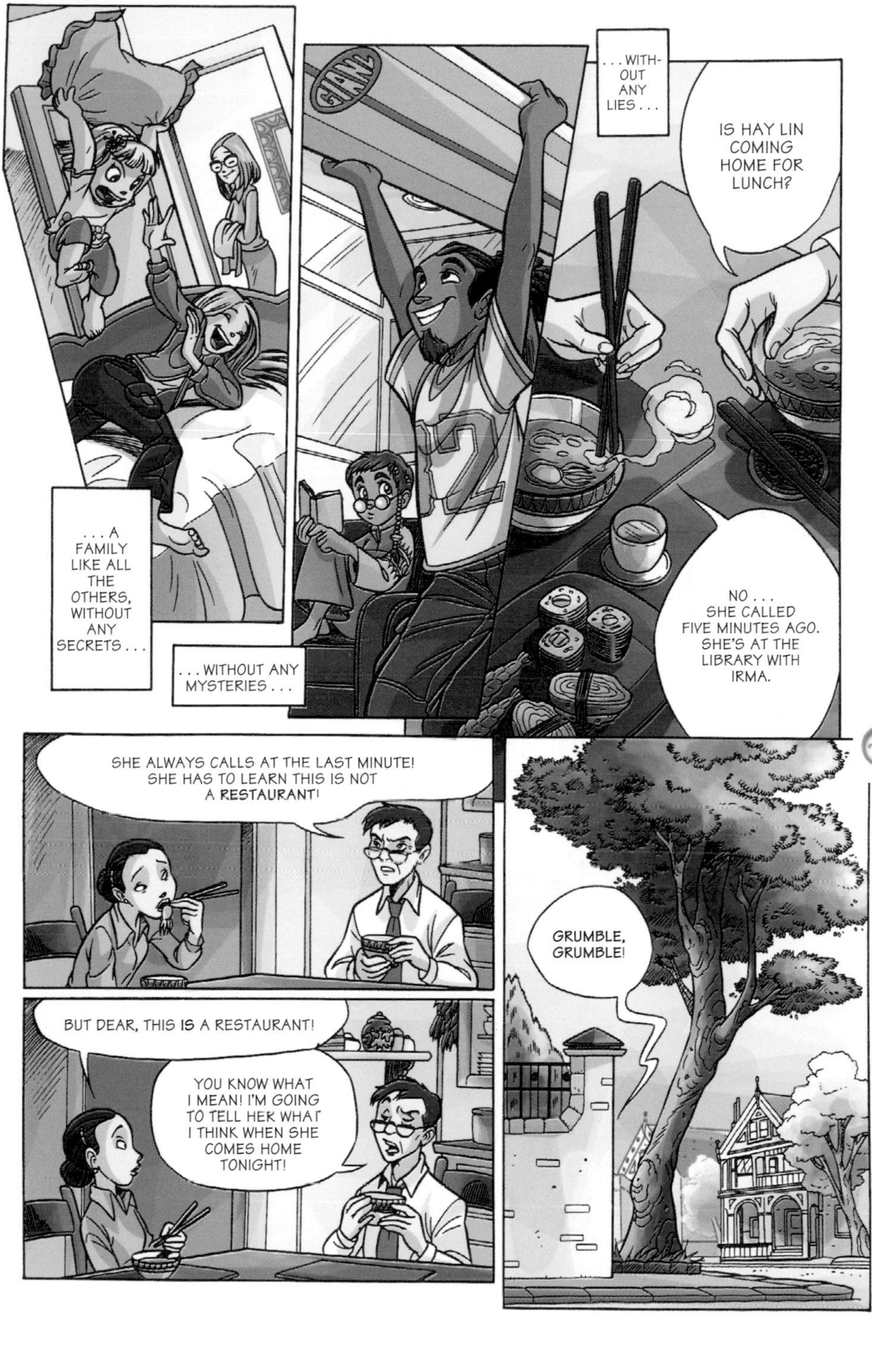

. . . A FAMILY LIKE ALL THE OTHERS, WITHOUT ANY SECRETS . . .
. . . WITHOUT ANY MYSTERIES . . .
. . . WITH-OUT ANY LIES . . .
IS HAY LIN COMING HOME FOR LUNCH?
NO . . . SHE CALLED FIVE MINUTES AGO. SHE'S AT THE LIBRARY WITH IRMA.
SHE ALWAYS CALLS AT THE LAST MINUTE! SHE HAS TO LEARN THIS IS NOT A RESTAURANT!
BUT DEAR, THIS IS A RESTAURANT!
YOU KNOW WHAT I MEAN! I'M GOING TO TELL HER WHAT I THINK WHEN SHE COMES HOME TONIGHT!
GRUMBLE, GRUMBLE!

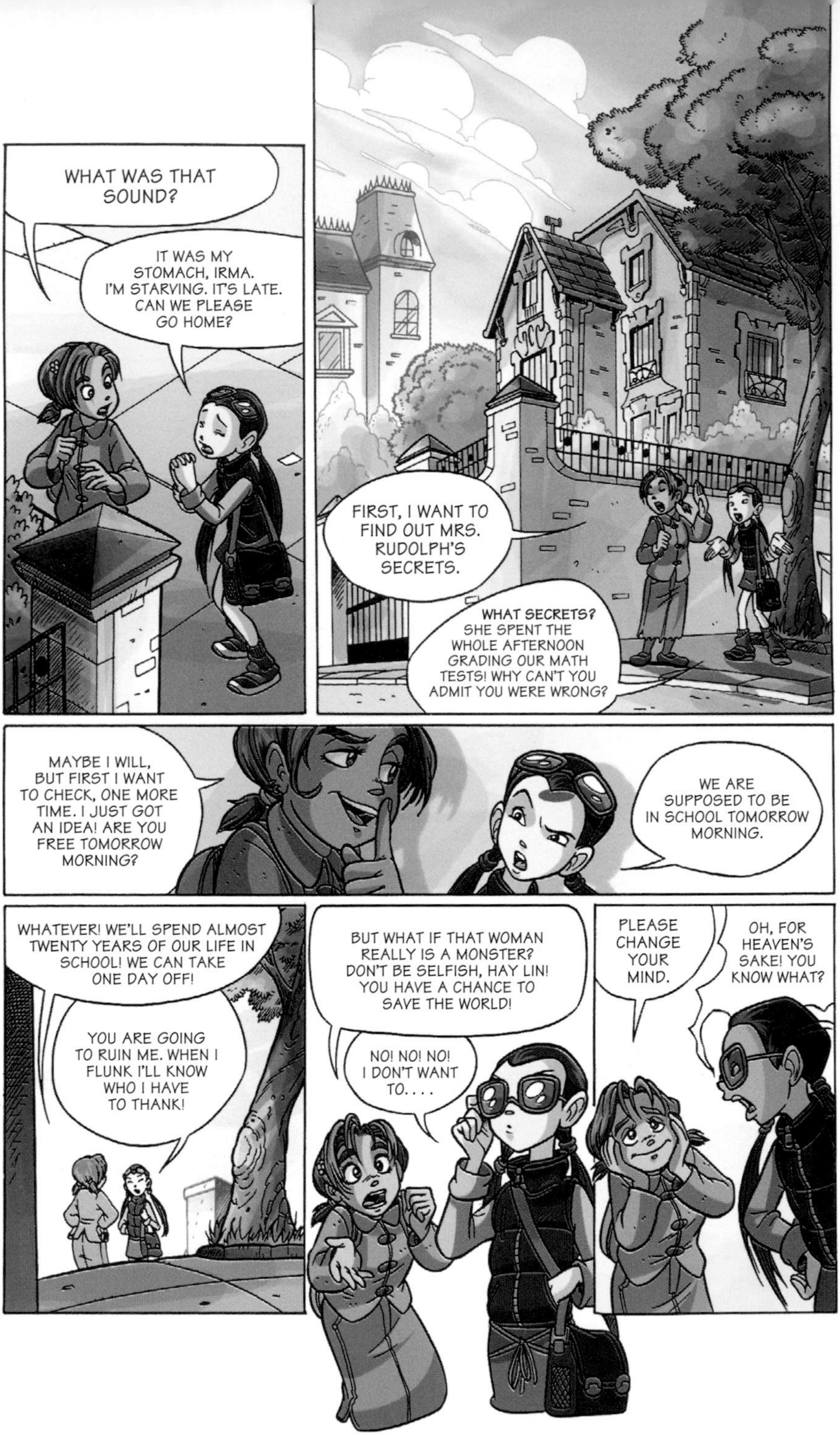
WHAT WAS THAT SOUND?
IT WAS MY STOMACH, IRMA. I'M STARVING. IT'S LATE. CAN WE PLEASE GO HOME?
FIRST, I WANT TO FIND OUT MRS. RUDOLPH'S SECRETS.
WHAT SECRETS? SHE SPENT THE WHOLE AFTERNOON GRADING OUR MATH TESTS! WHY CAN'T YOU ADMIT YOU WERE WRONG?
MAYBE I WILL, BUT FIRST I WANT TO CHECK, ONE MORE TIME. I JUST GOT AN IDEA! ARE YOU FREE TOMORROW MORNING?
WE ARE SUPPOSED TO BE IN SCHOOL TOMORROW MORNING.
WHATEVER! WE'LL SPEND ALMOST TWENTY YEARS OF OUR LIFE IN SCHOOL! WE CAN TAKE ONE DAY OFF!
YOU ARE GOING TO RUIN ME. WHEN I FLUNK I'LL KNOW WHO I HAVE TO THANK!
BUT WHAT IF THAT WOMAN REALLY IS A MONSTER? DON'T BE SELFISH, HAY LIN! YOU HAVE A CHANCE TO SAVE THE WORLD!
NO! NO! NO! I DON'T WANT TO. . . .
PLEASE CHANGE YOUR MIND.
OH, FOR HEAVEN'S SAKE! YOU KNOW WHAT?

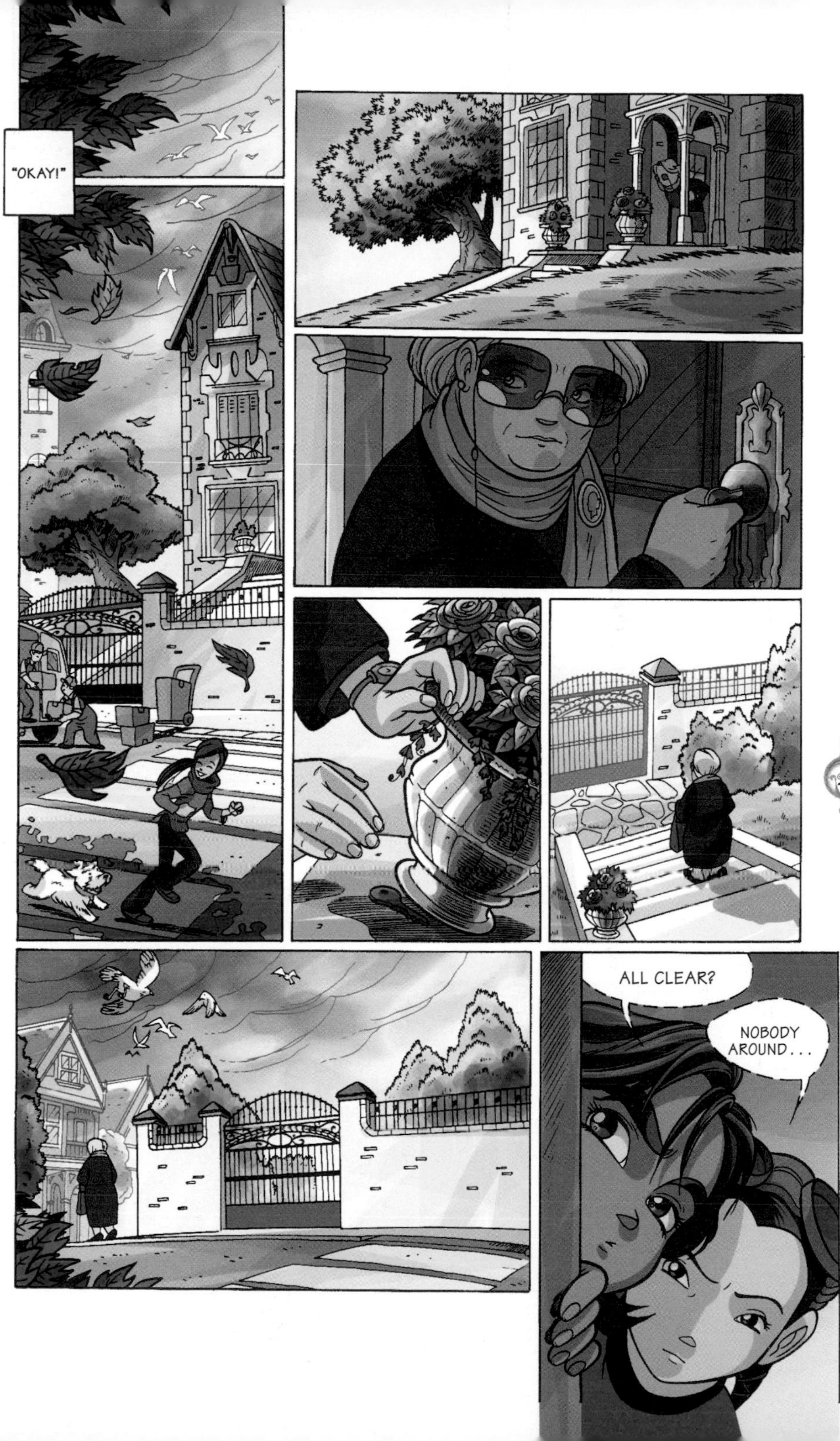
"OKAY!"
ALL CLEAR?
NOBODY AROUND...

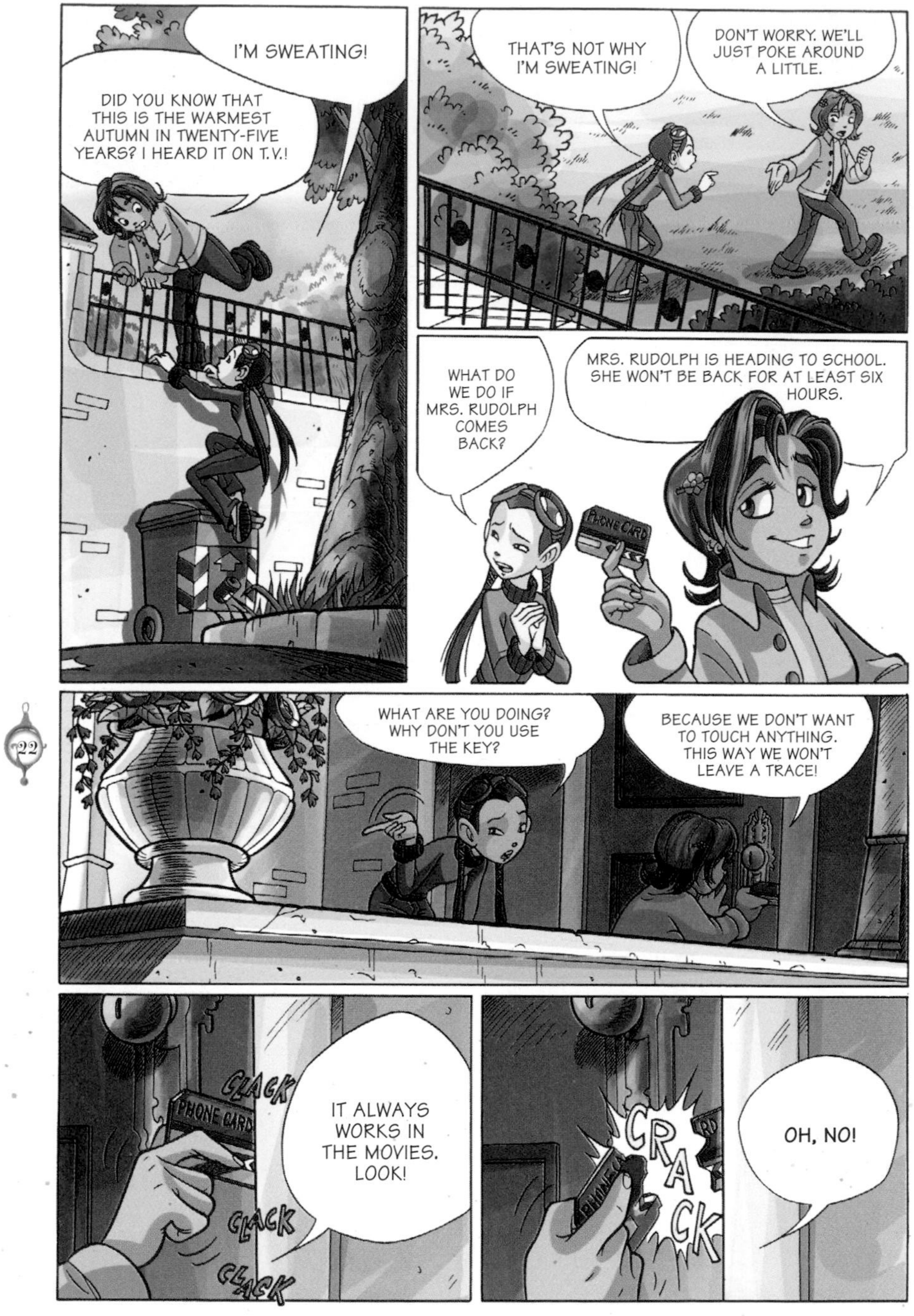
I'M SWEATING!
DID YOU KNOW THAT THIS IS THE WARMEST AUTUMN IN TWENTY-FIVE YEARS? I HEARD IT ON T.V.!
THAT'S NOT WHY I'M SWEATING!
DON'T WORRY. WE'LL JUST POKE AROUND A LITTLE.
WHAT DO WE DO IF MRS. RUDOLPH COMES BACK?
MRS. RUDOLPH IS HEADING TO SCHOOL. SHE WON'T BE BACK FOR AT LEAST SIX HOURS.
PHONE CARD
WHAT ARE YOU DOING? WHY DON'T YOU USE THE KEY?
BECAUSE WE DON'T WANT TO TOUCH ANYTHING. THIS WAY WE WON'T LEAVE A TRACE!
CLACK
PHONE CARD
IT ALWAYS WORKS IN THE MOVIES. LOOK!
CLACK
CLACK
CRACK
OH, NO!

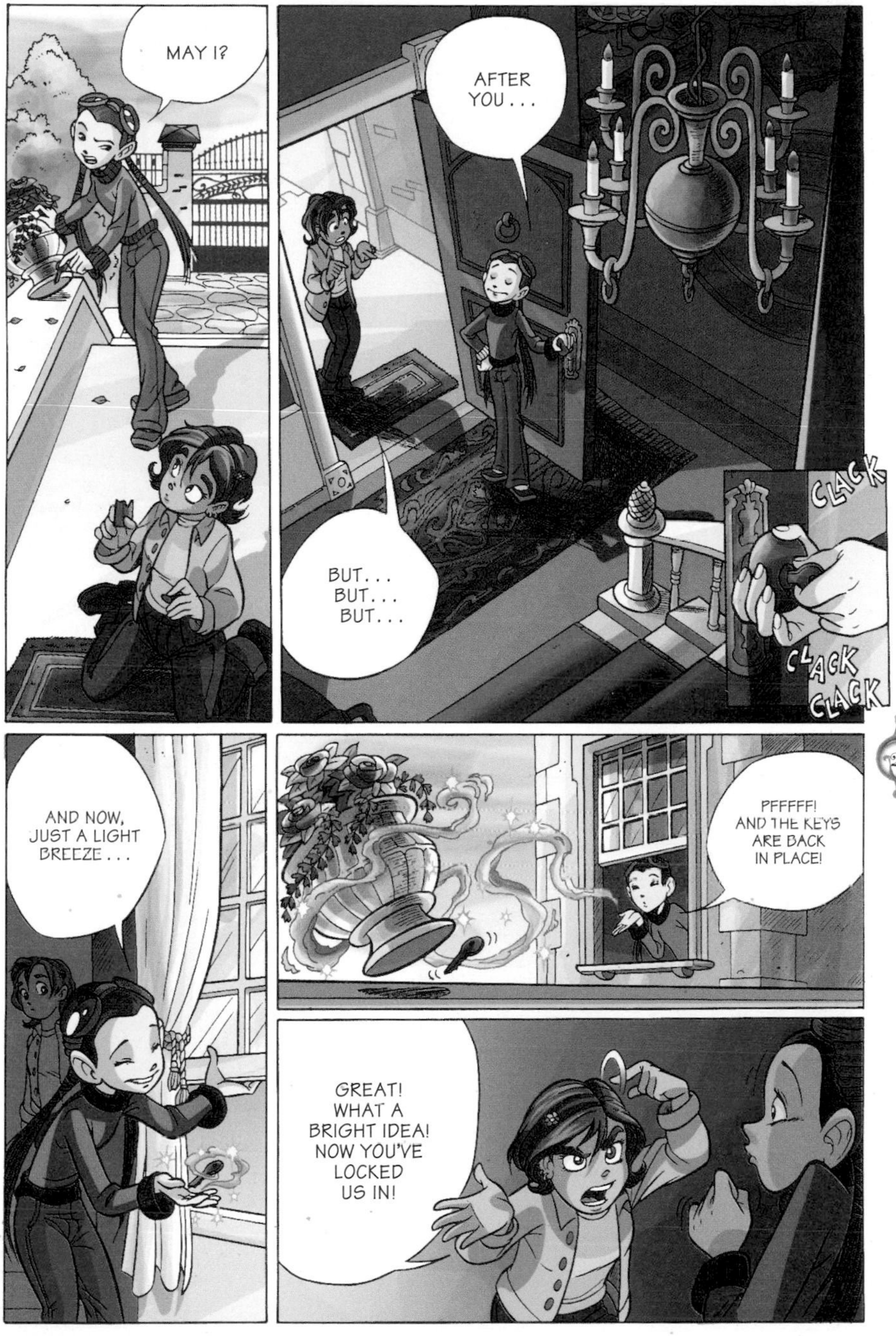
MAY I?
AFTER YOU . . .
BUT. . . BUT. . . BUT. . .
CLACK
CLACK
CLACK
AND NOW, JUST A LIGHT BREEZE . . .
PFFFFF! AND THE KEYS ARE BACK IN PLACE!
GREAT! WHAT A BRIGHT IDEA! NOW YOU'VE LOCKED US IN!

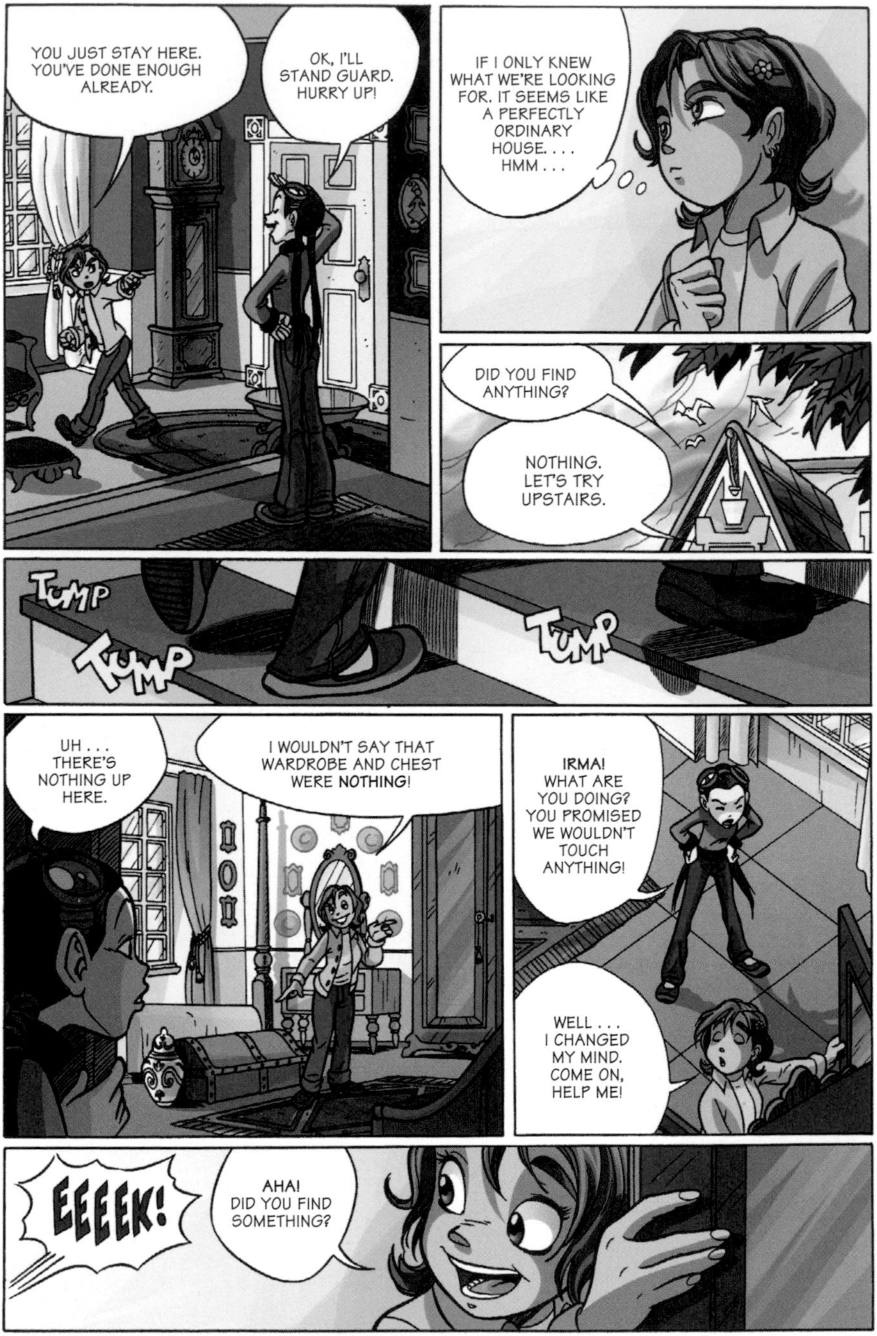
YOU JUST STAY HERE. YOU'VE DONE ENOUGH ALREADY.
OK, I'LL STAND GUARD. HURRY UP!
IF I ONLY KNEW WHAT WE'RE LOOKING FOR. IT SEEMS LIKE A PERFECTLY ORDINARY HOUSE. . . . HMM . . .
DID YOU FIND ANYTHING?
NOTHING. LET'S TRY UPSTAIRS.
TUMP
TUMP
TUMP
UH . . . THERE'S NOTHING UP HERE.
I WOULDN'T SAY THAT WARDROBE AND CHEST WERE **NOTHING**!
IRMA! WHAT ARE YOU DOING? YOU PROMISED WE WOULDN'T TOUCH ANYTHING!
WELL . . . I CHANGED MY MIND. COME ON, HELP ME!
EEEEK!
AHA! DID YOU FIND SOMETHING?

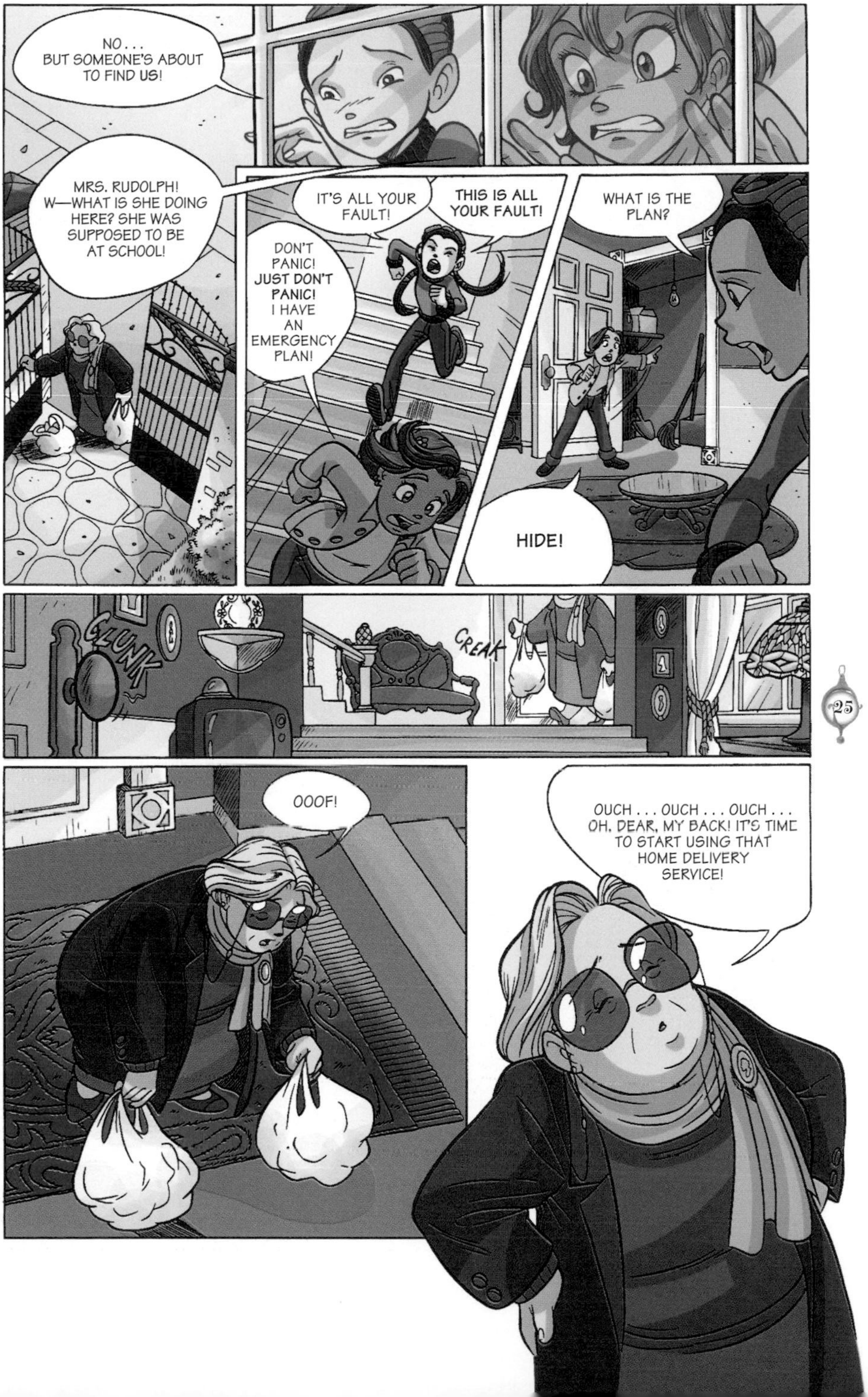
NO . . . BUT SOMEONE'S ABOUT TO FIND US!
MRS. RUDOLPH! W—WHAT IS SHE DOING HERE? SHE WAS SUPPOSED TO BE AT SCHOOL!
IT'S ALL YOUR FAULT!
THIS IS ALL YOUR FAULT!
DON'T PANIC! JUST DON'T PANIC! I HAVE AN EMERGENCY PLAN!
WHAT IS THE PLAN?
HIDE!
CLUNK
CREAK
OOOF!
OUCH . . . OUCH . . . OUCH . . . OH, DEAR, MY BACK! IT'S TIME TO START USING THAT HOME DELIVERY SERVICE!

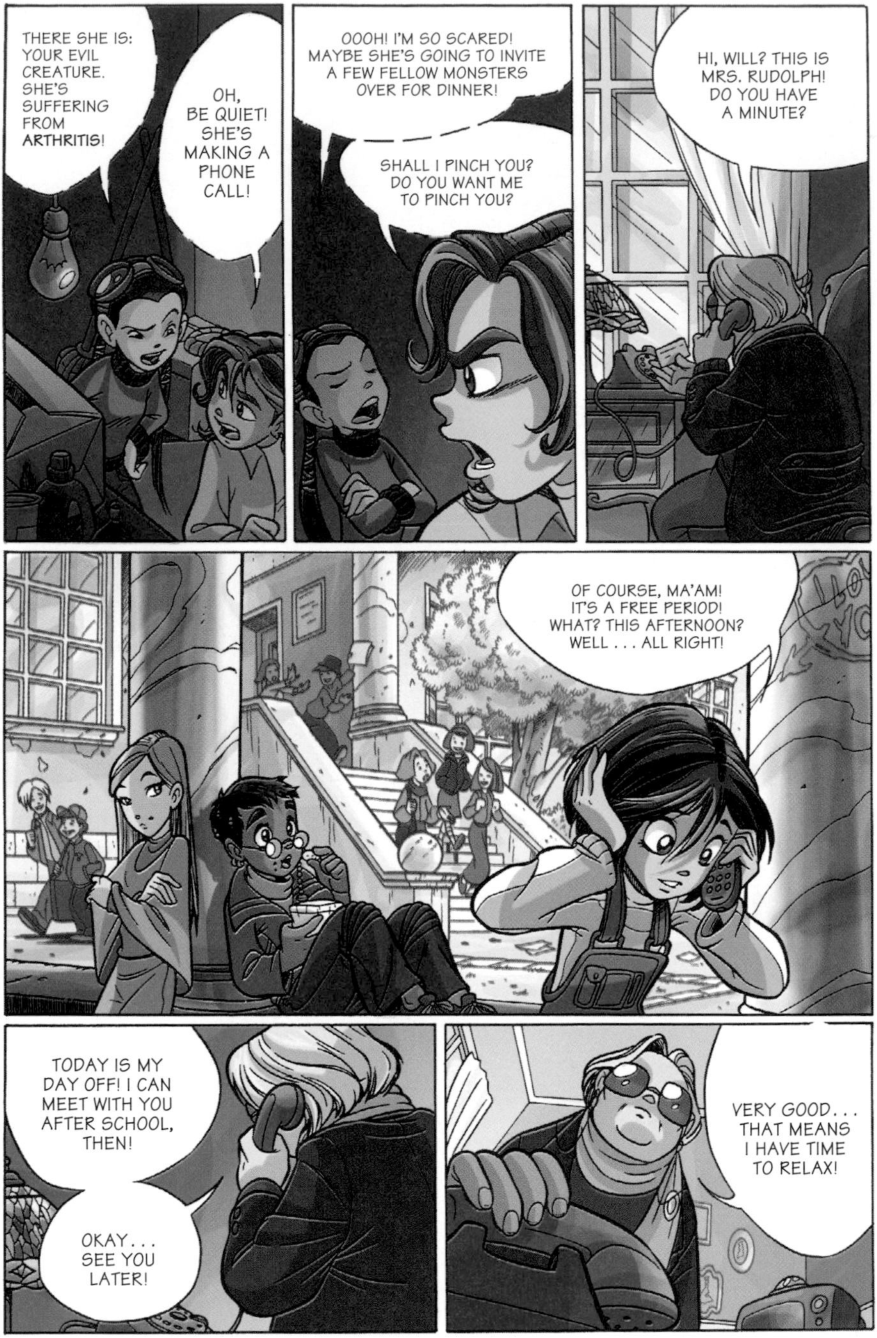

THERE SHE IS: YOUR EVIL CREATURE. SHE'S SUFFERING FROM ARTHRITIS!
OH, BE QUIET! SHE'S MAKING A PHONE CALL!
OOOH! I'M SO SCARED! MAYBE SHE'S GOING TO INVITE A FEW FELLOW MONSTERS OVER FOR DINNER!
SHALL I PINCH YOU? DO YOU WANT ME TO PINCH YOU?
HI, WILL? THIS IS MRS. RUDOLPH! DO YOU HAVE A MINUTE?
OF COURSE, MA'AM! IT'S A FREE PERIOD! WHAT? THIS AFTERNOON? WELL . . . ALL RIGHT!
TODAY IS MY DAY OFF! I CAN MEET WITH YOU AFTER SCHOOL, THEN!
OKAY . . . SEE YOU LATER!
VERY GOOD . . . THAT MEANS I HAVE TIME TO RELAX!

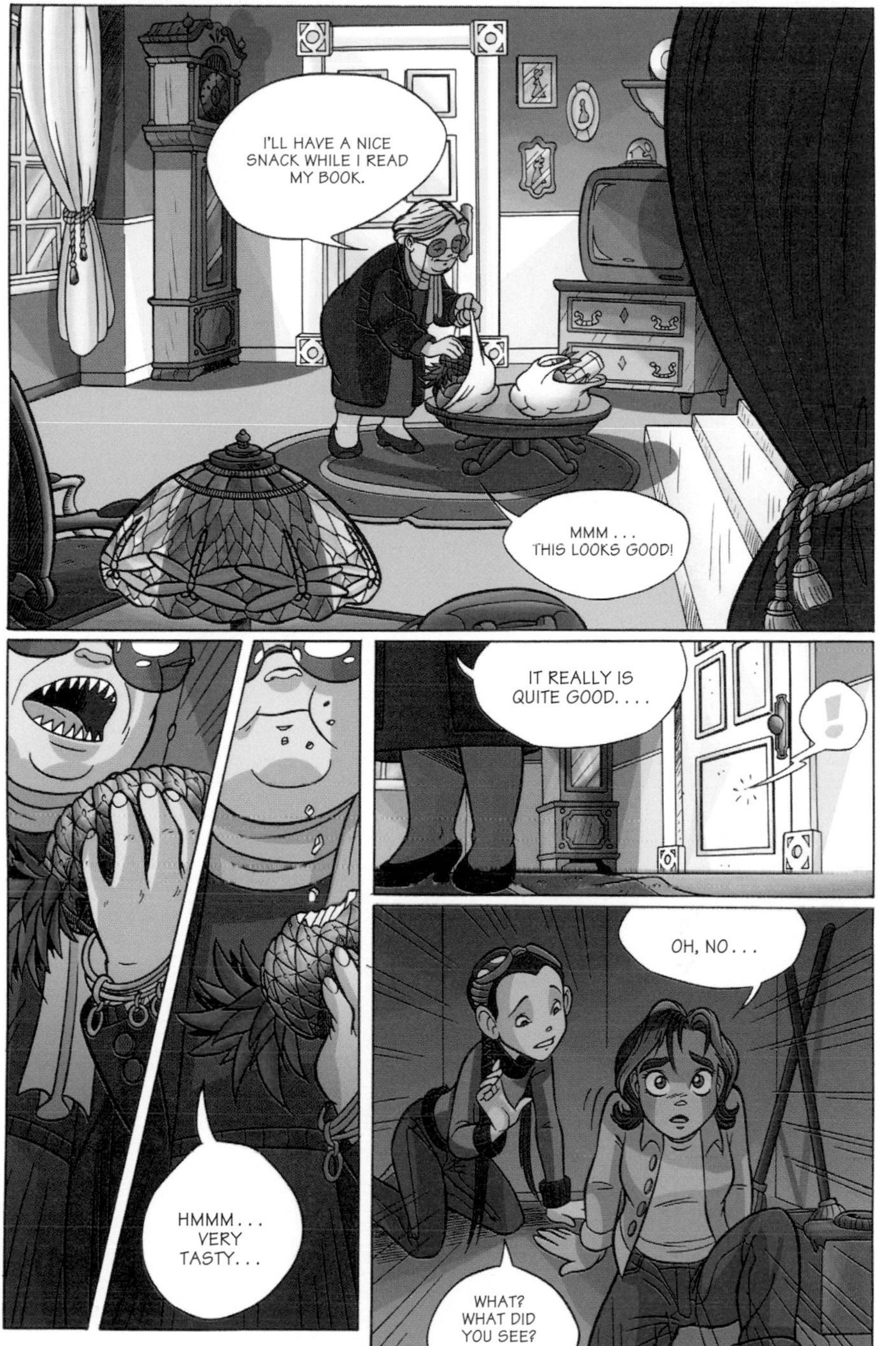
I'LL HAVE A NICE SNACK WHILE I READ MY BOOK.
MMM . . . THIS LOOKS GOOD!
HMMM . . . VERY TASTY. . .
IT REALLY IS QUITE GOOD. . . .
!
OH, NO . . .
WHAT? WHAT DID YOU SEE?

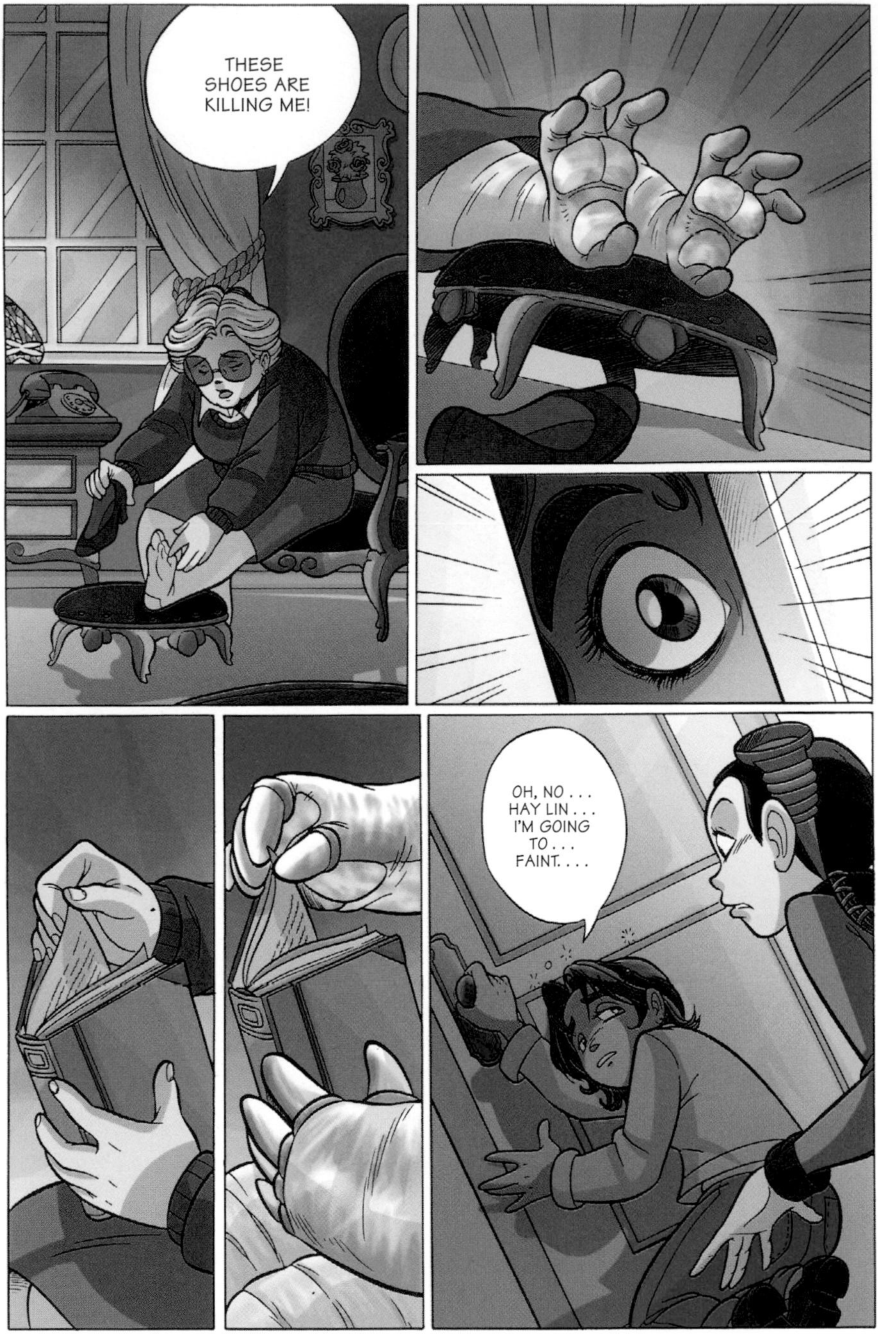
THESE SHOES ARE KILLING ME!
OH, NO . . . HAY LIN . . . I'M GOING TO . . . FAINT. . . .

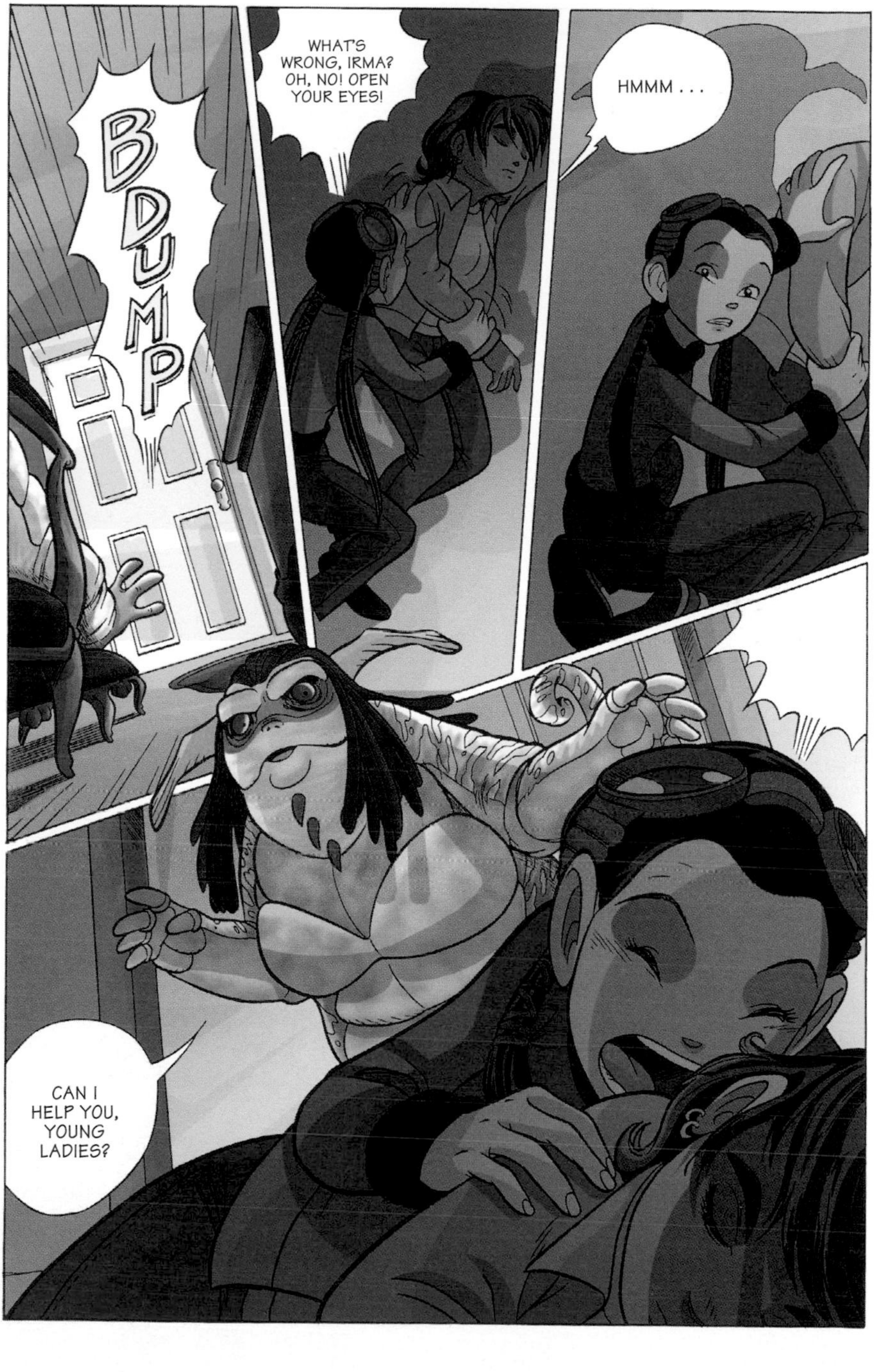
BDUMP
WHAT'S WRONG, IRMA? OH, NO! OPEN YOUR EYES!
HMMM . . .
CAN I HELP YOU, YOUNG LADIES?

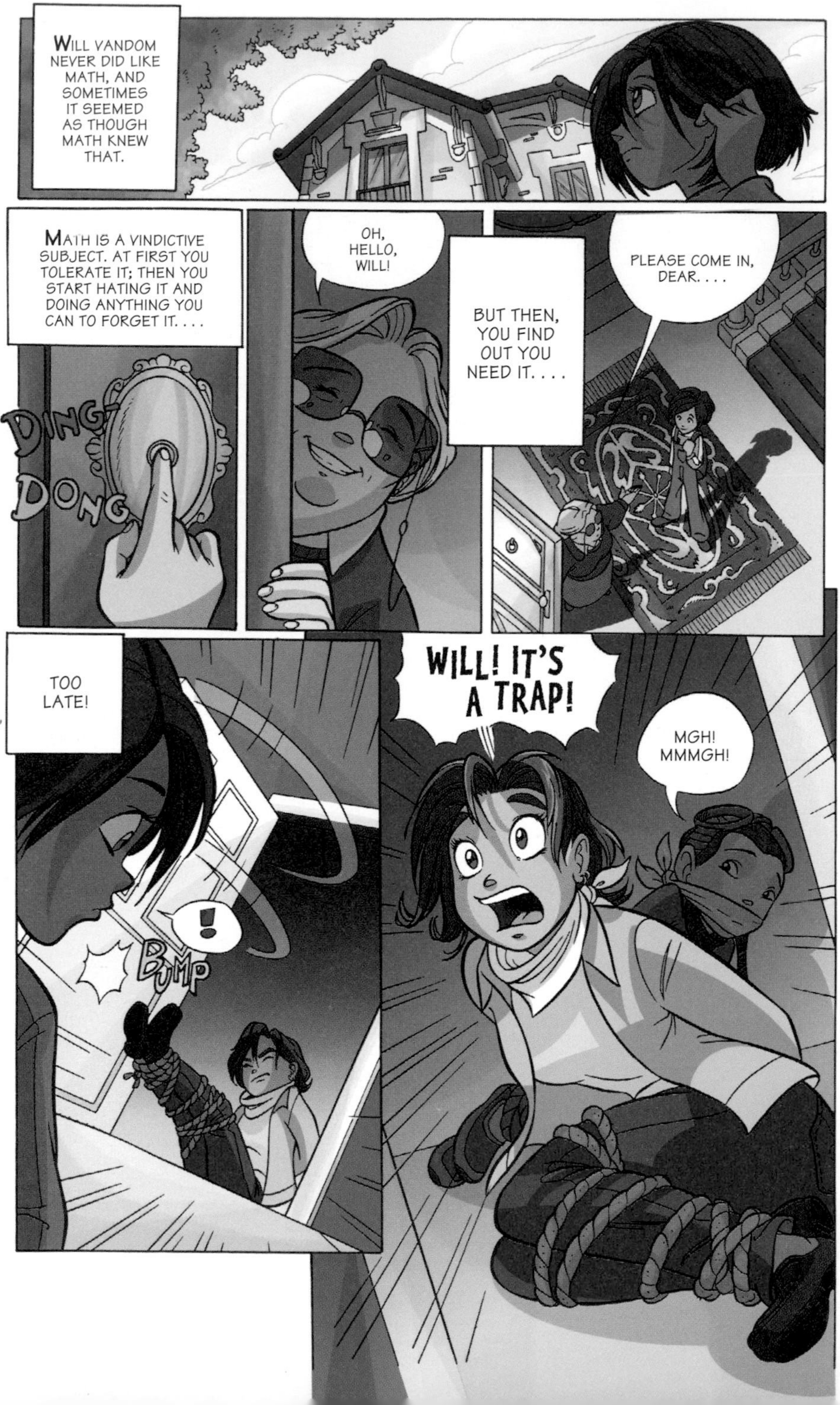
WILL VANDOM NEVER DID LIKE MATH, AND SOMETIMES IT SEEMED AS THOUGH MATH KNEW THAT.
MATH IS A VINDICTIVE SUBJECT. AT FIRST YOU TOLERATE IT; THEN YOU START HATING IT AND DOING ANYTHING YOU CAN TO FORGET IT. . . .
DING-DONG
OH, HELLO, WILL!
BUT THEN, YOU FIND OUT YOU NEED IT. . . .
PLEASE COME IN, DEAR. . . .
TOO LATE!
!
BUMP
WILL! IT'S A TRAP!
MGH! MMMGH!

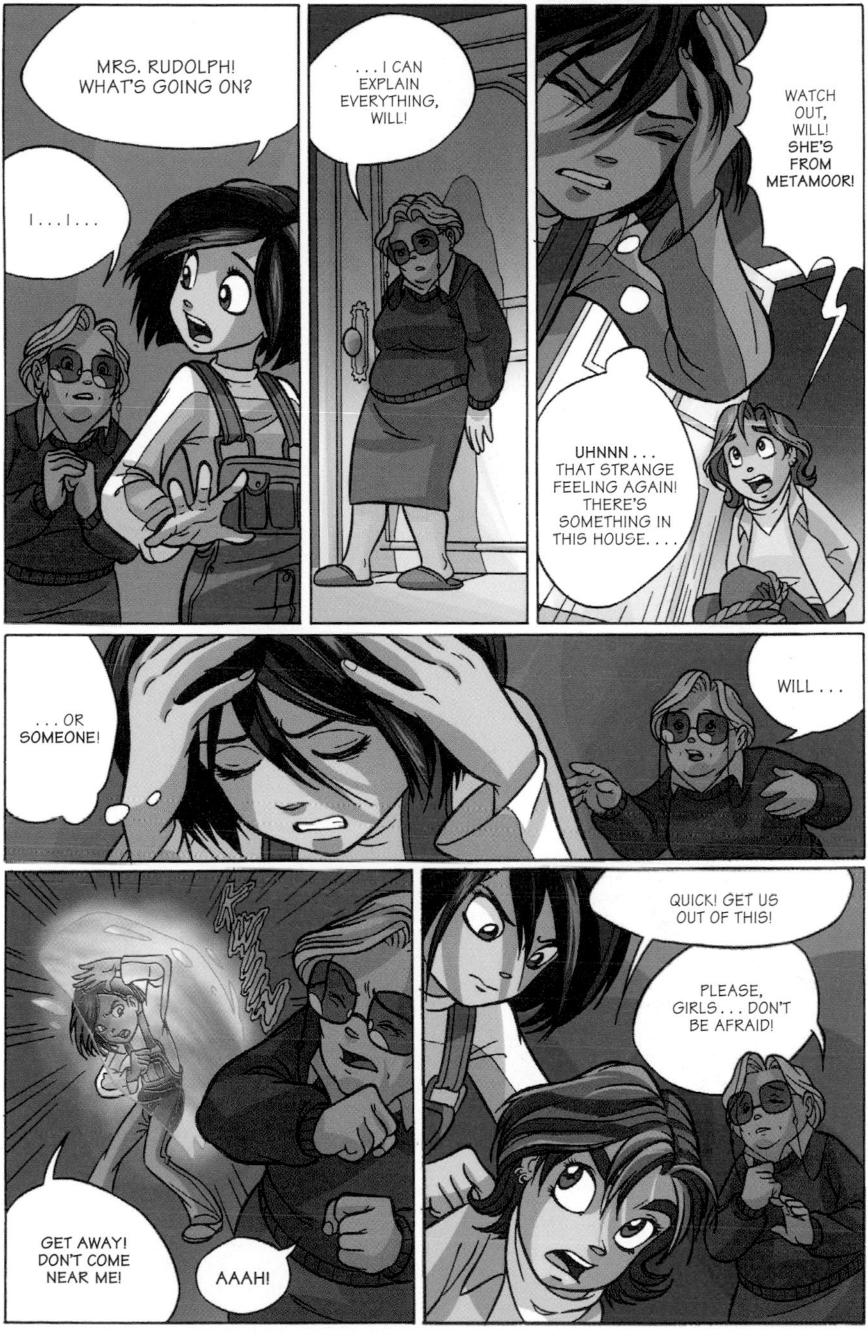

MRS. RUDOLPH! WHAT'S GOING ON?
I . . . I . . .
. . . I CAN EXPLAIN EVERYTHING, WILL!
WATCH OUT, WILL! SHE'S FROM METAMOOR!
UHNNN . . . THAT STRANGE FEELING AGAIN! THERE'S SOMETHING IN THIS HOUSE. . . .
. . . OR SOMEONE!
WILL . . .
GET AWAY! DON'T COME NEAR ME!
AAAH!
QUICK! GET US OUT OF THIS!
PLEASE, GIRLS . . . DON'T BE AFRAID!

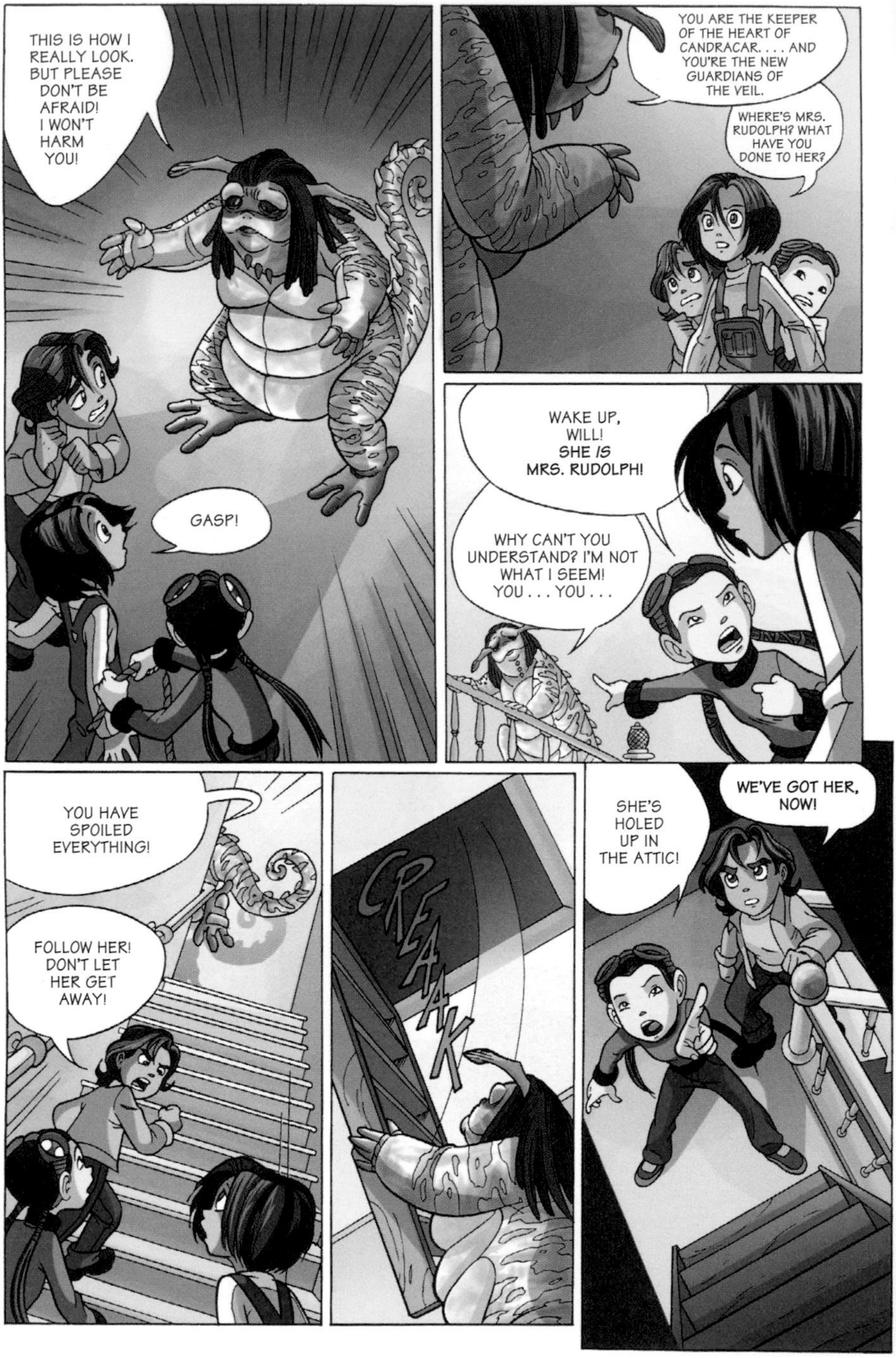
THIS IS HOW I REALLY LOOK. BUT PLEASE DON'T BE AFRAID! I WON'T HARM YOU!
GASP!
YOU ARE THE KEEPER OF THE HEART OF CANDRACAR. . . . AND YOU'RE THE NEW GUARDIANS OF THE VEIL.
WHERE'S MRS. RUDOLPH? WHAT HAVE YOU DONE TO HER?
WAKE UP, WILL! SHE *IS* MRS. RUDOLPH!
WHY CAN'T YOU UNDERSTAND? I'M NOT WHAT I SEEM! YOU . . . YOU . . .
YOU HAVE SPOILED EVERYTHING!
FOLLOW HER! DON'T LET HER GET AWAY!
CREAAAK
SHE'S HOLED UP IN THE ATTIC!
WE'VE GOT HER, NOW!

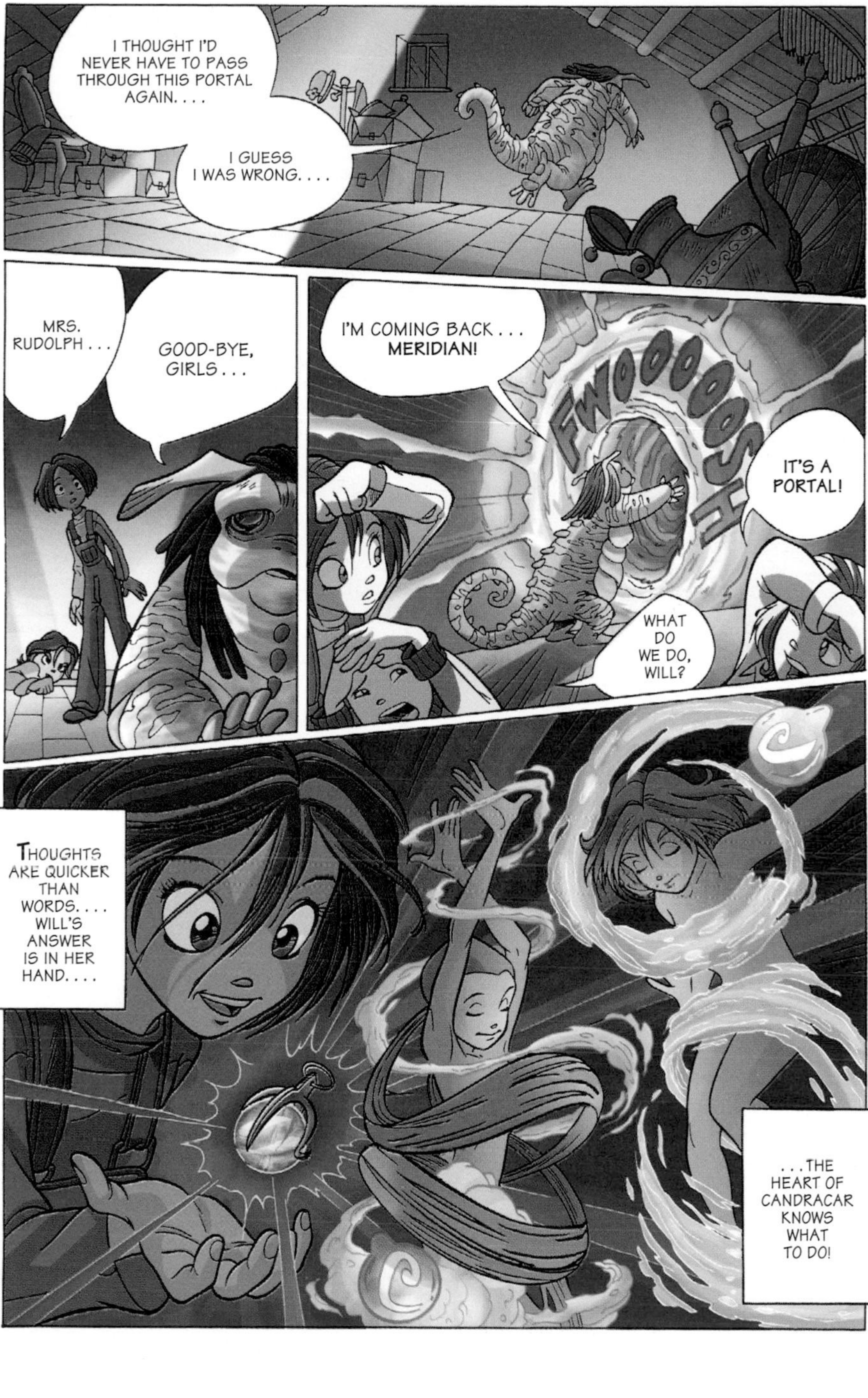
I THOUGHT I'D NEVER HAVE TO PASS THROUGH THIS PORTAL AGAIN. . . .
I GUESS I WAS WRONG. . . .
MRS. RUDOLPH . . .
GOOD-BYE, GIRLS . . .
I'M COMING BACK . . . MERIDIAN!
FWOOOOOSH
IT'S A PORTAL!
WHAT DO WE DO, WILL?
THOUGHTS ARE QUICKER THAN WORDS. . . . WILL'S ANSWER IS IN HER HAND. . . .
. . . THE HEART OF CANDRACAR KNOWS WHAT TO DO!

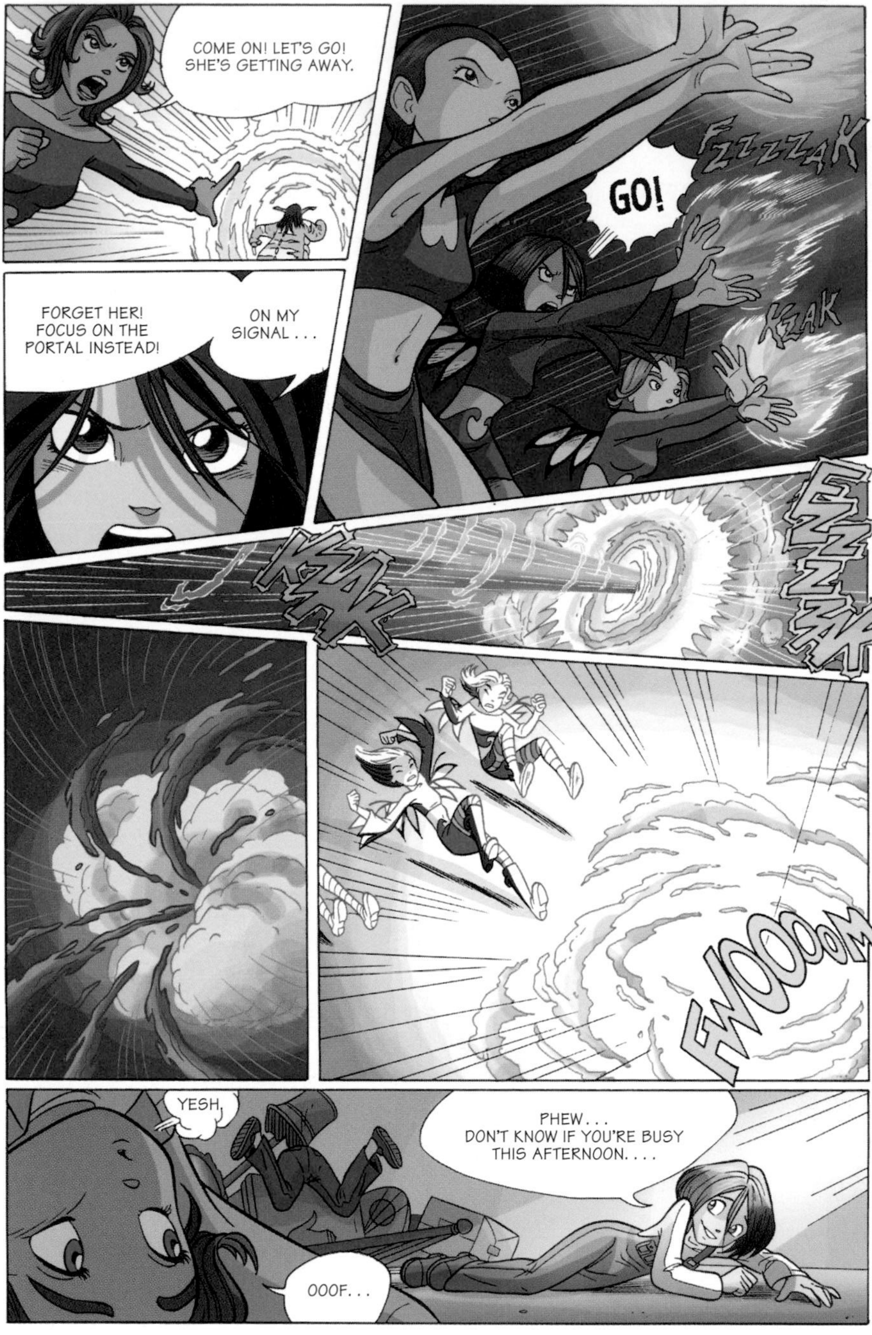
COME ON! LET'S GO! SHE'S GETTING AWAY.
FZZZZAK
GO!
KZAK
FORGET HER! FOCUS ON THE PORTAL INSTEAD!
ON MY SIGNAL . . .
KZAK
FZZZZAK
FWOOOOM
YESH.
PHEW . . . DON'T KNOW IF YOU'RE BUSY THIS AFTERNOON. . . .
OOOF. . .

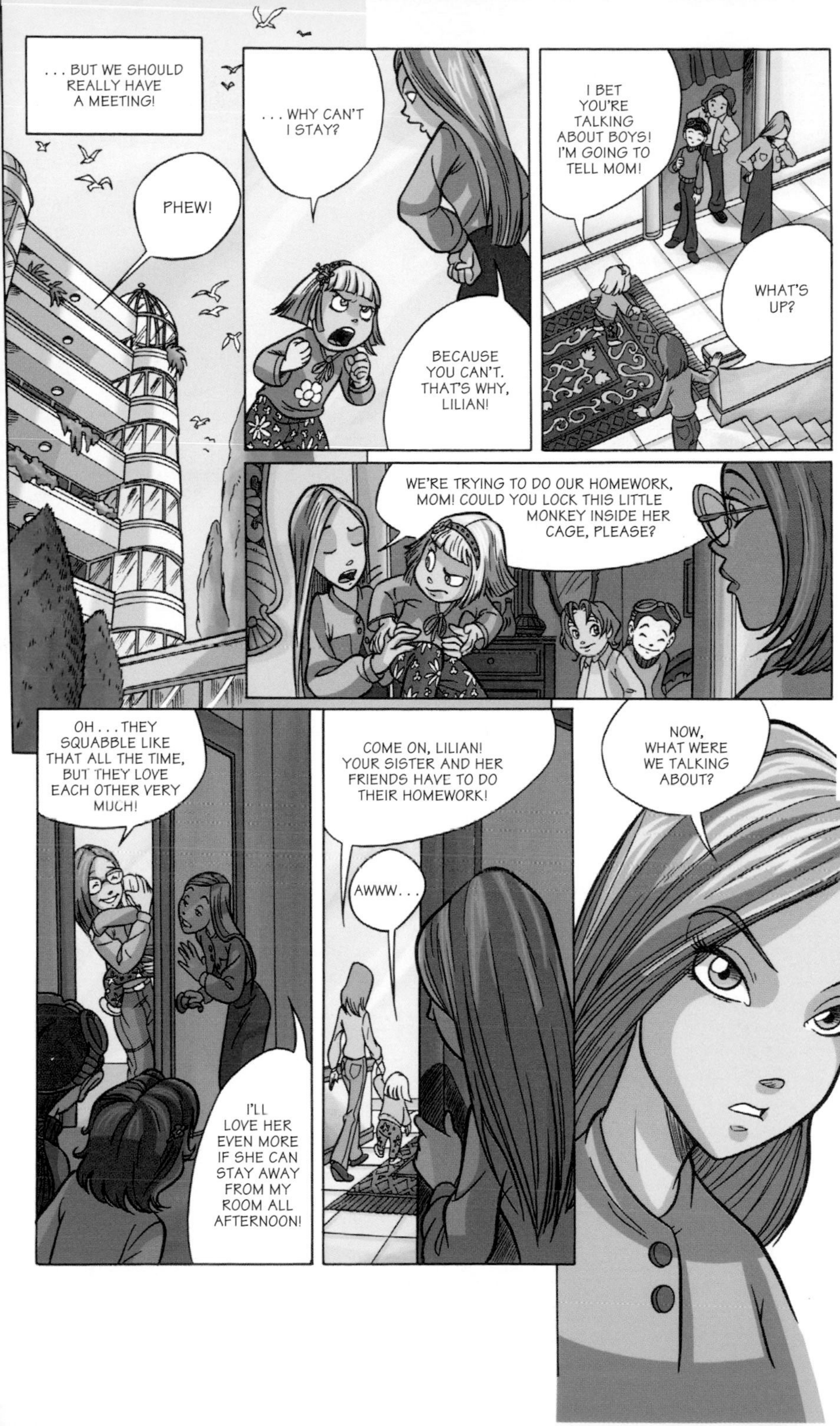

. . . BUT WE SHOULD REALLY HAVE A MEETING!
PHEW!
. . . WHY CAN'T I STAY?
BECAUSE YOU CAN'T. THAT'S WHY, LILIAN!
I BET YOU'RE TALKING ABOUT BOYS! I'M GOING TO TELL MOM!
WHAT'S UP?
WE'RE TRYING TO DO OUR HOMEWORK, MOM! COULD YOU LOCK THIS LITTLE MONKEY INSIDE HER CAGE, PLEASE?
OH . . . THEY SQUABBLE LIKE THAT ALL THE TIME, BUT THEY LOVE EACH OTHER VERY MUCH!
I'LL LOVE HER EVEN MORE IF SHE CAN STAY AWAY FROM MY ROOM ALL AFTERNOON!
COME ON, LILIAN! YOUR SISTER AND HER FRIENDS HAVE TO DO THEIR HOMEWORK!
AWWW. . .
NOW, WHAT WERE WE TALKING ABOUT?

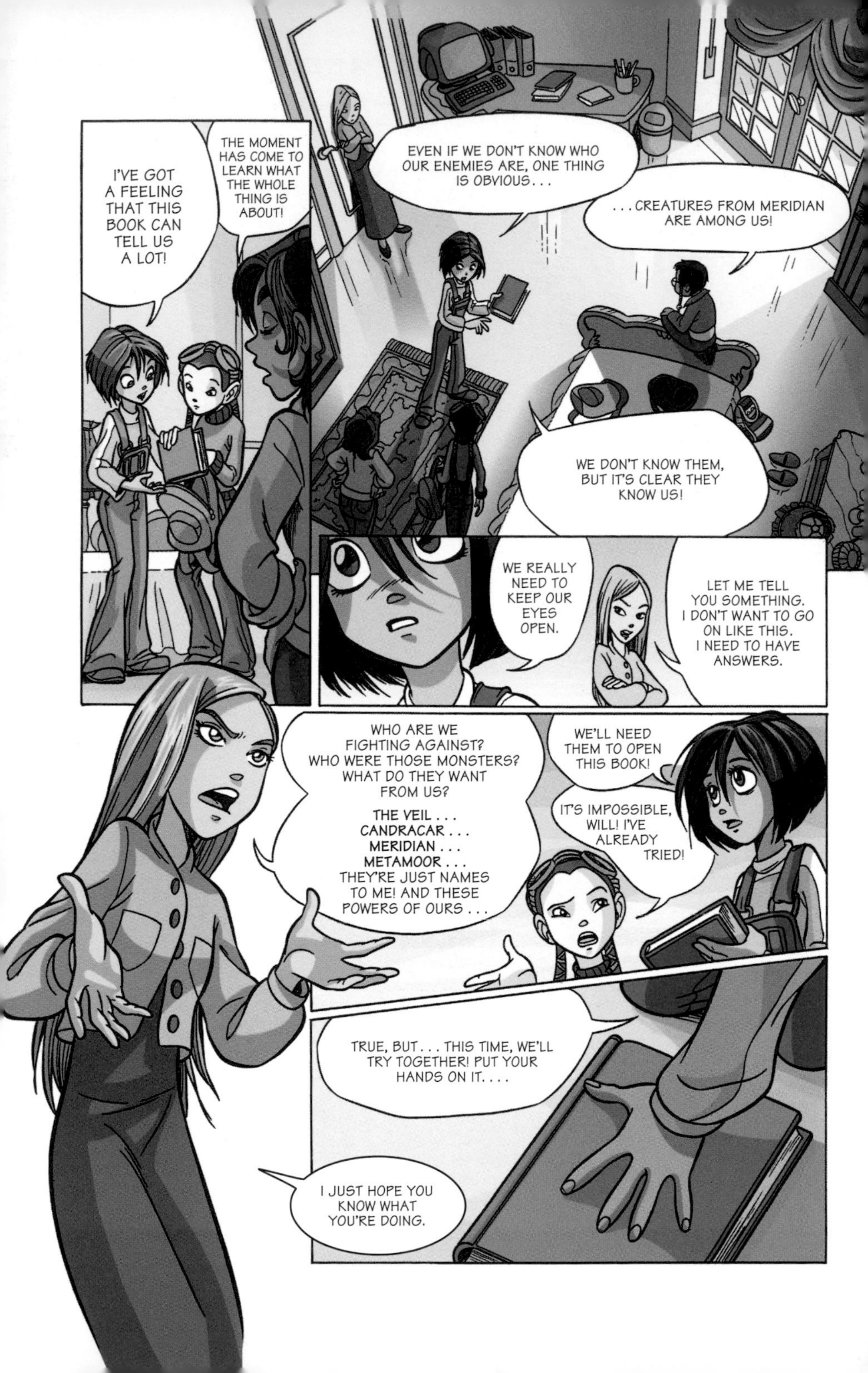

EVEN IF WE DON'T KNOW WHO OUR ENEMIES ARE, ONE THING IS OBVIOUS . . .
. . . CREATURES FROM MERIDIAN ARE AMONG US!
I'VE GOT A FEELING THAT THIS BOOK CAN TELL US A LOT!
THE MOMENT HAS COME TO LEARN WHAT THE WHOLE THING IS ABOUT!
WE DON'T KNOW THEM, BUT IT'S CLEAR THEY KNOW US!
WE REALLY NEED TO KEEP OUR EYES OPEN.
LET ME TELL YOU SOMETHING. I DON'T WANT TO GO ON LIKE THIS. I NEED TO HAVE ANSWERS.
WHO ARE WE FIGHTING AGAINST? WHO WERE THOSE MONSTERS? WHAT DO THEY WANT FROM US?
THE VEIL . . . CANDRACAR . . . MERIDIAN . . . METAMOOR . . . THEY'RE JUST NAMES TO ME! AND THESE POWERS OF OURS . . .
WE'LL NEED THEM TO OPEN THIS BOOK!
IT'S IMPOSSIBLE, WILL! I'VE ALREADY TRIED!
TRUE, BUT . . . THIS TIME, WE'LL TRY TOGETHER! PUT YOUR HANDS ON IT. . . .
I JUST HOPE YOU KNOW WHAT YOU'RE DOING.

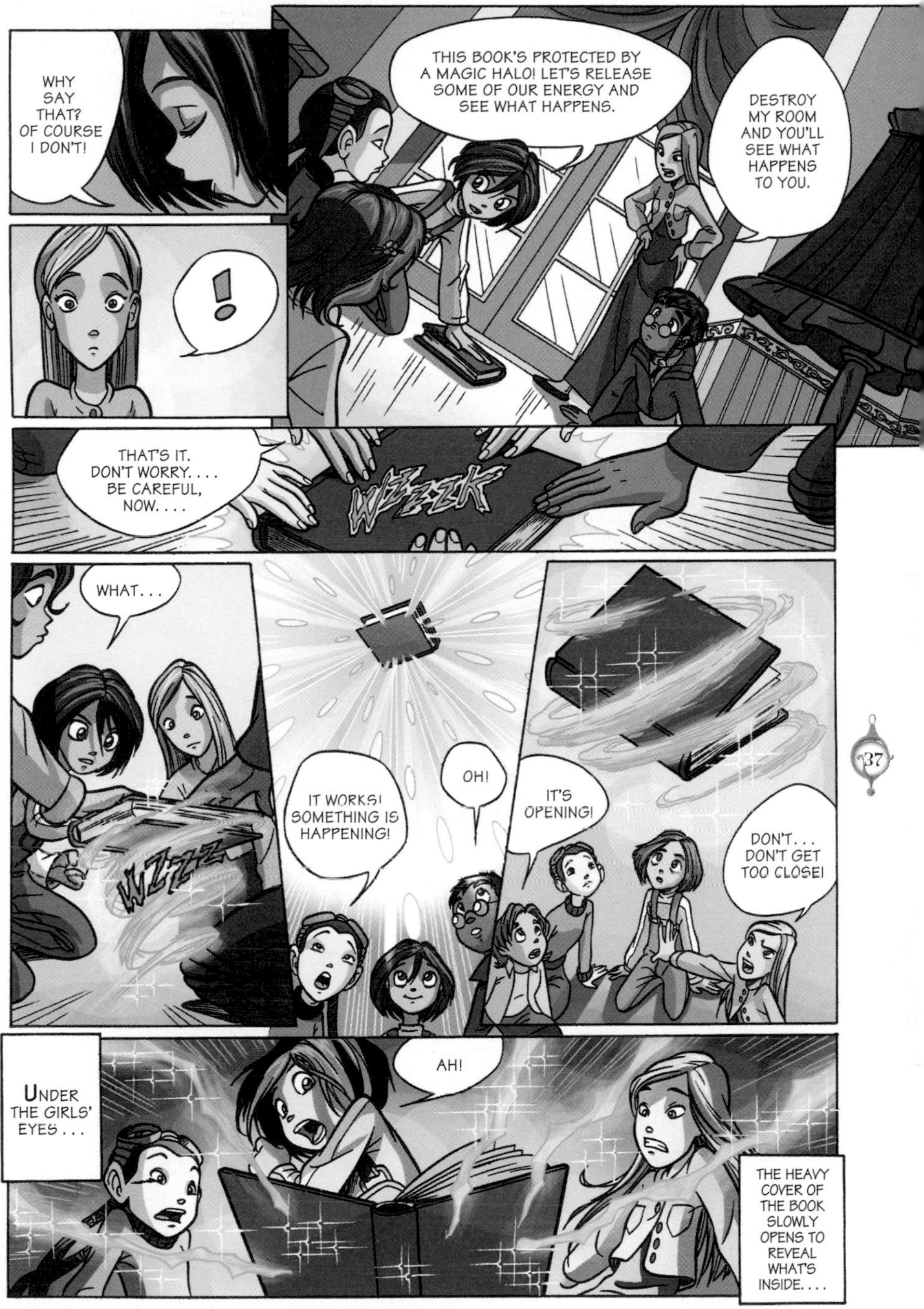
WHY SAY THAT? OF COURSE I DON'T!
THIS BOOK'S PROTECTED BY A MAGIC HALO! LET'S RELEASE SOME OF OUR ENERGY AND SEE WHAT HAPPENS.
DESTROY MY ROOM AND YOU'LL SEE WHAT HAPPENS TO YOU.
!
THAT'S IT. DON'T WORRY. . . . BE CAREFUL, NOW. . . .
WZZZK
WHAT. . .
WZZZ
IT WORKS! SOMETHING IS HAPPENING!
OH!
IT'S OPENING!
DON'T. . . DON'T GET TOO CLOSE!
UNDER THE GIRLS' EYES . . .
AH!
THE HEAVY COVER OF THE BOOK SLOWLY OPENS TO REVEAL WHAT'S INSIDE. . . .

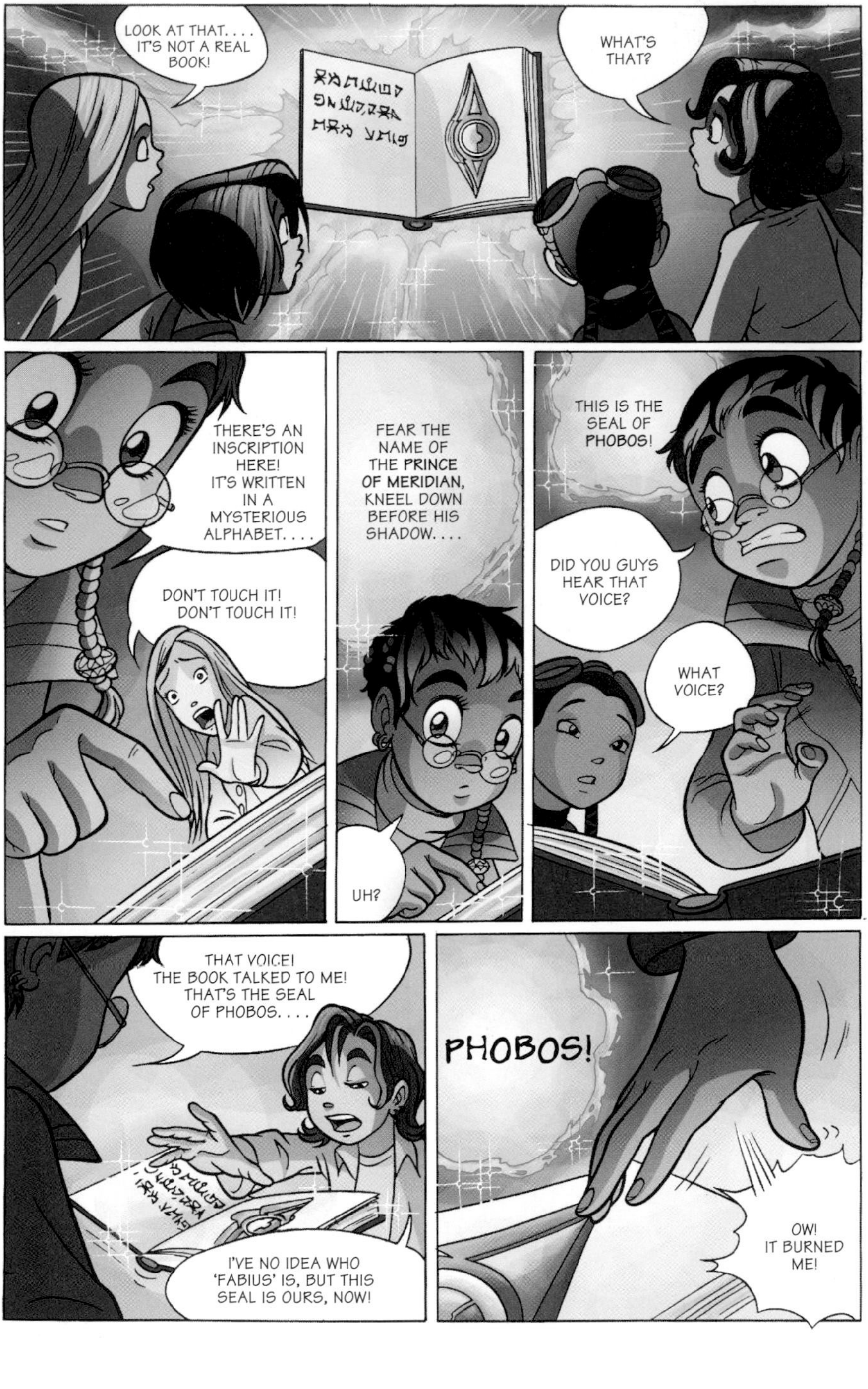
LOOK AT THAT. . . . IT'S NOT A REAL BOOK!
WHAT'S THAT?
THERE'S AN INSCRIPTION HERE! IT'S WRITTEN IN A MYSTERIOUS ALPHABET. . . .
DON'T TOUCH IT! DON'T TOUCH IT!
FEAR THE NAME OF THE **PRINCE OF MERIDIAN**, KNEEL DOWN BEFORE HIS SHADOW. . . .
UH?
THIS IS THE SEAL OF **PHOBOS**!
DID YOU GUYS HEAR THAT VOICE?
WHAT VOICE?
THAT VOICE! THE BOOK TALKED TO ME! THAT'S THE SEAL OF PHOBOS. . . .
I'VE NO IDEA WHO 'FABIUS' IS, BUT THIS SEAL IS OURS, NOW!
PHOBOS!
OW! IT BURNED ME!

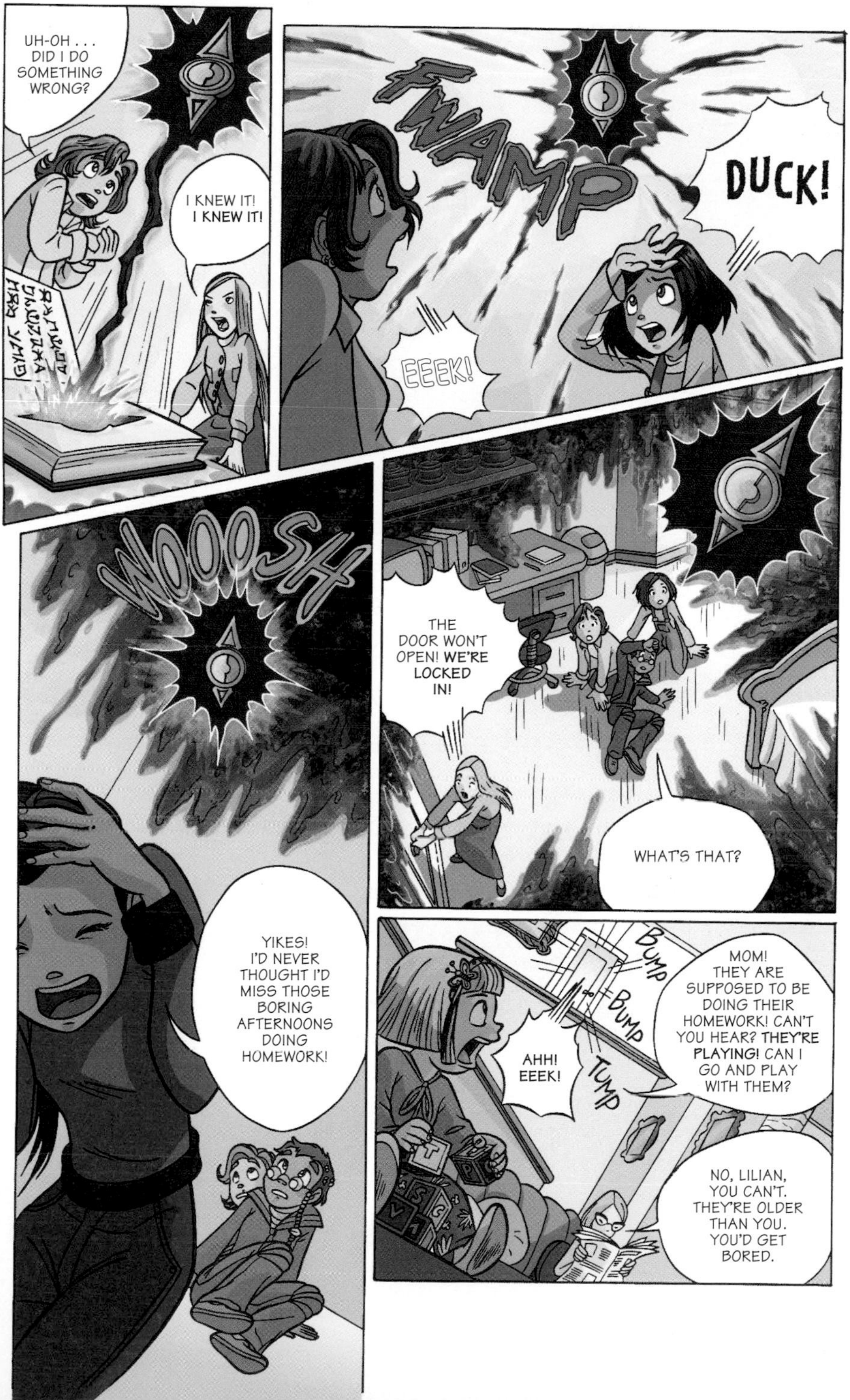
UH-OH . . . DID I DO SOMETHING WRONG?
I KNEW IT! I KNEW IT!
FWAMP
DUCK!
EEEK!
WOOOSH
THE DOOR WON'T OPEN! WE'RE LOCKED IN!
WHAT'S THAT?
YIKES! I'D NEVER THOUGHT I'D MISS THOSE BORING AFTERNOONS DOING HOMEWORK!
BUMP
BUMP
TUMP
AHH! EEEK!
MOM! THEY ARE SUPPOSED TO BE DOING THEIR HOMEWORK! CAN'T YOU HEAR? THEY'RE PLAYING! CAN I GO AND PLAY WITH THEM?
NO, LILIAN, YOU CAN'T. THEY'RE OLDER THAN YOU. YOU'D GET BORED.

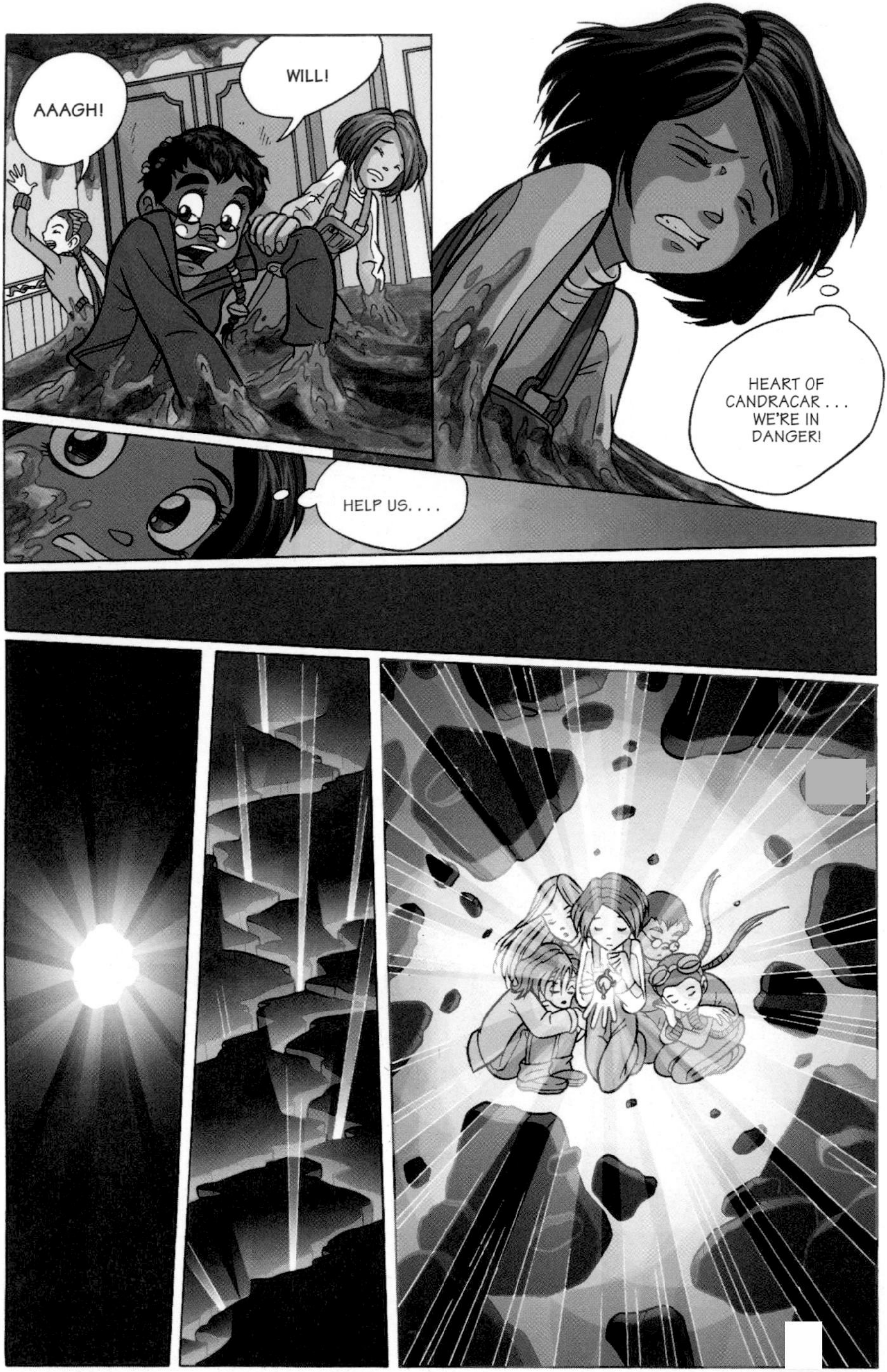
AAAGH!
WILL!
HEART OF CANDRACAR . . . WE'RE IN DANGER!
HELP US. . . .

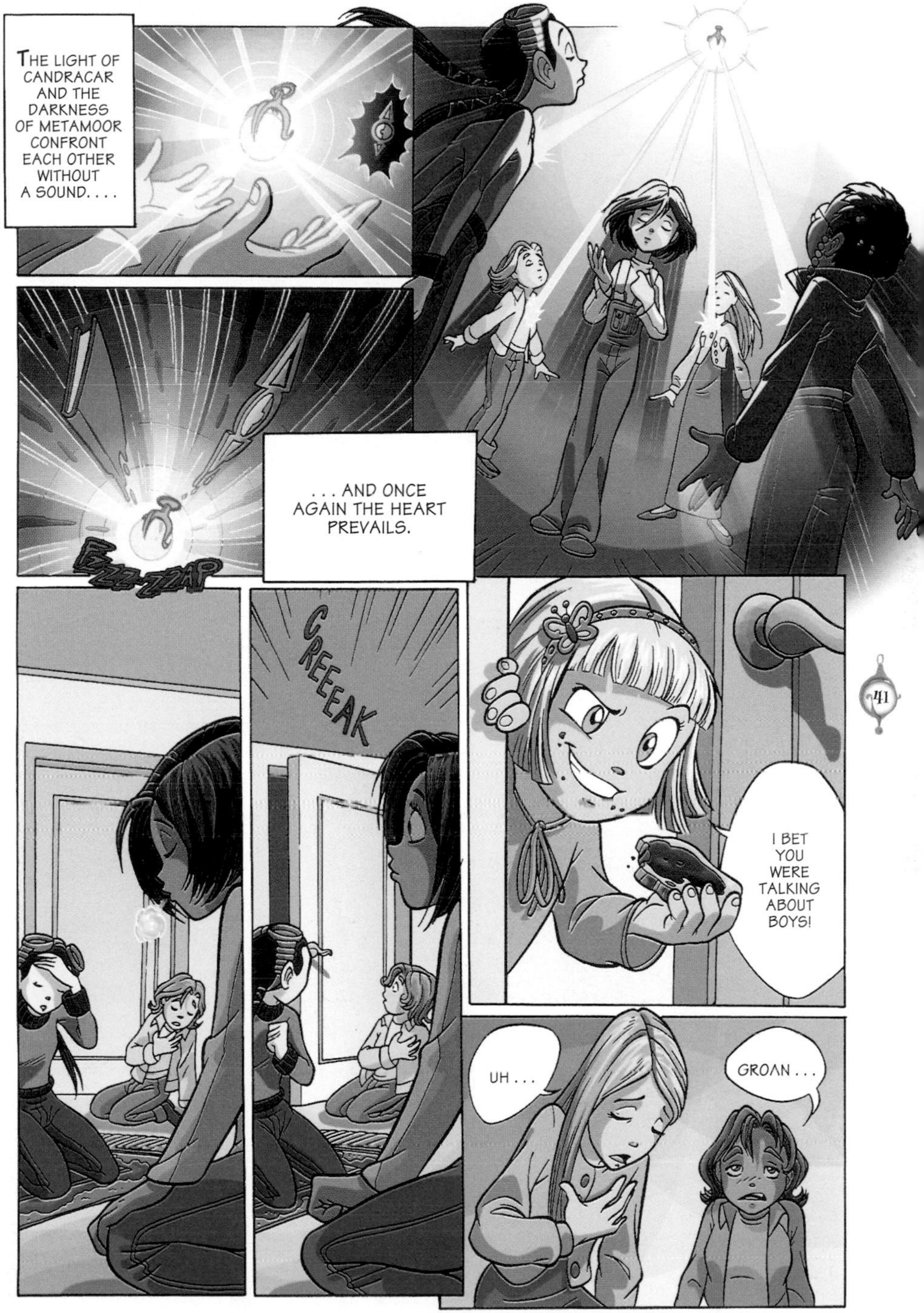
THE LIGHT OF CANDRACAR AND THE DARKNESS OF METAMOOR CONFRONT EACH OTHER WITHOUT A SOUND. . . .
. . . AND ONCE AGAIN THE HEART PREVAILS.
EZZZ-ZZZAP
CREEEAK
I BET YOU WERE TALKING ABOUT BOYS!
UH . . .
GROAN . . .

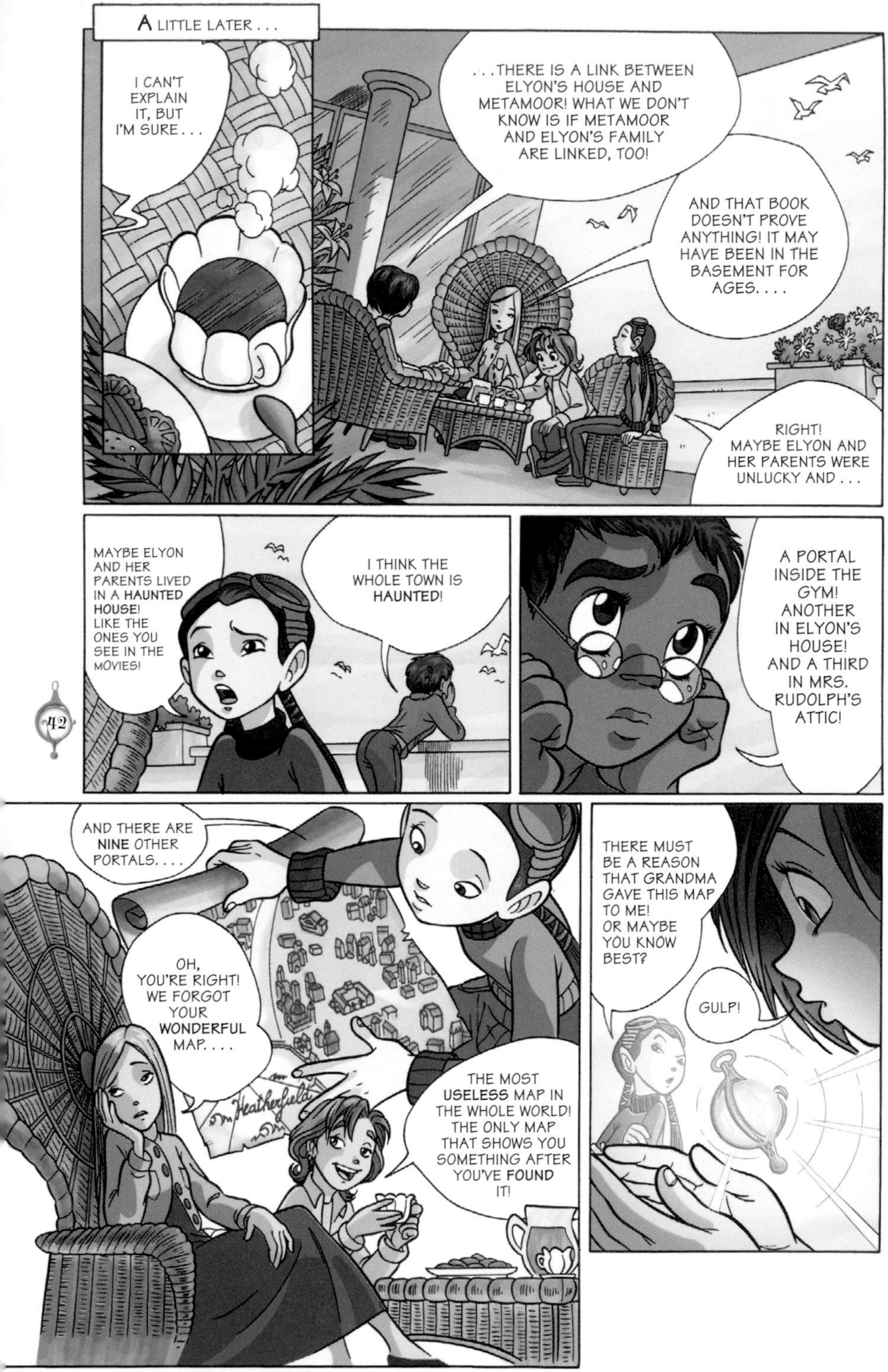
A LITTLE LATER . . .
I CAN'T EXPLAIN IT, BUT I'M SURE . . .
. . .THERE IS A LINK BETWEEN ELYON'S HOUSE AND METAMOOR! WHAT WE DON'T KNOW IS IF METAMOOR AND ELYON'S FAMILY ARE LINKED, TOO!
AND THAT BOOK DOESN'T PROVE ANYTHING! IT MAY HAVE BEEN IN THE BASEMENT FOR AGES. . . .
RIGHT! MAYBE ELYON AND HER PARENTS WERE UNLUCKY AND . . .
MAYBE ELYON AND HER PARENTS LIVED IN A **HAUNTED HOUSE**! LIKE THE ONES YOU SEE IN THE MOVIES!
I THINK THE WHOLE TOWN IS **HAUNTED**!
A PORTAL INSIDE THE GYM! ANOTHER IN ELYON'S HOUSE! AND A THIRD IN MRS. RUDOLPH'S ATTIC!
AND THERE ARE **NINE** OTHER PORTALS. . . .
OH, YOU'RE RIGHT! WE FORGOT YOUR **WONDERFUL** MAP. . . .
Heatherfield
THE MOST **USELESS** MAP IN THE WHOLE WORLD! THE ONLY MAP THAT SHOWS YOU SOMETHING AFTER YOU'VE **FOUND** IT!
THERE MUST BE A REASON THAT GRANDMA GAVE THIS MAP TO ME! OR MAYBE YOU KNOW BEST?
GULP!

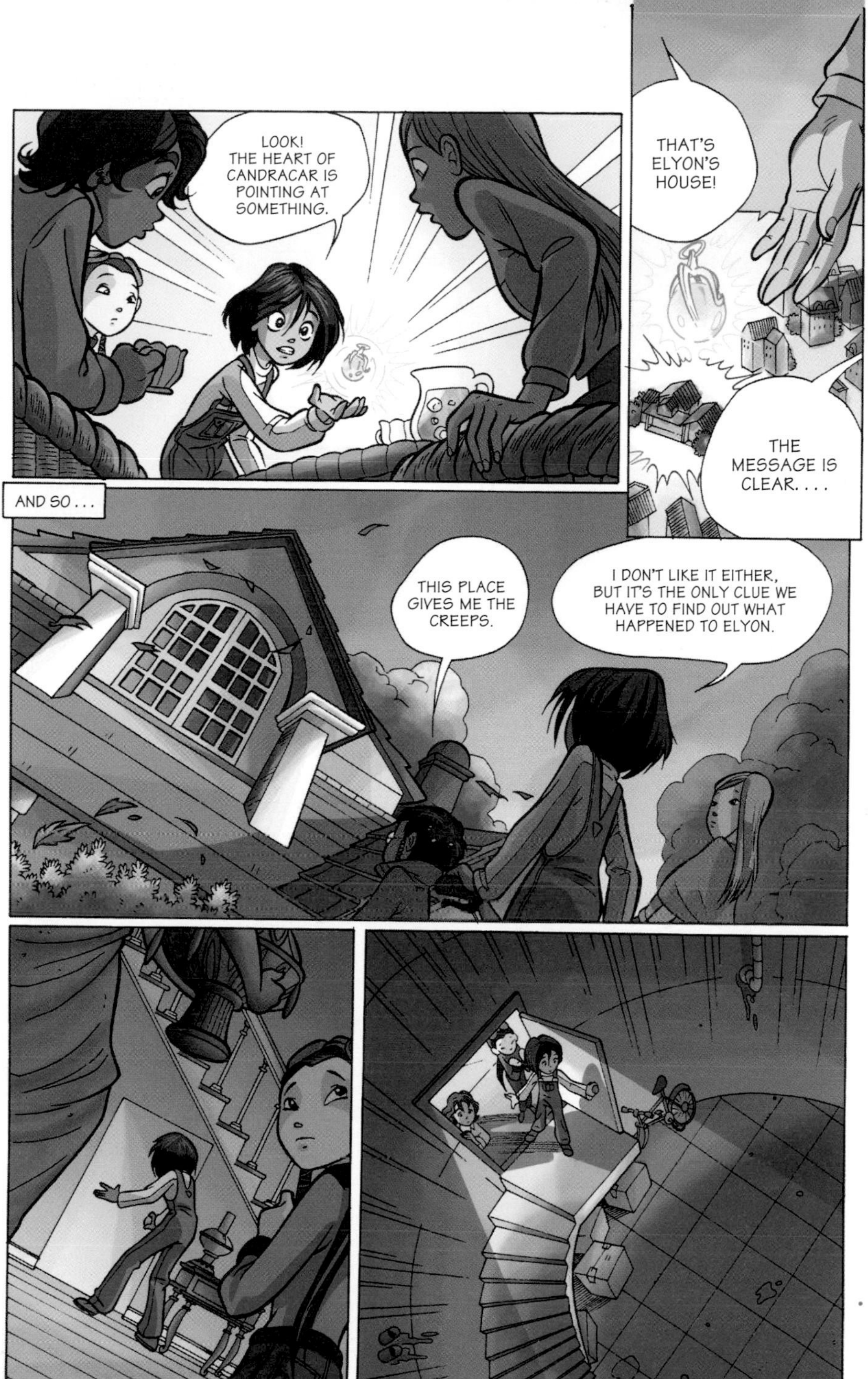
LOOK! THE HEART OF CANDRACAR IS POINTING AT SOMETHING.
THAT'S ELYON'S HOUSE!
THE MESSAGE IS CLEAR. . . .
AND SO . . .
THIS PLACE GIVES ME THE CREEPS.
I DON'T LIKE IT EITHER, BUT IT'S THE ONLY CLUE WE HAVE TO FIND OUT WHAT HAPPENED TO ELYON.

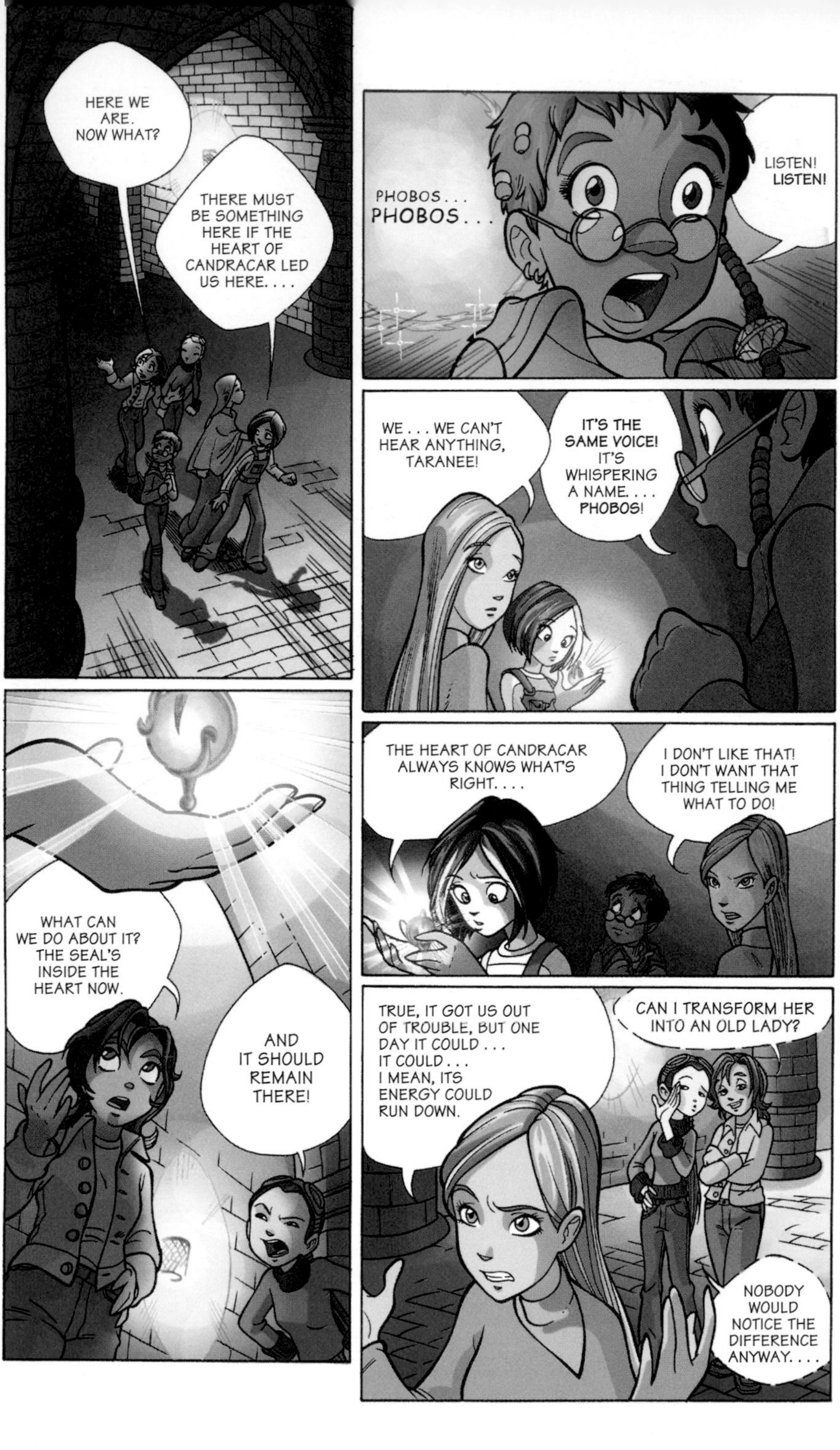
HERE WE ARE. NOW WHAT?
THERE MUST BE SOMETHING HERE IF THE HEART OF CANDRACAR LED US HERE. . . .
PHOBOS . . . PHOBOS . . .
LISTEN! LISTEN!
WE . . . WE CAN'T HEAR ANYTHING, TARANEE!
IT'S THE SAME VOICE! IT'S WHISPERING A NAME. . . . PHOBOS!
WHAT CAN WE DO ABOUT IT? THE SEAL'S INSIDE THE HEART NOW.
AND IT SHOULD REMAIN THERE!
THE HEART OF CANDRACAR ALWAYS KNOWS WHAT'S RIGHT. . . .
I DON'T LIKE THAT! I DON'T WANT THAT THING TELLING ME WHAT TO DO!
TRUE, IT GOT US OUT OF TROUBLE, BUT ONE DAY IT COULD . . . IT COULD . . . I MEAN, ITS ENERGY COULD RUN DOWN.
CAN I TRANSFORM HER INTO AN OLD LADY?
NOBODY WOULD NOTICE THE DIFFERENCE ANYWAY. . . .

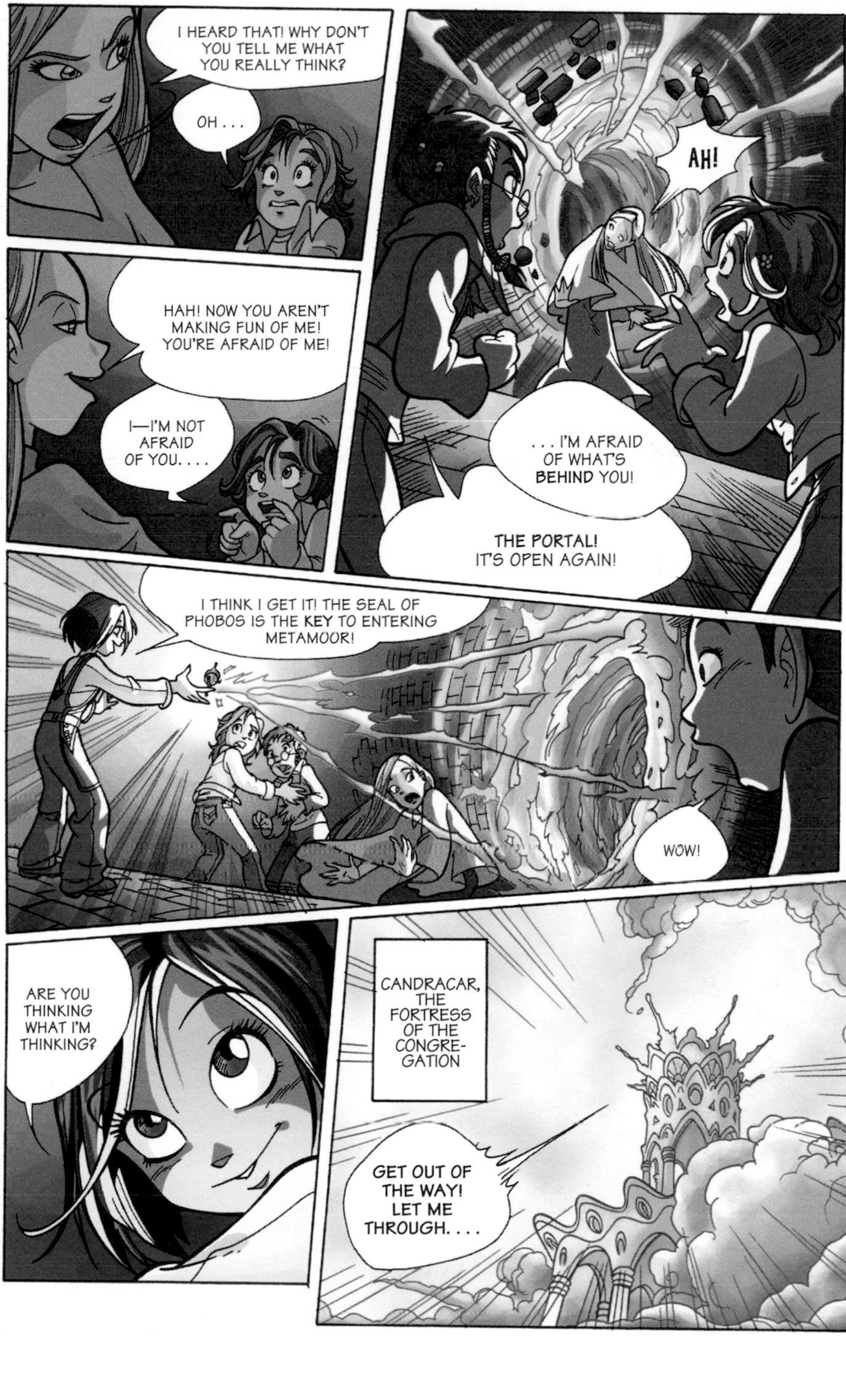
I HEARD THAT! WHY DON'T YOU TELL ME WHAT YOU REALLY THINK?
OH . . .
AH!
HAH! NOW YOU AREN'T MAKING FUN OF ME! YOU'RE AFRAID OF ME!
I—I'M NOT AFRAID OF YOU. . . .
. . . I'M AFRAID OF WHAT'S BEHIND YOU!
THE PORTAL! IT'S OPEN AGAIN!
I THINK I GET IT! THE SEAL OF PHOBOS IS THE KEY TO ENTERING METAMOOR!
WOW!
ARE YOU THINKING WHAT I'M THINKING?
CANDRACAR, THE FORTRESS OF THE CONGRE-GATION
GET OUT OF THE WAY! LET ME THROUGH. . . .

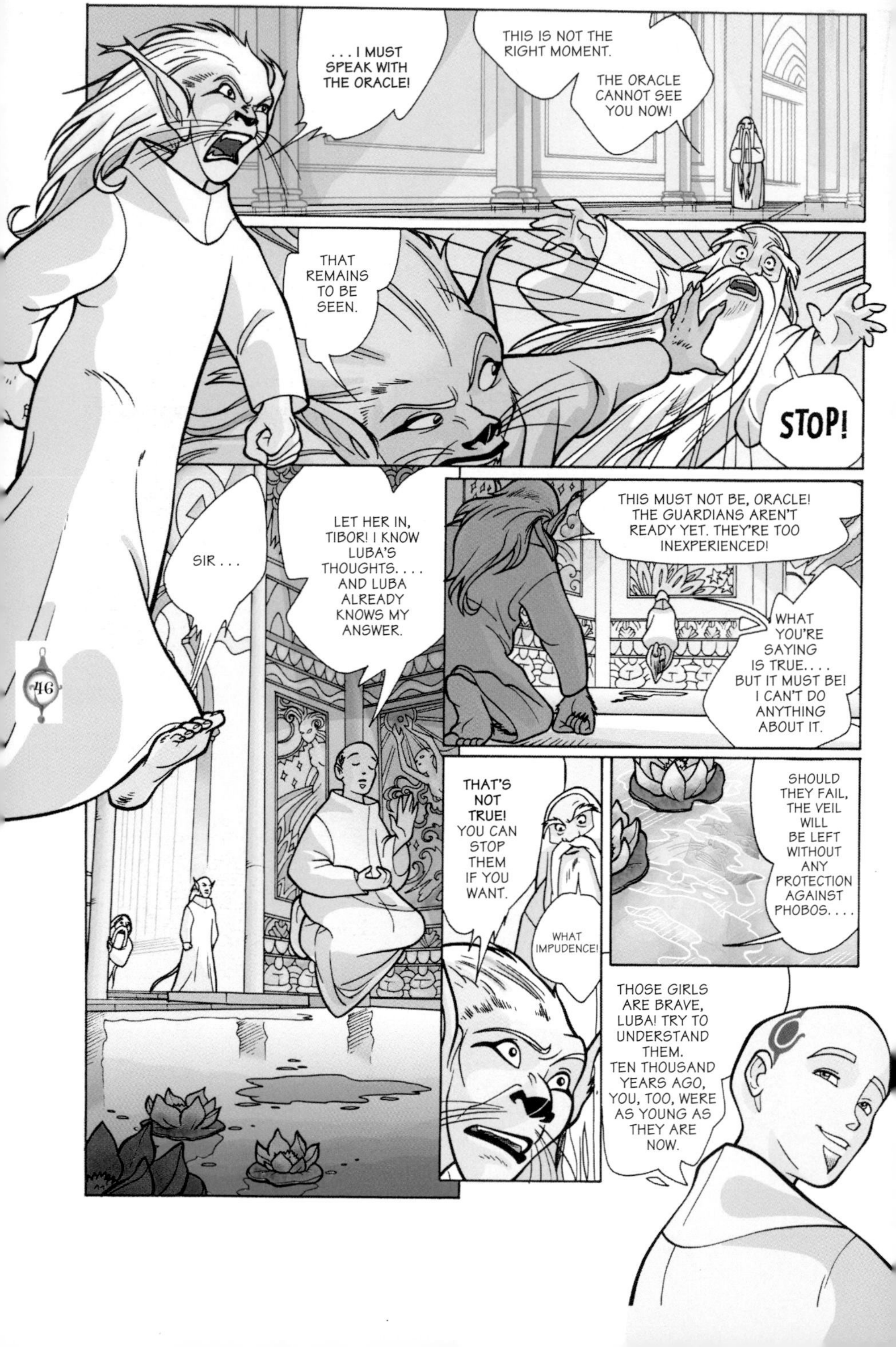

. . . I MUST SPEAK WITH THE ORACLE!
THIS IS NOT THE RIGHT MOMENT.
THE ORACLE CANNOT SEE YOU NOW!
THAT REMAINS TO BE SEEN.
STOP!
SIR . . .
LET HER IN, TIBOR! I KNOW LUBA'S THOUGHTS. . . . AND LUBA ALREADY KNOWS MY ANSWER.
THIS MUST NOT BE, ORACLE! THE GUARDIANS AREN'T READY YET. THEY'RE TOO INEXPERIENCED!
WHAT YOU'RE SAYING IS TRUE. . . . BUT IT MUST BE! I CAN'T DO ANYTHING ABOUT IT.
THAT'S NOT TRUE! YOU CAN STOP THEM IF YOU WANT.
WHAT IMPUDENCE!
SHOULD THEY FAIL, THE VEIL WILL BE LEFT WITHOUT ANY PROTECTION AGAINST PHOBOS. . . .
THOSE GIRLS ARE BRAVE, LUBA! TRY TO UNDERSTAND THEM. TEN THOUSAND YEARS AGO, YOU, TOO, WERE AS YOUNG AS THEY ARE NOW.

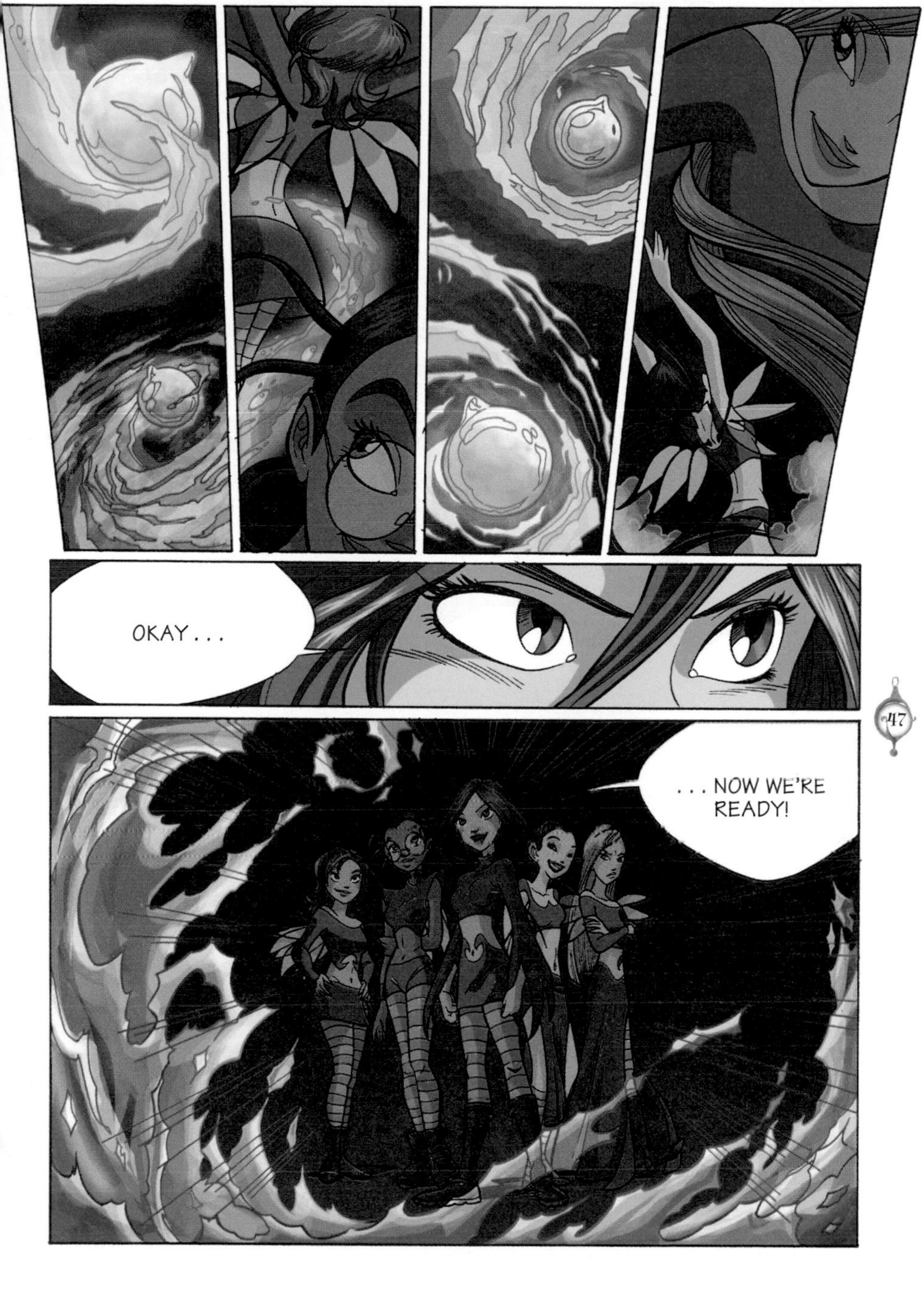
OKAY . . .
. . . NOW WE'RE READY!

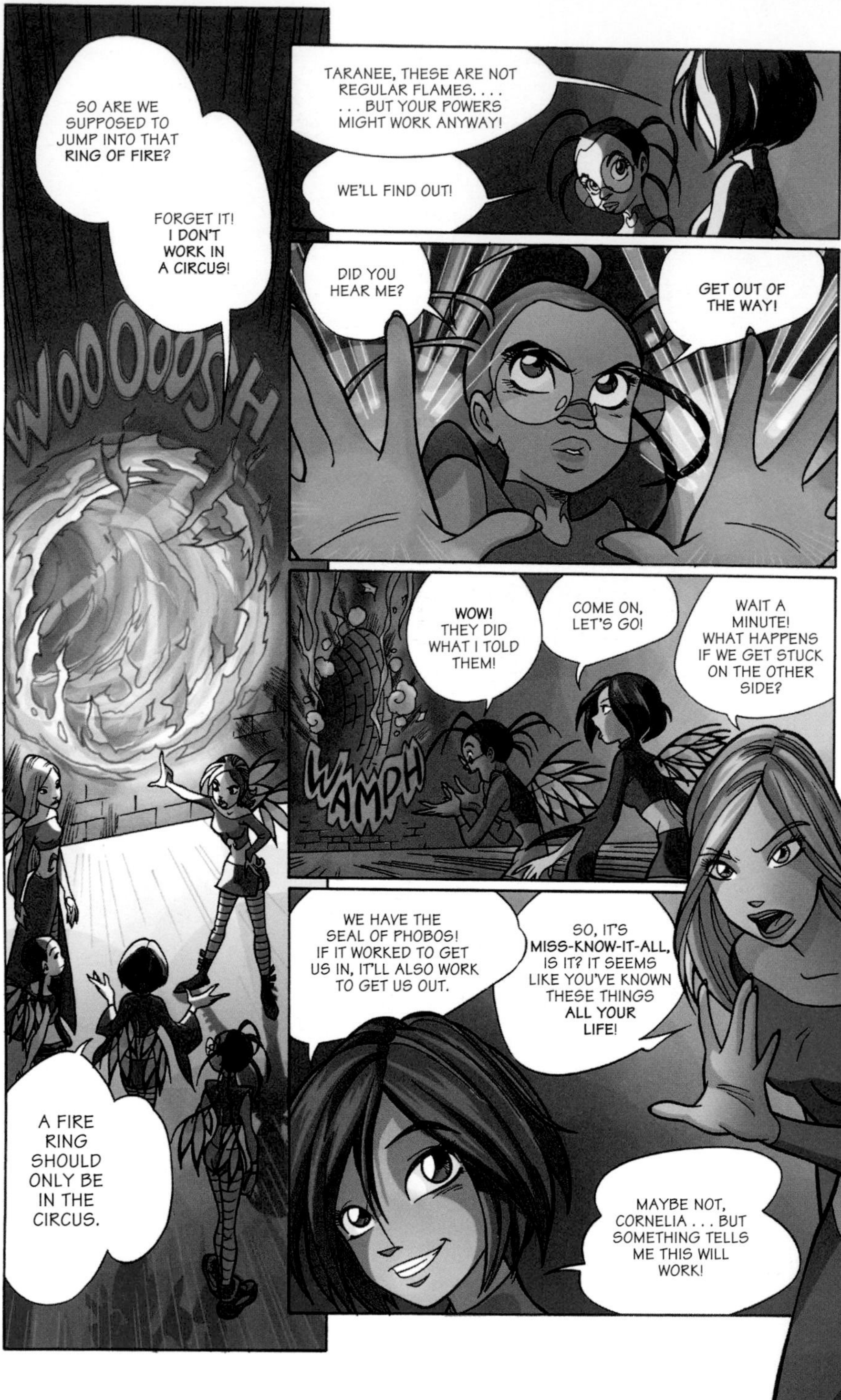

SO ARE WE SUPPOSED TO JUMP INTO THAT RING OF FIRE?
FORGET IT! I DON'T WORK IN A CIRCUS!
WOOOOOSH
A FIRE RING SHOULD ONLY BE IN THE CIRCUS.
TARANEE, THESE ARE NOT REGULAR FLAMES. . . . . . . BUT YOUR POWERS MIGHT WORK ANYWAY!
WE'LL FIND OUT!
DID YOU HEAR ME?
GET OUT OF THE WAY!
WAMPH
WOW! THEY DID WHAT I TOLD THEM!
COME ON, LET'S GO!
WAIT A MINUTE! WHAT HAPPENS IF WE GET STUCK ON THE OTHER SIDE?
WE HAVE THE SEAL OF PHOBOS! IF IT WORKED TO GET US IN, IT'LL ALSO WORK TO GET US OUT.
SO, IT'S MISS-KNOW-IT-ALL, IS IT? IT SEEMS LIKE YOU'VE KNOWN THESE THINGS ALL YOUR LIFE!
MAYBE NOT, CORNELIA . . . BUT SOMETHING TELLS ME THIS WILL WORK!

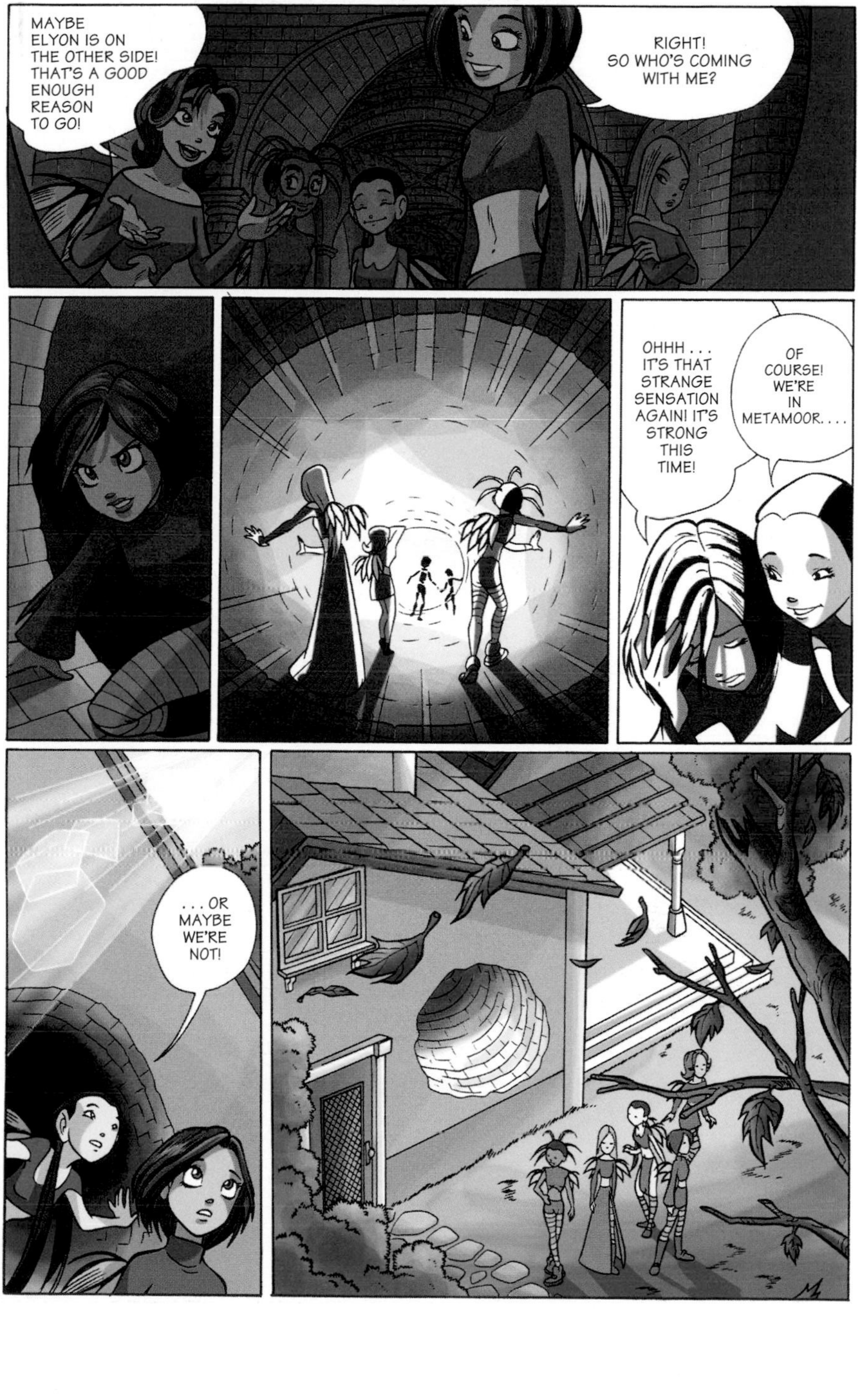
MAYBE ELYON IS ON THE OTHER SIDE! THAT'S A GOOD ENOUGH REASON TO GO!
RIGHT! SO WHO'S COMING WITH ME?
OHHH . . . IT'S THAT STRANGE SENSATION AGAIN! IT'S STRONG THIS TIME!
OF COURSE! WE'RE IN METAMOOR. . . .
. . . OR MAYBE WE'RE NOT!

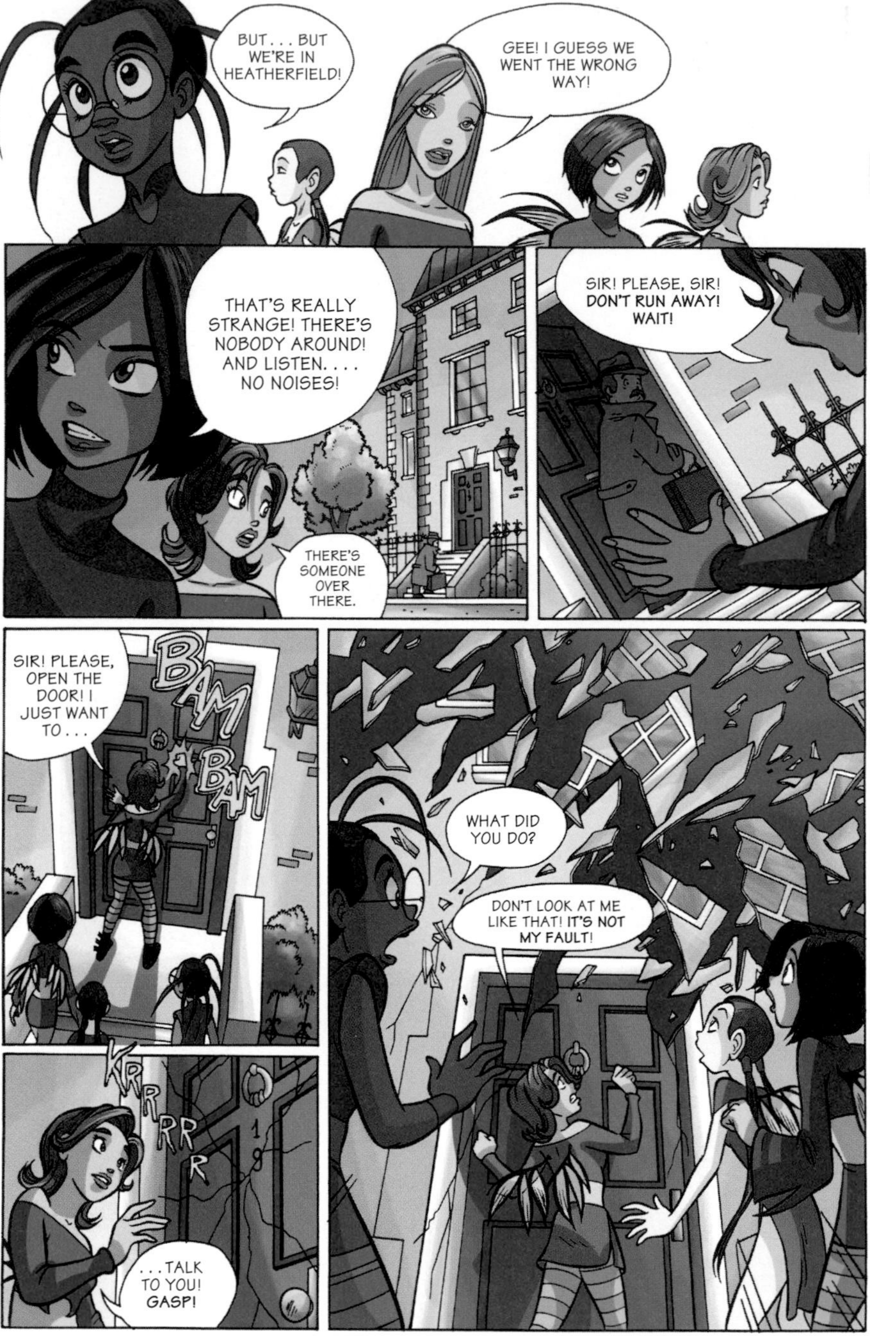

BUT . . . BUT WE'RE IN HEATHERFIELD!
GEE! I GUESS WE WENT THE WRONG WAY!
THAT'S REALLY STRANGE! THERE'S NOBODY AROUND! AND LISTEN. . . . NO NOISES!
THERE'S SOMEONE OVER THERE.
SIR! PLEASE, SIR! DON'T RUN AWAY! WAIT!
SIR! PLEASE, OPEN THE DOOR! I JUST WANT TO . . .
BAM
BAM
KRRRRR
. . . TALK TO YOU! GASP!
WHAT DID YOU DO?
DON'T LOOK AT ME LIKE THAT! IT'S NOT MY FAULT!

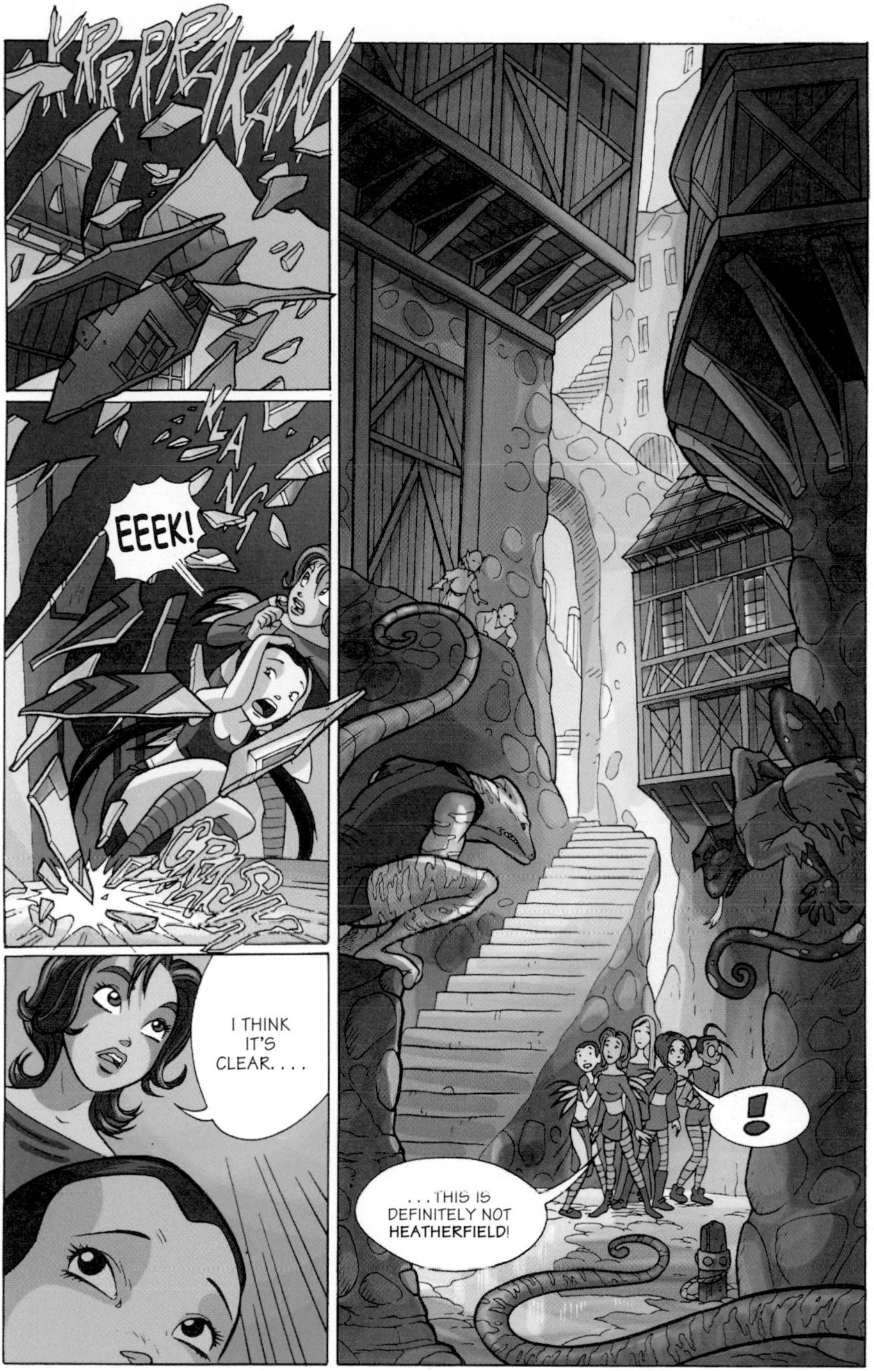
KRRRAKAW
KLANG
EEEK!
CRASH
I THINK IT'S CLEAR. . . .
!
. . .THIS IS DEFINITELY NOT HEATHERFIELD!

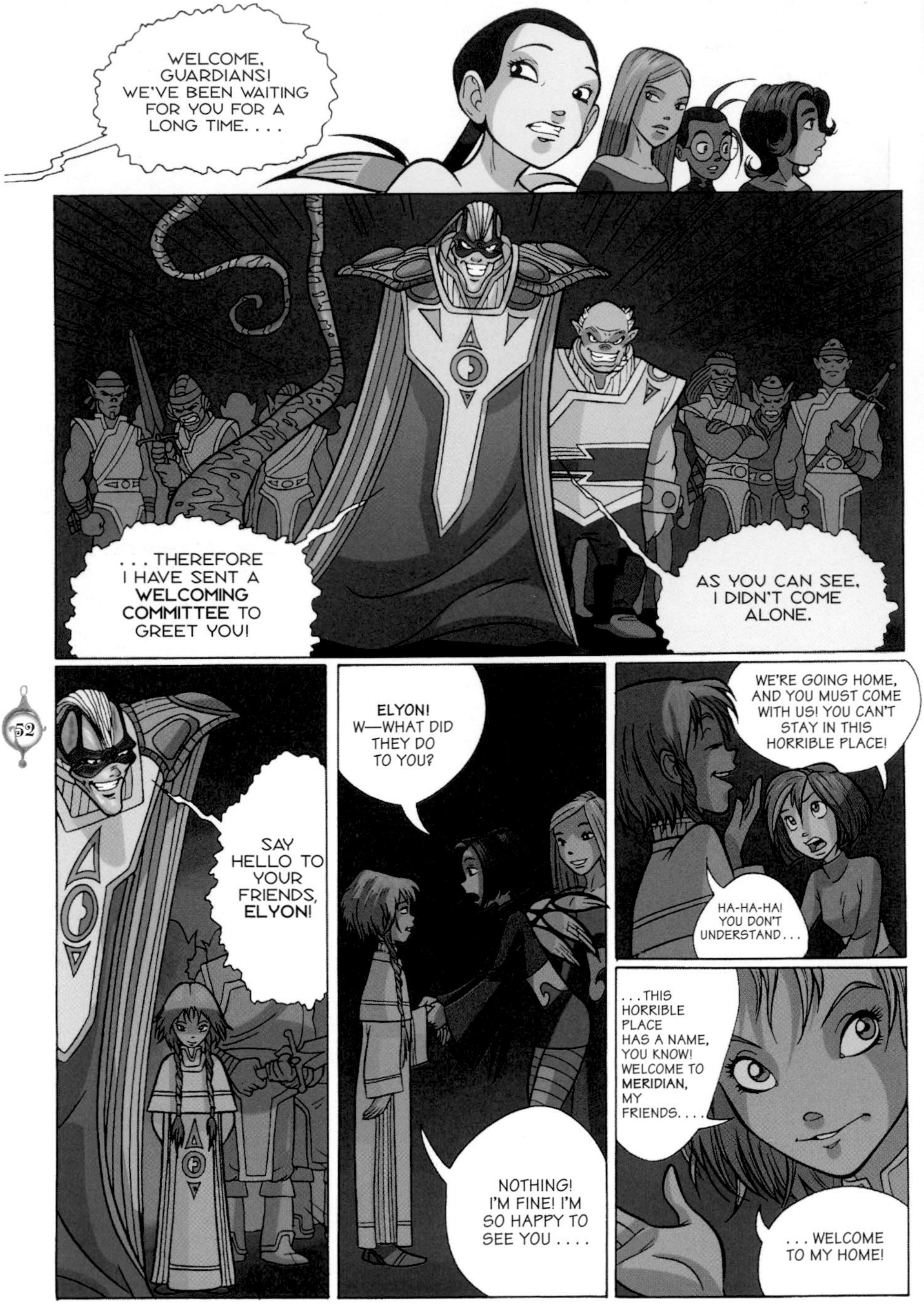
WELCOME, GUARDIANS! WE'VE BEEN WAITING FOR YOU FOR A LONG TIME. . . .
. . . THEREFORE I HAVE SENT A WELCOMING COMMITTEE TO GREET YOU!
AS YOU CAN SEE, I DIDN'T COME ALONE.
SAY HELLO TO YOUR FRIENDS, ELYON!
ELYON! W—WHAT DID THEY DO TO YOU?
NOTHING! I'M FINE! I'M SO HAPPY TO SEE YOU . . . .
WE'RE GOING HOME, AND YOU MUST COME WITH US! YOU CAN'T STAY IN THIS HORRIBLE PLACE!
HA-HA-HA! YOU DON'T UNDERSTAND . . .
. . . THIS HORRIBLE PLACE HAS A NAME, YOU KNOW! WELCOME TO MERIDIAN, MY FRIENDS. . . .
. . . WELCOME TO MY HOME!

STAY! YOU'LL LIKE IT!

SURE! I'LL ASK MY PARENTS TO RENT A HOUSE HERE FOR THE SUMMER!

YOU DON'T WANT TO STAY? I'M SO SORRY.

YOU LEAVE US WITH NO CHOICE. . . .

GUARDS! SEIZE THEM!

I KNEW HE WAS GOING TO SAY THAT! I KNEW IT!

DON'T LET THEM GET ANY CLOSER!

BZZT BZZAP

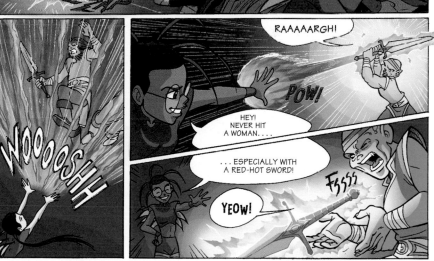

RAAAAARGH!

POW!

HEY! NEVER HIT A WOMAN. . . .

. . . ESPECIALLY WITH A RED-HOT SWORD!

WOOOOSHH

FSSSS

YEOW!

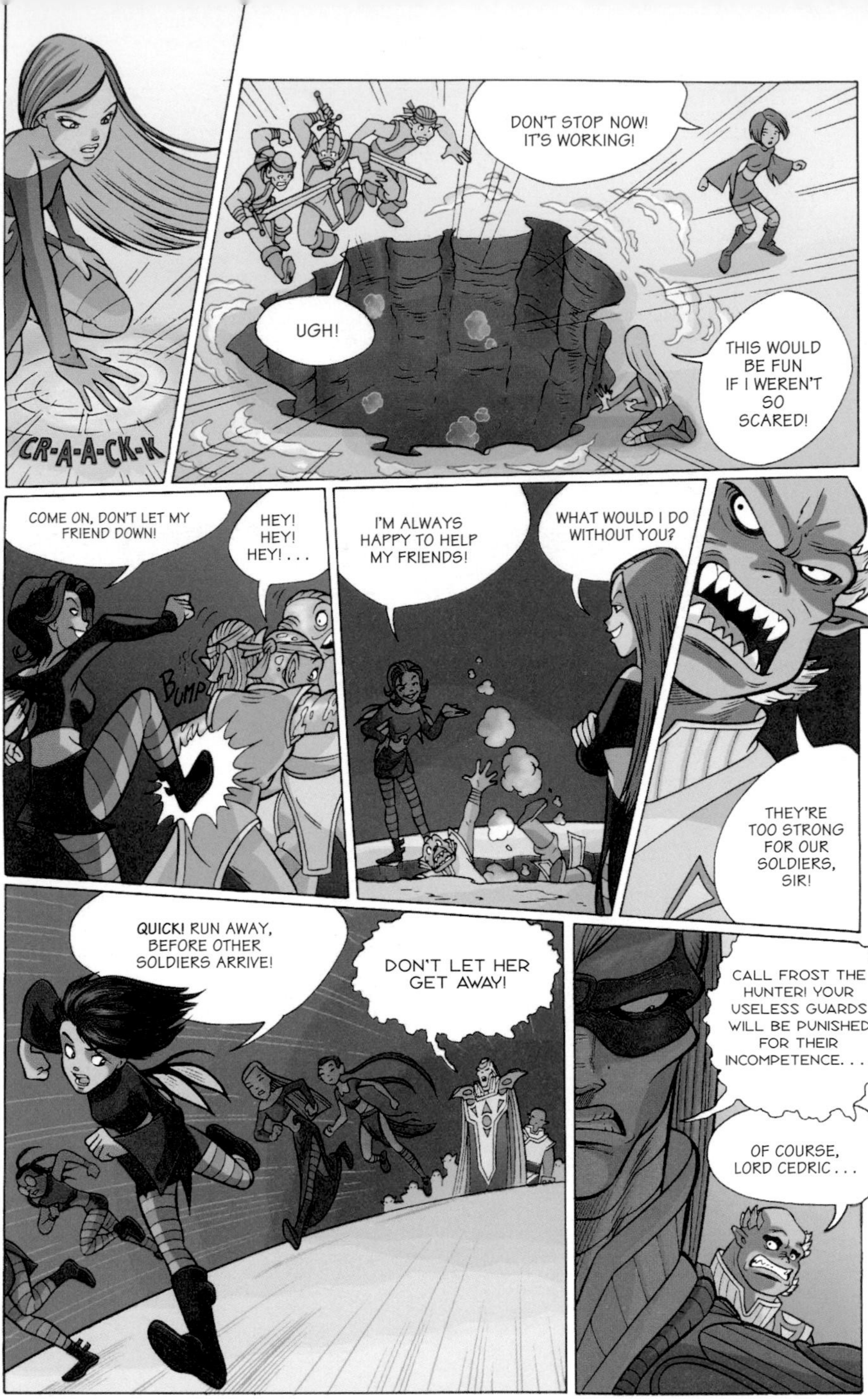
CR-A-A-CK-K
DON'T STOP NOW! IT'S WORKING!
UGH!
THIS WOULD BE FUN IF I WEREN'T SO SCARED!
COME ON, DON'T LET MY FRIEND DOWN!
HEY! HEY! HEY! . . .
BUMP
I'M ALWAYS HAPPY TO HELP MY FRIENDS!
WHAT WOULD I DO WITHOUT YOU?
THEY'RE TOO STRONG FOR OUR SOLDIERS, SIR!
QUICK! RUN AWAY, BEFORE OTHER SOLDIERS ARRIVE!
DON'T LET HER GET AWAY!
CALL FROST THE HUNTER! YOUR USELESS GUARDS WILL BE PUNISHED FOR THEIR INCOMPETENCE. . . .
OF COURSE, LORD CEDRIC . . .

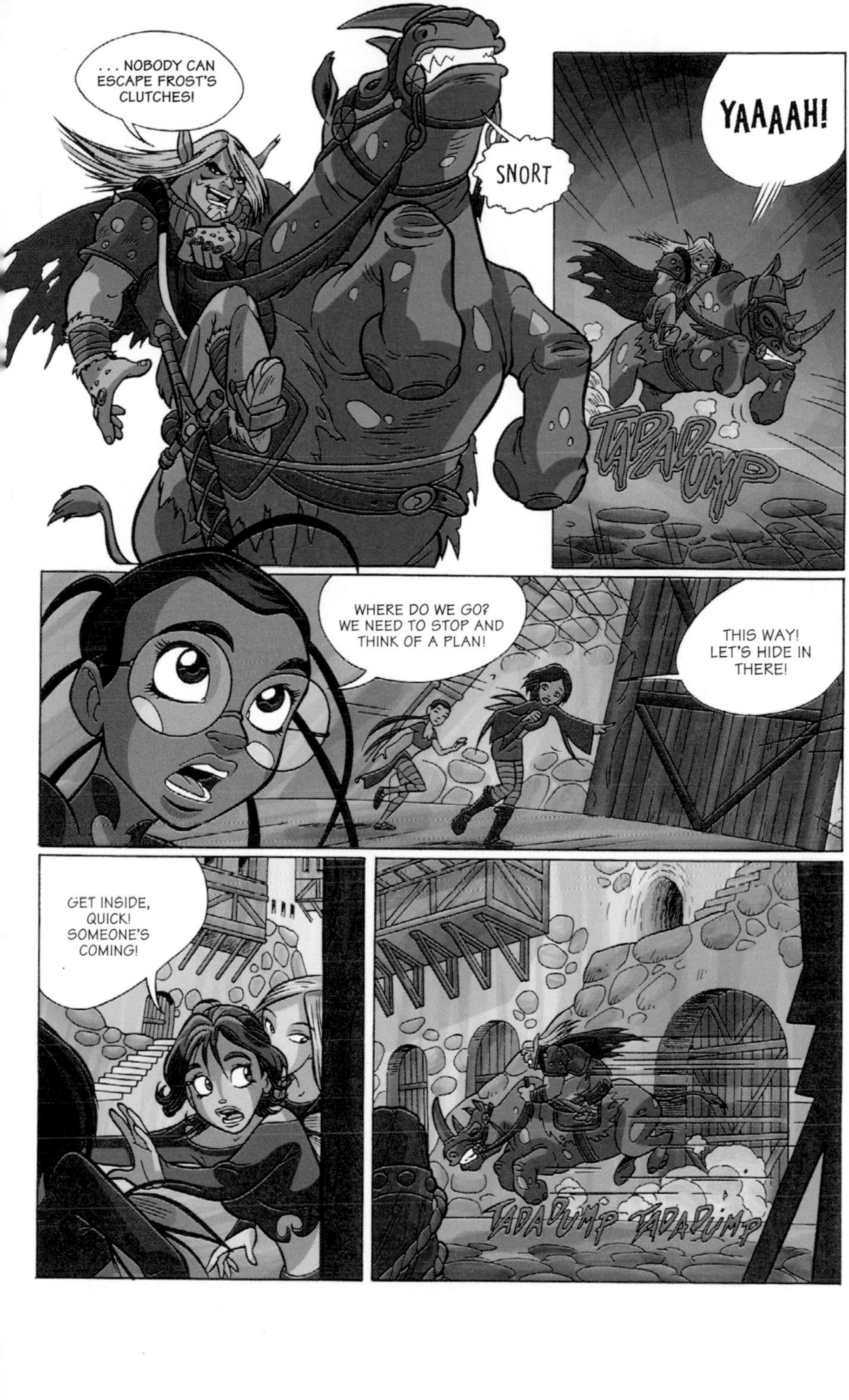

. . . NOBODY CAN ESCAPE FROST'S CLUTCHES!
SNORT
YAAAAH!
TAPADUMP
WHERE DO WE GO? WE NEED TO STOP AND THINK OF A PLAN!
THIS WAY! LET'S HIDE IN THERE!
GET INSIDE, QUICK! SOMEONE'S COMING!
TADADUMP TADADUMP

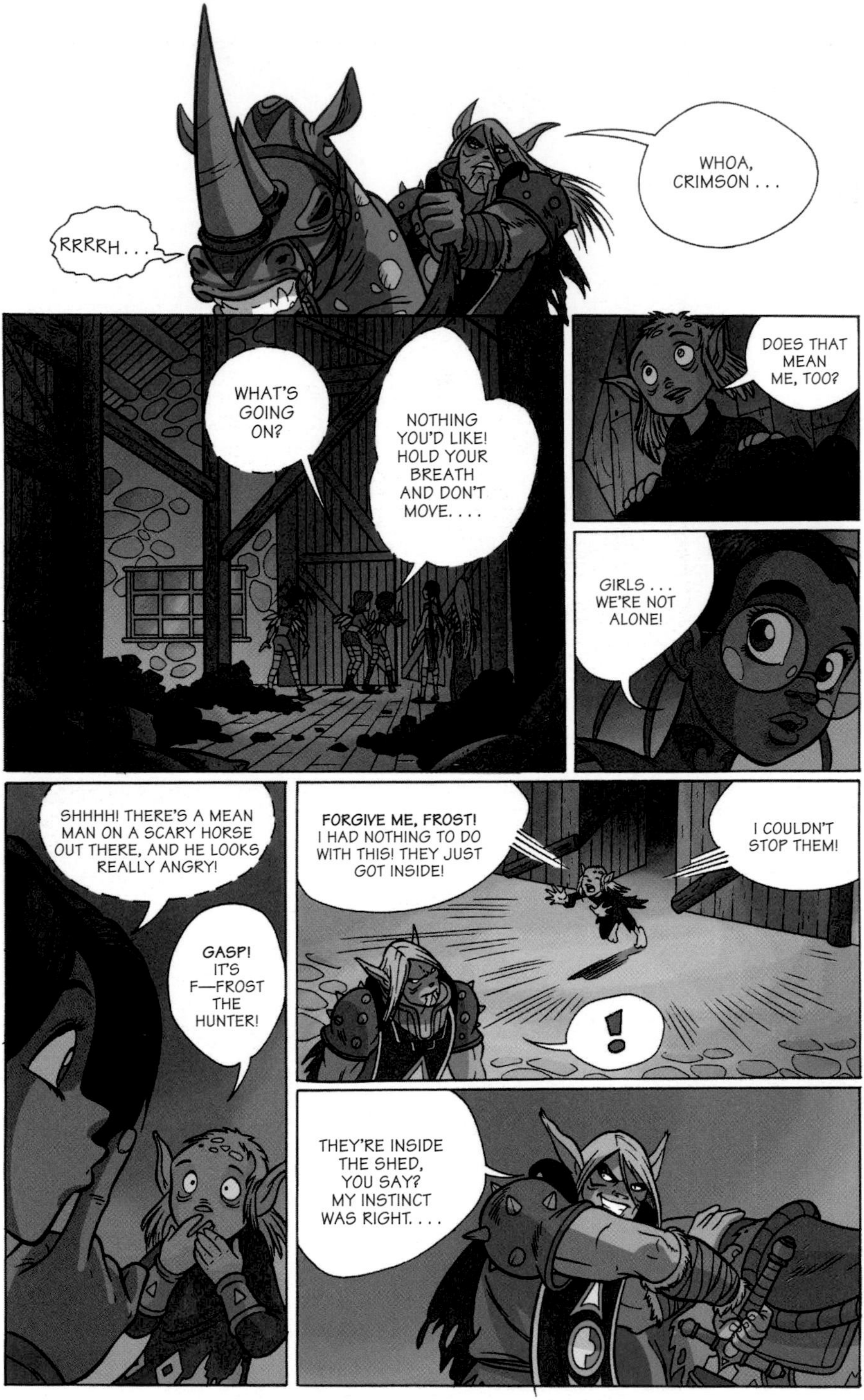

WHOA, CRIMSON . . .
RRRRH . . .
WHAT'S GOING ON?
NOTHING YOU'D LIKE! HOLD YOUR BREATH AND DON'T MOVE. . . .
DOES THAT MEAN ME, TOO?
GIRLS . . . WE'RE NOT ALONE!
SHHHH! THERE'S A MEAN MAN ON A SCARY HORSE OUT THERE, AND HE LOOKS REALLY ANGRY!
GASP! IT'S F—FROST THE HUNTER!
FORGIVE ME, FROST! I HAD NOTHING TO DO WITH THIS! THEY JUST GOT INSIDE!
I COULDN'T STOP THEM!
!
THEY'RE INSIDE THE SHED, YOU SAY? MY INSTINCT WAS RIGHT. . . .

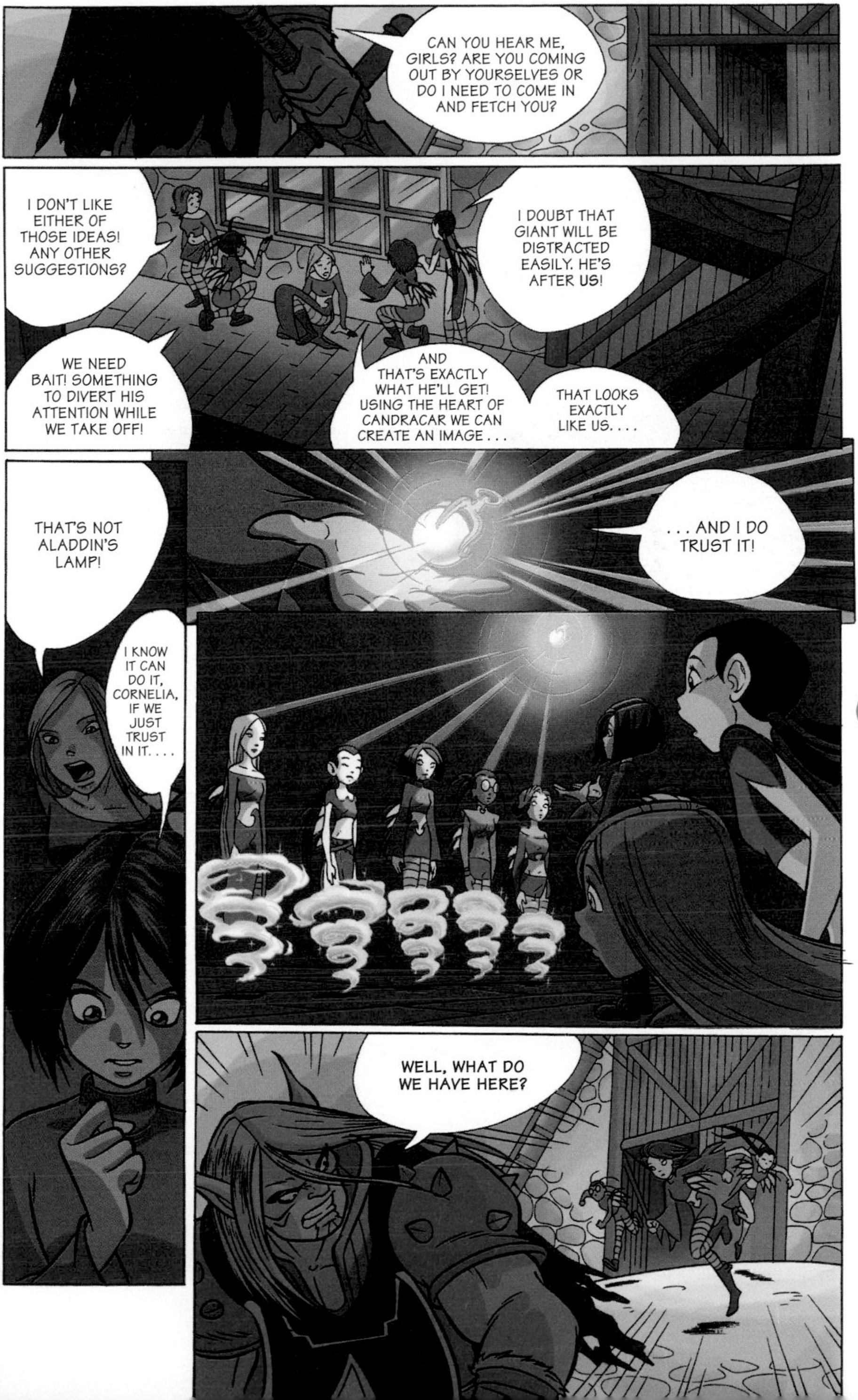
CAN YOU HEAR ME, GIRLS? ARE YOU COMING OUT BY YOURSELVES OR DO I NEED TO COME IN AND FETCH YOU?
I DON'T LIKE EITHER OF THOSE IDEAS! ANY OTHER SUGGESTIONS?
I DOUBT THAT GIANT WILL BE DISTRACTED EASILY. HE'S AFTER US!
WE NEED BAIT! SOMETHING TO DIVERT HIS ATTENTION WHILE WE TAKE OFF!
AND THAT'S EXACTLY WHAT HE'LL GET! USING THE HEART OF CANDRACAR WE CAN CREATE AN IMAGE . . .
THAT LOOKS EXACTLY LIKE US. . . .
THAT'S NOT ALADDIN'S LAMP!
. . . AND I DO TRUST IT!
I KNOW IT CAN DO IT, CORNELIA, IF WE JUST TRUST IN IT. . . .
WELL, WHAT DO WE HAVE HERE?

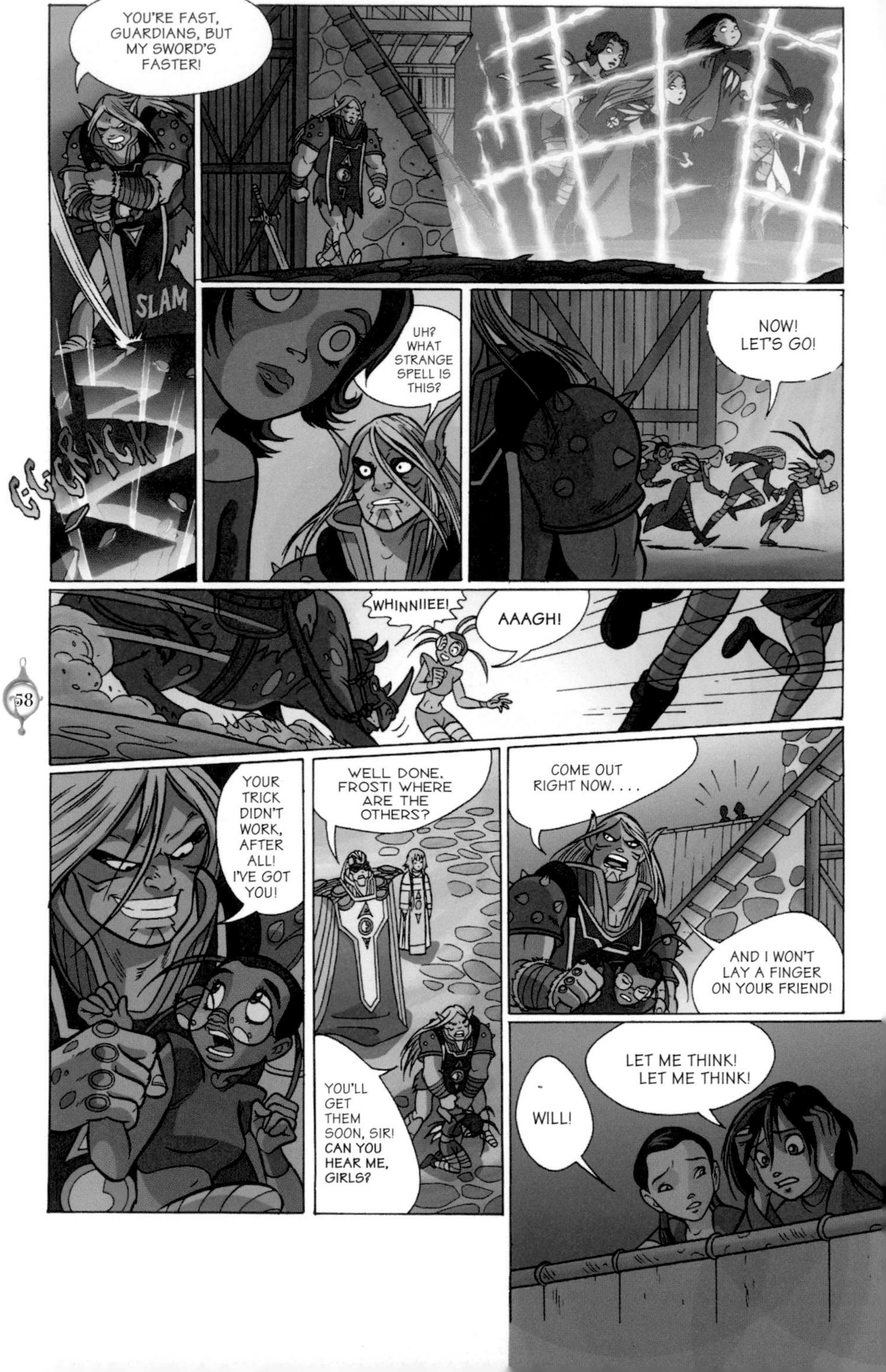
YOU'RE FAST, GUARDIANS, BUT MY SWORD'S FASTER!
SLAM
C-C-CRACK
UH? WHAT STRANGE SPELL IS THIS?
NOW! LET'S GO!
WHINNIIEE!
AAAGH!
YOUR TRICK DIDN'T WORK, AFTER ALL! I'VE GOT YOU!
WELL DONE, FROST! WHERE ARE THE OTHERS?
YOU'LL GET THEM SOON, SIR! CAN YOU HEAR ME, GIRLS?
COME OUT RIGHT NOW. . . .
AND I WON'T LAY A FINGER ON YOUR FRIEND!
LET ME THINK! LET ME THINK!
WILL!

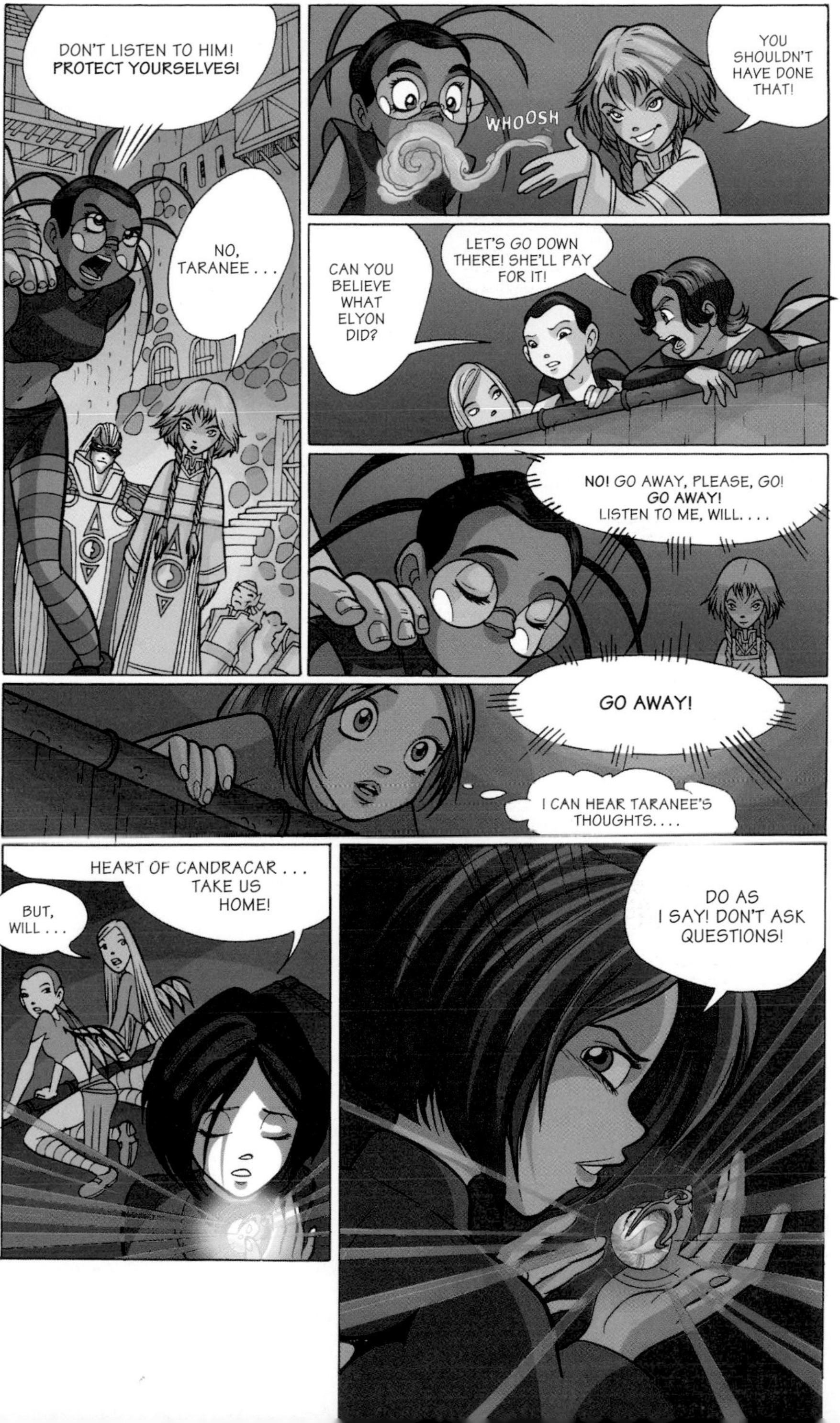
DON'T LISTEN TO HIM! PROTECT YOURSELVES!
NO, TARANEE . . .
YOU SHOULDN'T HAVE DONE THAT!
WHOOSH
CAN YOU BELIEVE WHAT ELYON DID?
LET'S GO DOWN THERE! SHE'LL PAY FOR IT!
NO! GO AWAY, PLEASE, GO! GO AWAY! LISTEN TO ME, WILL. . . .
GO AWAY!
I CAN HEAR TARANEE'S THOUGHTS. . . .
HEART OF CANDRACAR . . . TAKE US HOME!
BUT, WILL . . .
DO AS I SAY! DON'T ASK QUESTIONS!

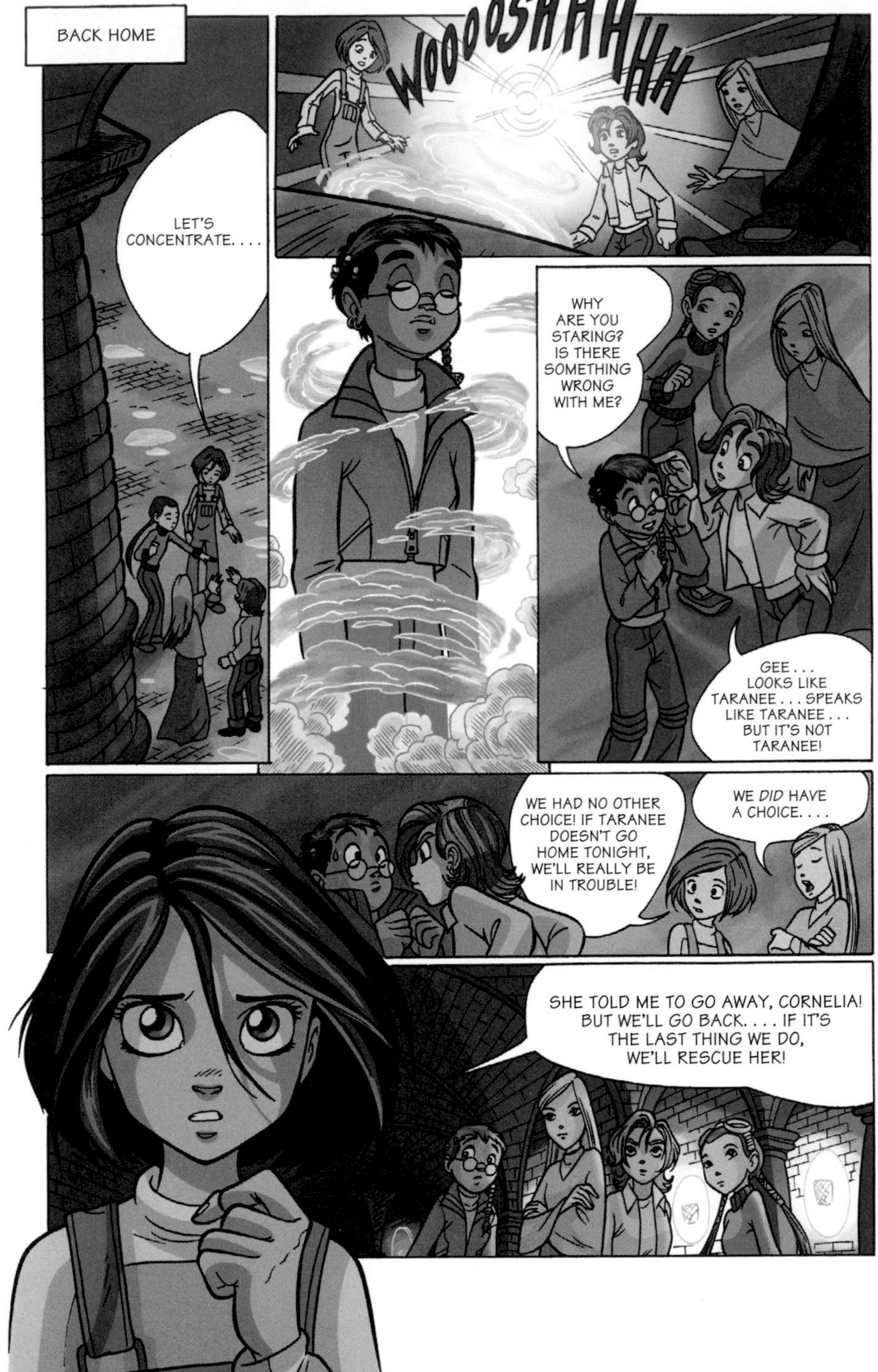
BACK HOME
WOOOOSHHHHHH
LET'S CONCENTRATE. . . .
WHY ARE YOU STARING? IS THERE SOMETHING WRONG WITH ME?
GEE . . . LOOKS LIKE TARANEE . . . SPEAKS LIKE TARANEE . . . BUT IT'S NOT TARANEE!
WE HAD NO OTHER CHOICE! IF TARANEE DOESN'T GO HOME TONIGHT, WE'LL REALLY BE IN TROUBLE!
WE *DID* HAVE A CHOICE. . . .
SHE TOLD ME TO GO AWAY, CORNELIA! BUT WE'LL GO BACK. . . . IF IT'S THE LAST THING WE DO, WE'LL RESCUE HER!

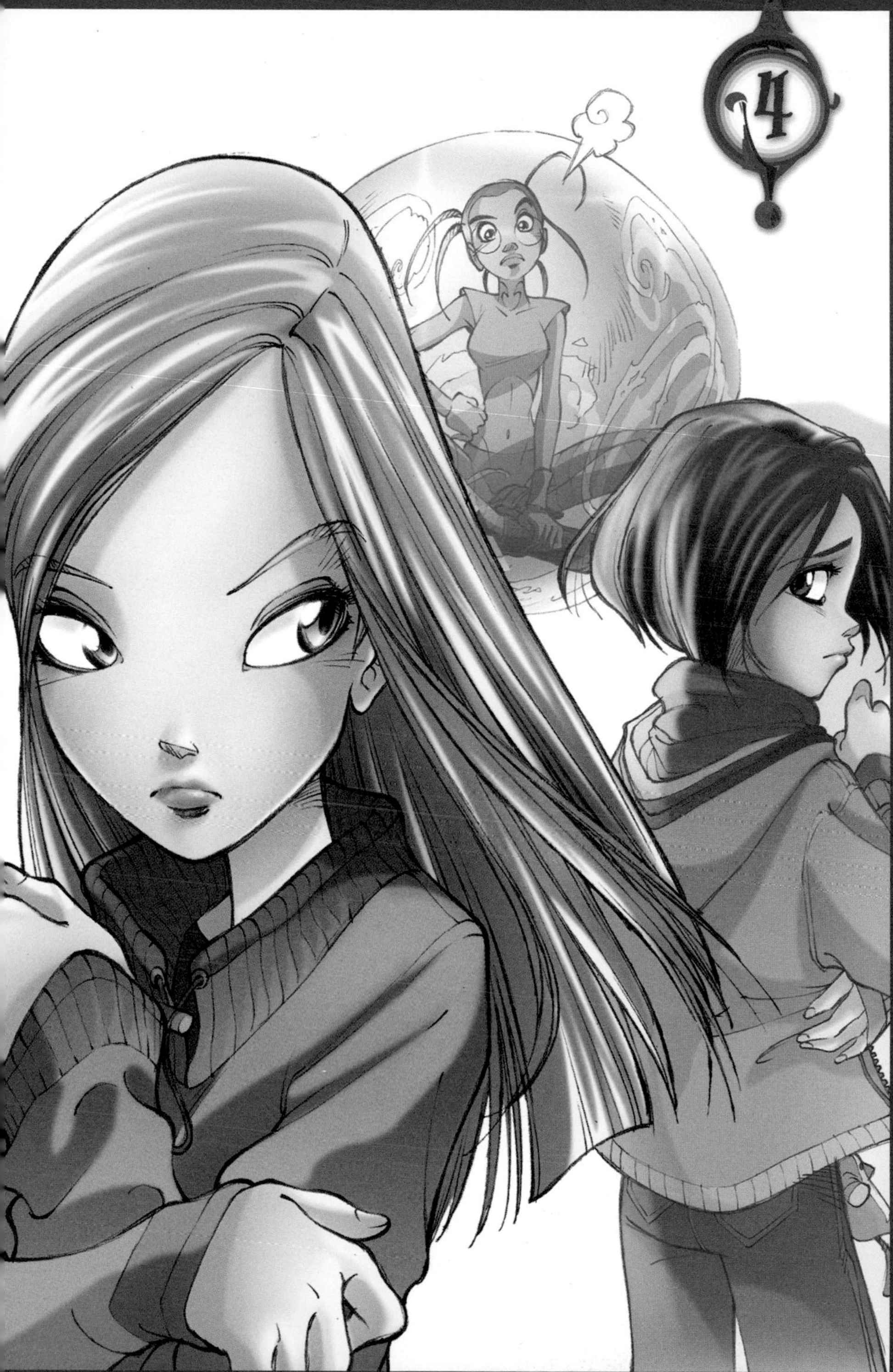
4

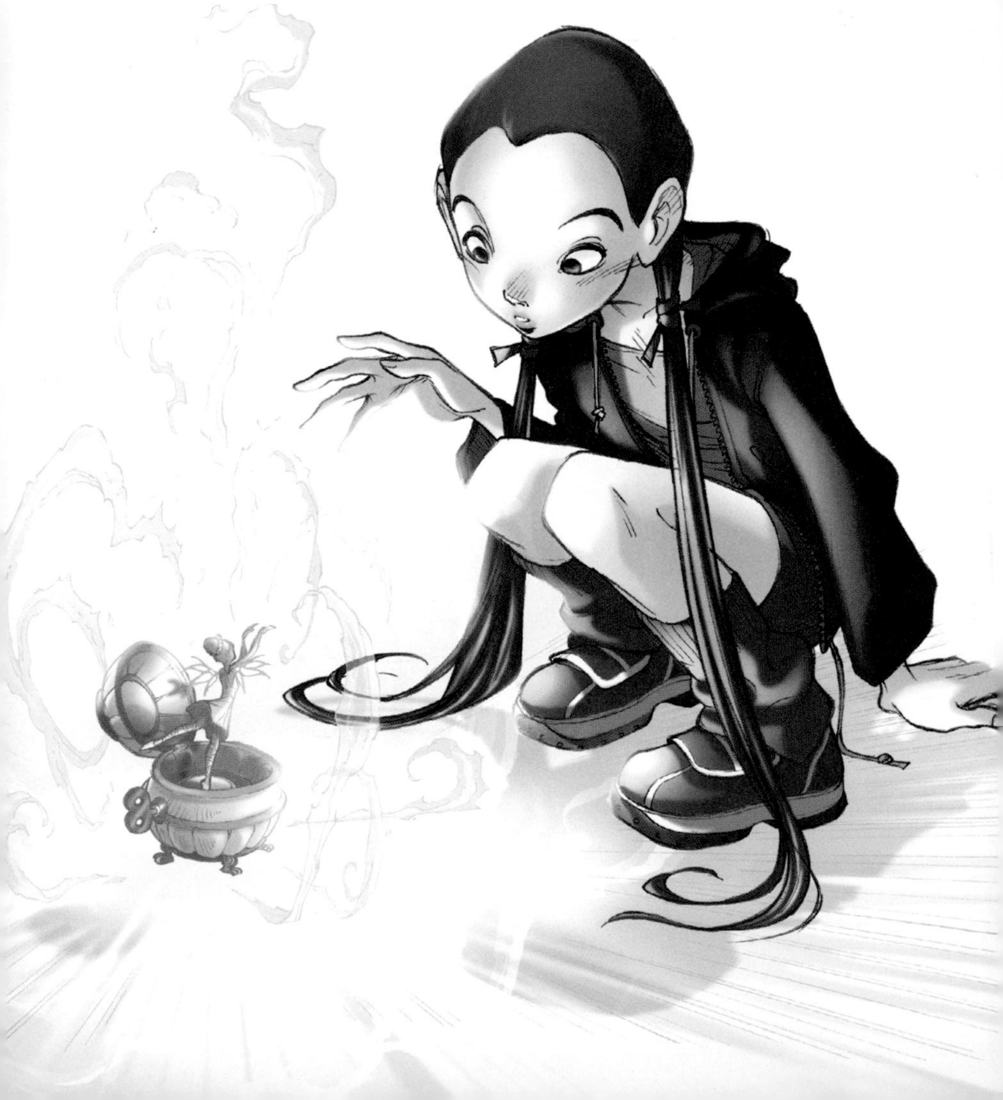

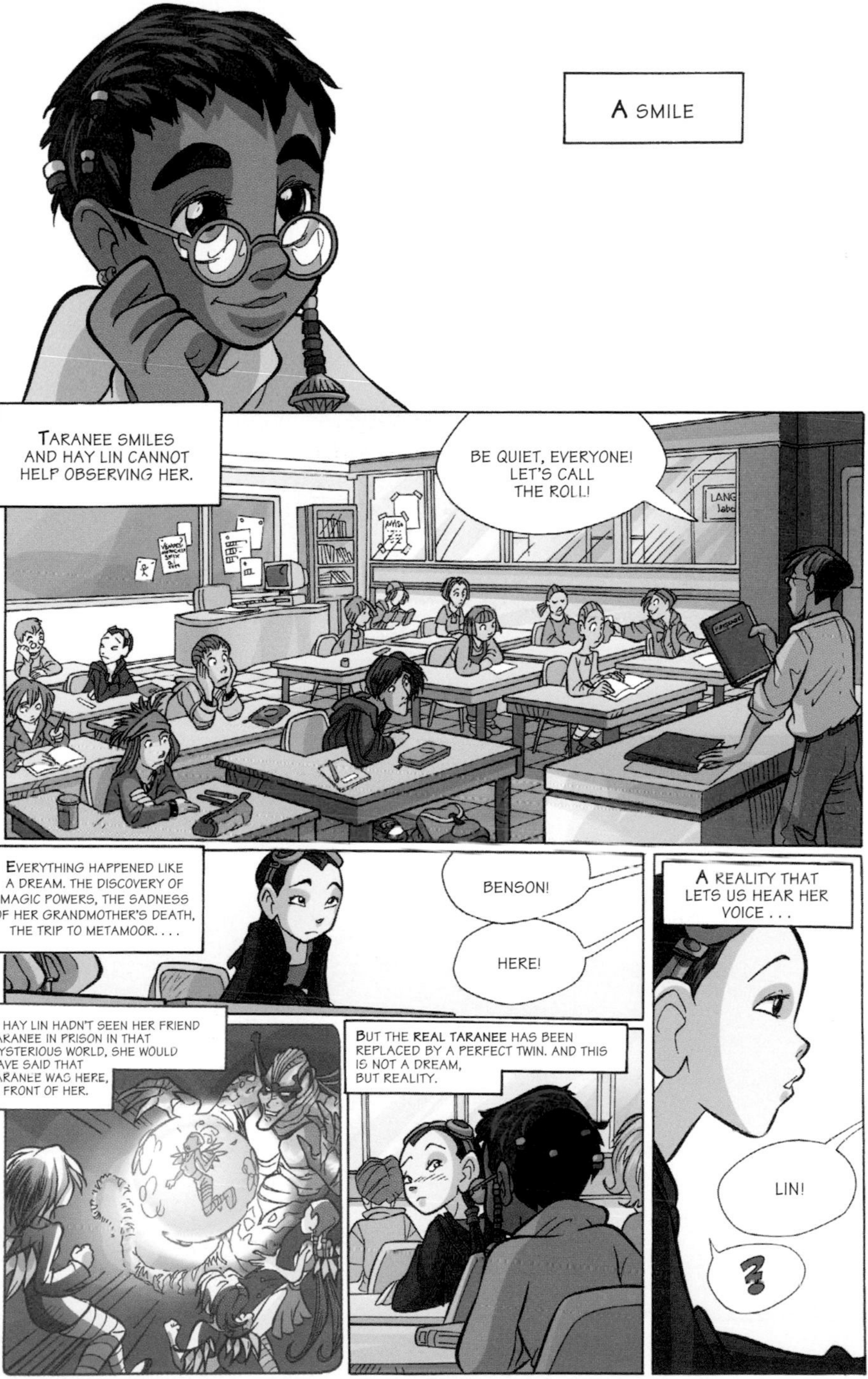
A SMILE
TARANEE SMILES AND HAY LIN CANNOT HELP OBSERVING HER.
BE QUIET, EVERYONE! LET'S CALL THE ROLL!
EVERYTHING HAPPENED LIKE A DREAM. THE DISCOVERY OF MAGIC POWERS, THE SADNESS OF HER GRANDMOTHER'S DEATH, THE TRIP TO METAMOOR. . . .
BENSON!
HERE!
A REALITY THAT LETS US HEAR HER VOICE . . .
IF HAY LIN HADN'T SEEN HER FRIEND TARANEE IN PRISON IN THAT MYSTERIOUS WORLD, SHE WOULD HAVE SAID THAT TARANEE WAS HERE, IN FRONT OF HER.
BUT THE REAL TARANEE HAS BEEN REPLACED BY A PERFECT TWIN. AND THIS IS NOT A DREAM, BUT REALITY.
LIN!
?

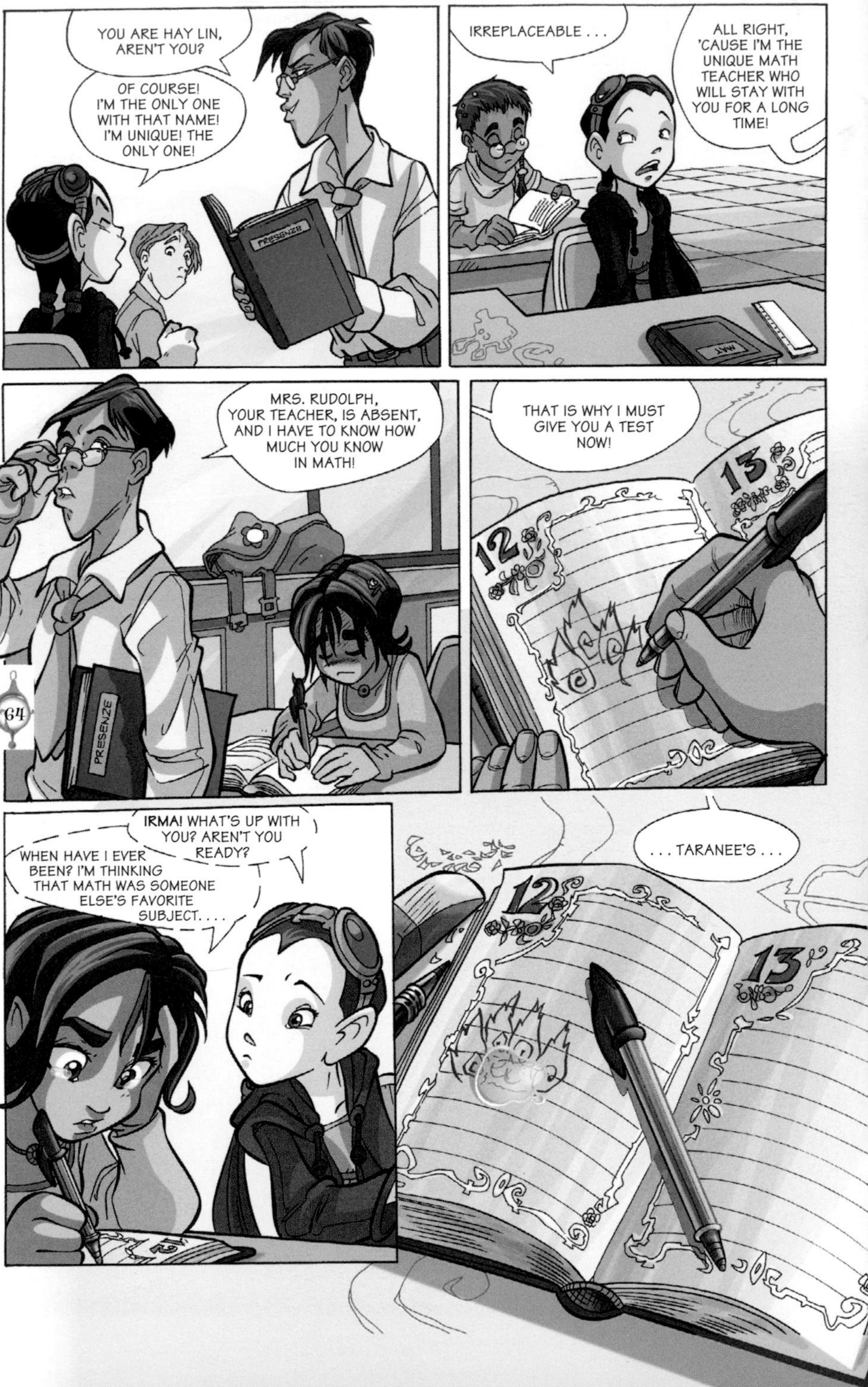
YOU ARE HAY LIN, AREN'T YOU?
OF COURSE! I'M THE ONLY ONE WITH THAT NAME! I'M UNIQUE! THE ONLY ONE!
PRESENZE
IRREPLACEABLE . . .
ALL RIGHT, 'CAUSE I'M THE UNIQUE MATH TEACHER WHO WILL STAY WITH YOU FOR A LONG TIME!
MRS. RUDOLPH, YOUR TEACHER, IS ABSENT, AND I HAVE TO KNOW HOW MUCH YOU KNOW IN MATH!
PRESENZE
THAT IS WHY I MUST GIVE YOU A TEST NOW!
12
13
IRMA! WHAT'S UP WITH YOU? AREN'T YOU READY?
WHEN HAVE I EVER BEEN? I'M THINKING THAT MATH WAS SOMEONE ELSE'S FAVORITE SUBJECT. . . .
. . . TARANEE'S . . .
12
13

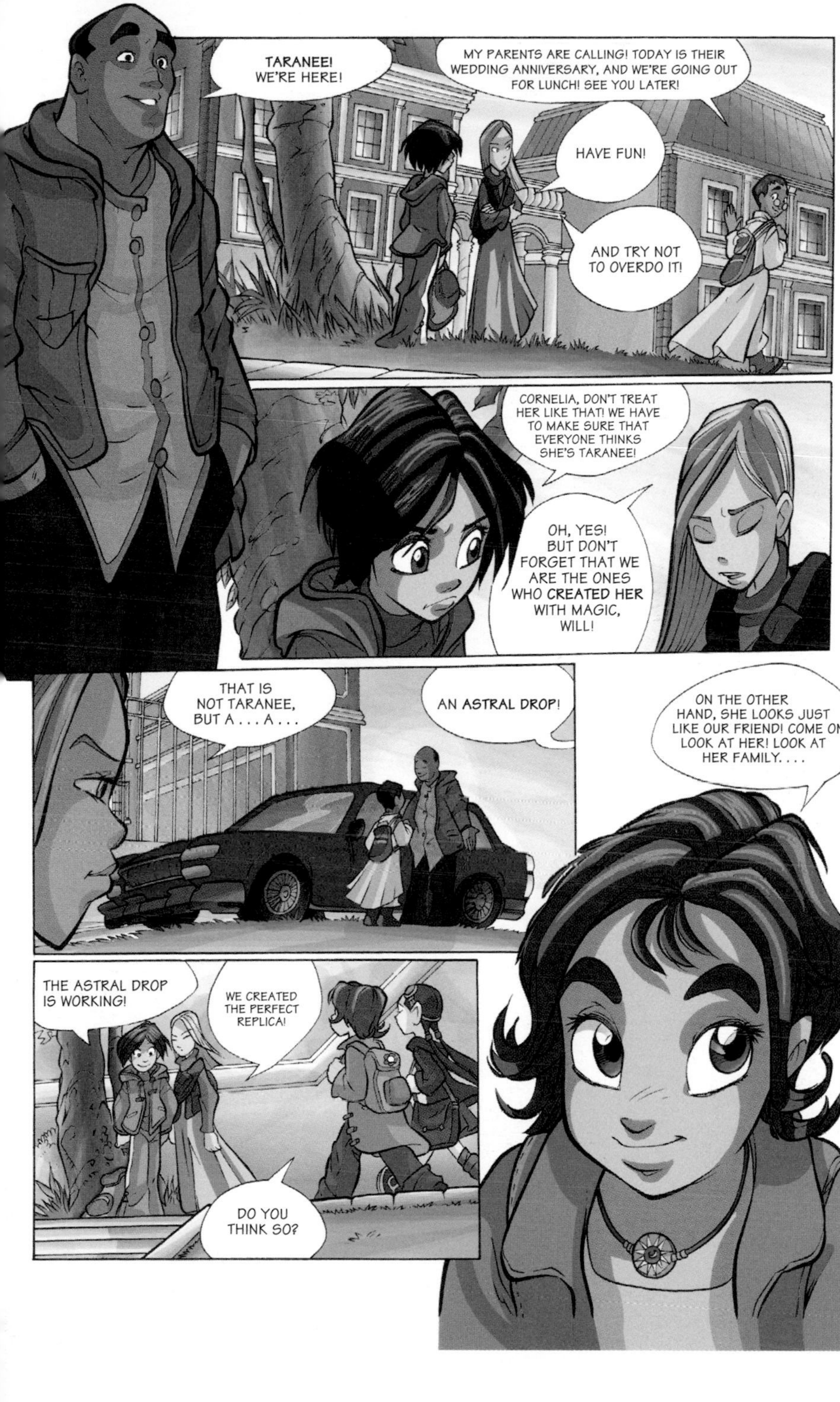
TARANEE!
WE'RE HERE!
MY PARENTS ARE CALLING! TODAY IS THEIR WEDDING ANNIVERSARY, AND WE'RE GOING OUT FOR LUNCH! SEE YOU LATER!
HAVE FUN!
AND TRY NOT TO OVERDO IT!
CORNELIA, DON'T TREAT HER LIKE THAT! WE HAVE TO MAKE SURE THAT EVERYONE THINKS SHE'S TARANEE!
OH, YES! BUT DON'T FORGET THAT WE ARE THE ONES WHO CREATED HER WITH MAGIC, WILL!
THAT IS NOT TARANEE, BUT A . . . A . . .
AN ASTRAL DROP!
ON THE OTHER HAND, SHE LOOKS JUST LIKE OUR FRIEND! COME ON, LOOK AT HER! LOOK AT HER FAMILY. . . .
THE ASTRAL DROP IS WORKING!
WE CREATED THE PERFECT REPLICA!
DO YOU THINK SO?

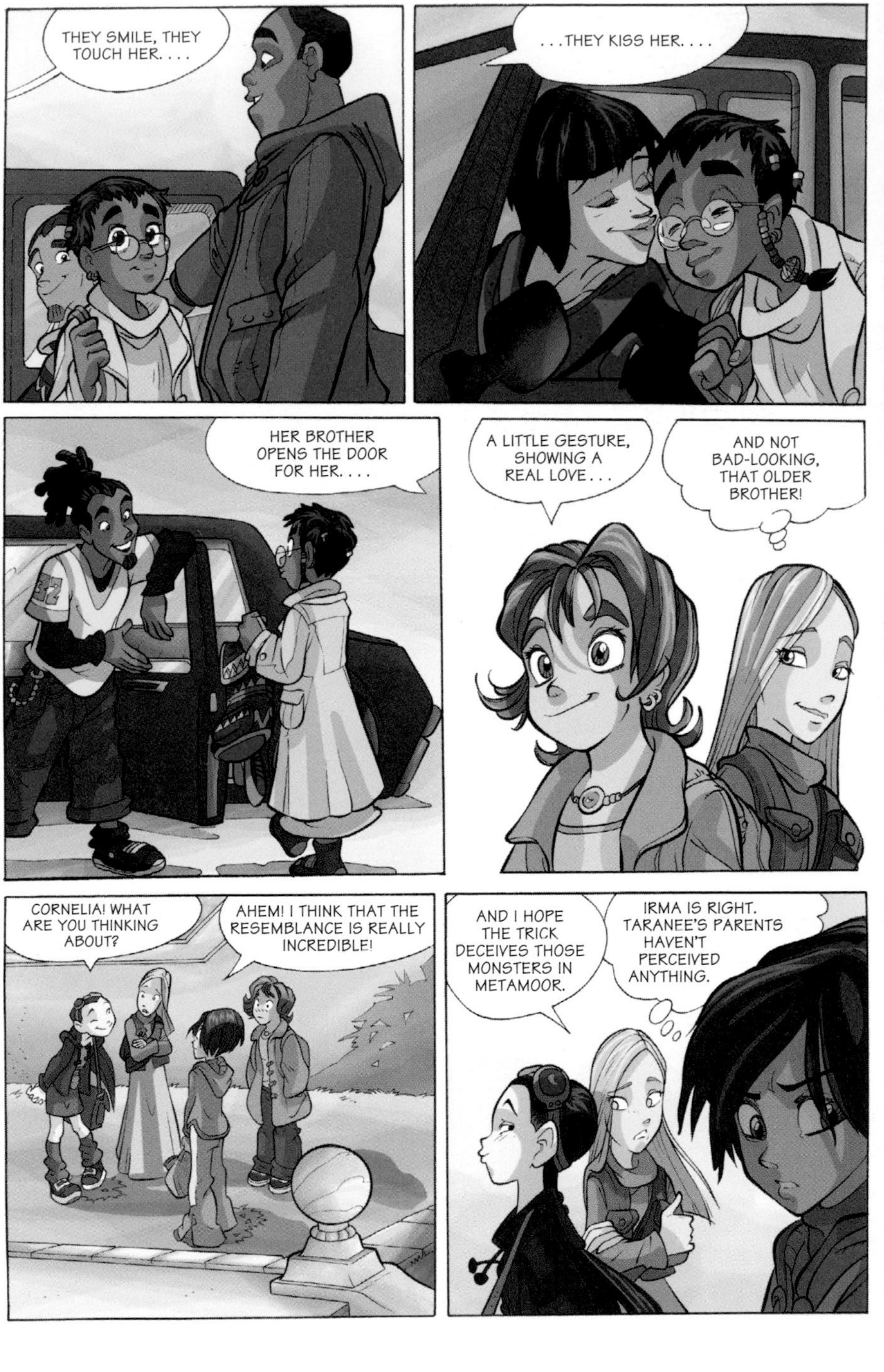
THEY SMILE, THEY TOUCH HER. . . .
. . .THEY KISS HER. . . .
HER BROTHER OPENS THE DOOR FOR HER. . . .
A LITTLE GESTURE, SHOWING A REAL LOVE . . .
AND NOT BAD-LOOKING, THAT OLDER BROTHER!
CORNELIA! WHAT ARE YOU THINKING ABOUT?
AHEM! I THINK THAT THE RESEMBLANCE IS REALLY INCREDIBLE!
AND I HOPE THE TRICK DECEIVES THOSE MONSTERS IN METAMOOR.
IRMA IS RIGHT. TARANEE'S PARENTS HAVEN'T PERCEIVED ANYTHING.

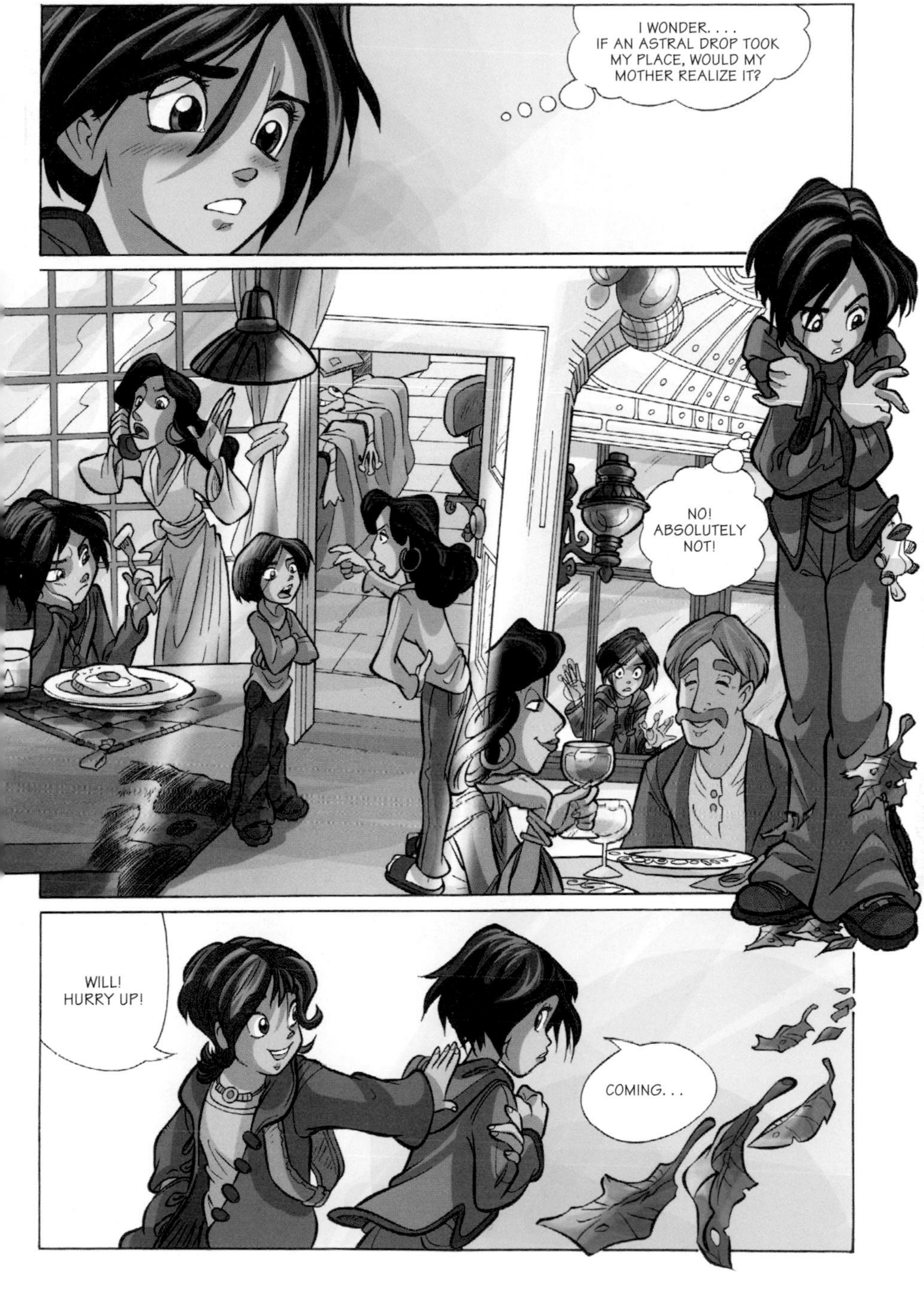
I WONDER. . . .
IF AN ASTRAL DROP TOOK MY PLACE, WOULD MY MOTHER REALIZE IT?
NO! ABSOLUTELY NOT!
WILL! HURRY UP!
COMING. . .

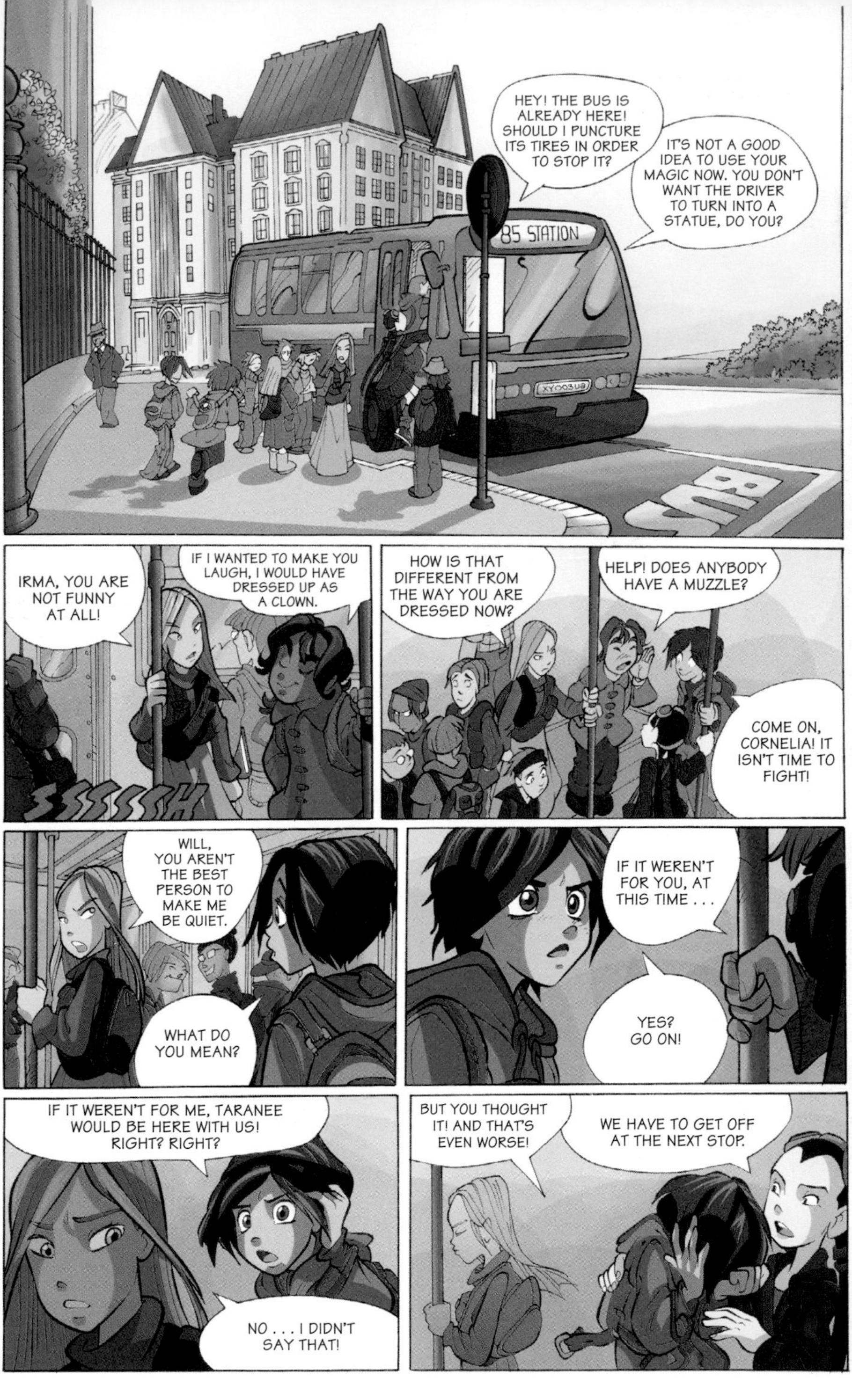
HEY! THE BUS IS ALREADY HERE! SHOULD I PUNCTURE ITS TIRES IN ORDER TO STOP IT?
IT'S NOT A GOOD IDEA TO USE YOUR MAGIC NOW. YOU DON'T WANT THE DRIVER TO TURN INTO A STATUE, DO YOU?
85 STATION
BUS
IRMA, YOU ARE NOT FUNNY AT ALL!
IF I WANTED TO MAKE YOU LAUGH, I WOULD HAVE DRESSED UP AS A CLOWN.
SSSSSCH
HOW IS THAT DIFFERENT FROM THE WAY YOU ARE DRESSED NOW?
HELP! DOES ANYBODY HAVE A MUZZLE?
COME ON, CORNELIA! IT ISN'T TIME TO FIGHT!
WILL, YOU AREN'T THE BEST PERSON TO MAKE ME BE QUIET.
WHAT DO YOU MEAN?
IF IT WEREN'T FOR YOU, AT THIS TIME . . .
YES? GO ON!
IF IT WEREN'T FOR ME, TARANEE WOULD BE HERE WITH US! RIGHT? RIGHT?
NO . . . I DIDN'T SAY THAT!
BUT YOU THOUGHT IT! AND THAT'S EVEN WORSE!
WE HAVE TO GET OFF AT THE NEXT STOP.

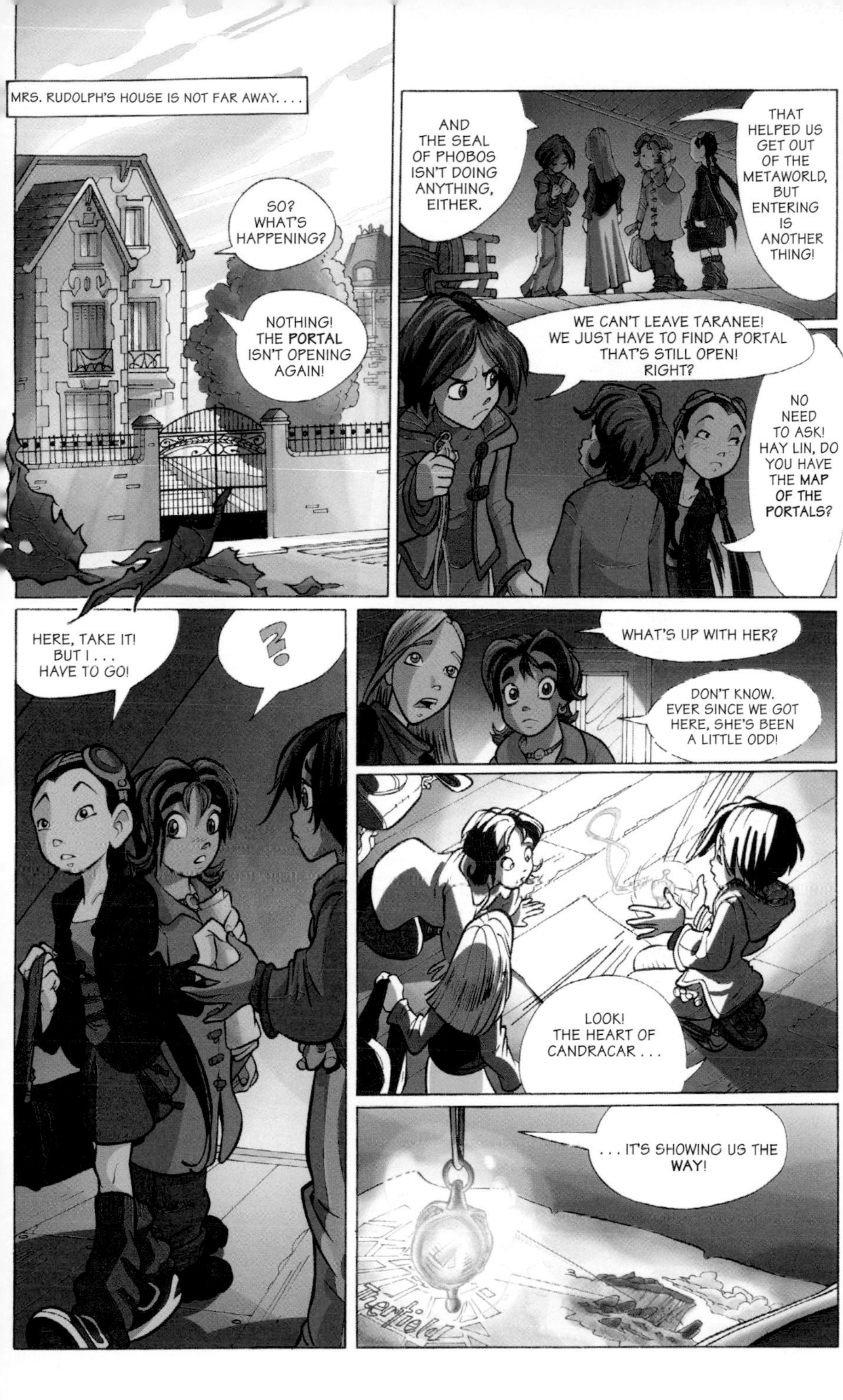
MRS. RUDOLPH'S HOUSE IS NOT FAR AWAY. . . .
SO? WHAT'S HAPPENING?
NOTHING! THE PORTAL ISN'T OPENING AGAIN!
AND THE SEAL OF PHOBOS ISN'T DOING ANYTHING, EITHER.
THAT HELPED US GET OUT OF THE METAWORLD, BUT ENTERING IS ANOTHER THING!
WE CAN'T LEAVE TARANEE! WE JUST HAVE TO FIND A PORTAL THAT'S STILL OPEN! RIGHT?
NO NEED TO ASK! HAY LIN, DO YOU HAVE THE MAP OF THE PORTALS?
HERE, TAKE IT! BUT I . . . HAVE TO GO!
?
WHAT'S UP WITH HER?
DON'T KNOW. EVER SINCE WE GOT HERE, SHE'S BEEN A LITTLE ODD!
LOOK! THE HEART OF CANDRACAR . . .
. . . IT'S SHOWING US THE WAY!

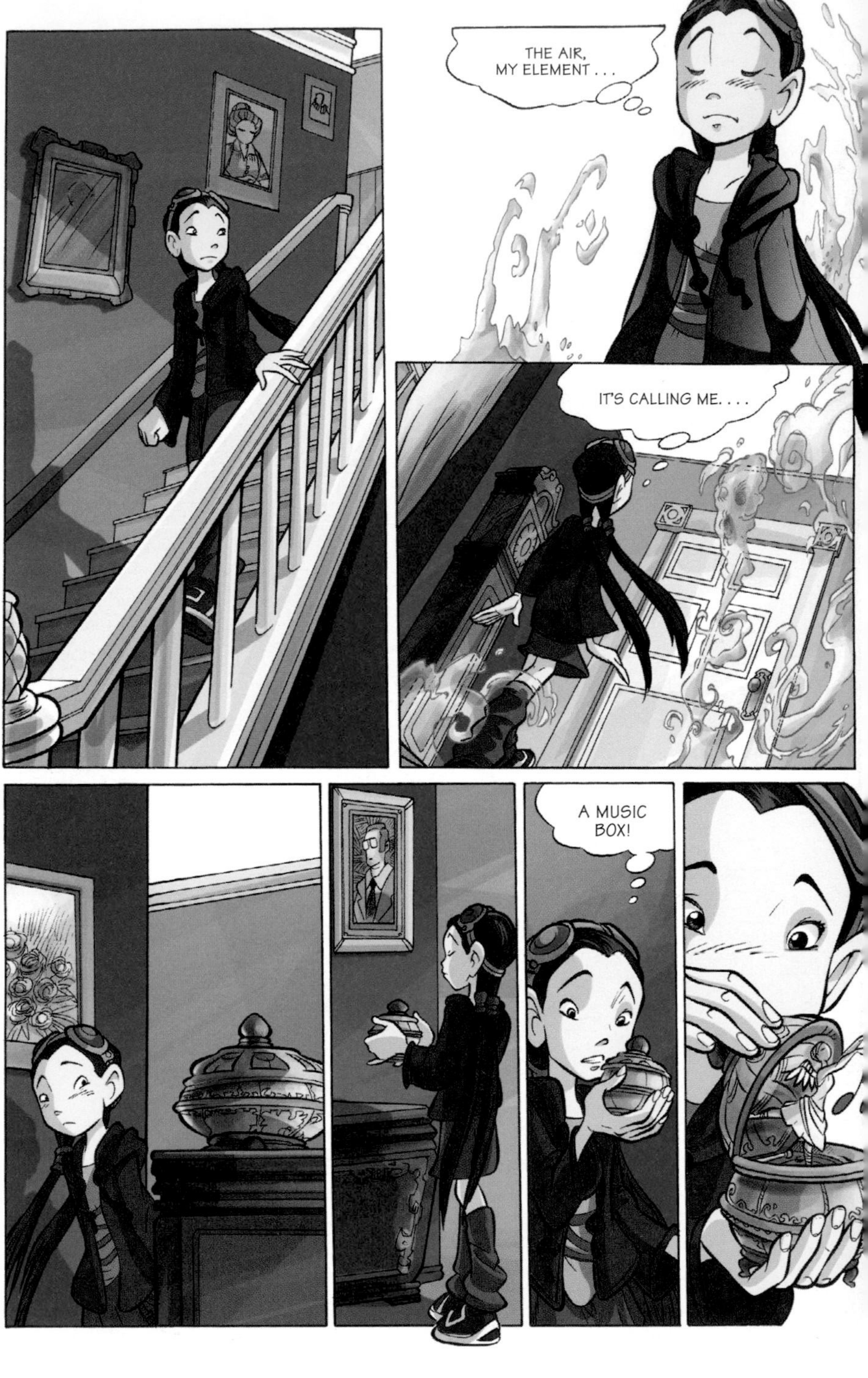
THE AIR, MY ELEMENT . . .
IT'S CALLING ME. . . .
A MUSIC BOX!

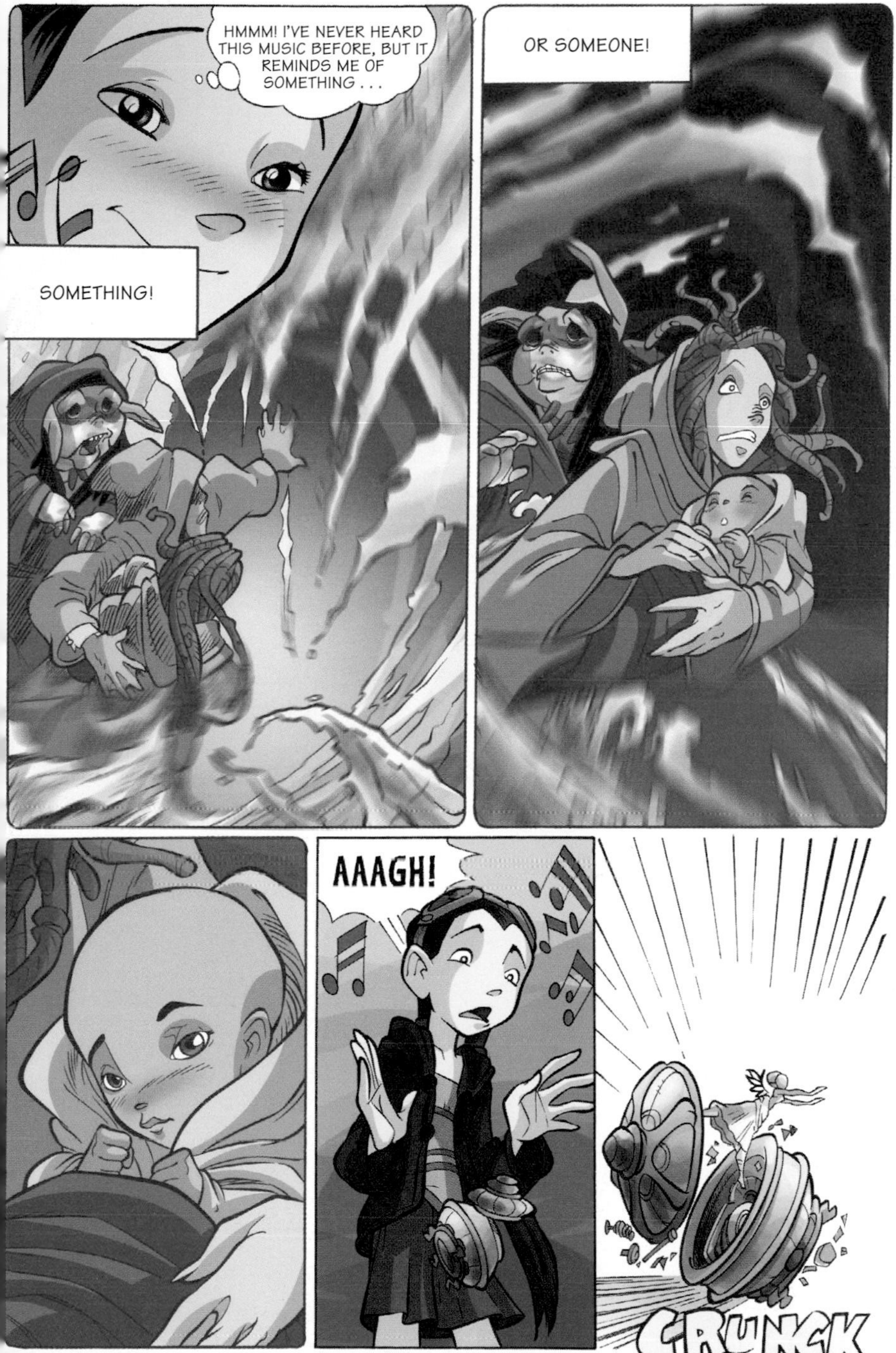
HMMM! I'VE NEVER HEARD THIS MUSIC BEFORE, BUT IT REMINDS ME OF SOMETHING . . .
SOMETHING!
OR SOMEONE!
AAAGH!
CRUNCK

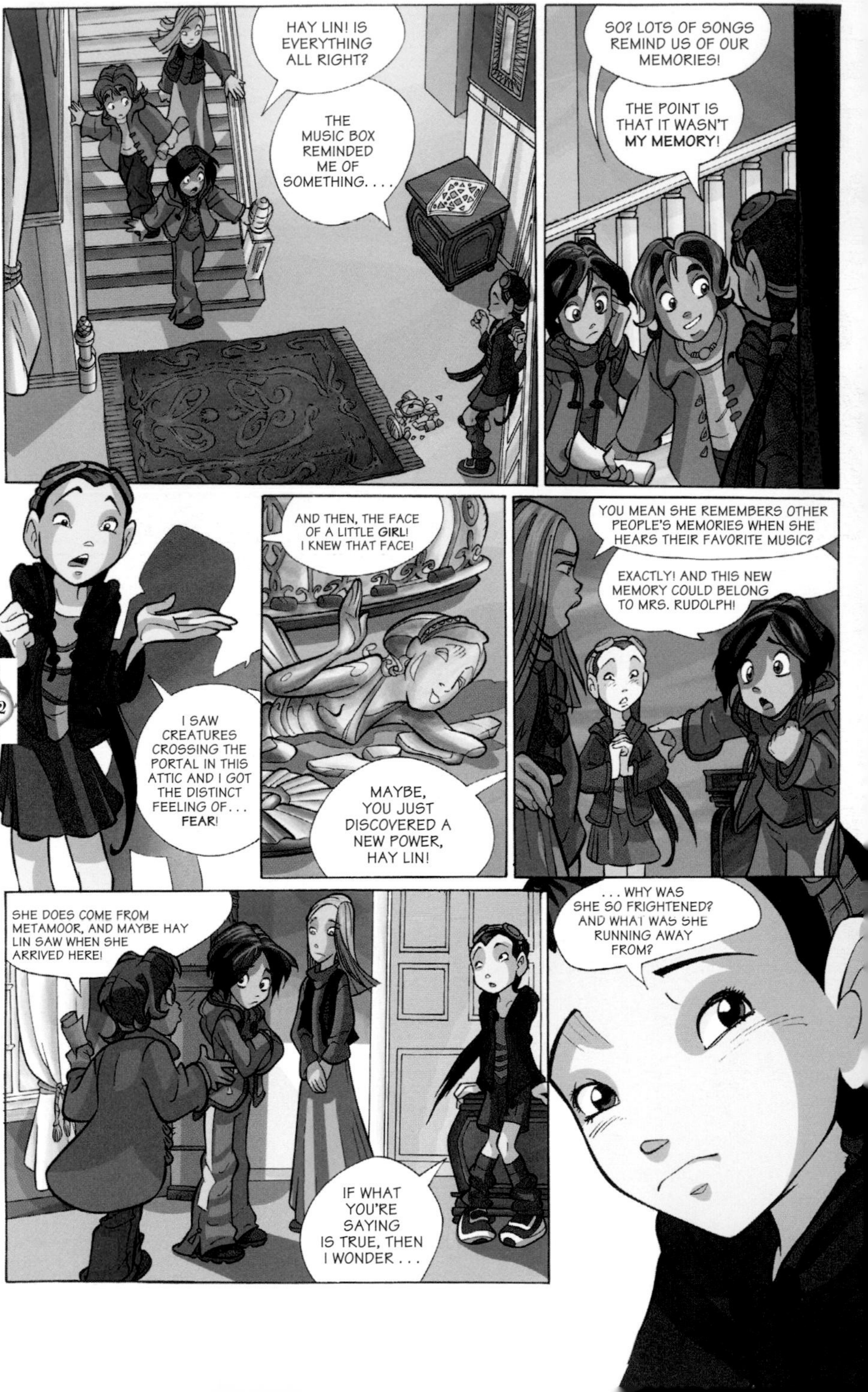
HAY LIN! IS EVERYTHING ALL RIGHT?
THE MUSIC BOX REMINDED ME OF SOMETHING. . . .
SO? LOTS OF SONGS REMIND US OF OUR MEMORIES!
THE POINT IS THAT IT WASN'T MY MEMORY!
I SAW CREATURES CROSSING THE PORTAL IN THIS ATTIC AND I GOT THE DISTINCT FEELING OF . . . FEAR!
AND THEN, THE FACE OF A LITTLE GIRL! I KNEW THAT FACE!
MAYBE, YOU JUST DISCOVERED A NEW POWER, HAY LIN!
YOU MEAN SHE REMEMBERS OTHER PEOPLE'S MEMORIES WHEN SHE HEARS THEIR FAVORITE MUSIC?
EXACTLY! AND THIS NEW MEMORY COULD BELONG TO MRS. RUDOLPH!
SHE DOES COME FROM METAMOOR, AND MAYBE HAY LIN SAW WHEN SHE ARRIVED HERE!
IF WHAT YOU'RE SAYING IS TRUE, THEN I WONDER . . .
. . . WHY WAS SHE SO FRIGHTENED? AND WHAT WAS SHE RUNNING AWAY FROM?

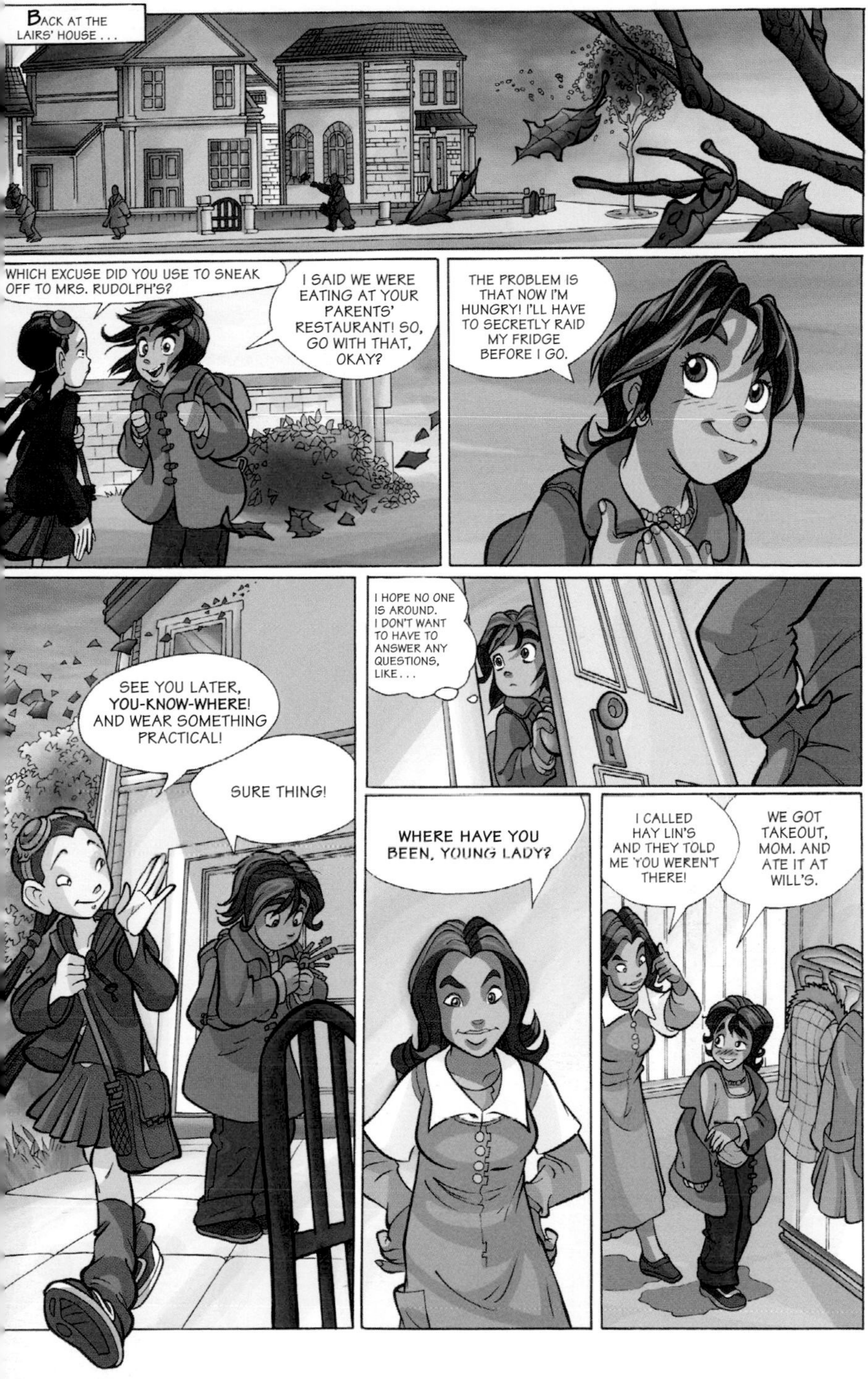
BACK AT THE LAIRS' HOUSE . . .
WHICH EXCUSE DID YOU USE TO SNEAK OFF TO MRS. RUDOLPH'S?
I SAID WE WERE EATING AT YOUR PARENTS' RESTAURANT! SO, GO WITH THAT, OKAY?
THE PROBLEM IS THAT NOW I'M HUNGRY! I'LL HAVE TO SECRETLY RAID MY FRIDGE BEFORE I GO.
SEE YOU LATER, YOU-KNOW-WHERE! AND WEAR SOMETHING PRACTICAL!
SURE THING!
I HOPE NO ONE IS AROUND. I DON'T WANT TO HAVE TO ANSWER ANY QUESTIONS, LIKE . . .
WHERE HAVE YOU BEEN, YOUNG LADY?
I CALLED HAY LIN'S AND THEY TOLD ME YOU WEREN'T THERE!
WE GOT TAKEOUT, MOM. AND ATE IT AT WILL'S.

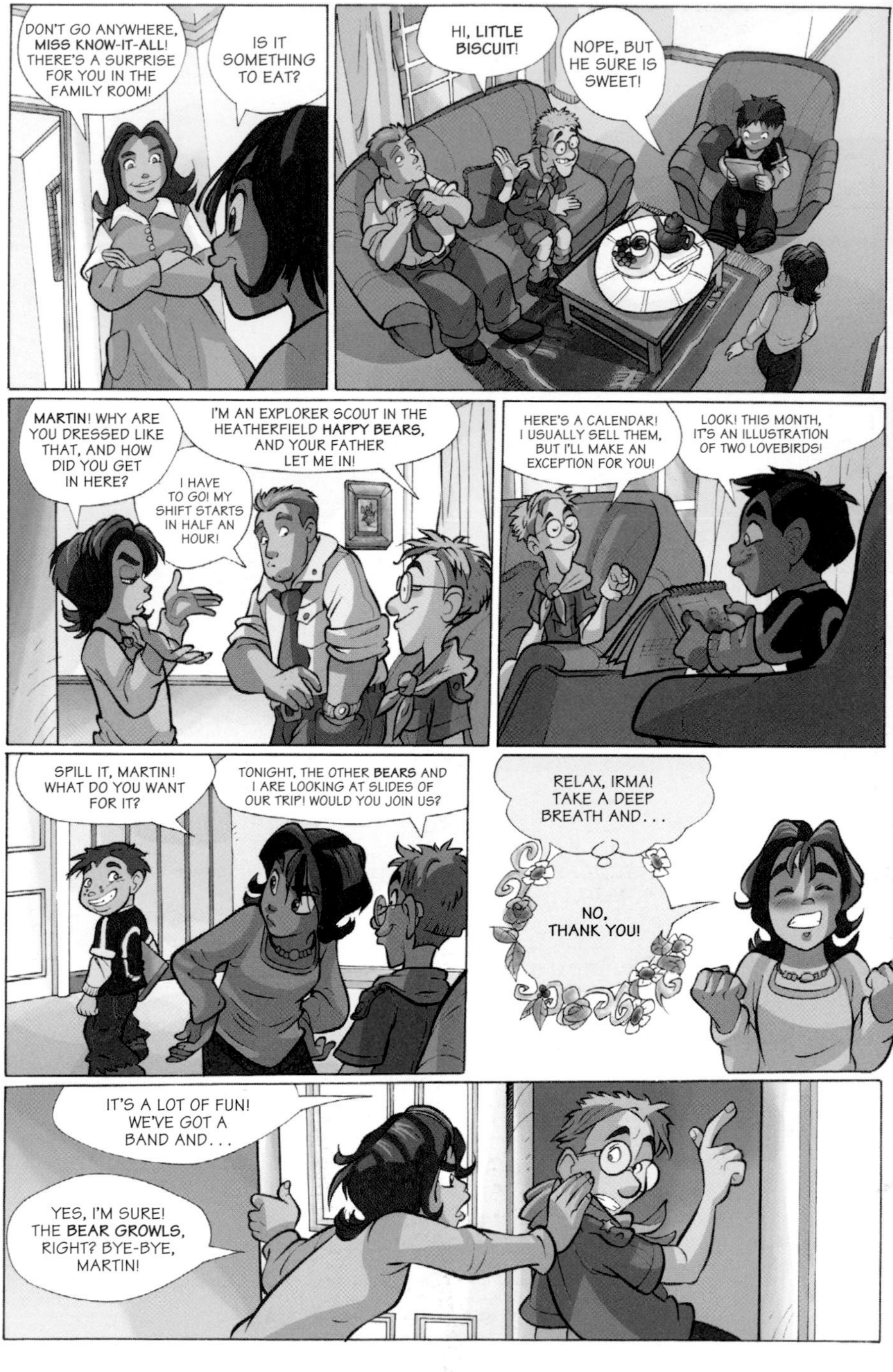
DON'T GO ANYWHERE, MISS KNOW-IT-ALL! THERE'S A SURPRISE FOR YOU IN THE FAMILY ROOM!
IS IT SOMETHING TO EAT?
HI, LITTLE BISCUIT!
NOPE, BUT HE SURE IS SWEET!
MARTIN! WHY ARE YOU DRESSED LIKE THAT, AND HOW DID YOU GET IN HERE?
I'M AN EXPLORER SCOUT IN THE HEATHERFIELD HAPPY BEARS, AND YOUR FATHER LET ME IN!
I HAVE TO GO! MY SHIFT STARTS IN HALF AN HOUR!
HERE'S A CALENDAR! I USUALLY SELL THEM, BUT I'LL MAKE AN EXCEPTION FOR YOU!
LOOK! THIS MONTH, IT'S AN ILLUSTRATION OF TWO LOVEBIRDS!
SPILL IT, MARTIN! WHAT DO YOU WANT FOR IT?
TONIGHT, THE OTHER BEARS AND I ARE LOOKING AT SLIDES OF OUR TRIP! WOULD YOU JOIN US?
RELAX, IRMA! TAKE A DEEP BREATH AND. . .
NO, THANK YOU!
IT'S A LOT OF FUN! WE'VE GOT A BAND AND. . .
YES, I'M SURE! THE BEAR GROWLS, RIGHT? BYE-BYE, MARTIN!

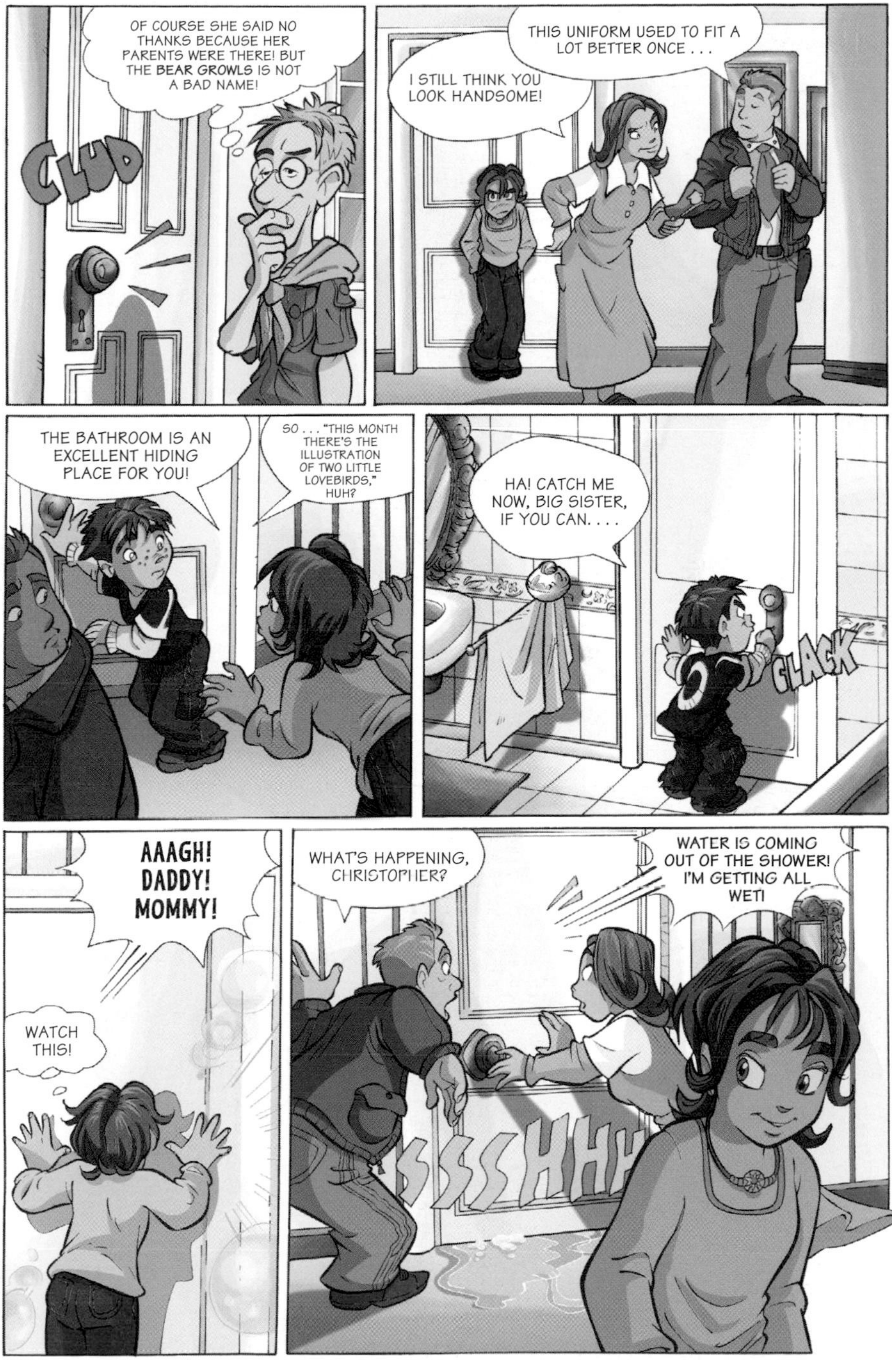
OF COURSE SHE SAID NO THANKS BECAUSE HER PARENTS WERE THERE! BUT THE BEAR GROWLS IS NOT A BAD NAME!
CLUD
THIS UNIFORM USED TO FIT A LOT BETTER ONCE . . .
I STILL THINK YOU LOOK HANDSOME!
THE BATHROOM IS AN EXCELLENT HIDING PLACE FOR YOU!
SO . . . "THIS MONTH THERE'S THE ILLUSTRATION OF TWO LITTLE LOVEBIRDS," HUH?
HA! CATCH ME NOW, BIG SISTER, IF YOU CAN. . . .
CLACK
AAAGH! DADDY! MOMMY!
WATCH THIS!
WHAT'S HAPPENING, CHRISTOPHER?
WATER IS COMING OUT OF THE SHOWER! I'M GETTING ALL WET!
SSSHHH

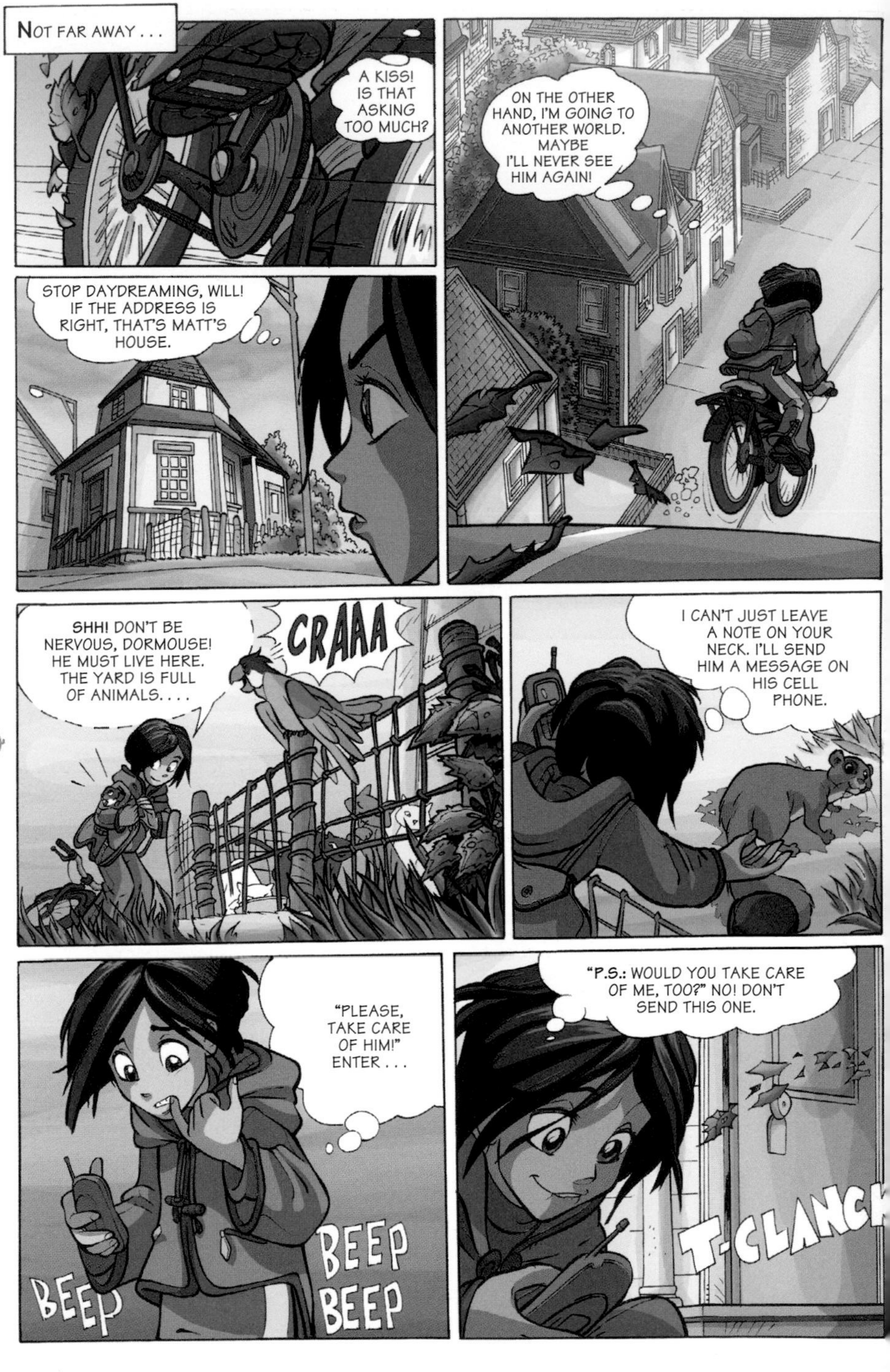
NOT FAR AWAY . . .
A KISS! IS THAT ASKING TOO MUCH?
ON THE OTHER HAND, I'M GOING TO ANOTHER WORLD. MAYBE I'LL NEVER SEE HIM AGAIN!
STOP DAYDREAMING, WILL! IF THE ADDRESS IS RIGHT, THAT'S MATT'S HOUSE.
SHH! DON'T BE NERVOUS, DORMOUSE! HE MUST LIVE HERE. THE YARD IS FULL OF ANIMALS. . . .
CRAAA
I CAN'T JUST LEAVE A NOTE ON YOUR NECK. I'LL SEND HIM A MESSAGE ON HIS CELL PHONE.
"PLEASE, TAKE CARE OF HIM!" ENTER . . .
BEEP
BEEP
BEEP
"P.S.: WOULD YOU TAKE CARE OF ME, TOO?" NO! DON'T SEND THIS ONE.
T-CLANCH

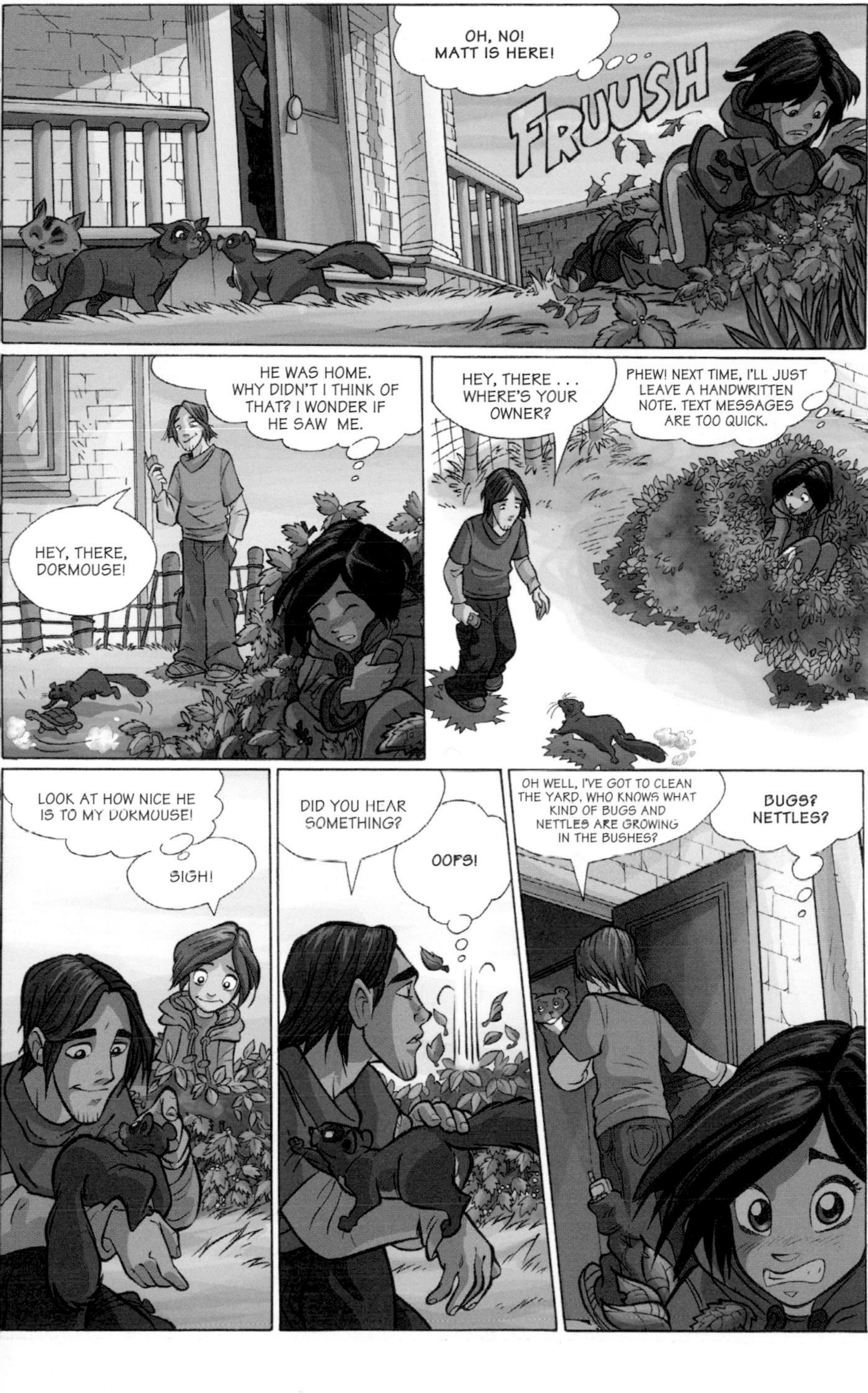
OH, NO!
MATT IS HERE!
FRUUSH
HE WAS HOME. WHY DIDN'T I THINK OF THAT? I WONDER IF HE SAW ME.
HEY, THERE, DORMOUSE!
HEY, THERE . . . WHERE'S YOUR OWNER?
PHEW! NEXT TIME, I'LL JUST LEAVE A HANDWRITTEN NOTE. TEXT MESSAGES ARE TOO QUICK.
LOOK AT HOW NICE HE IS TO MY DORMOUSE!
SIGH!
DID YOU HEAR SOMETHING?
OOPS!
OH WELL, I'VE GOT TO CLEAN THE YARD, WHO KNOWS WHAT KIND OF BUGS AND NETTLES ARE GROWING IN THE BUSHES?
BUGS? NETTLES?

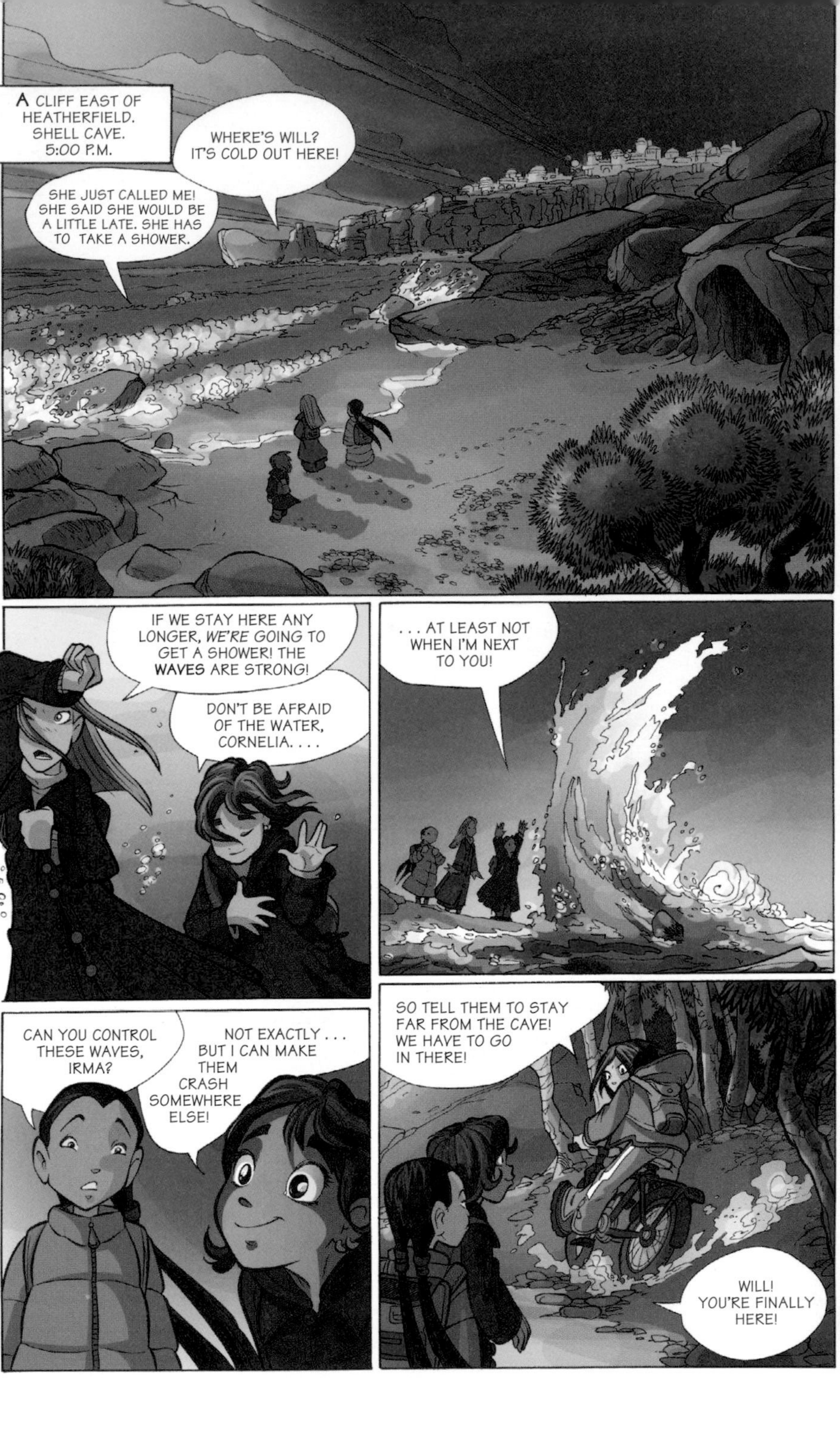
A CLIFF EAST OF HEATHERFIELD. SHELL CAVE. 5:00 P.M.
WHERE'S WILL? IT'S COLD OUT HERE!
SHE JUST CALLED ME! SHE SAID SHE WOULD BE A LITTLE LATE. SHE HAS TO TAKE A SHOWER.
IF WE STAY HERE ANY LONGER, *WE'RE* GOING TO GET A SHOWER! THE **WAVES** ARE STRONG!
DON'T BE AFRAID OF THE WATER, CORNELIA. . . .
. . . AT LEAST NOT WHEN I'M NEXT TO YOU!
CAN YOU CONTROL THESE WAVES, IRMA?
NOT EXACTLY . . . BUT I CAN MAKE THEM CRASH SOMEWHERE ELSE!
SO TELL THEM TO STAY FAR FROM THE CAVE! WE HAVE TO GO IN THERE!
WILL! YOU'RE FINALLY HERE!

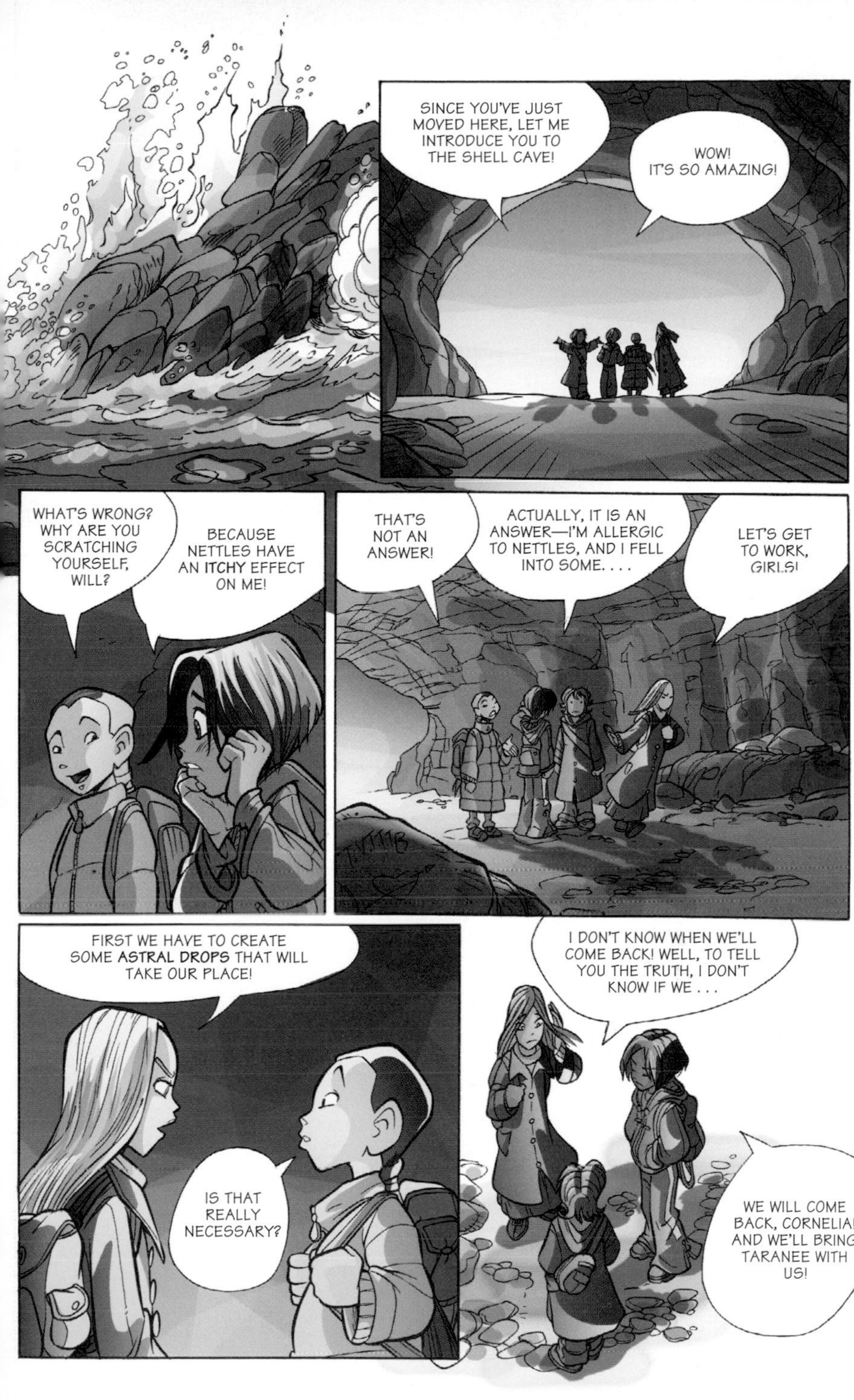
SINCE YOU'VE JUST MOVED HERE, LET ME INTRODUCE YOU TO THE SHELL CAVE!
WOW! IT'S SO AMAZING!
WHAT'S WRONG? WHY ARE YOU SCRATCHING YOURSELF, WILL?
BECAUSE NETTLES HAVE AN ITCHY EFFECT ON ME!
THAT'S NOT AN ANSWER!
ACTUALLY, IT IS AN ANSWER—I'M ALLERGIC TO NETTLES, AND I FELL INTO SOME. . . .
LET'S GET TO WORK, GIRLS!
FIRST WE HAVE TO CREATE SOME ASTRAL DROPS THAT WILL TAKE OUR PLACE!
IS THAT REALLY NECESSARY?
I DON'T KNOW WHEN WE'LL COME BACK! WELL, TO TELL YOU THE TRUTH, I DON'T KNOW IF WE . . .
WE WILL COME BACK, CORNELIA! AND WE'LL BRING TARANEE WITH US!

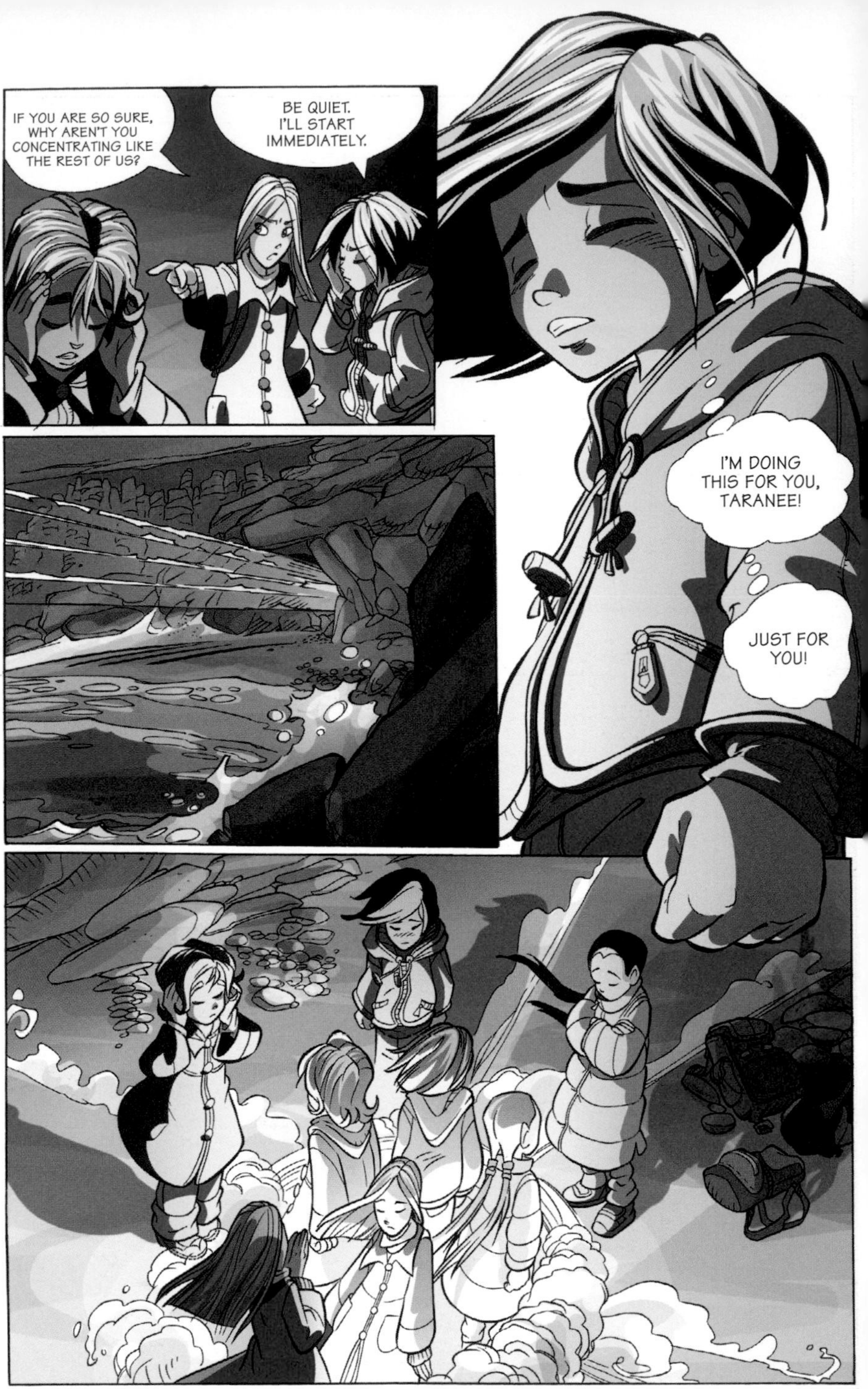
IF YOU ARE SO SURE, WHY AREN'T YOU CONCENTRATING LIKE THE REST OF US?
BE QUIET. I'LL START IMMEDIATELY.
I'M DOING THIS FOR YOU, TARANEE!
JUST FOR YOU!

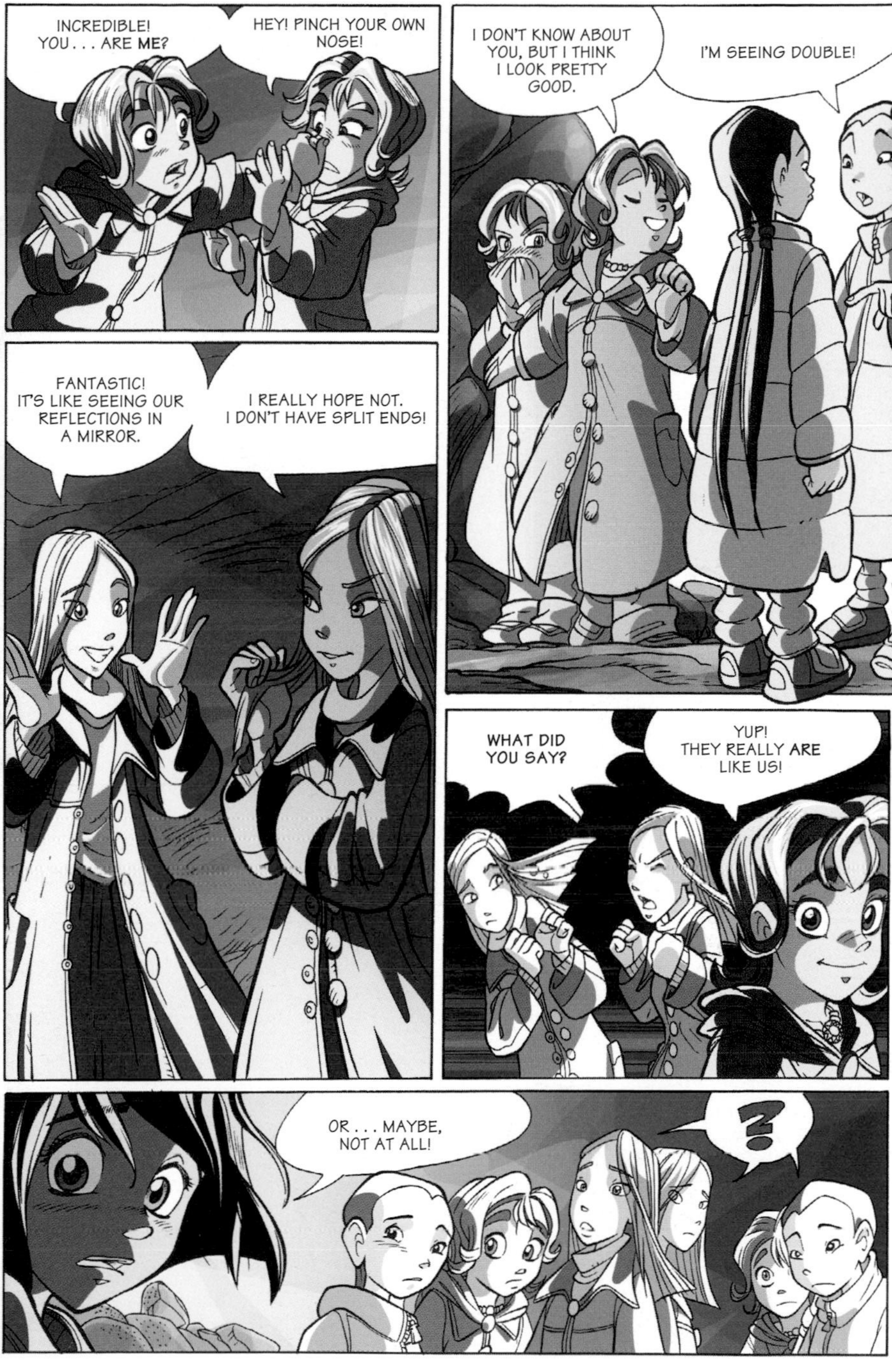

INCREDIBLE! YOU . . . ARE ME?
HEY! PINCH YOUR OWN NOSE!
I DON'T KNOW ABOUT YOU, BUT I THINK I LOOK PRETTY GOOD.
I'M SEEING DOUBLE!
FANTASTIC! IT'S LIKE SEEING OUR REFLECTIONS IN A MIRROR.
I REALLY HOPE NOT. I DON'T HAVE SPLIT ENDS!
WHAT DID YOU SAY?
YUP! THEY REALLY ARE LIKE US!
OR . . . MAYBE, NOT AT ALL!
?

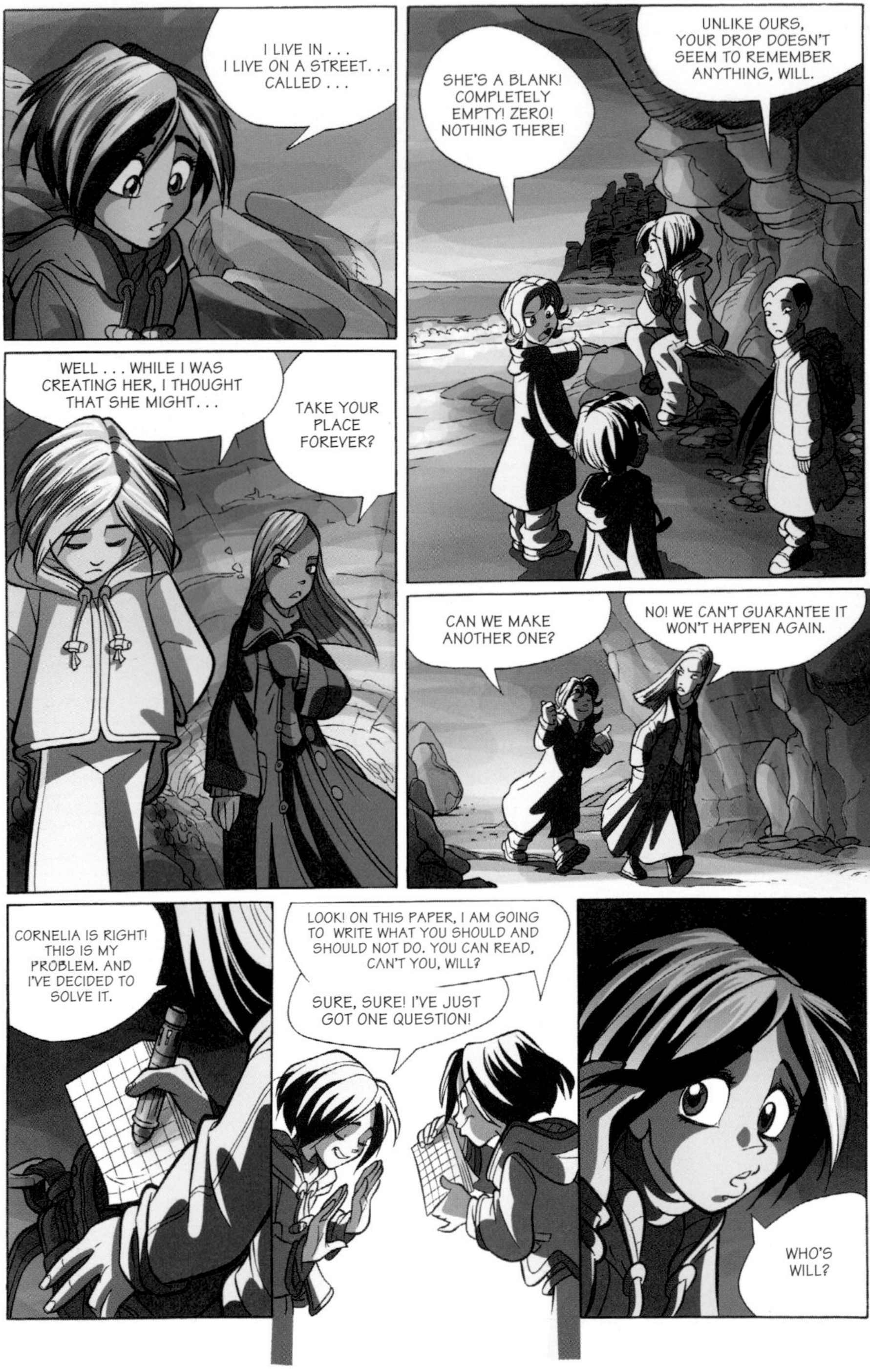

I LIVE IN . . .
I LIVE ON A STREET. . .
CALLED . . .
SHE'S A BLANK! COMPLETELY EMPTY! ZERO! NOTHING THERE!
UNLIKE OURS, YOUR DROP DOESN'T SEEM TO REMEMBER ANYTHING, WILL.
WELL . . . WHILE I WAS CREATING HER, I THOUGHT THAT SHE MIGHT. . .
TAKE YOUR PLACE FOREVER?
CAN WE MAKE ANOTHER ONE?
NO! WE CAN'T GUARANTEE IT WON'T HAPPEN AGAIN.
CORNELIA IS RIGHT! THIS IS MY PROBLEM. AND I'VE DECIDED TO SOLVE IT.
LOOK! ON THIS PAPER, I AM GOING TO WRITE WHAT YOU SHOULD AND SHOULD NOT DO. YOU CAN READ, CAN'T YOU, WILL?
SURE, SURE! I'VE JUST GOT ONE QUESTION!
WHO'S WILL?

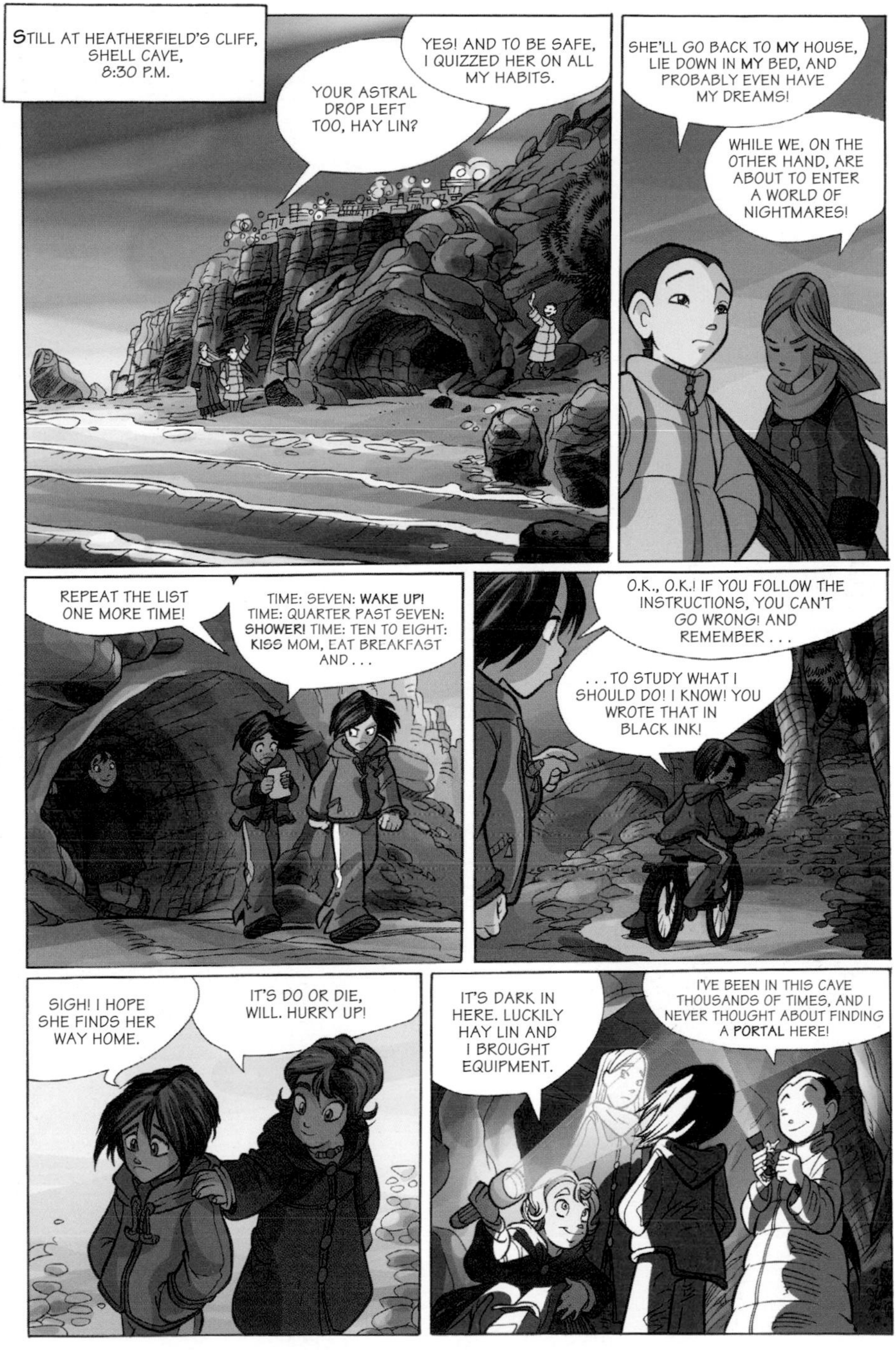

STILL AT HEATHERFIELD'S CLIFF, SHELL CAVE, 8:30 P.M.
YOUR ASTRAL DROP LEFT TOO, HAY LIN?
YES! AND TO BE SAFE, I QUIZZED HER ON ALL MY HABITS.
SHE'LL GO BACK TO MY HOUSE, LIE DOWN IN MY BED, AND PROBABLY EVEN HAVE MY DREAMS!
WHILE WE, ON THE OTHER HAND, ARE ABOUT TO ENTER A WORLD OF NIGHTMARES!
REPEAT THE LIST ONE MORE TIME!
TIME: SEVEN: WAKE UP! TIME: QUARTER PAST SEVEN: SHOWER! TIME: TEN TO EIGHT: KISS MOM, EAT BREAKFAST AND . . .
O.K., O.K.! IF YOU FOLLOW THE INSTRUCTIONS, YOU CAN'T GO WRONG! AND REMEMBER . . .
. . . TO STUDY WHAT I SHOULD DO! I KNOW! YOU WROTE THAT IN BLACK INK!
SIGH! I HOPE SHE FINDS HER WAY HOME.
IT'S DO OR DIE, WILL. HURRY UP!
IT'S DARK IN HERE. LUCKILY HAY LIN AND I BROUGHT EQUIPMENT.
I'VE BEEN IN THIS CAVE THOUSANDS OF TIMES, AND I NEVER THOUGHT ABOUT FINDING A PORTAL HERE!

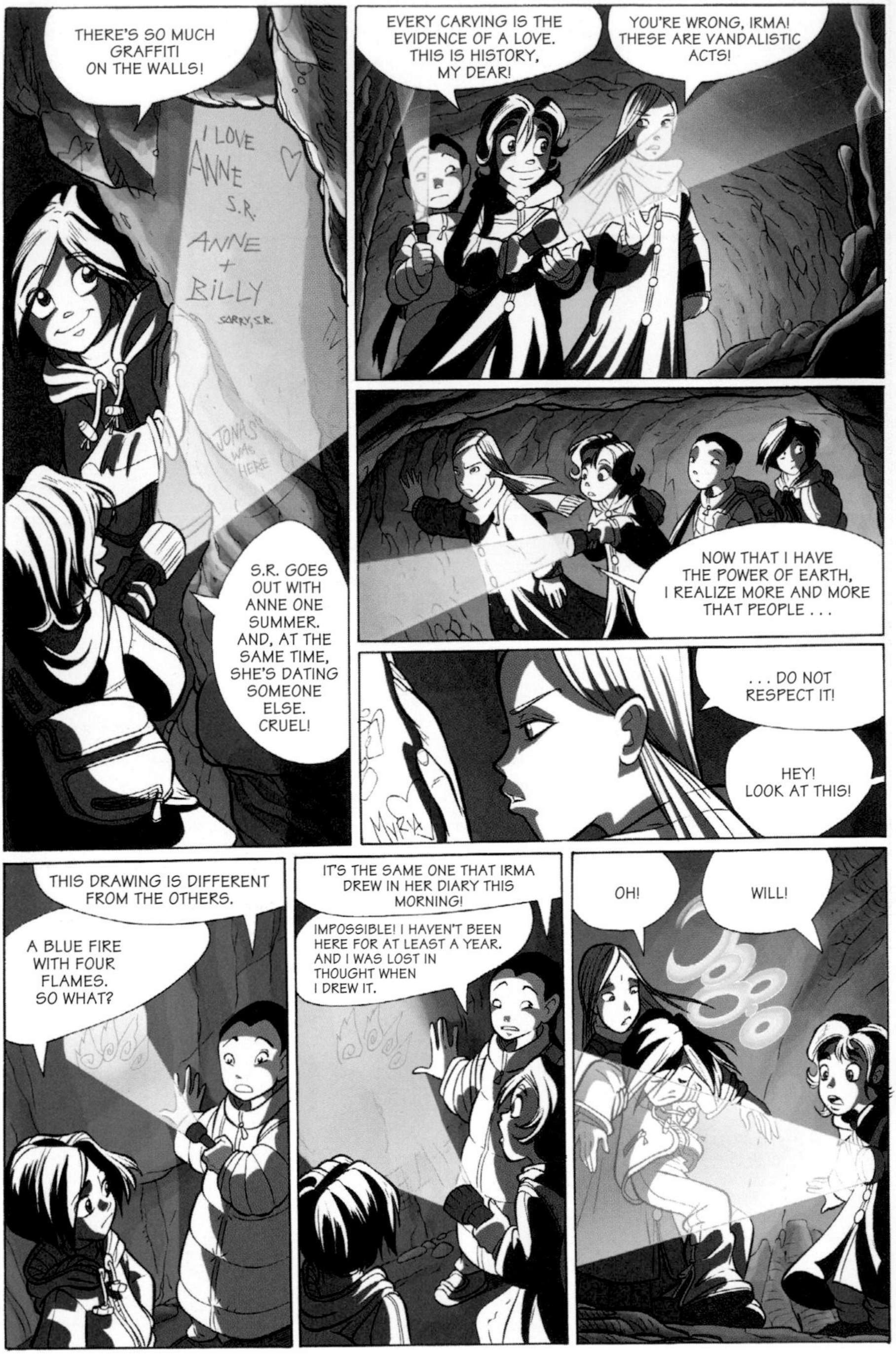
THERE'S SO MUCH GRAFFITI ON THE WALLS!
I LOVE ANNE S.R.
ANNE + BILLY
SORRY, S.R.
JONAS WAS HERE
S.R. GOES OUT WITH ANNE ONE SUMMER. AND, AT THE SAME TIME, SHE'S DATING SOMEONE ELSE. CRUEL!
EVERY CARVING IS THE EVIDENCE OF A LOVE. THIS IS HISTORY, MY DEAR!
YOU'RE WRONG, IRMA! THESE ARE VANDALISTIC ACTS!
NOW THAT I HAVE THE POWER OF EARTH, I REALIZE MORE AND MORE THAT PEOPLE . . .
. . . DO NOT RESPECT IT!
HEY! LOOK AT THIS!
THIS DRAWING IS DIFFERENT FROM THE OTHERS.
A BLUE FIRE WITH FOUR FLAMES. SO WHAT?
IT'S THE SAME ONE THAT IRMA DREW IN HER DIARY THIS MORNING!
IMPOSSIBLE! I HAVEN'T BEEN HERE FOR AT LEAST A YEAR. AND I WAS LOST IN THOUGHT WHEN I DREW IT.
OH!
WILL!

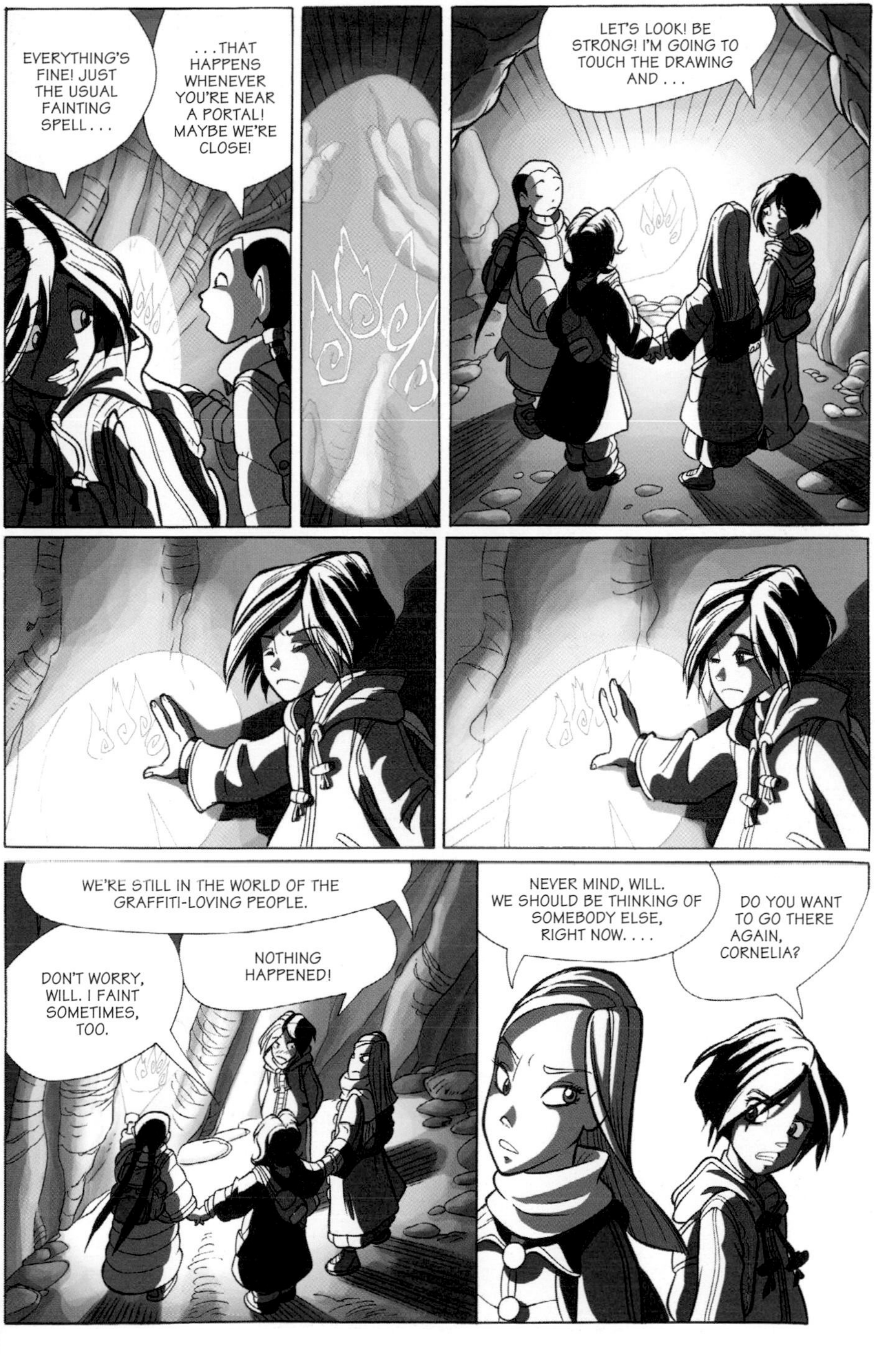

EVERYTHING'S FINE! JUST THE USUAL FAINTING SPELL . . .
. . .THAT HAPPENS WHENEVER YOU'RE NEAR A PORTAL! MAYBE WE'RE CLOSE!
LET'S LOOK! BE STRONG! I'M GOING TO TOUCH THE DRAWING AND . . .
WE'RE STILL IN THE WORLD OF THE GRAFFITI-LOVING PEOPLE.
NOTHING HAPPENED!
DON'T WORRY, WILL. I FAINT SOMETIMES, TOO.
DO YOU WANT TO GO THERE AGAIN, CORNELIA?
NEVER MIND, WILL. WE SHOULD BE THINKING OF SOMEBODY ELSE, RIGHT NOW. . . .

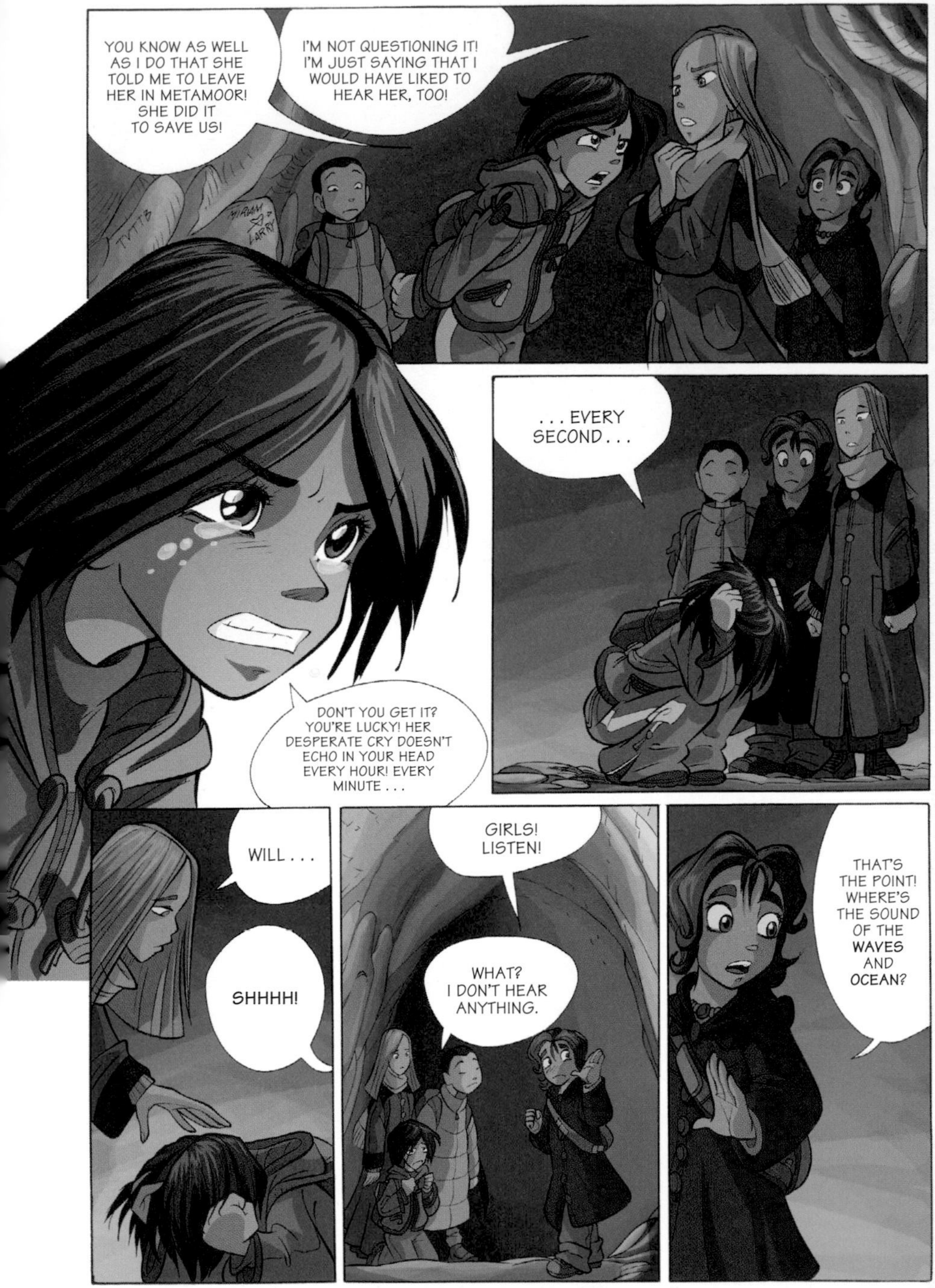
YOU KNOW AS WELL AS I DO THAT SHE TOLD ME TO LEAVE HER IN METAMOOR! SHE DID IT TO SAVE US!
I'M NOT QUESTIONING IT! I'M JUST SAYING THAT I WOULD HAVE LIKED TO HEAR HER, TOO!
DON'T YOU GET IT? YOU'RE LUCKY! HER DESPERATE CRY DOESN'T ECHO IN YOUR HEAD EVERY HOUR! EVERY MINUTE . . .
. . . EVERY SECOND . . .
WILL . . .
SHHHH!
GIRLS! LISTEN!
WHAT? I DON'T HEAR ANYTHING.
THAT'S THE POINT! WHERE'S THE SOUND OF THE WAVES AND OCEAN?

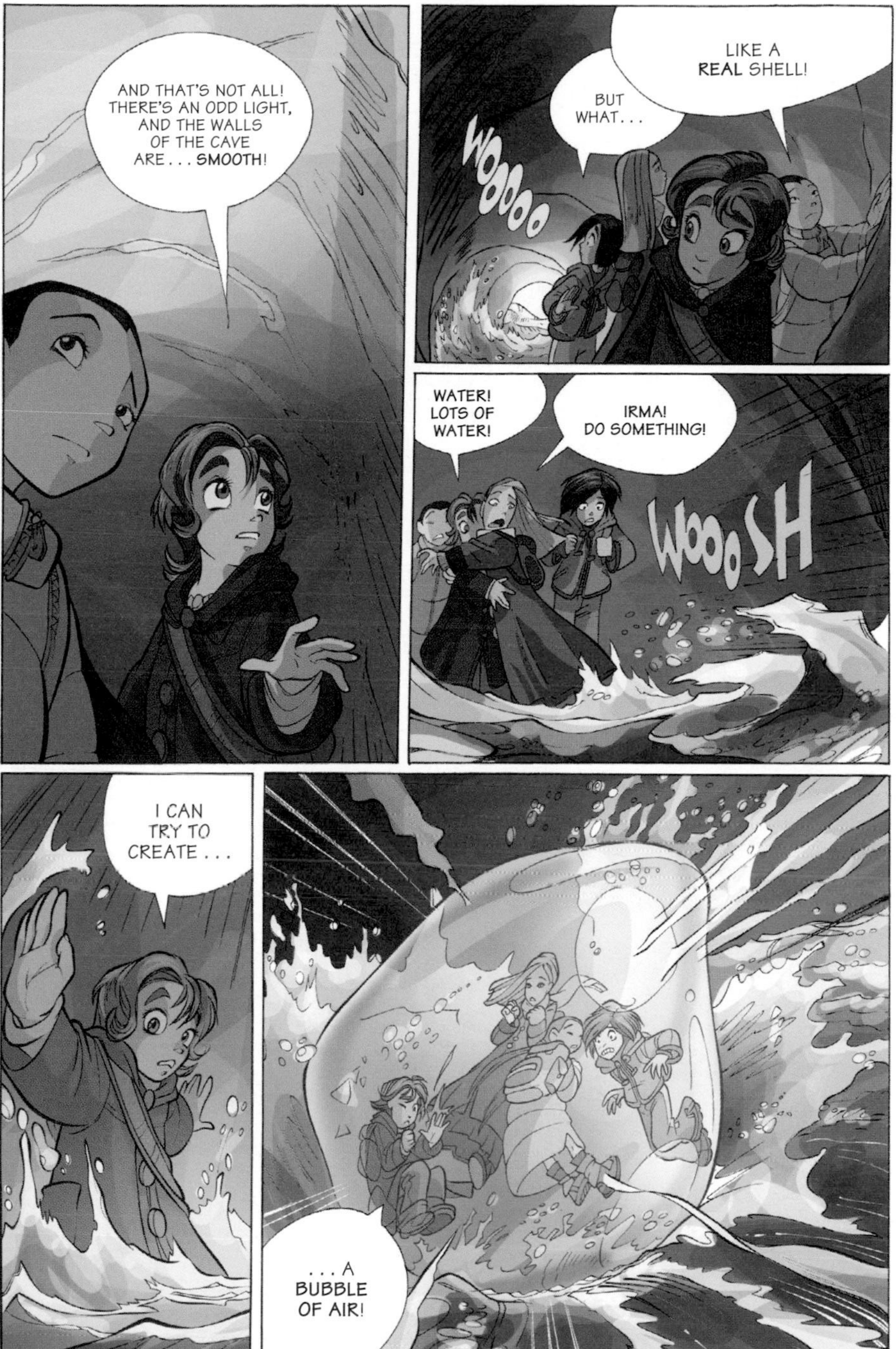
AND THAT'S NOT ALL! THERE'S AN ODD LIGHT, AND THE WALLS OF THE CAVE ARE . . . SMOOTH!
LIKE A REAL SHELL!
BUT WHAT. . .
WOOOOO
WATER! LOTS OF WATER!
IRMA! DO SOMETHING!
WOOOSH
I CAN TRY TO CREATE . . .
. . . A BUBBLE OF AIR!

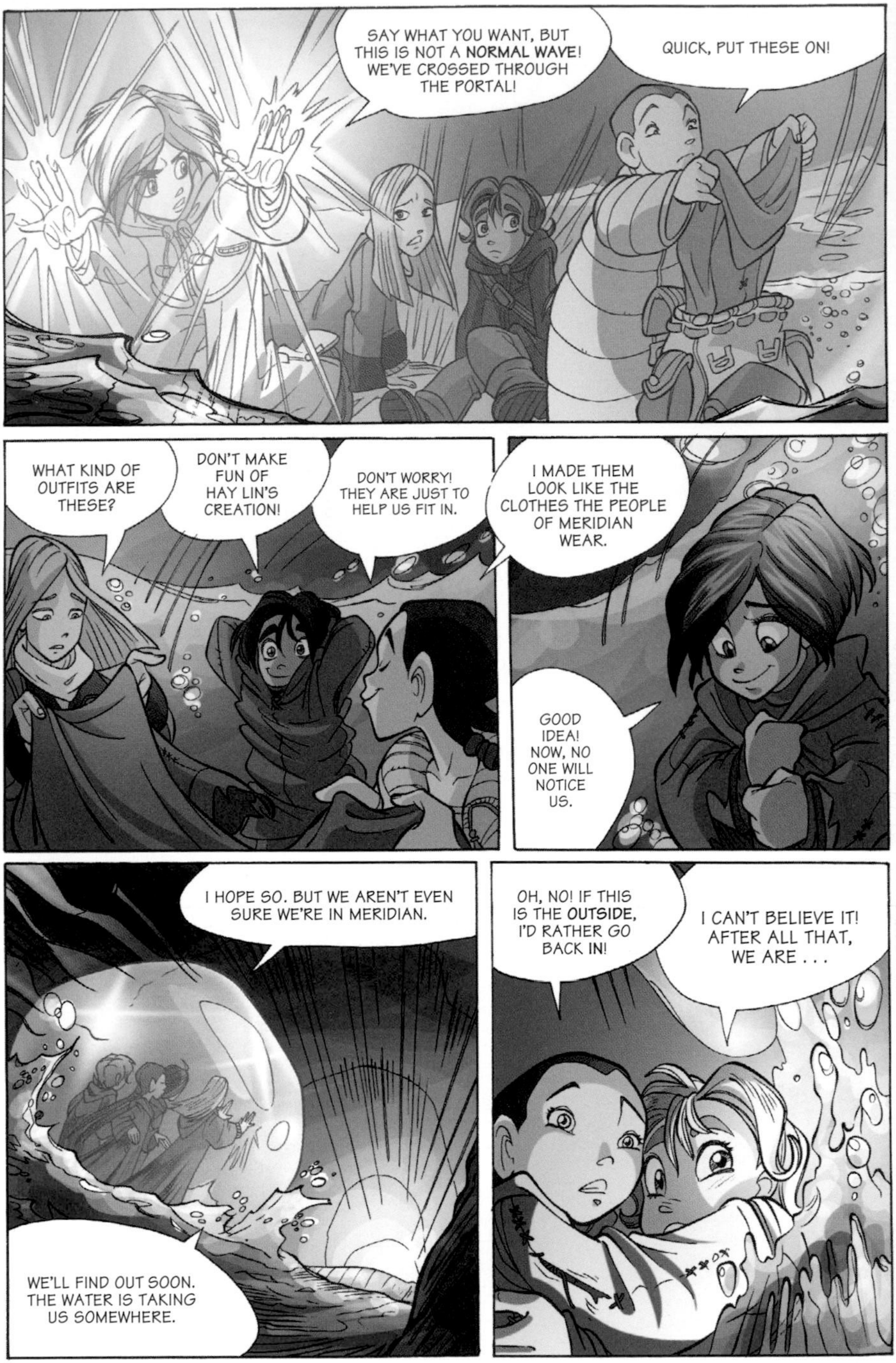
SAY WHAT YOU WANT, BUT THIS IS NOT A **NORMAL WAVE**! WE'VE CROSSED THROUGH THE PORTAL!
QUICK, PUT THESE ON!
WHAT KIND OF OUTFITS ARE THESE?
DON'T MAKE FUN OF HAY LIN'S CREATION!
DON'T WORRY! THEY ARE JUST TO HELP US FIT IN.
I MADE THEM LOOK LIKE THE CLOTHES THE PEOPLE OF MERIDIAN WEAR.
GOOD IDEA! NOW, NO ONE WILL NOTICE US.
I HOPE SO. BUT WE AREN'T EVEN SURE WE'RE IN MERIDIAN.
WE'LL FIND OUT SOON. THE WATER IS TAKING US SOMEWHERE.
OH, NO! IF THIS IS THE **OUTSIDE**, I'D RATHER GO BACK **IN**!
I CAN'T BELIEVE IT! AFTER ALL THAT, WE ARE . . .

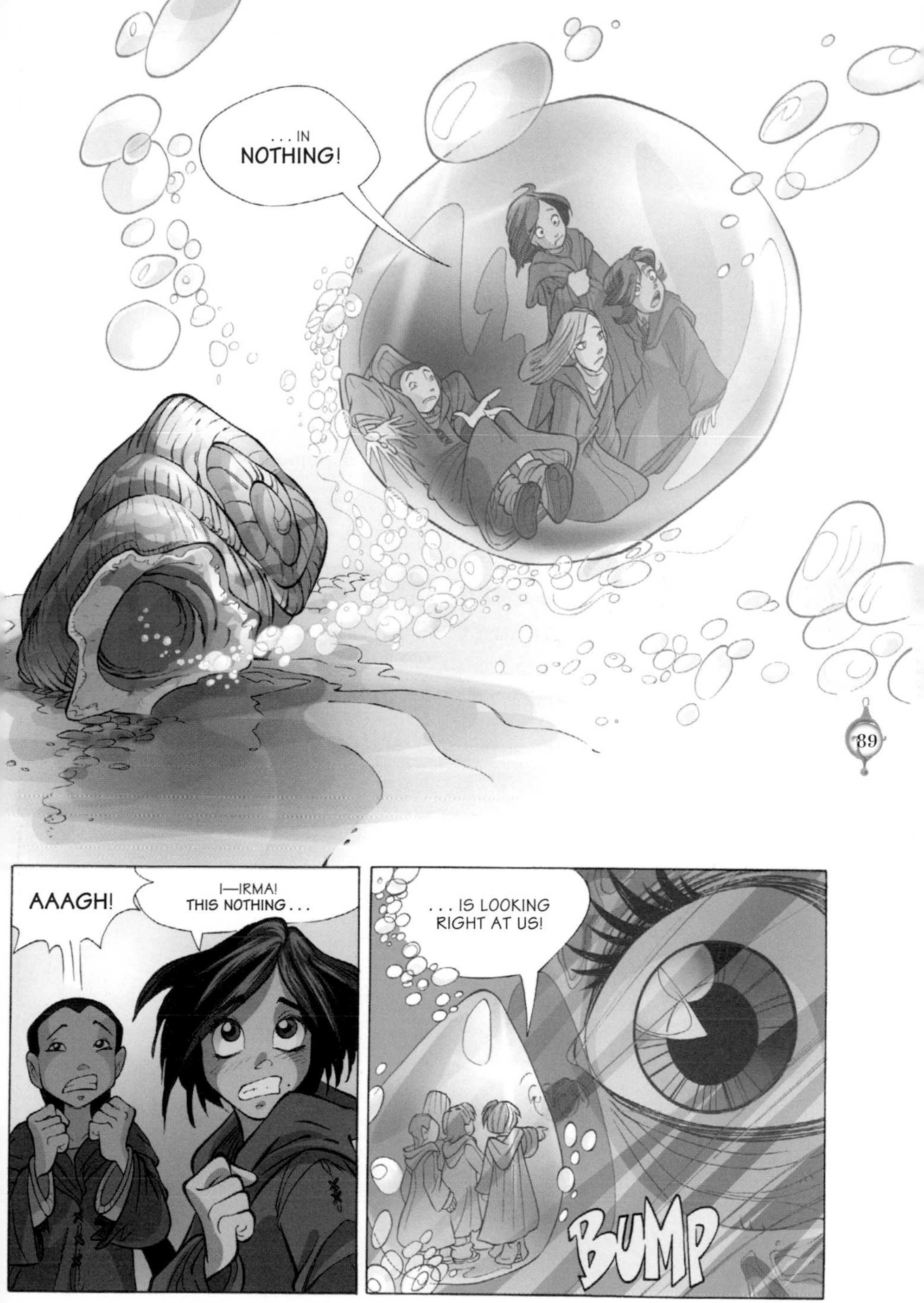

. . . IN NOTHING!
AAAGH!
I—IRMA! THIS NOTHING . . .
. . . IS LOOKING RIGHT AT US!
BUMP

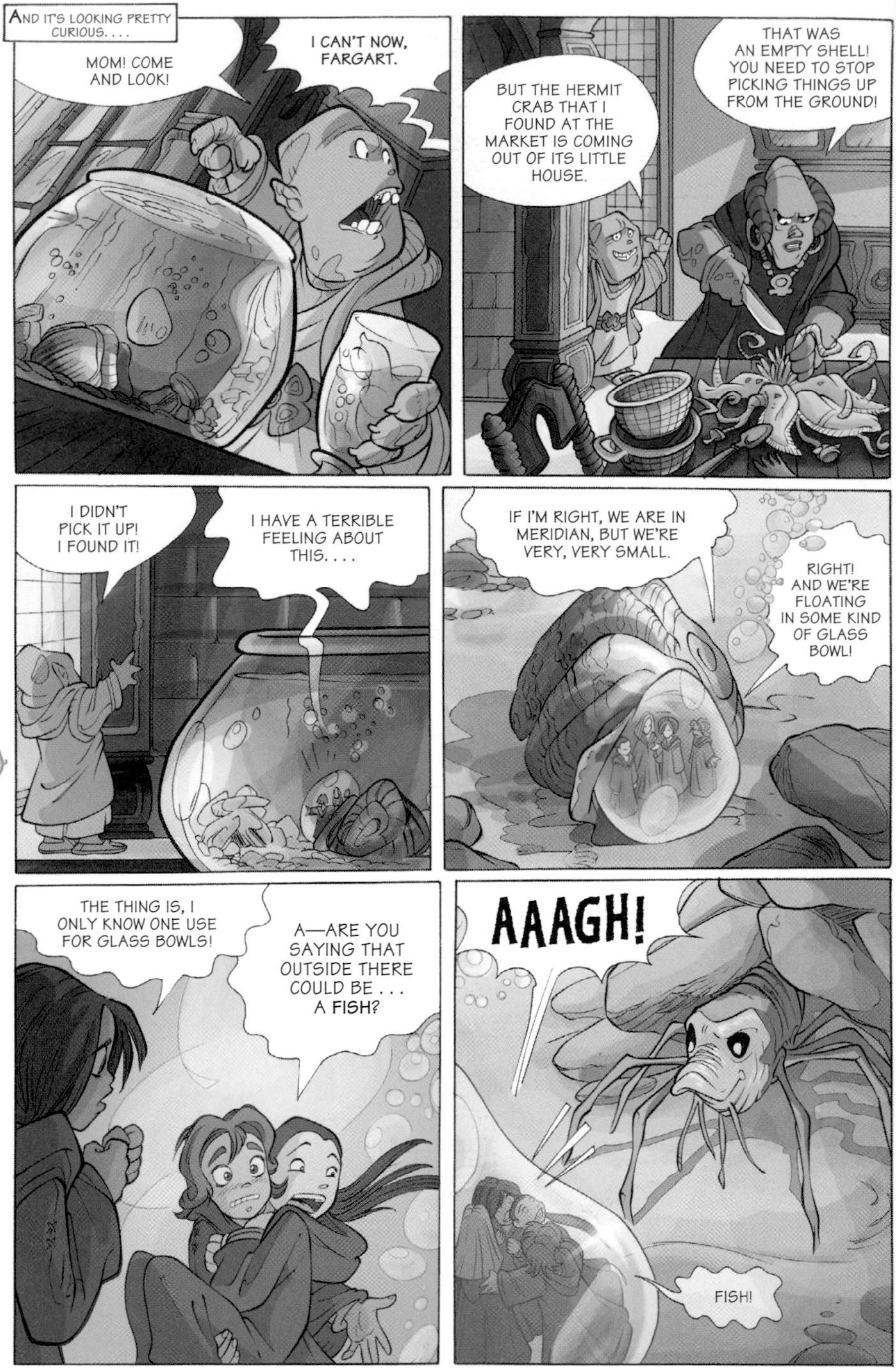
AND IT'S LOOKING PRETTY CURIOUS. . . .
MOM! COME AND LOOK!
I CAN'T NOW, FARGART.
BUT THE HERMIT CRAB THAT I FOUND AT THE MARKET IS COMING OUT OF ITS LITTLE HOUSE.
THAT WAS AN EMPTY SHELL! YOU NEED TO STOP PICKING THINGS UP FROM THE GROUND!
I DIDN'T PICK IT UP! I FOUND IT!
I HAVE A TERRIBLE FEELING ABOUT THIS. . . .
IF I'M RIGHT, WE ARE IN MERIDIAN, BUT WE'RE VERY, VERY SMALL.
RIGHT! AND WE'RE FLOATING IN SOME KIND OF GLASS BOWL!
THE THING IS, I ONLY KNOW ONE USE FOR GLASS BOWLS!
A—ARE YOU SAYING THAT OUTSIDE THERE COULD BE . . . A FISH?
AAAGH!
FISH!

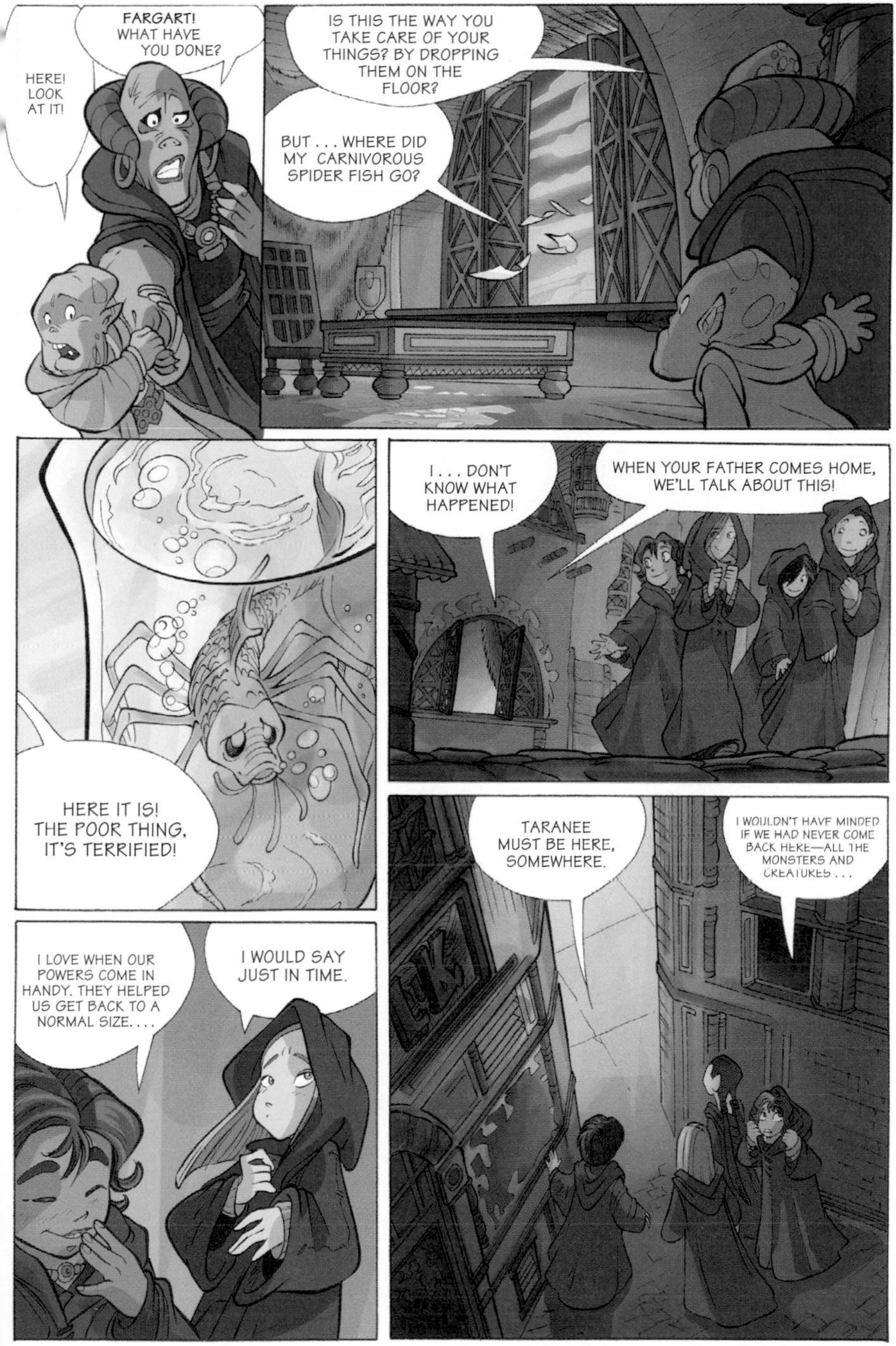
HERE! LOOK AT IT!
FARGART! WHAT HAVE YOU DONE?
IS THIS THE WAY YOU TAKE CARE OF YOUR THINGS? BY DROPPING THEM ON THE FLOOR?
BUT . . . WHERE DID MY CARNIVOROUS SPIDER FISH GO?
HERE IT IS! THE POOR THING, IT'S TERRIFIED!
I . . . DON'T KNOW WHAT HAPPENED!
WHEN YOUR FATHER COMES HOME, WE'LL TALK ABOUT THIS!
I LOVE WHEN OUR POWERS COME IN HANDY. THEY HELPED US GET BACK TO A NORMAL SIZE. . . .
I WOULD SAY JUST IN TIME.
TARANEE MUST BE HERE, SOMEWHERE.
I WOULDN'T HAVE MINDED IF WE HAD NEVER COME BACK HERE—ALL THE MONSTERS AND CREATURES . . .

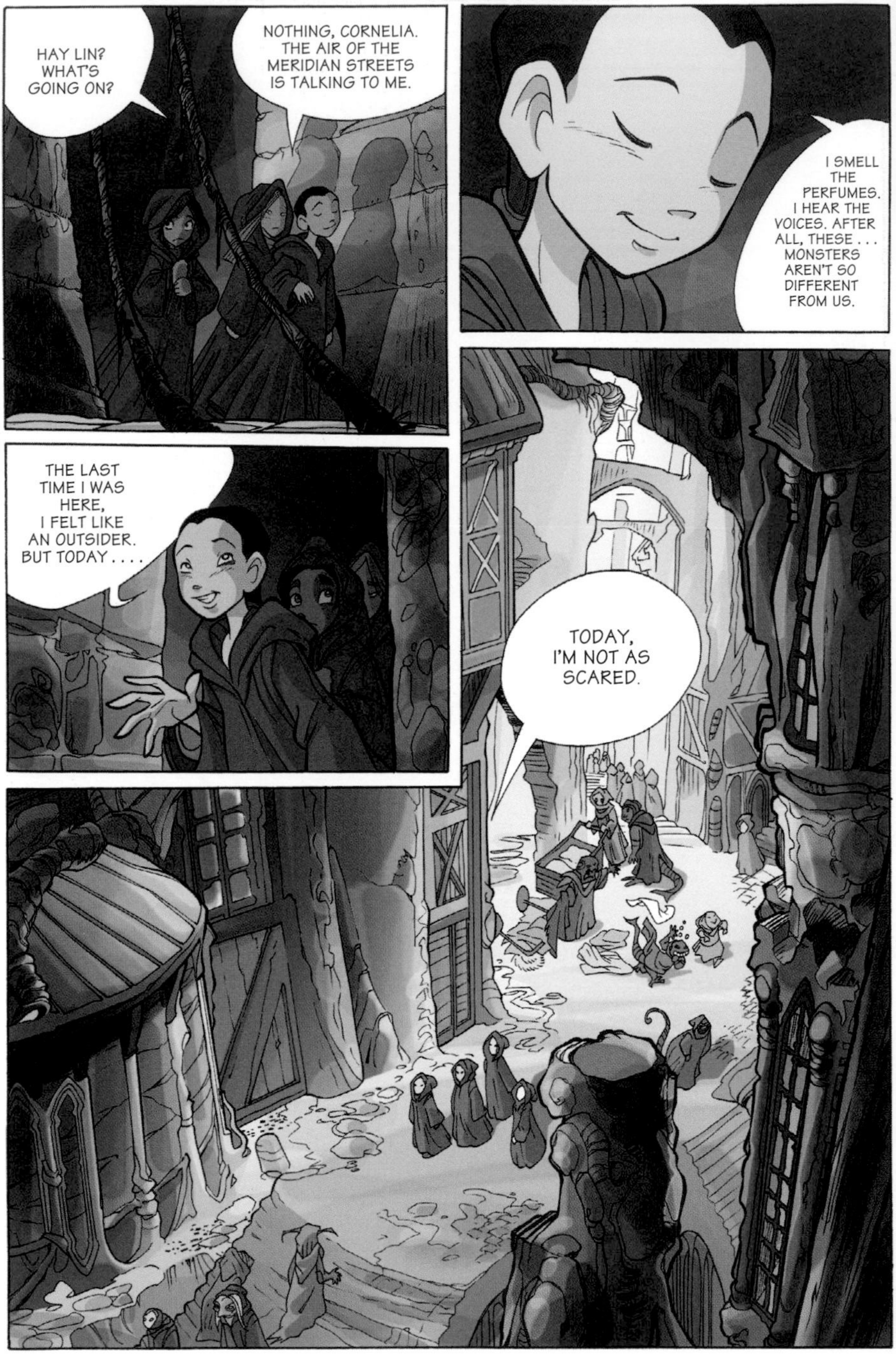
HAY LIN? WHAT'S GOING ON?
NOTHING, CORNELIA. THE AIR OF THE MERIDIAN STREETS IS TALKING TO ME.
I SMELL THE PERFUMES. I HEAR THE VOICES. AFTER ALL, THESE . . . MONSTERS AREN'T SO DIFFERENT FROM US.
THE LAST TIME I WAS HERE, I FELT LIKE AN OUTSIDER. BUT TODAY . . . .
TODAY, I'M NOT AS SCARED.

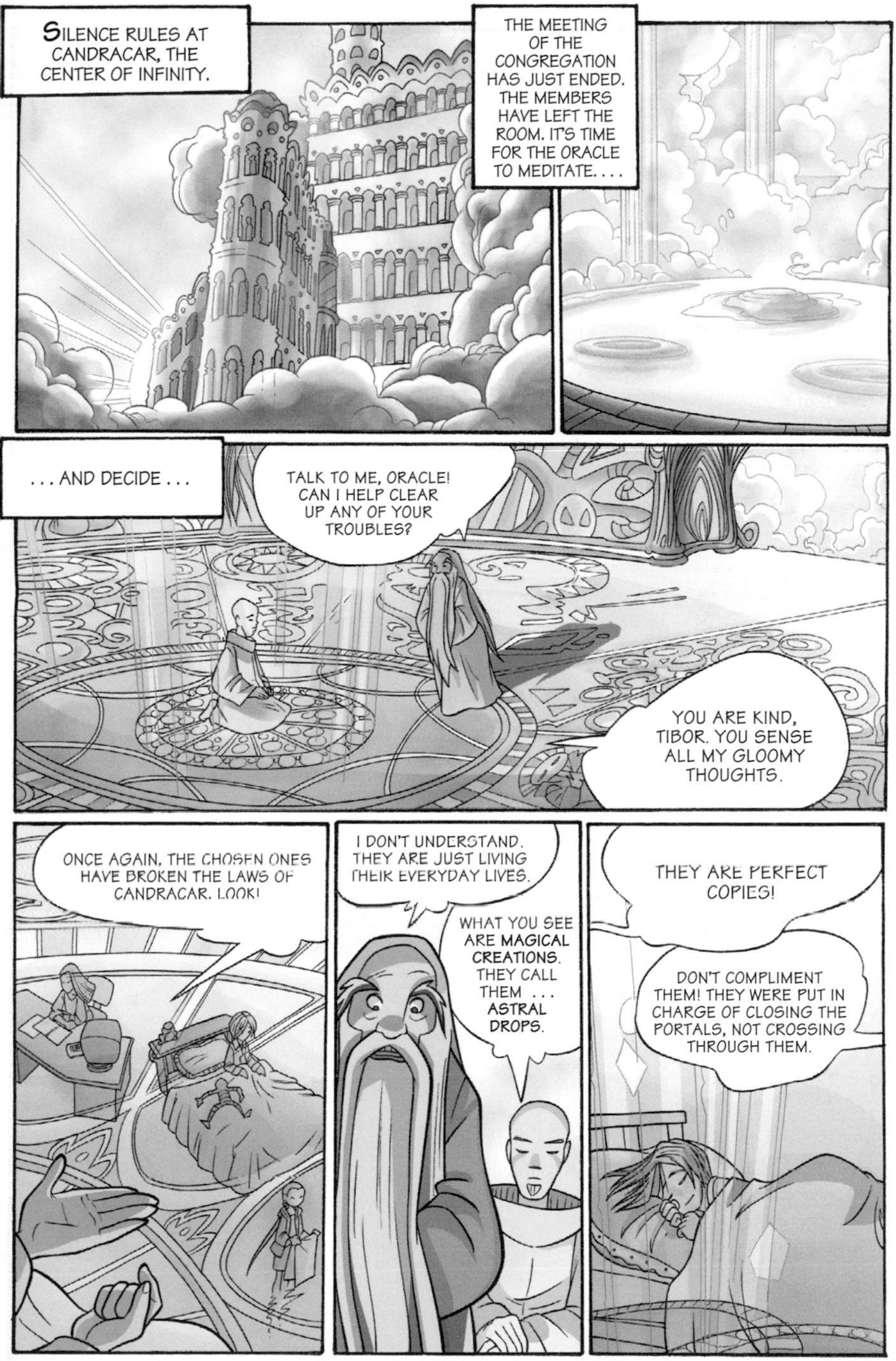
SILENCE RULES AT CANDRACAR, THE CENTER OF INFINITY.
THE MEETING OF THE CONGREGATION HAS JUST ENDED. THE MEMBERS HAVE LEFT THE ROOM. IT'S TIME FOR THE ORACLE TO MEDITATE. . . .
. . . AND DECIDE . . .
TALK TO ME, ORACLE! CAN I HELP CLEAR UP ANY OF YOUR TROUBLES?
YOU ARE KIND, TIBOR. YOU SENSE ALL MY GLOOMY THOUGHTS.
ONCE AGAIN, THE CHOSEN ONES HAVE BROKEN THE LAWS OF CANDRACAR. LOOK!
I DON'T UNDERSTAND. THEY ARE JUST LIVING THEIR EVERYDAY LIVES.
WHAT YOU SEE ARE MAGICAL CREATIONS. THEY CALL THEM . . . ASTRAL DROPS.
THEY ARE PERFECT COPIES!
DON'T COMPLIMENT THEM! THEY WERE PUT IN CHARGE OF CLOSING THE PORTALS, NOT CROSSING THROUGH THEM.

ARE YOU GOING TO PUNISH THEM?

I HAVEN'T MADE UP MY MIND. RIGHT NOW, THEY ARE WALKING THROUGH THE LAND OF PRINCE PHOBOS.

WHY ARE THEY RISKING **EVERYTHING**?

FOR A FEELING MORE POWERFUL THAN AIR, EARTH, WATER, OR FIRE . . .

FRIENDSHIP!

WHAT DOES THAT WORD MEAN TO YOU, TARANEE?

PROBABLY NOT WHAT IT MEANS TO YOU, ELYON!

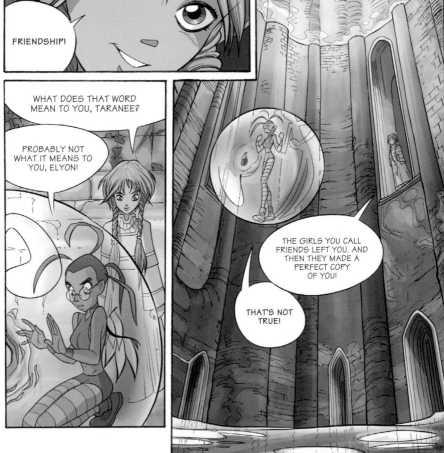

THE GIRLS YOU CALL FRIENDS LEFT YOU. AND THEN THEY MADE A PERFECT COPY OF YOU!

THAT'S NOT TRUE!

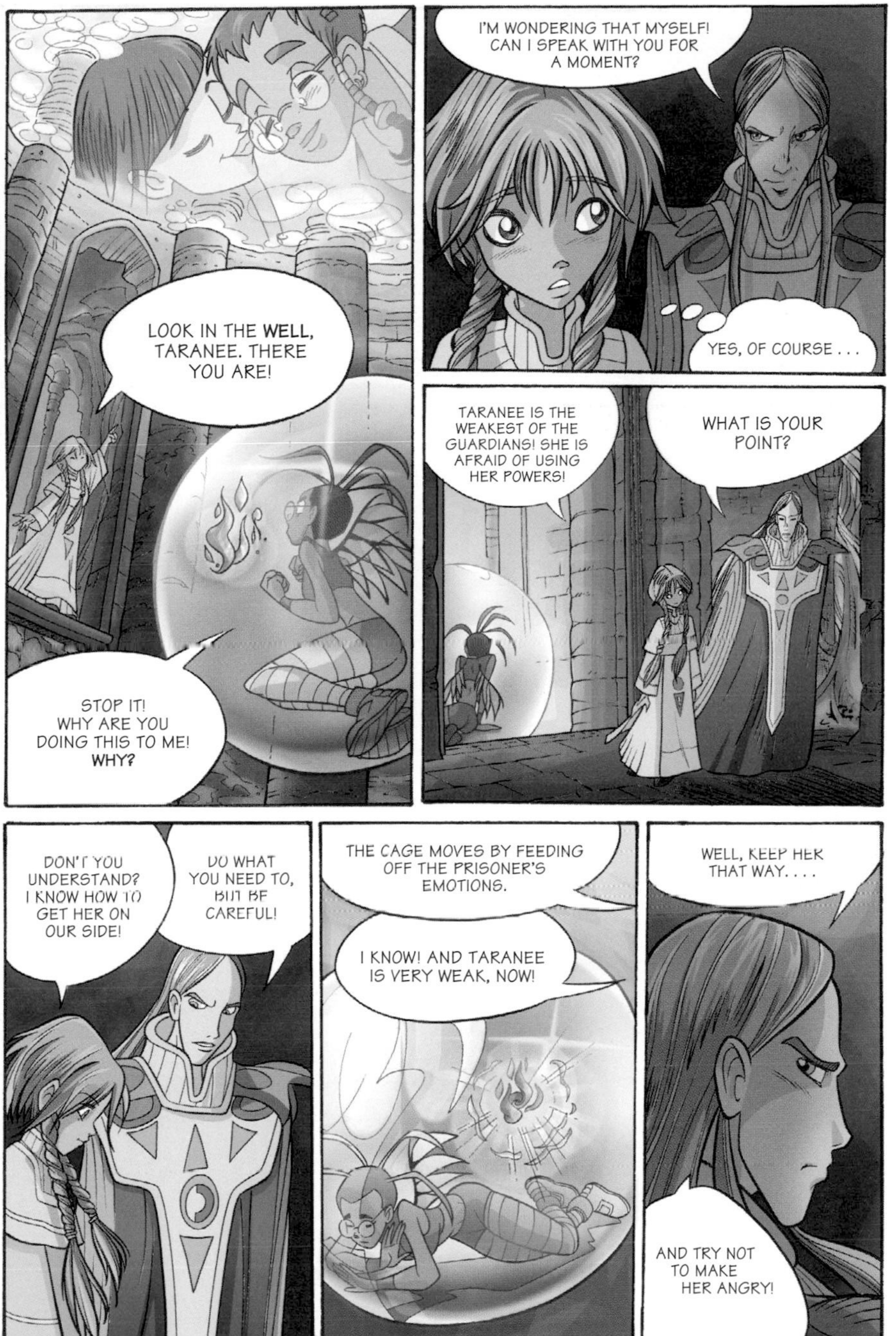

LOOK IN THE **WELL**, TARANEE. THERE YOU ARE!
STOP IT! WHY ARE YOU DOING THIS TO ME! **WHY?**
I'M WONDERING THAT MYSELF! CAN I SPEAK WITH YOU FOR A MOMENT?
YES, OF COURSE . . .
TARANEE IS THE WEAKEST OF THE GUARDIANS! SHE IS AFRAID OF USING HER POWERS!
WHAT IS YOUR POINT?
DON'T YOU UNDERSTAND? I KNOW HOW TO GET HER ON OUR SIDE!
DO WHAT YOU NEED TO, BUT BE CAREFUL!
THE CAGE MOVES BY FEEDING OFF THE PRISONER'S EMOTIONS.
I KNOW! AND TARANEE IS VERY WEAK, NOW!
WELL, KEEP HER THAT WAY. . . .
AND TRY NOT TO MAKE HER ANGRY!

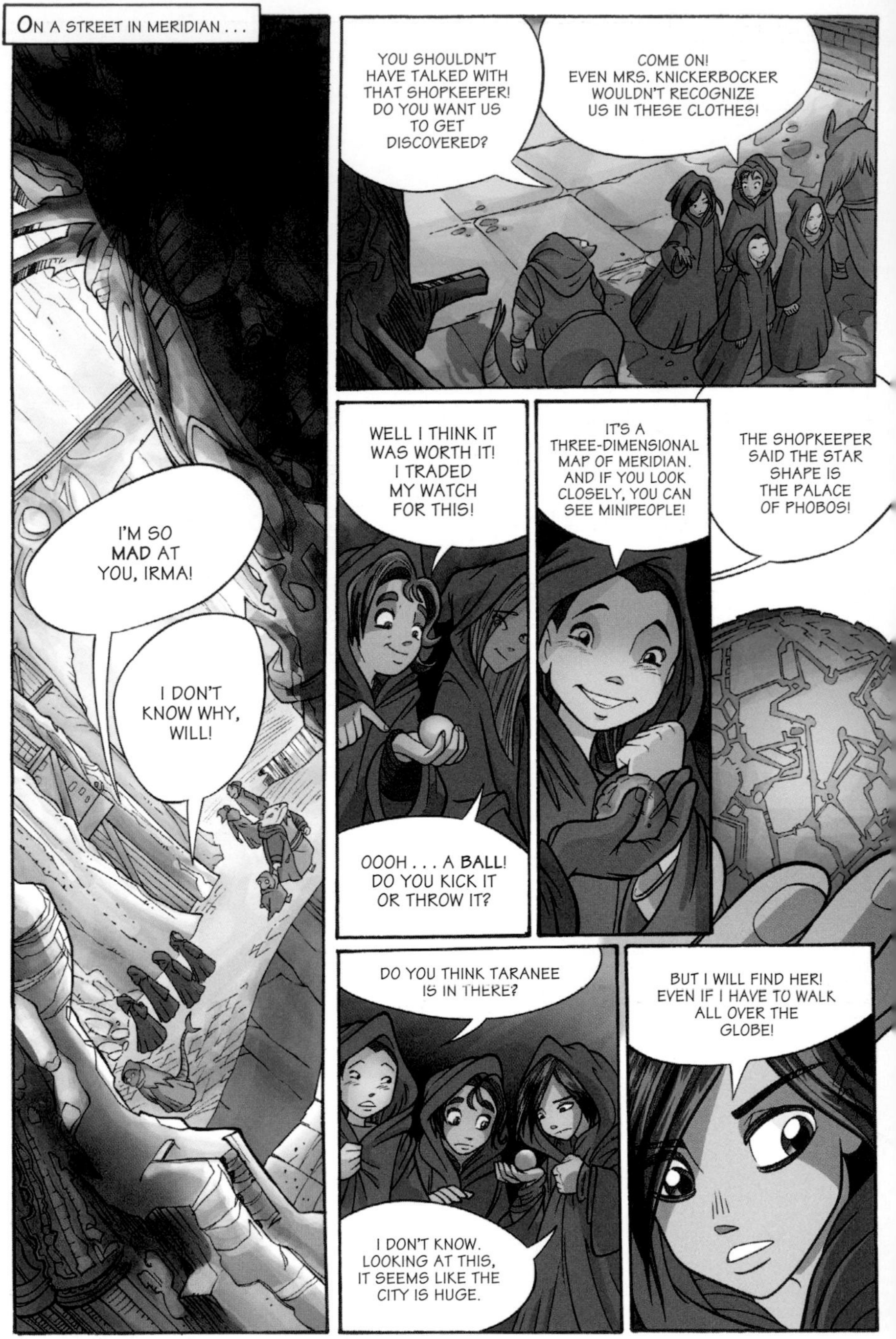
ON A STREET IN MERIDIAN . . .
I'M SO MAD AT YOU, IRMA!
I DON'T KNOW WHY, WILL!
YOU SHOULDN'T HAVE TALKED WITH THAT SHOPKEEPER! DO YOU WANT US TO GET DISCOVERED?
COME ON! EVEN MRS. KNICKERBOCKER WOULDN'T RECOGNIZE US IN THESE CLOTHES!
WELL I THINK IT WAS WORTH IT! I TRADED MY WATCH FOR THIS!
OOOH . . . A BALL! DO YOU KICK IT OR THROW IT?
IT'S A THREE-DIMENSIONAL MAP OF MERIDIAN. AND IF YOU LOOK CLOSELY, YOU CAN SEE MINIPEOPLE!
THE SHOPKEEPER SAID THE STAR SHAPE IS THE PALACE OF PHOBOS!
DO YOU THINK TARANEE IS IN THERE?
I DON'T KNOW. LOOKING AT THIS, IT SEEMS LIKE THE CITY IS HUGE.
BUT I WILL FIND HER! EVEN IF I HAVE TO WALK ALL OVER THE GLOBE!

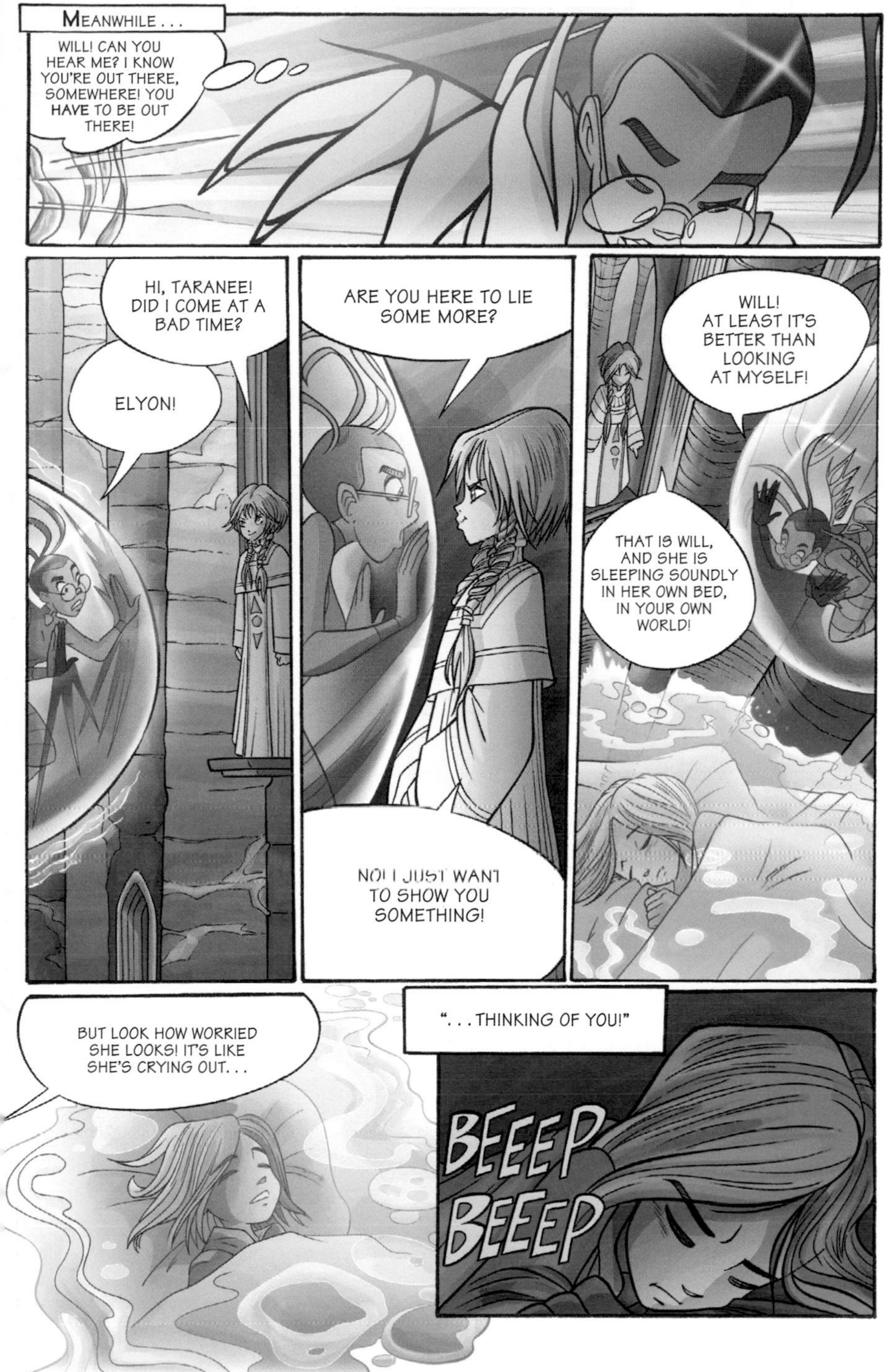
MEANWHILE . . .
WILL! CAN YOU HEAR ME? I KNOW YOU'RE OUT THERE, SOMEWHERE! YOU HAVE TO BE OUT THERE!
HI, TARANEE! DID I COME AT A BAD TIME?
ELYON!
ARE YOU HERE TO LIE SOME MORE?
NO! I JUST WANT TO SHOW YOU SOMETHING!
WILL! AT LEAST IT'S BETTER THAN LOOKING AT MYSELF!
THAT IS WILL, AND SHE IS SLEEPING SOUNDLY IN HER OWN BED, IN YOUR OWN WORLD!
BUT LOOK HOW WORRIED SHE LOOKS! IT'S LIKE SHE'S CRYING OUT. . .
". . . THINKING OF YOU!"
BEEEP
BEEEP

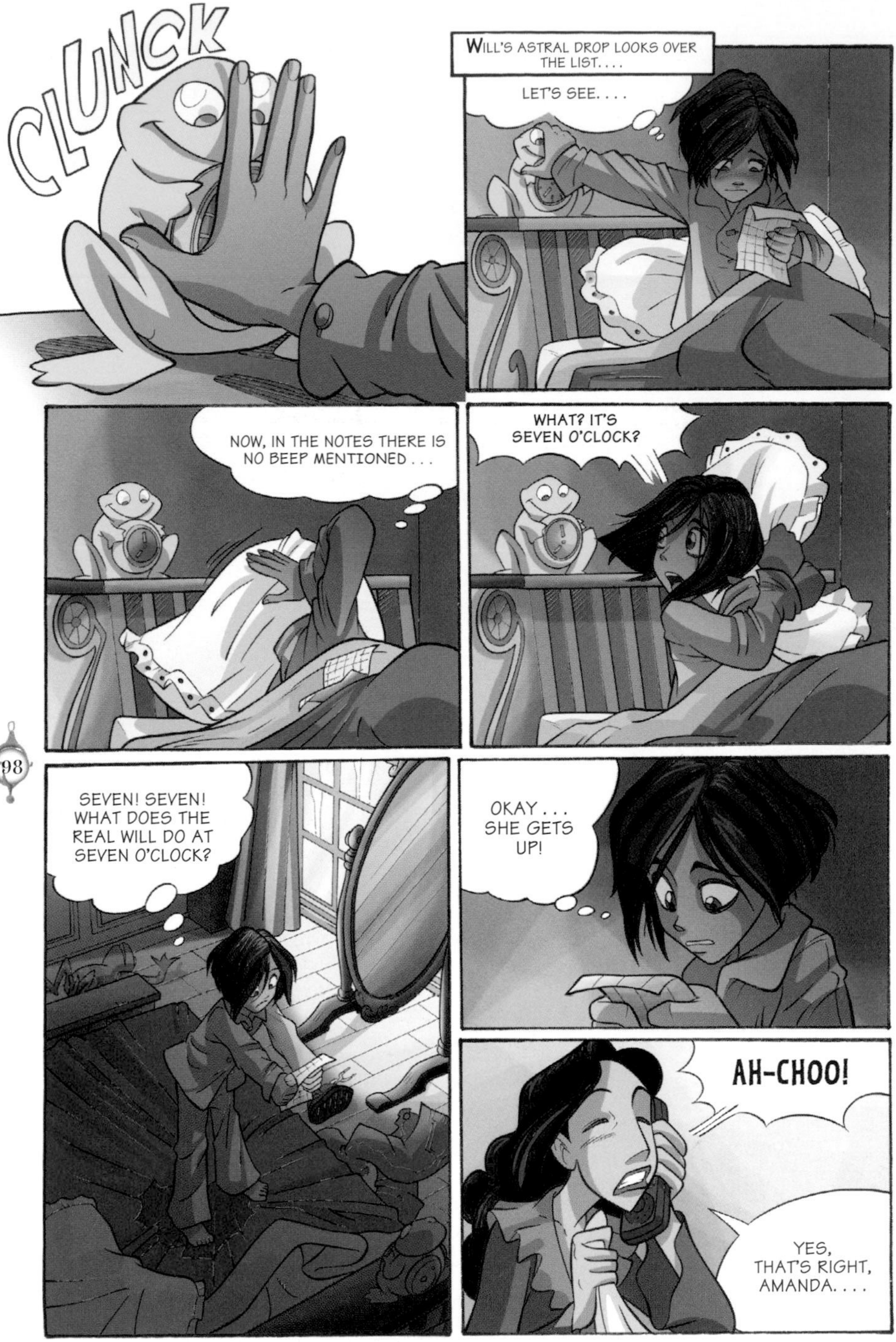
CLUNCK
WILL'S ASTRAL DROP LOOKS OVER THE LIST. . . .
LET'S SEE. . . .
NOW, IN THE NOTES THERE IS NO BEEP MENTIONED . . .
WHAT? IT'S SEVEN O'CLOCK?
SEVEN! SEVEN! WHAT DOES THE REAL WILL DO AT SEVEN O'CLOCK?
OKAY . . . SHE GETS UP!
AH-CHOO!
YES, THAT'S RIGHT, AMANDA. . . .

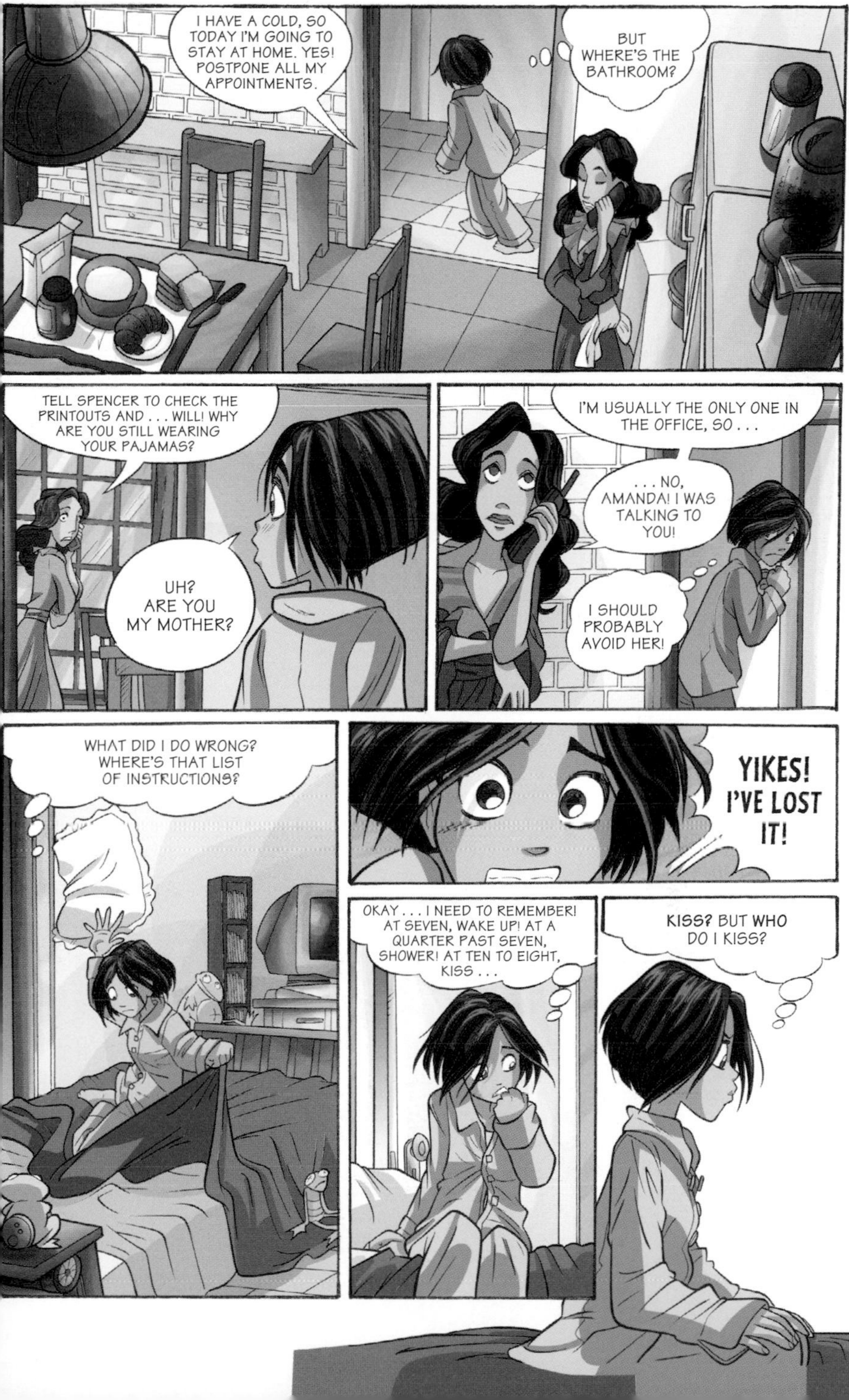
I HAVE A COLD, SO TODAY I'M GOING TO STAY AT HOME. YES! POSTPONE ALL MY APPOINTMENTS.
BUT WHERE'S THE BATHROOM?
TELL SPENCER TO CHECK THE PRINTOUTS AND . . . WILL! WHY ARE YOU STILL WEARING YOUR PAJAMAS?
UH? ARE YOU MY MOTHER?
I'M USUALLY THE ONLY ONE IN THE OFFICE, SO . . .
. . . NO, AMANDA! I WAS TALKING TO YOU!
I SHOULD PROBABLY AVOID HER!
WHAT DID I DO WRONG? WHERE'S THAT LIST OF INSTRUCTIONS?
YIKES! I'VE LOST IT!
OKAY . . . I NEED TO REMEMBER! AT SEVEN, WAKE UP! AT A QUARTER PAST SEVEN, SHOWER! AT TEN TO EIGHT, KISS . . .
KISS? BUT WHO DO I KISS?

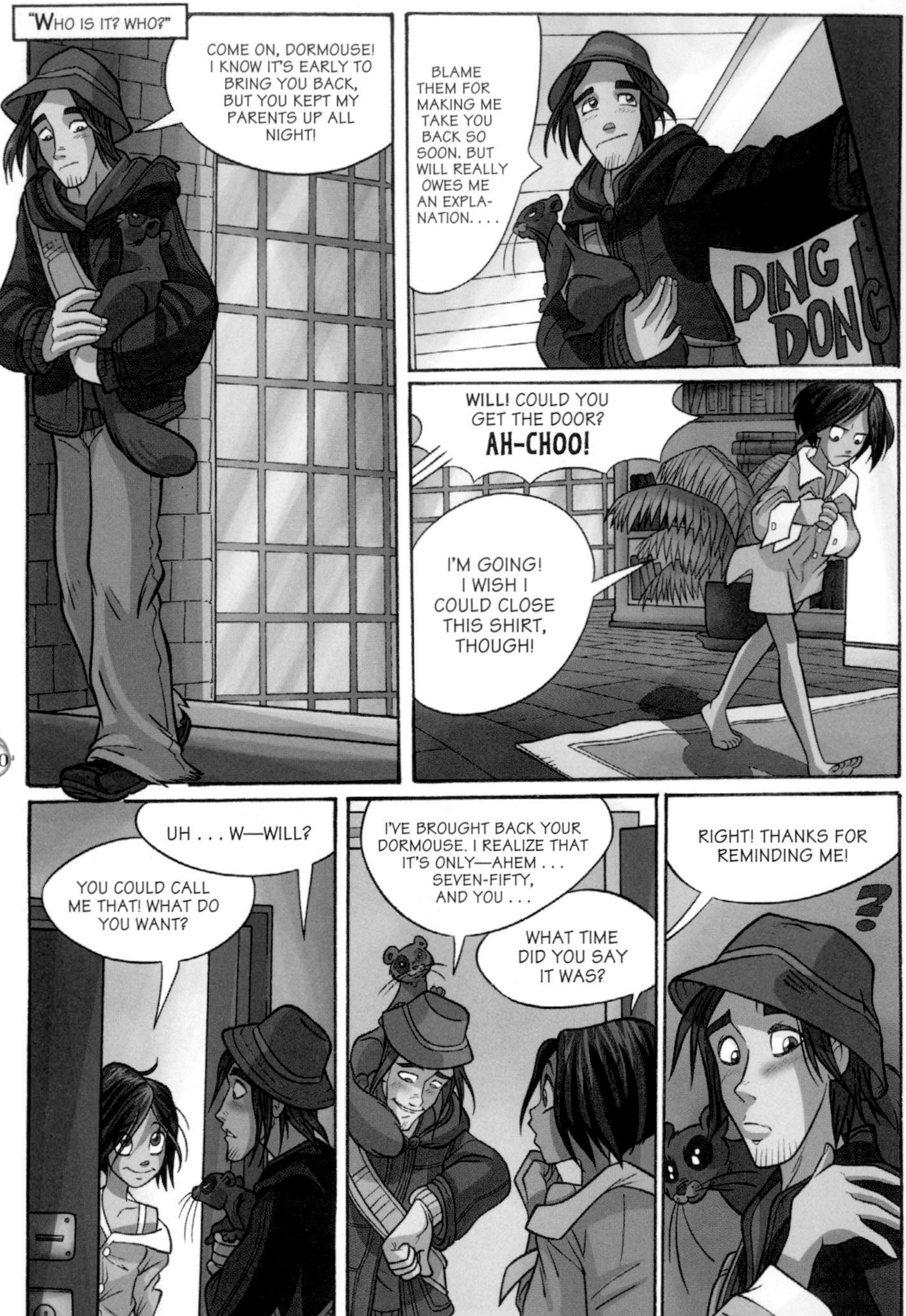
"WHO IS IT? WHO?"
COME ON, DORMOUSE! I KNOW IT'S EARLY TO BRING YOU BACK, BUT YOU KEPT MY PARENTS UP ALL NIGHT!
BLAME THEM FOR MAKING ME TAKE YOU BACK SO SOON. BUT WILL REALLY OWES ME AN EXPLANATION. . . .
DING DONG
WILL! COULD YOU GET THE DOOR? AH-CHOO!
I'M GOING! I WISH I COULD CLOSE THIS SHIRT, THOUGH!
UH . . . W—WILL?
YOU COULD CALL ME THAT! WHAT DO YOU WANT?
I'VE BROUGHT BACK YOUR DORMOUSE. I REALIZE THAT IT'S ONLY—AHEM . . . SEVEN-FIFTY, AND YOU . . .
WHAT TIME DID YOU SAY IT WAS?
RIGHT! THANKS FOR REMINDING ME!
?

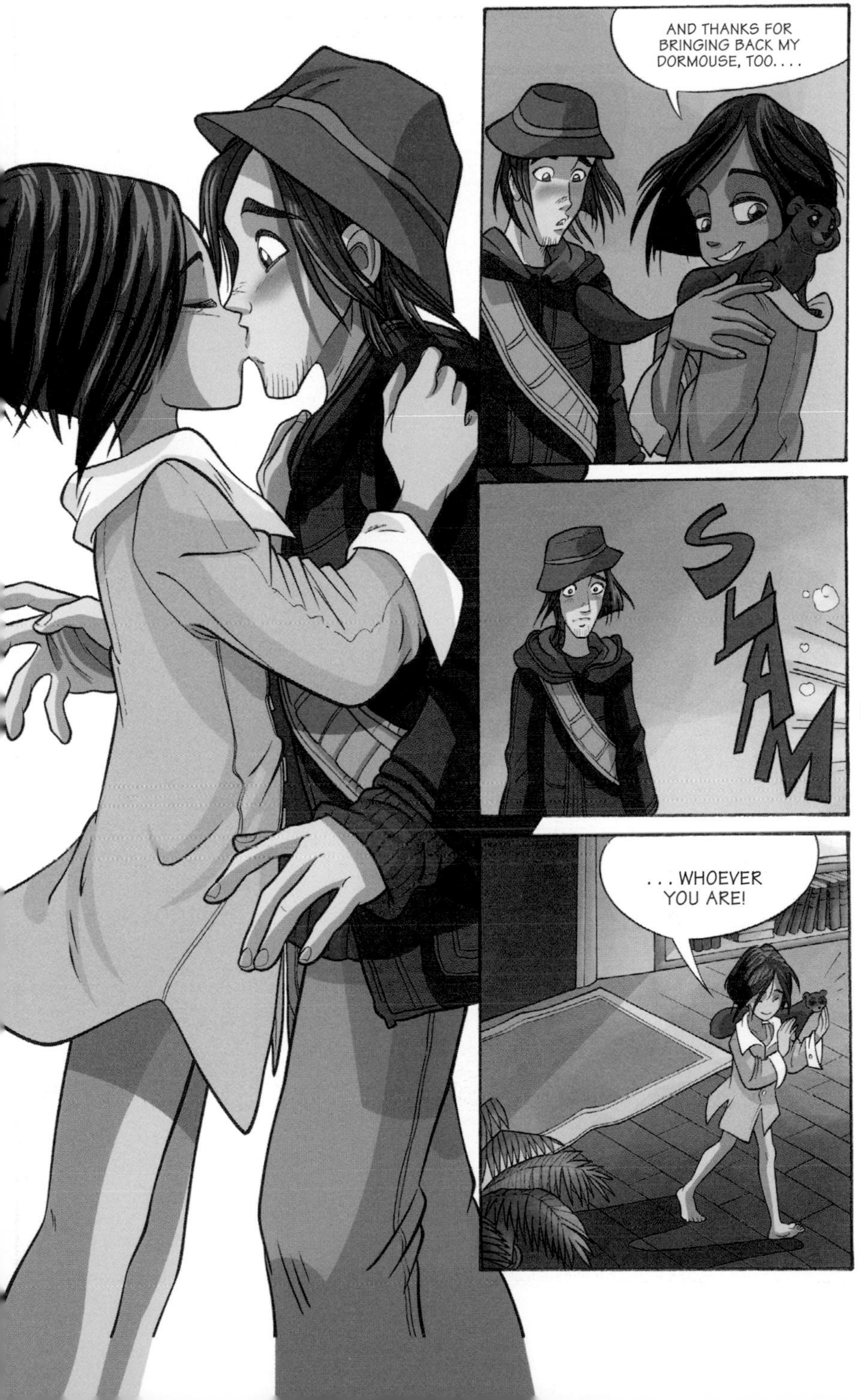

AND THANKS FOR BRINGING BACK MY DORMOUSE, TOO. . . .
SLAM
. . . WHOEVER YOU ARE!

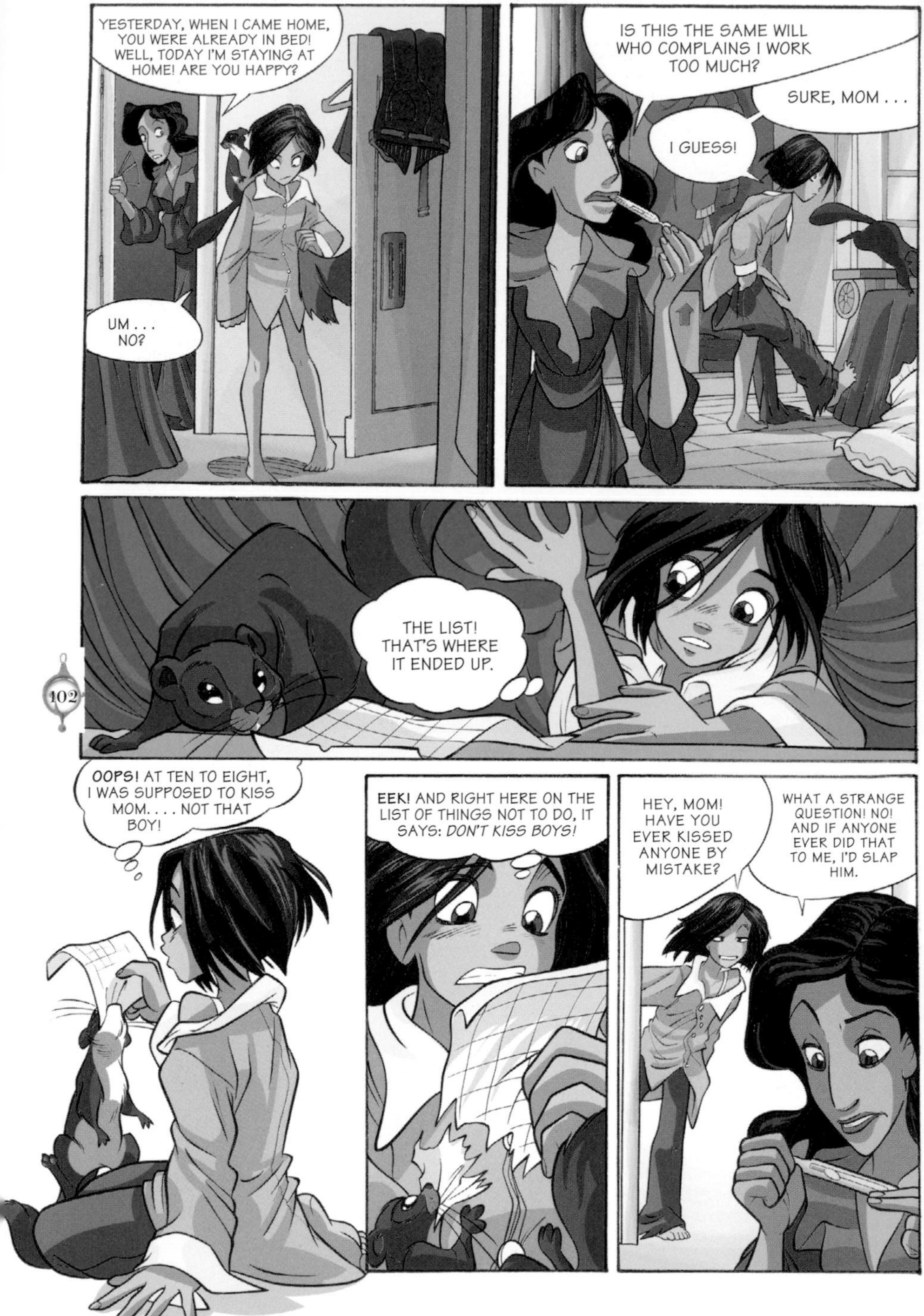
YESTERDAY, WHEN I CAME HOME, YOU WERE ALREADY IN BED! WELL, TODAY I'M STAYING AT HOME! ARE YOU HAPPY?
UM . . . NO?
IS THIS THE SAME WILL WHO COMPLAINS I WORK TOO MUCH?
SURE, MOM . . .
I GUESS!
THE LIST! THAT'S WHERE IT ENDED UP.
OOPS! AT TEN TO EIGHT, I WAS SUPPOSED TO KISS MOM. . . . NOT THAT BOY!
EEK! AND RIGHT HERE ON THE LIST OF THINGS NOT TO DO, IT SAYS: *DON'T KISS BOYS!*
HEY, MOM! HAVE YOU EVER KISSED ANYONE BY MISTAKE?
WHAT A STRANGE QUESTION! NO! AND IF ANYONE EVER DID THAT TO ME, I'D SLAP HIM.

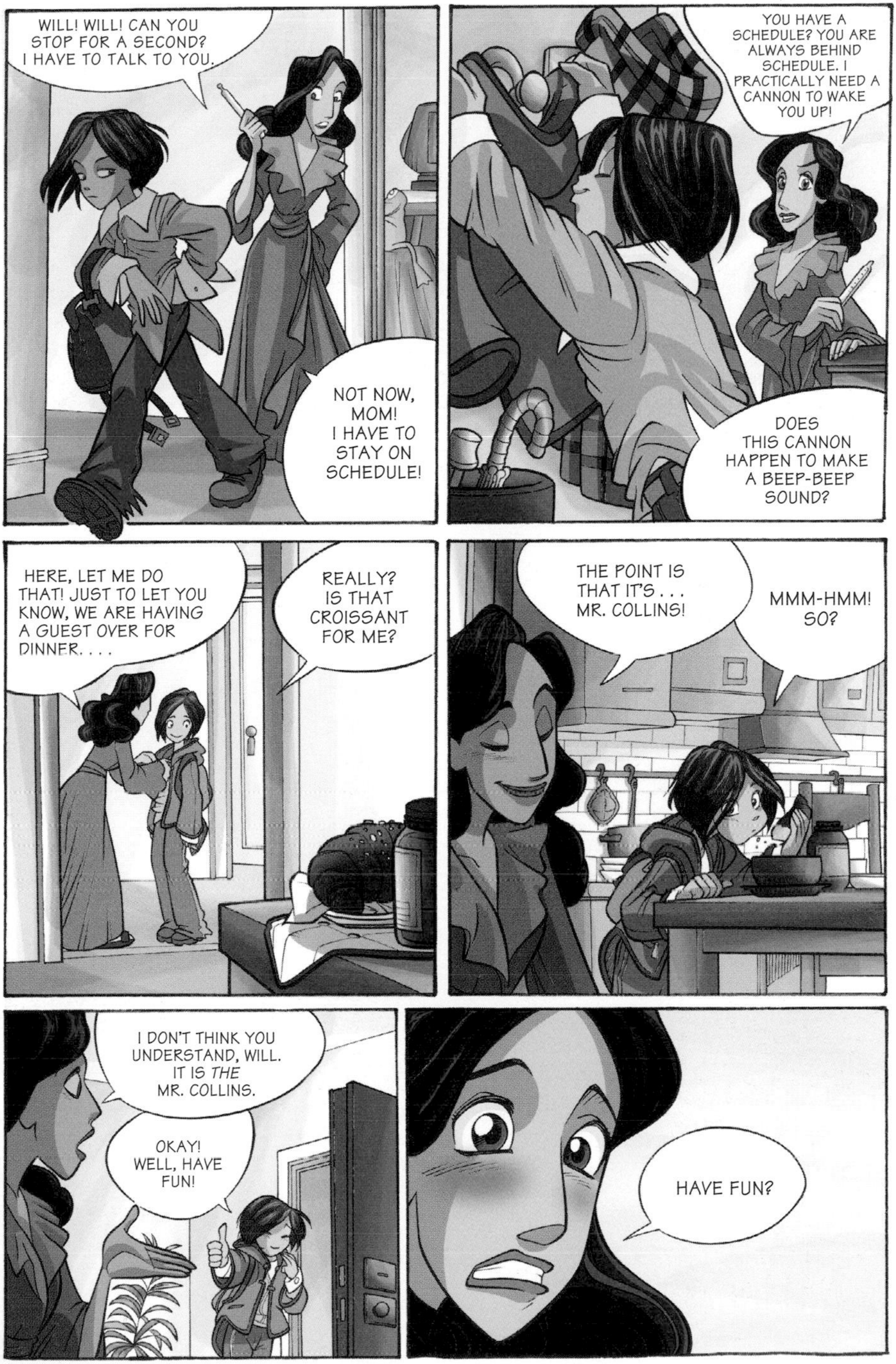

WILL! WILL! CAN YOU STOP FOR A SECOND? I HAVE TO TALK TO YOU.
NOT NOW, MOM! I HAVE TO STAY ON SCHEDULE!
YOU HAVE A SCHEDULE? YOU ARE ALWAYS BEHIND SCHEDULE. I PRACTICALLY NEED A CANNON TO WAKE YOU UP!
DOES THIS CANNON HAPPEN TO MAKE A BEEP-BEEP SOUND?
HERE, LET ME DO THAT! JUST TO LET YOU KNOW, WE ARE HAVING A GUEST OVER FOR DINNER. . . .
REALLY? IS THAT CROISSANT FOR ME?
THE POINT IS THAT IT'S . . . MR. COLLINS!
MMM-HMM! SO?
I DON'T THINK YOU UNDERSTAND, WILL. IT IS *THE* MR. COLLINS.
OKAY! WELL, HAVE FUN!
HAVE FUN?

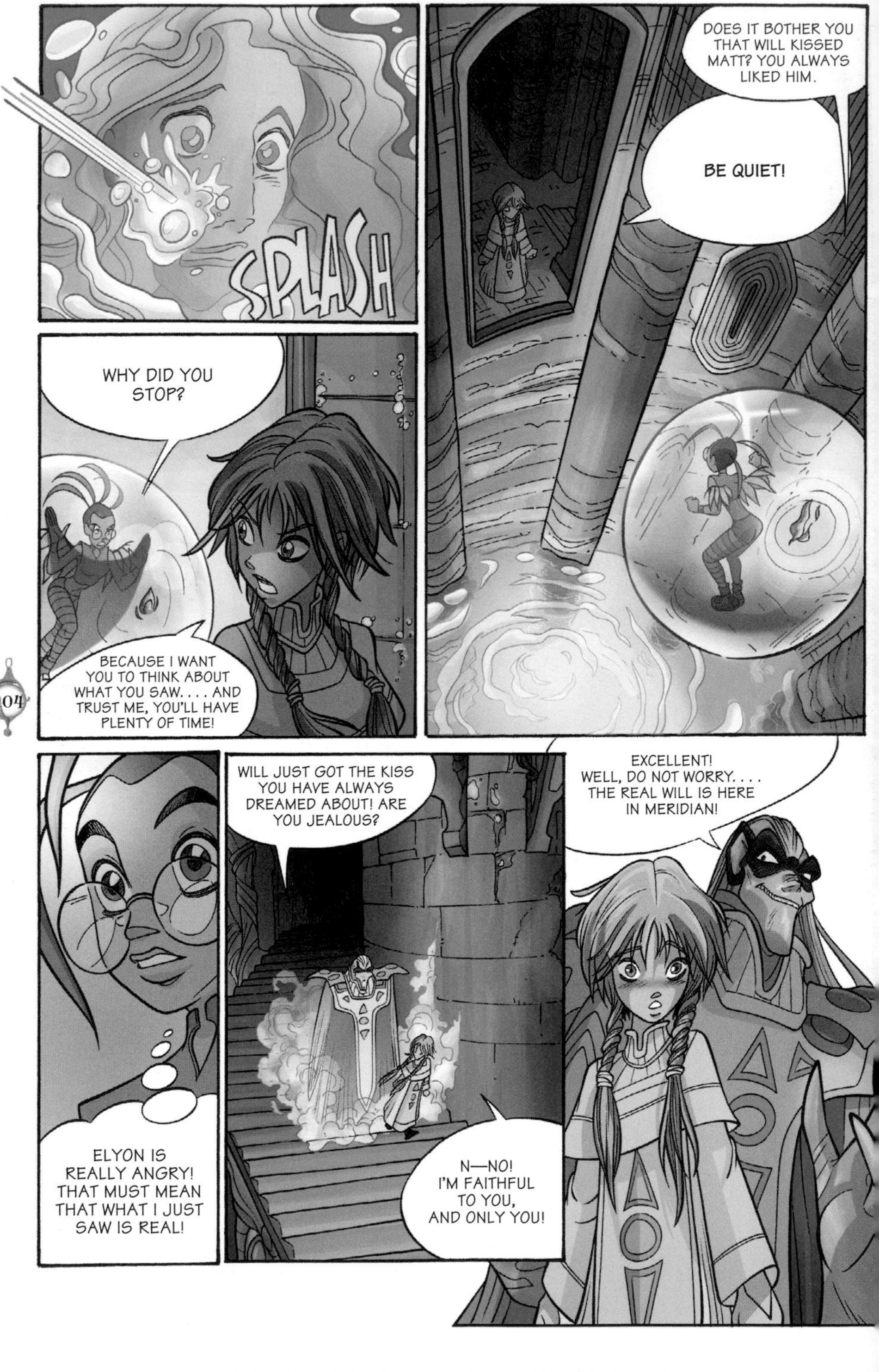
SPLASH
DOES IT BOTHER YOU THAT WILL KISSED MATT? YOU ALWAYS LIKED HIM.
BE QUIET!
WHY DID YOU STOP?
BECAUSE I WANT YOU TO THINK ABOUT WHAT YOU SAW. . . . AND TRUST ME, YOU'LL HAVE PLENTY OF TIME!
ELYON IS REALLY ANGRY! THAT MUST MEAN THAT WHAT I JUST SAW IS REAL!
WILL JUST GOT THE KISS YOU HAVE ALWAYS DREAMED ABOUT! ARE YOU JEALOUS?
N—NO! I'M FAITHFUL TO YOU, AND ONLY YOU!
EXCELLENT! WELL, DO NOT WORRY. . . . THE REAL WILL IS HERE IN MERIDIAN!

"STOP THEM!"

THERE SHE IS!

AH! THERE HE IS!

IRMA? WHO'S THAT GUY HEADING TOWARD US WITH A LOT OF OTHER ANGRY-LOOKING SOLDIERS?

THAT'S THE SHOPKEEPER! THE ONE WHO SOLD ME THE MAP OF THE CITY!

I GUESS HE DIDN'T LIKE YOUR WATCH!

I DON'T SEE WHY! I WON IT IN A BAG OF CHIPS!

WILL! DON'T YOU THINK IT'S ABOUT TIME WE TRANSFORM OURSELVES?

NO! NOT YET!

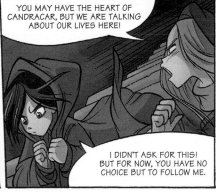

YOU MAY HAVE THE HEART OF CANDRACAR, BUT WE ARE TALKING ABOUT OUR LIVES HERE!

I DIDN'T ASK FOR THIS! BUT FOR NOW, YOU HAVE NO CHOICE BUT TO FOLLOW ME.

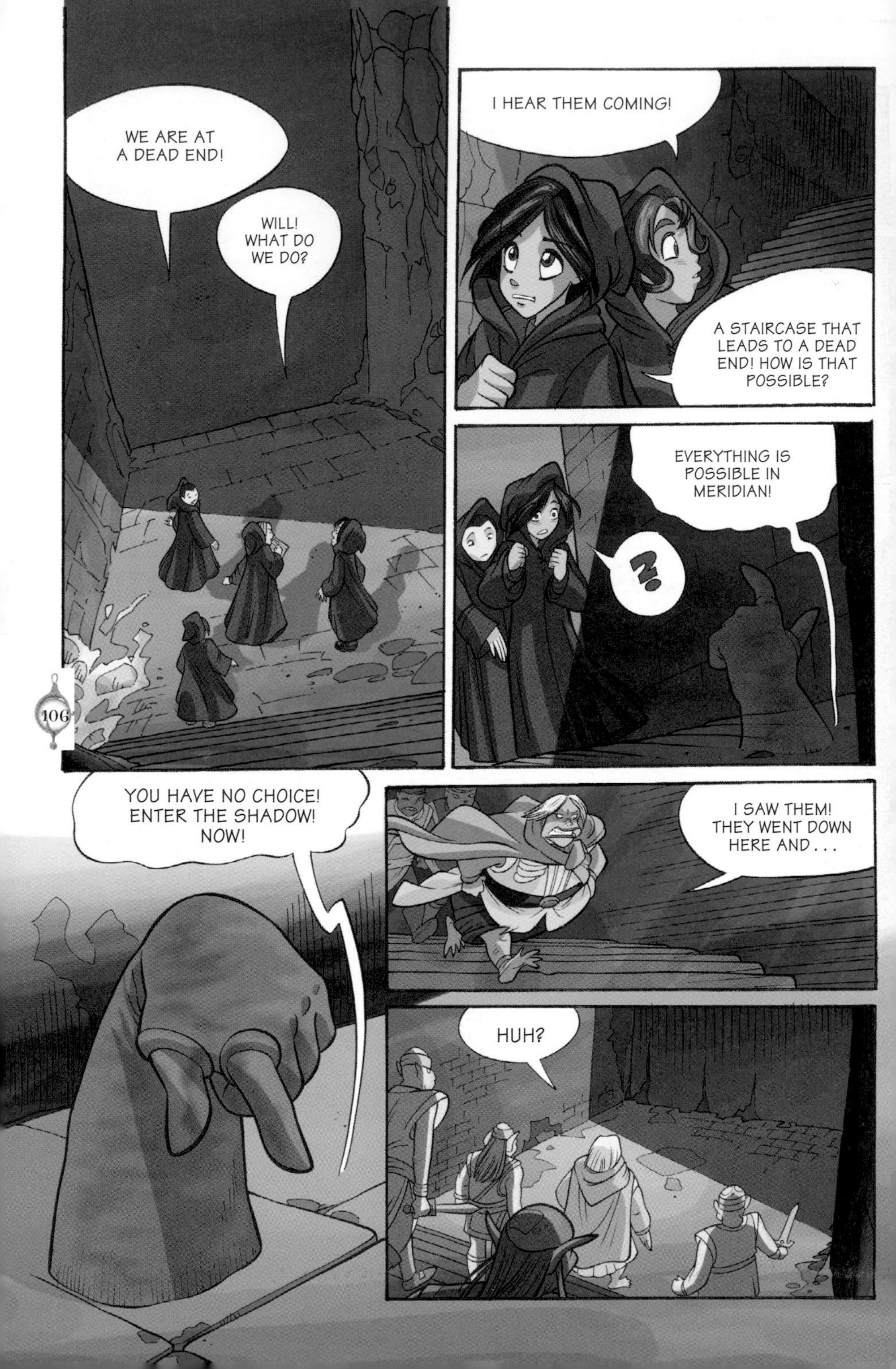
WE ARE AT A DEAD END!
WILL! WHAT DO WE DO?
I HEAR THEM COMING!
A STAIRCASE THAT LEADS TO A DEAD END! HOW IS THAT POSSIBLE?
EVERYTHING IS POSSIBLE IN MERIDIAN!
?
YOU HAVE NO CHOICE! ENTER THE SHADOW! NOW!
I SAW THEM! THEY WENT DOWN HERE AND . . .
HUH?

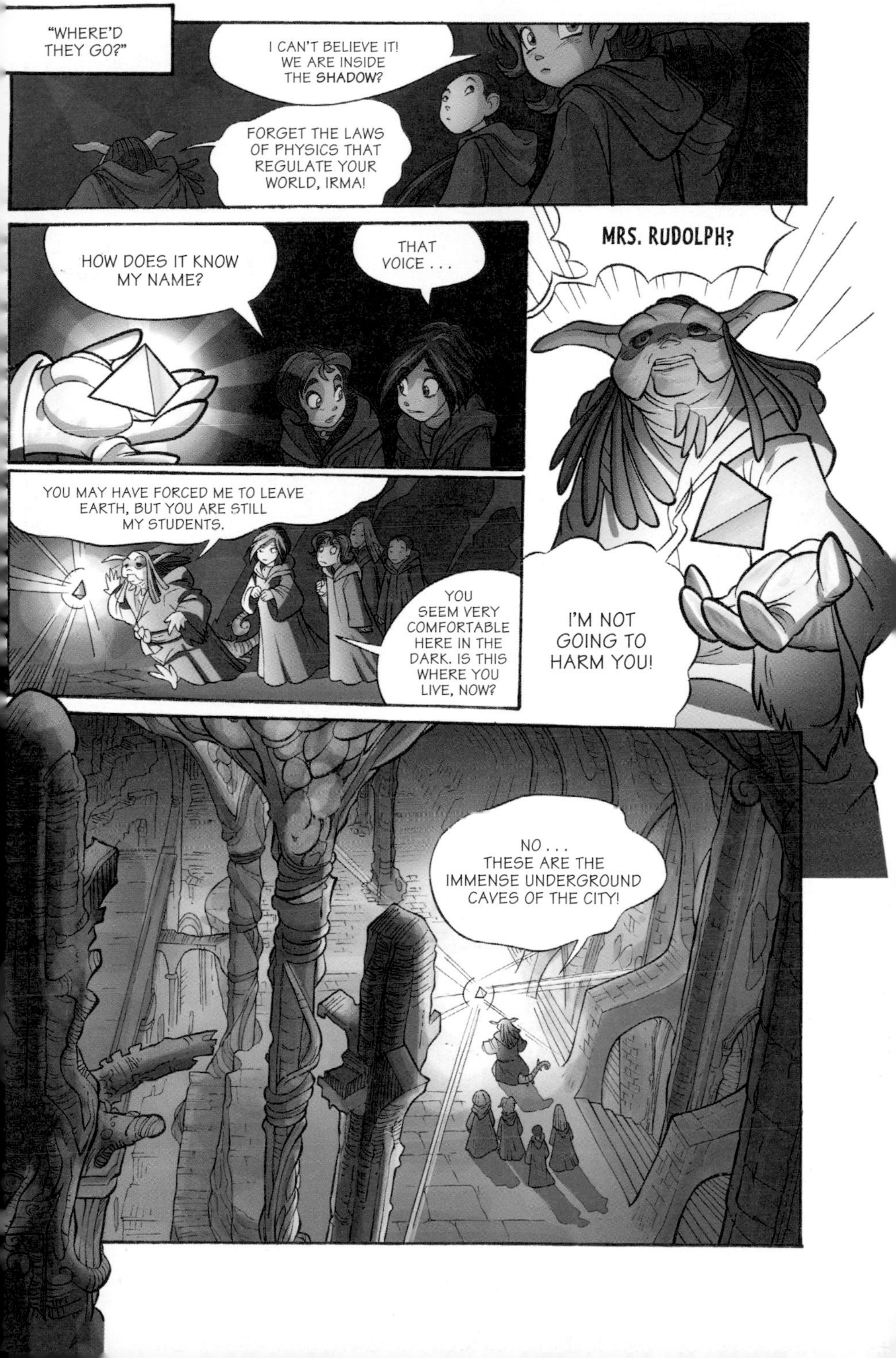
"WHERE'D THEY GO?"
I CAN'T BELIEVE IT! WE ARE INSIDE THE SHADOW?
FORGET THE LAWS OF PHYSICS THAT REGULATE YOUR WORLD, IRMA!
HOW DOES IT KNOW MY NAME?
THAT VOICE . . .
MRS. RUDOLPH?
I'M NOT GOING TO HARM YOU!
YOU MAY HAVE FORCED ME TO LEAVE EARTH, BUT YOU ARE STILL MY STUDENTS.
YOU SEEM VERY COMFORTABLE HERE IN THE DARK. IS THIS WHERE YOU LIVE, NOW?
NO . . . THESE ARE THE IMMENSE UNDERGROUND CAVES OF THE CITY!

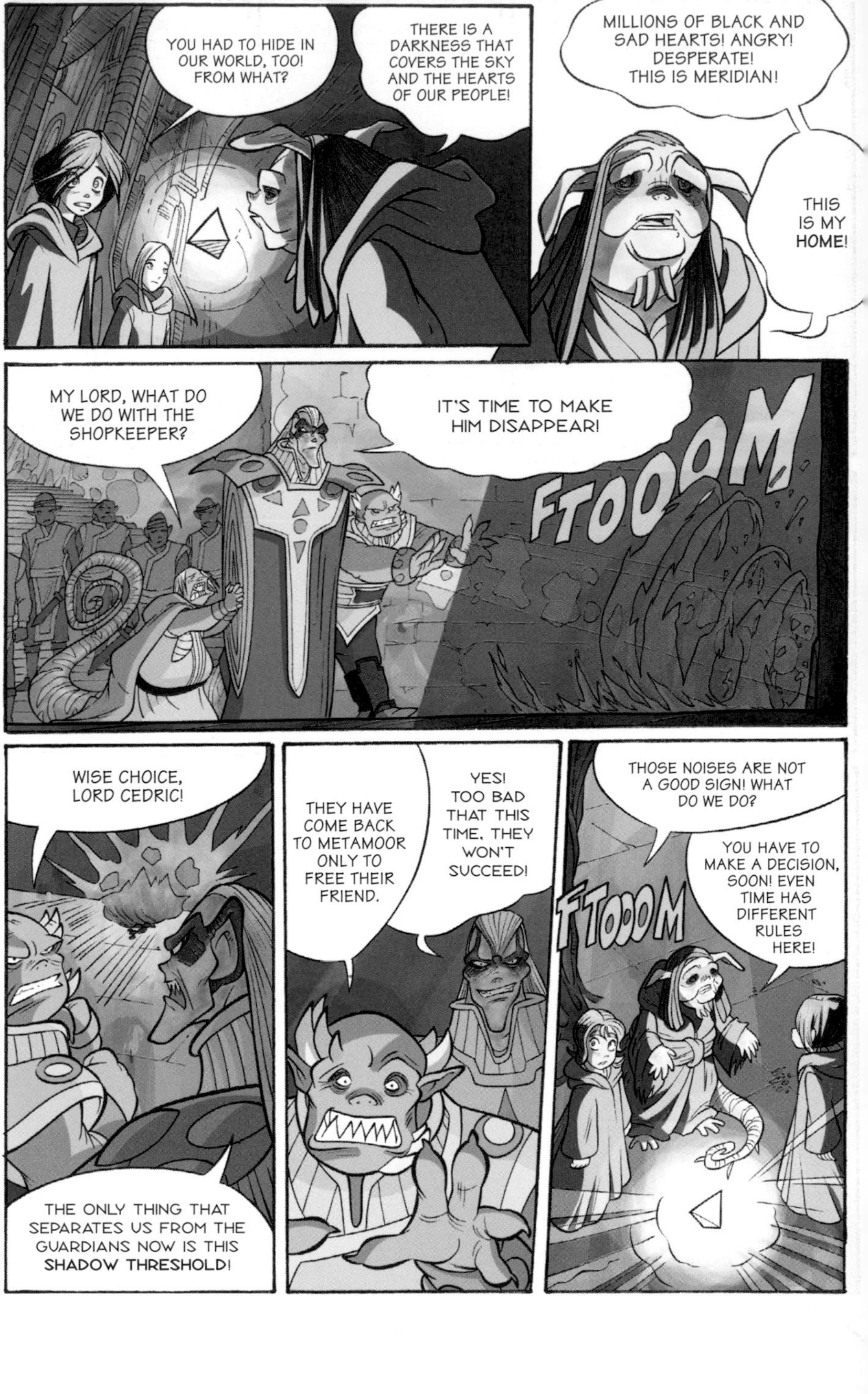

YOU HAD TO HIDE IN OUR WORLD, TOO! FROM WHAT?
THERE IS A DARKNESS THAT COVERS THE SKY AND THE HEARTS OF OUR PEOPLE!
MILLIONS OF BLACK AND SAD HEARTS! ANGRY! DESPERATE! THIS IS MERIDIAN!
THIS IS MY HOME!
MY LORD, WHAT DO WE DO WITH THE SHOPKEEPER?
IT'S TIME TO MAKE HIM DISAPPEAR!
FTOOOM
WISE CHOICE, LORD CEDRIC!
THE ONLY THING THAT SEPARATES US FROM THE GUARDIANS NOW IS THIS SHADOW THRESHOLD!
THEY HAVE COME BACK TO METAMOOR ONLY TO FREE THEIR FRIEND.
YES! TOO BAD THAT THIS TIME, THEY WON'T SUCCEED!
THOSE NOISES ARE NOT A GOOD SIGN! WHAT DO WE DO?
FTOOOM
YOU HAVE TO MAKE A DECISION, SOON! EVEN TIME HAS DIFFERENT RULES HERE!

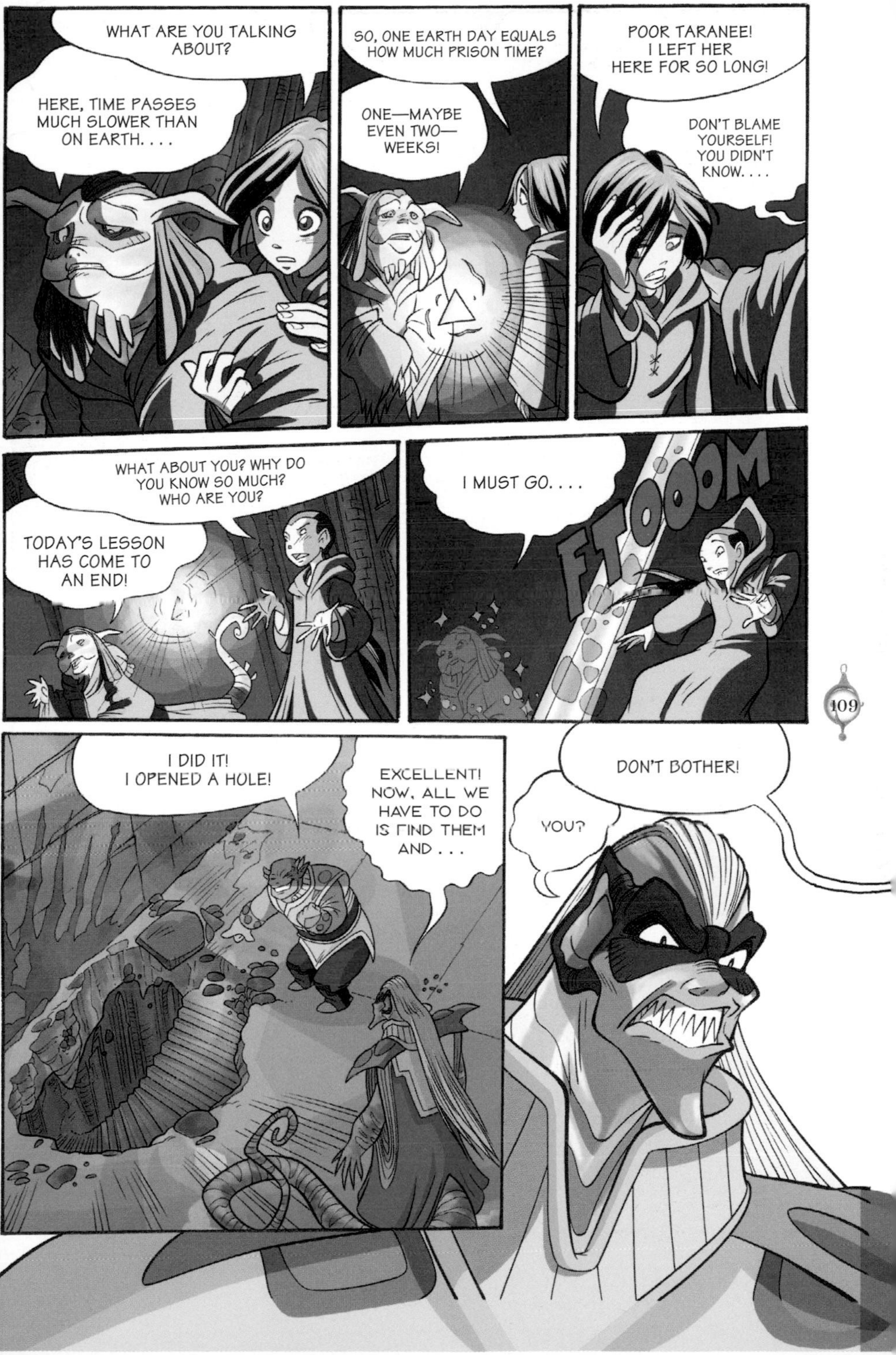
WHAT ARE YOU TALKING ABOUT?
HERE, TIME PASSES MUCH SLOWER THAN ON EARTH. . . .
SO, ONE EARTH DAY EQUALS HOW MUCH PRISON TIME?
ONE—MAYBE EVEN TWO— WEEKS!
POOR TARANEE! I LEFT HER HERE FOR SO LONG!
DON'T BLAME YOURSELF! YOU DIDN'T KNOW. . . .
WHAT ABOUT YOU? WHY DO YOU KNOW SO MUCH? WHO ARE YOU?
TODAY'S LESSON HAS COME TO AN END!
I MUST GO. . . .
FTOOOM
I DID IT! I OPENED A HOLE!
EXCELLENT! NOW, ALL WE HAVE TO DO IS FIND THEM AND . . .
DON'T BOTHER!
YOU?

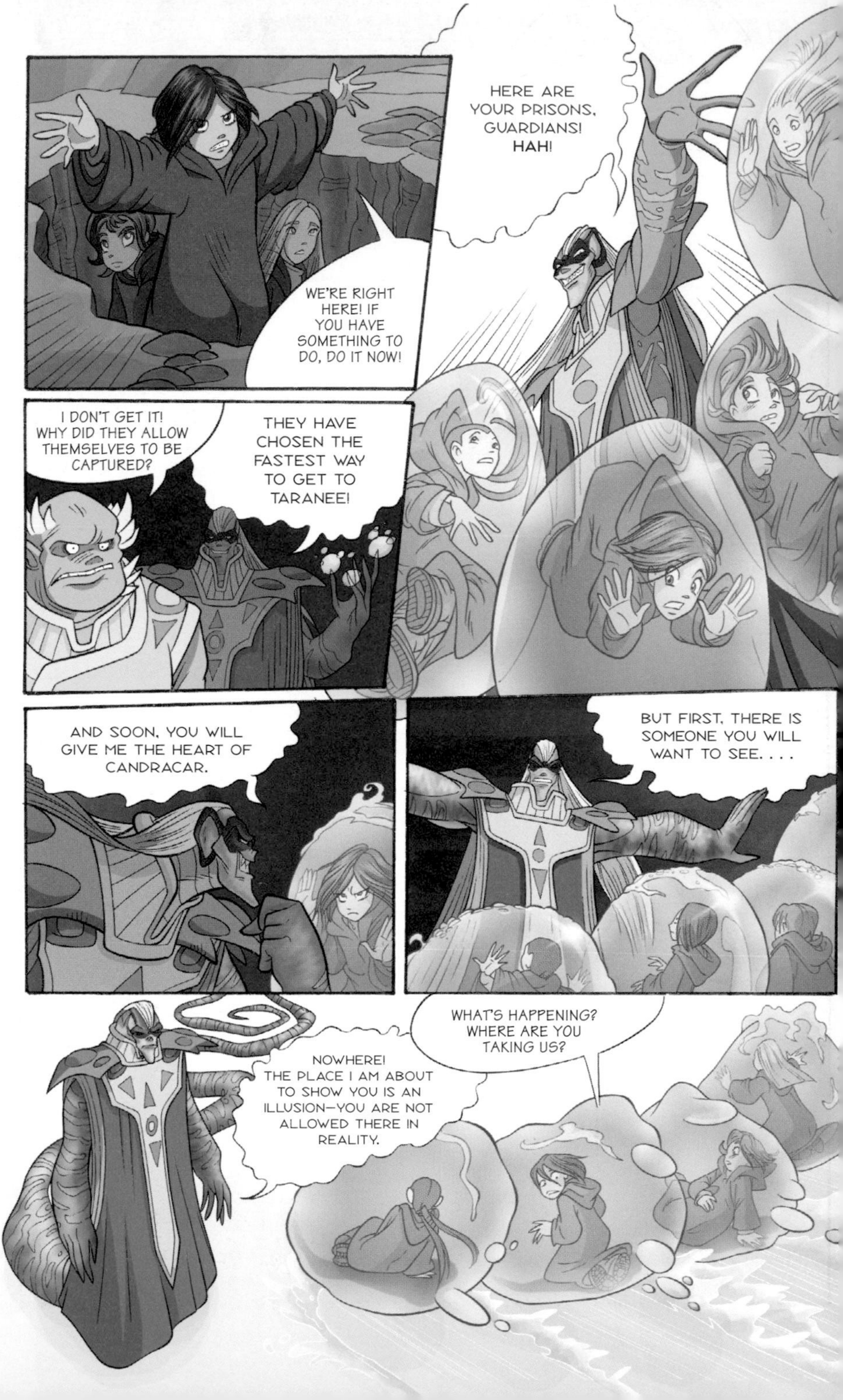
WE'RE RIGHT HERE! IF YOU HAVE SOMETHING TO DO, DO IT NOW!
HERE ARE YOUR PRISONS, GUARDIANS! HAH!
I DON'T GET IT! WHY DID THEY ALLOW THEMSELVES TO BE CAPTURED?
THEY HAVE CHOSEN THE FASTEST WAY TO GET TO TARANEE!
AND SOON, YOU WILL GIVE ME THE HEART OF CANDRACAR.
BUT FIRST, THERE IS SOMEONE YOU WILL WANT TO SEE. . . .
WHAT'S HAPPENING? WHERE ARE YOU TAKING US?
NOWHERE! THE PLACE I AM ABOUT TO SHOW YOU IS AN ILLUSION—YOU ARE NOT ALLOWED THERE IN REALITY.

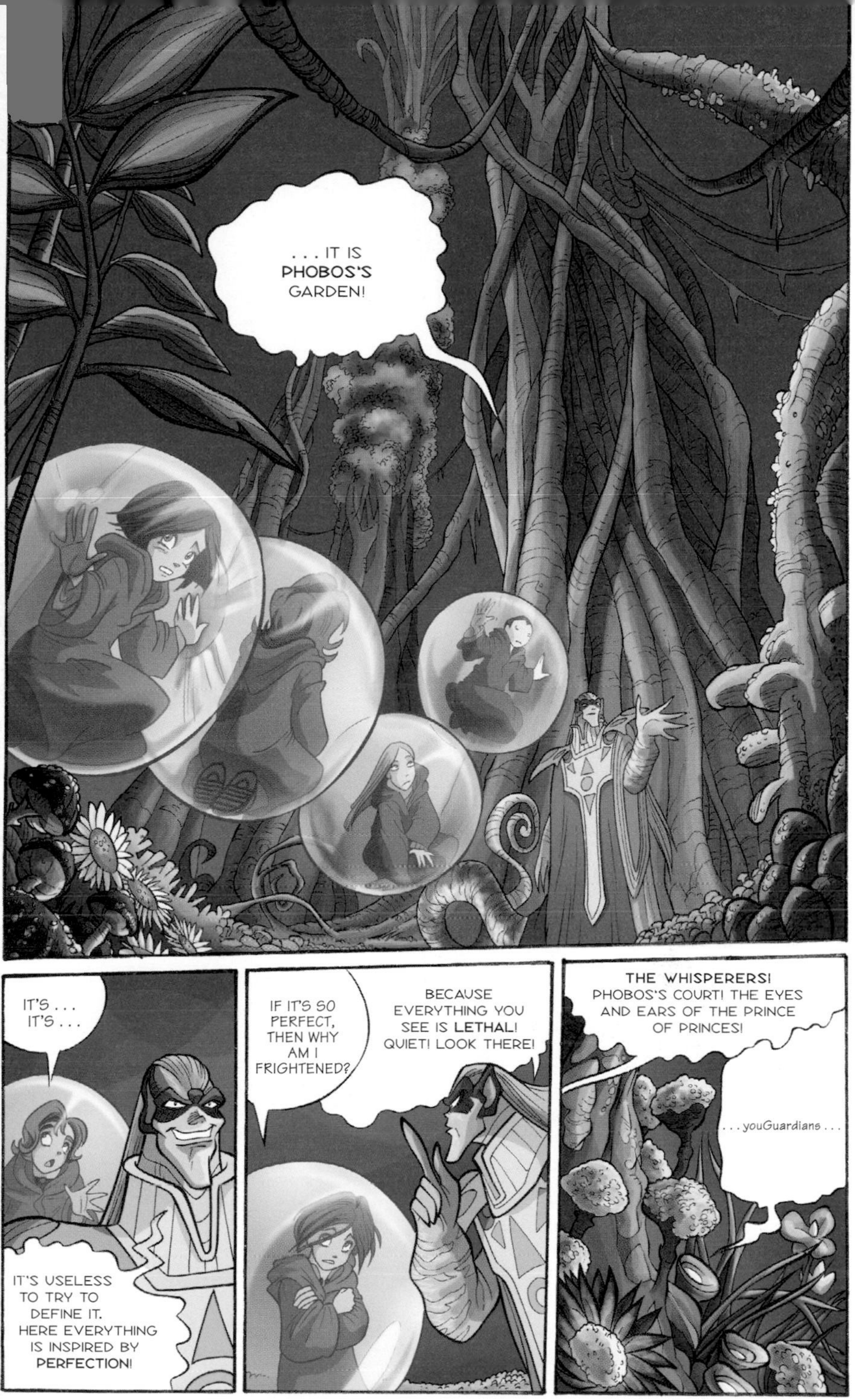
. . . IT IS PHOBOS'S GARDEN!
IT'S . . . IT'S . . .
IT'S USELESS TO TRY TO DEFINE IT. HERE EVERYTHING IS INSPIRED BY PERFECTION!
IF IT'S SO PERFECT, THEN WHY AM I FRIGHTENED?
BECAUSE EVERYTHING YOU SEE IS LETHAL! QUIET! LOOK THERE!
THE WHISPERERS! PHOBOS'S COURT! THE EYES AND EARS OF THE PRINCE OF PRINCES!
. . . youGuardians . . .

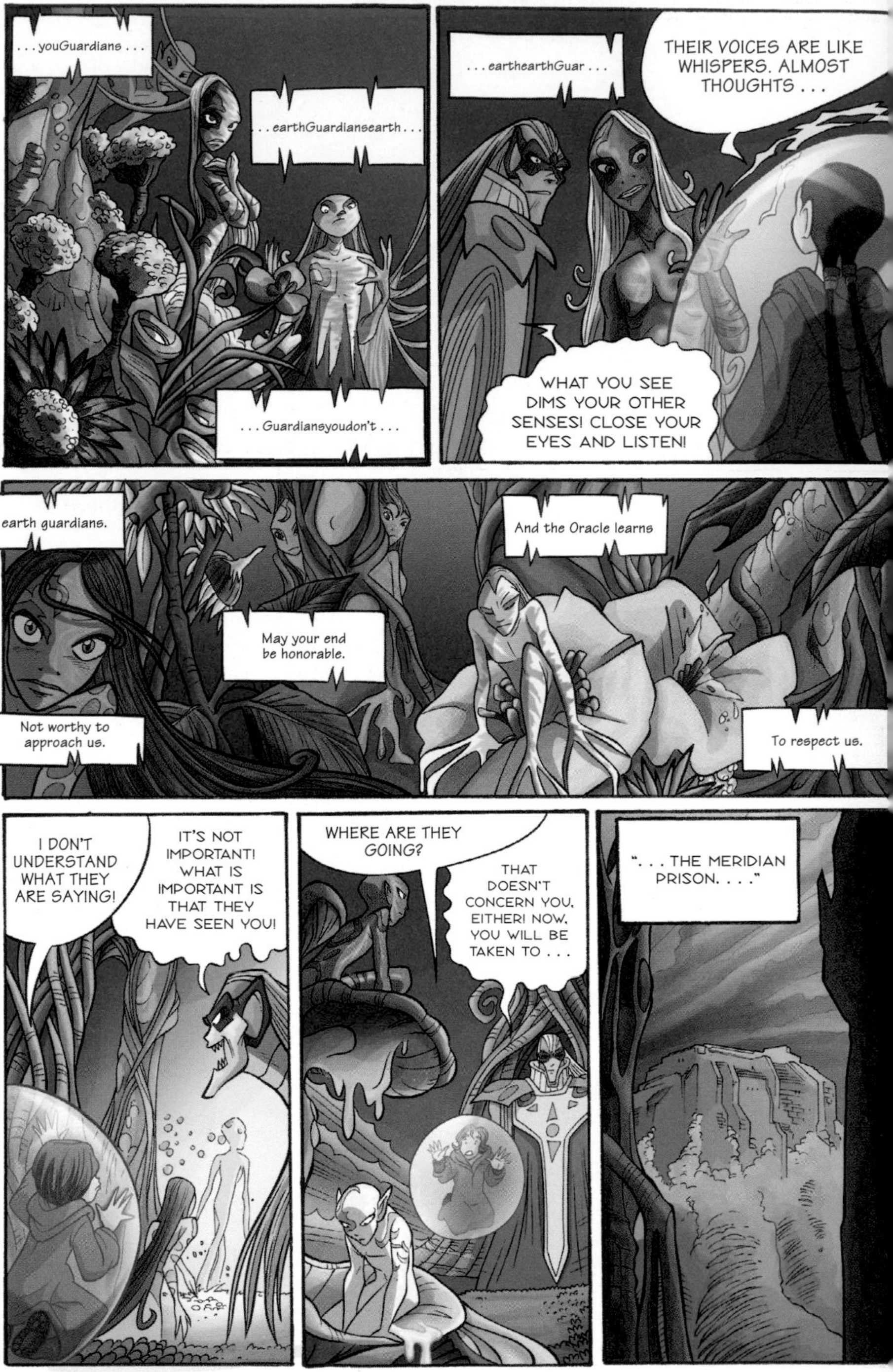

. . . youGuardians . . .
. . . earthGuardiansearth . . .
. . . Guardiansyoudon't . . .
. . . earthearthGuar . . .
THEIR VOICES ARE LIKE WHISPERS. ALMOST THOUGHTS . . .
WHAT YOU SEE DIMS YOUR OTHER SENSES! CLOSE YOUR EYES AND LISTEN!
You, earth guardians.
May your end be honorable.
Not worthy to approach us.
And the Oracle learns
To respect us.
I DON'T UNDERSTAND WHAT THEY ARE SAYING!
IT'S NOT IMPORTANT! WHAT IS IMPORTANT IS THAT THEY HAVE SEEN YOU!
WHERE ARE THEY GOING?
THAT DOESN'T CONCERN YOU, EITHER! NOW, YOU WILL BE TAKEN TO . . .
". . . THE MERIDIAN PRISON. . . ."

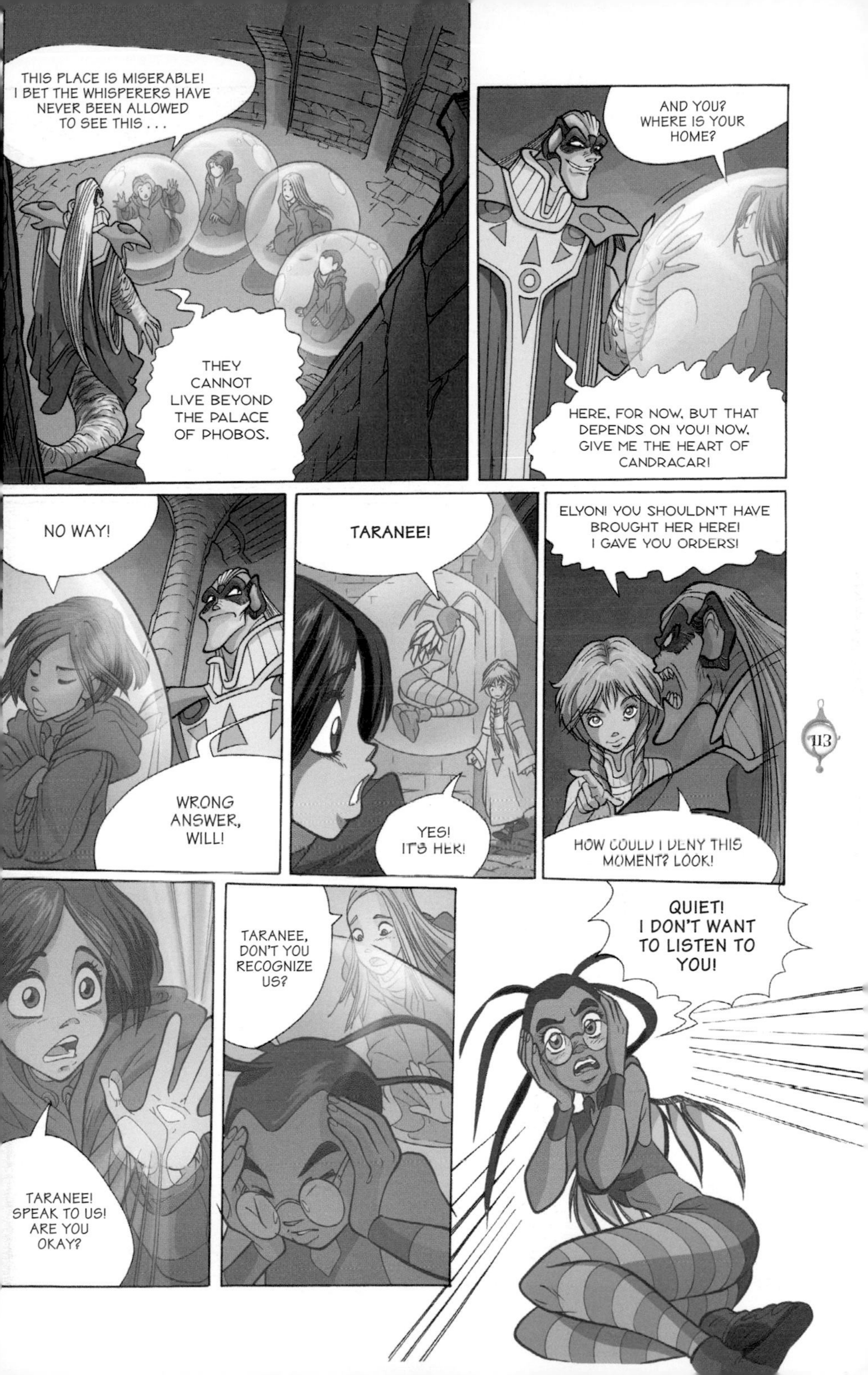
THIS PLACE IS MISERABLE! I BET THE WHISPERERS HAVE NEVER BEEN ALLOWED TO SEE THIS . . .
THEY CANNOT LIVE BEYOND THE PALACE OF PHOBOS.
AND YOU? WHERE IS YOUR HOME?
HERE, FOR NOW, BUT THAT DEPENDS ON YOU! NOW, GIVE ME THE HEART OF CANDRACAR!
NO WAY!
WRONG ANSWER, WILL!
TARANEE!
YES! IT'S HER!
ELYON! YOU SHOULDN'T HAVE BROUGHT HER HERE! I GAVE YOU ORDERS!
HOW COULD I DENY THIS MOMENT? LOOK!
TARANEE! SPEAK TO US! ARE YOU OKAY?
TARANEE, DON'T YOU RECOGNIZE US?
QUIET! I DON'T WANT TO LISTEN TO YOU!

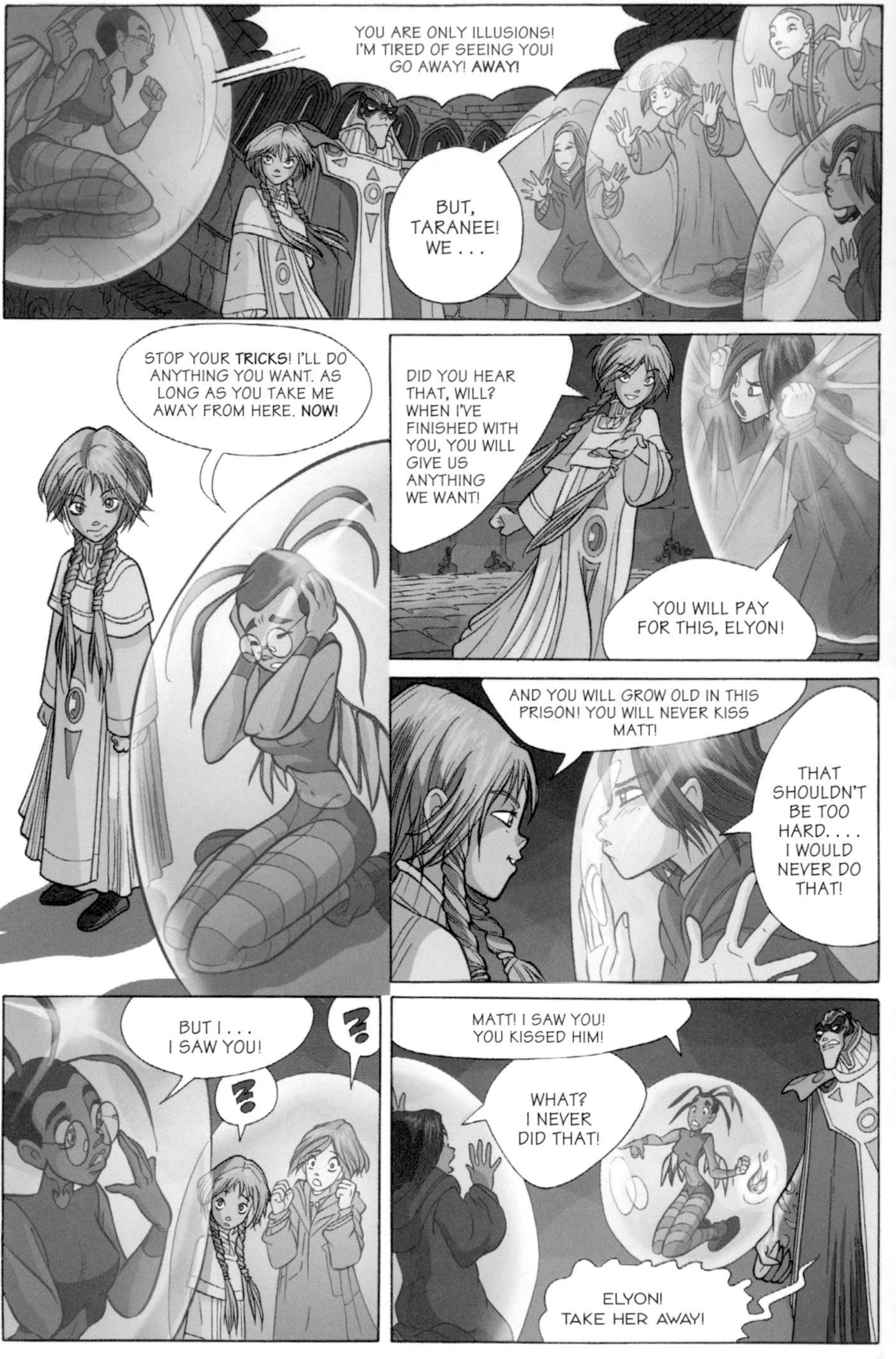
YOU ARE ONLY ILLUSIONS! I'M TIRED OF SEEING YOU! GO AWAY! **AWAY!**
BUT, TARANEE! WE . . .
STOP YOUR **TRICKS**! I'LL DO ANYTHING YOU WANT. AS LONG AS YOU TAKE ME AWAY FROM HERE. **NOW!**
DID YOU HEAR THAT, WILL? WHEN I'VE FINISHED WITH YOU, YOU WILL GIVE US ANYTHING WE WANT!
YOU WILL PAY FOR THIS, ELYON!
AND YOU WILL GROW OLD IN THIS PRISON! YOU WILL NEVER KISS MATT!
THAT SHOULDN'T BE TOO HARD. . . . I WOULD NEVER DO THAT!
BUT I . . . I SAW YOU!
?
?
MATT! I SAW YOU! YOU KISSED HIM!
WHAT? I NEVER DID THAT!
ELYON! TAKE HER AWAY!

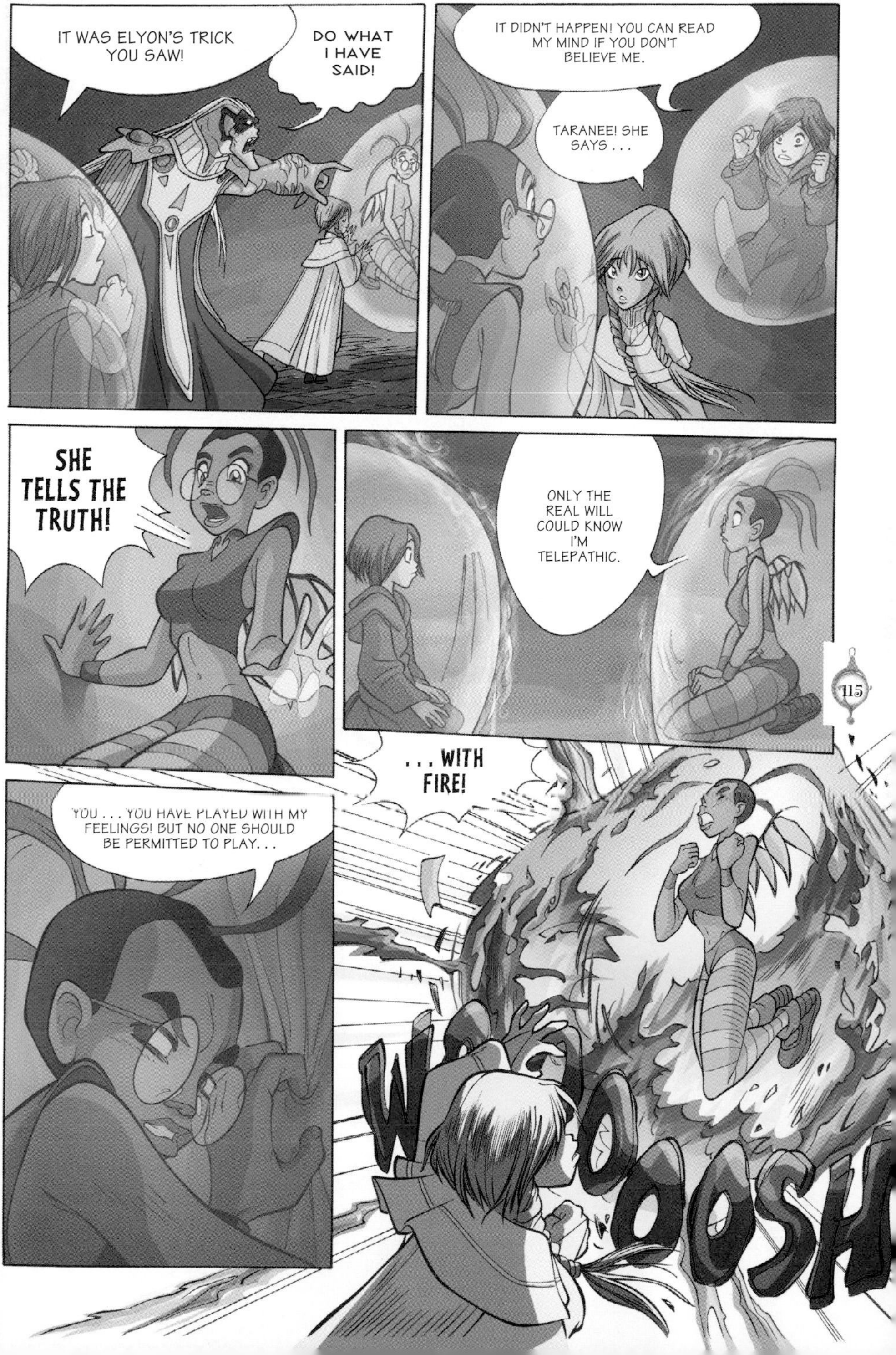
IT WAS ELYON'S TRICK YOU SAW!
DO WHAT I HAVE SAID!
IT DIDN'T HAPPEN! YOU CAN READ MY MIND IF YOU DON'T BELIEVE ME.
TARANEE! SHE SAYS . . .
SHE TELLS THE TRUTH!
ONLY THE REAL WILL COULD KNOW I'M TELEPATHIC.
YOU . . . YOU HAVE PLAYED WITH MY FEELINGS! BUT NO ONE SHOULD BE PERMITTED TO PLAY. . .
. . . WITH FIRE!
WHOOOSH

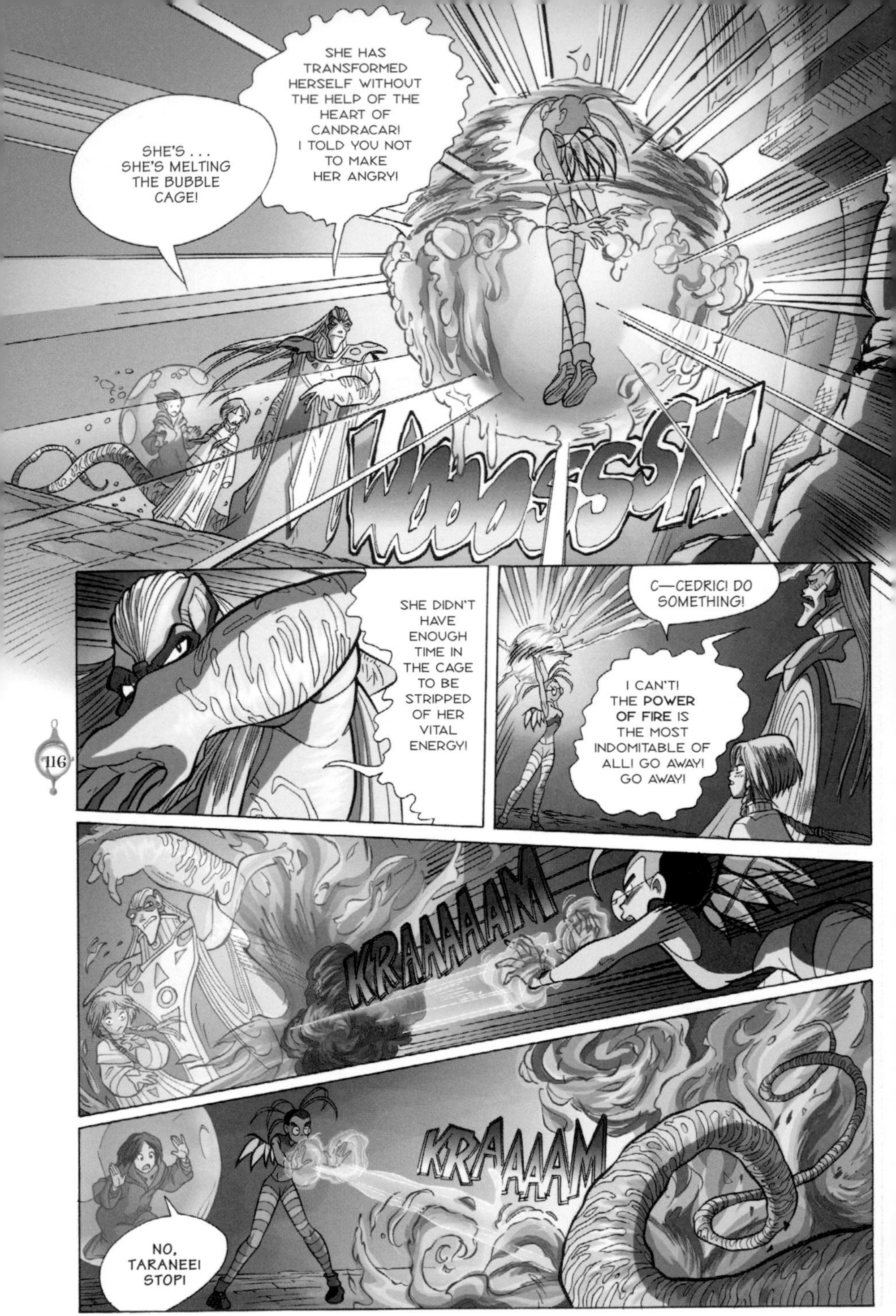
SHE'S . . . SHE'S MELTING THE BUBBLE CAGE!
SHE HAS TRANSFORMED HERSELF WITHOUT THE HELP OF THE HEART OF CANDRACAR! I TOLD YOU NOT TO MAKE HER ANGRY!
WHOOSSH!
SHE DIDN'T HAVE ENOUGH TIME IN THE CAGE TO BE STRIPPED OF HER VITAL ENERGY!
C—CEDRIC! DO SOMETHING!
I CAN'T! THE POWER OF FIRE IS THE MOST INDOMITABLE OF ALL! GO AWAY! GO AWAY!
KRAAAAAM
KRAAAAM
NO, TARANEE! STOP!

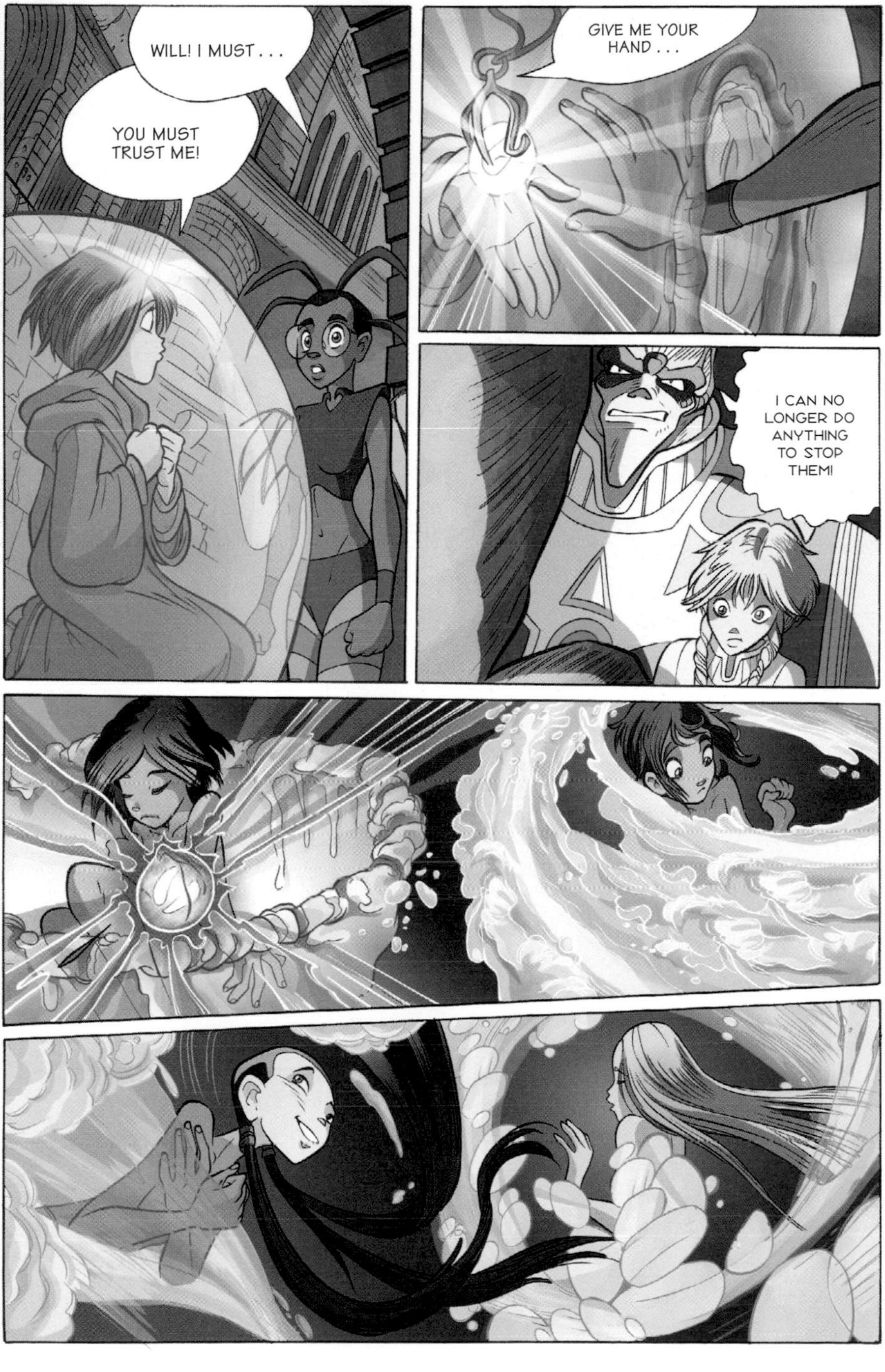
WILL! I MUST . . .
YOU MUST TRUST ME!
GIVE ME YOUR HAND . . .
I CAN NO LONGER DO ANYTHING TO STOP THEM!

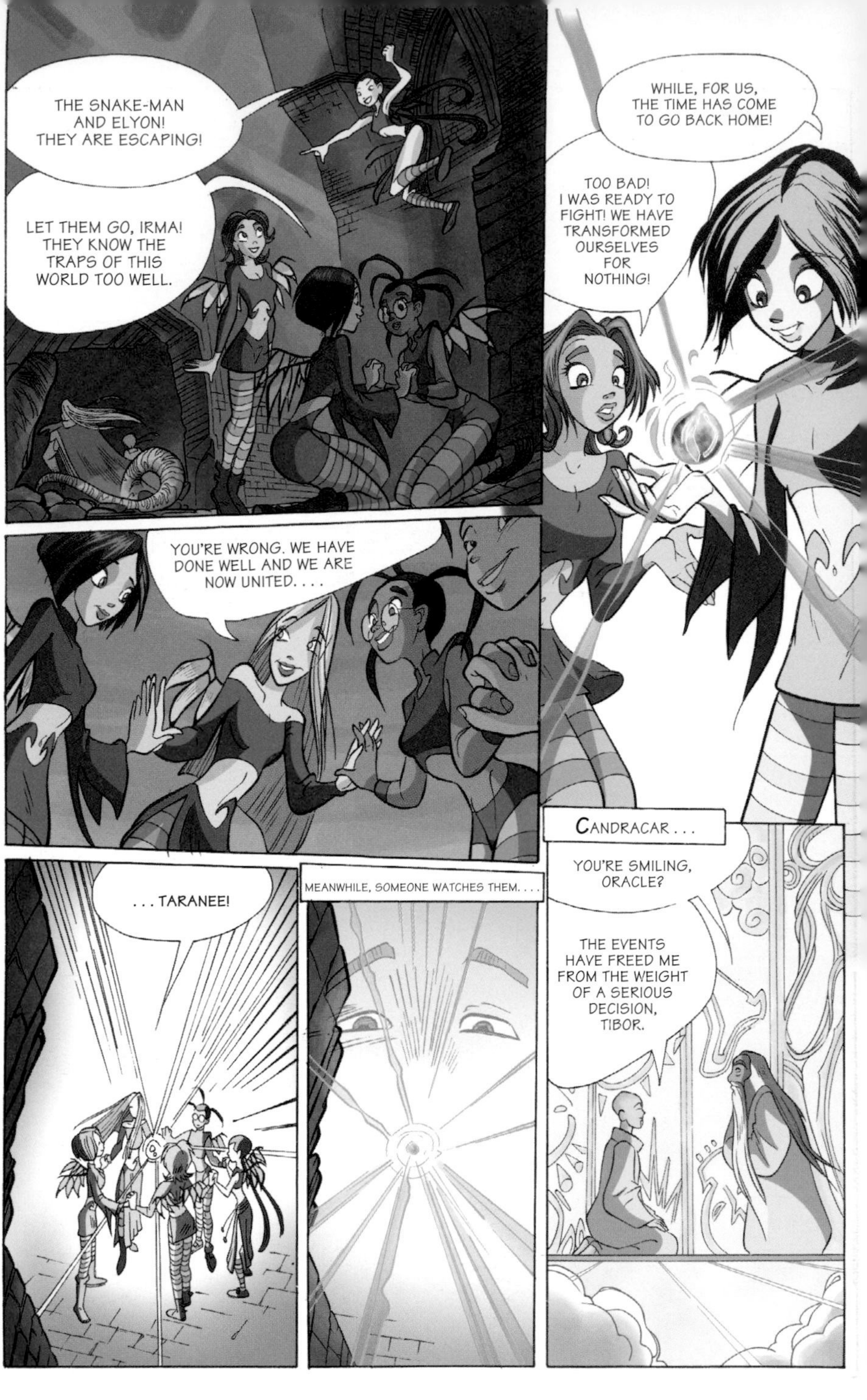

THE SNAKE-MAN AND ELYON! THEY ARE ESCAPING!
LET THEM GO, IRMA! THEY KNOW THE TRAPS OF THIS WORLD TOO WELL.
YOU'RE WRONG. WE HAVE DONE WELL AND WE ARE NOW UNITED. . . .
WHILE, FOR US, THE TIME HAS COME TO GO BACK HOME!
TOO BAD! I WAS READY TO FIGHT! WE HAVE TRANSFORMED OURSELVES FOR NOTHING!
. . . TARANEE!
MEANWHILE, SOMEONE WATCHES THEM. . . .
CANDRACAR . . .
YOU'RE SMILING, ORACLE?
THE EVENTS HAVE FREED ME FROM THE WEIGHT OF A SERIOUS DECISION, TIBOR.

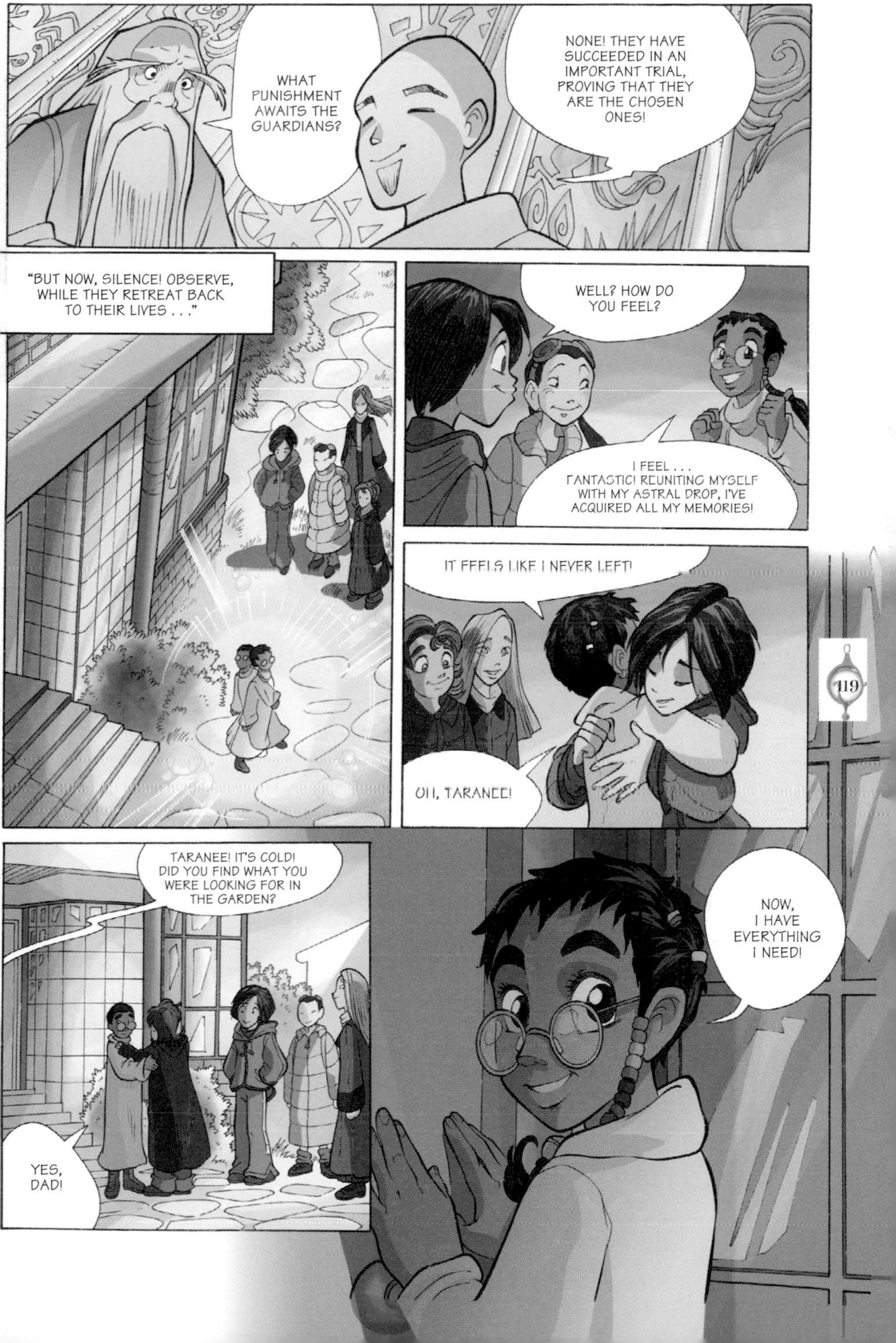
WHAT PUNISHMENT AWAITS THE GUARDIANS?
NONE! THEY HAVE SUCCEEDED IN AN IMPORTANT TRIAL, PROVING THAT THEY ARE THE CHOSEN ONES!
"BUT NOW, SILENCE! OBSERVE, WHILE THEY RETREAT BACK TO THEIR LIVES . . ."
WELL? HOW DO YOU FEEL?
I FEEL . . . FANTASTIC! REUNITING MYSELF WITH MY ASTRAL DROP, I'VE ACQUIRED ALL MY MEMORIES!
IT FEELS LIKE I NEVER LEFT!
OH, TARANEE!
TARANEE! IT'S COLD! DID YOU FIND WHAT YOU WERE LOOKING FOR IN THE GARDEN?
YES, DAD!
NOW, I HAVE EVERYTHING I NEED!

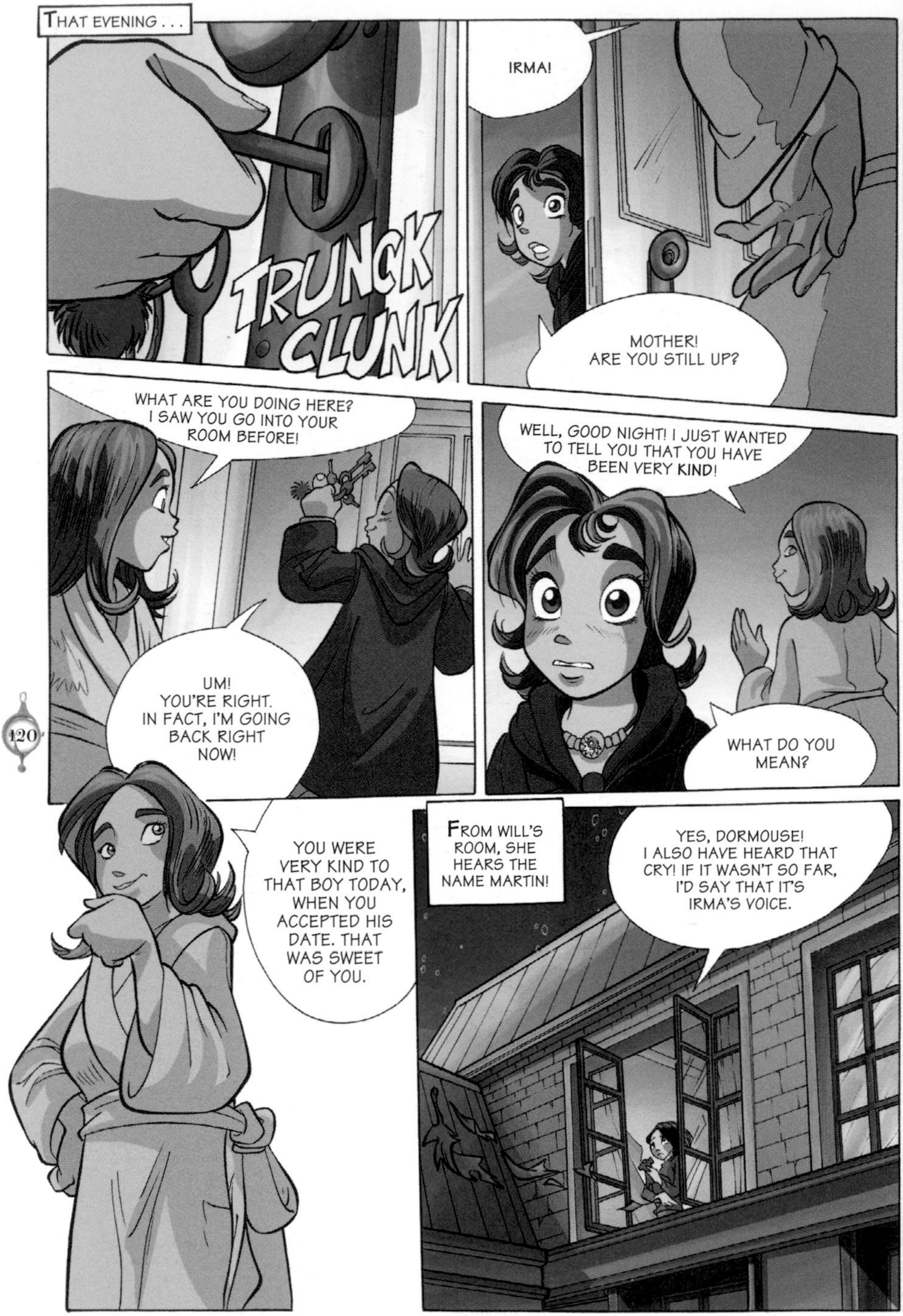
THAT EVENING . . .
TRUNCK CLUNK
IRMA!
MOTHER! ARE YOU STILL UP?
WHAT ARE YOU DOING HERE? I SAW YOU GO INTO YOUR ROOM BEFORE!
UM! YOU'RE RIGHT. IN FACT, I'M GOING BACK RIGHT NOW!
WELL, GOOD NIGHT! I JUST WANTED TO TELL YOU THAT YOU HAVE BEEN VERY KIND!
WHAT DO YOU MEAN?
YOU WERE VERY KIND TO THAT BOY TODAY, WHEN YOU ACCEPTED HIS DATE. THAT WAS SWEET OF YOU.
FROM WILL'S ROOM, SHE HEARS THE NAME MARTIN!
YES, DORMOUSE! I ALSO HAVE HEARD THAT CRY! IF IT WASN'T SO FAR, I'D SAY THAT IT'S IRMA'S VOICE.

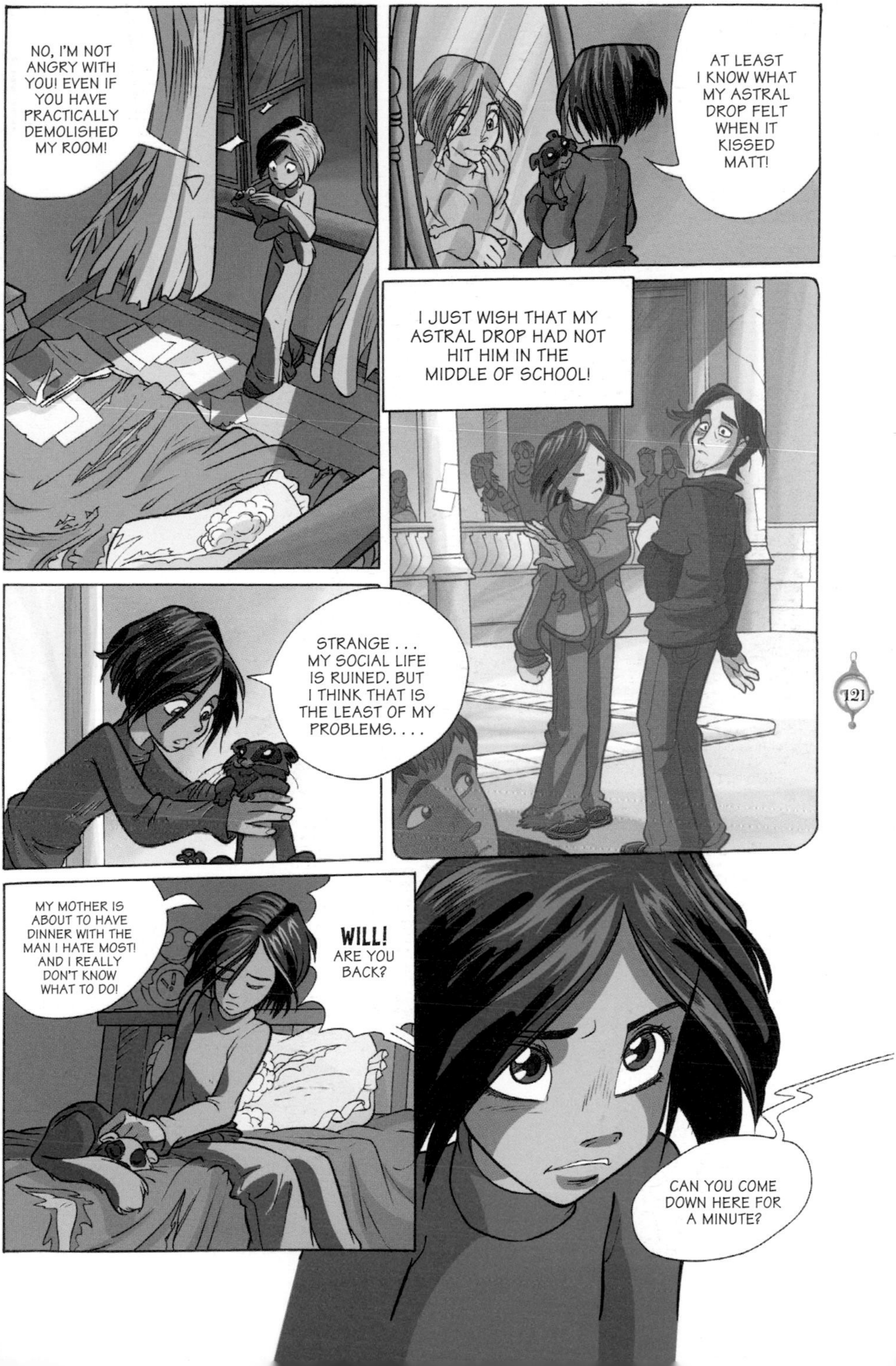
NO, I'M NOT ANGRY WITH YOU! EVEN IF YOU HAVE PRACTICALLY DEMOLISHED MY ROOM!
AT LEAST I KNOW WHAT MY ASTRAL DROP FELT WHEN IT KISSED MATT!
I JUST WISH THAT MY ASTRAL DROP HAD NOT HIT HIM IN THE MIDDLE OF SCHOOL!
STRANGE . . . MY SOCIAL LIFE IS RUINED. BUT I THINK THAT IS THE LEAST OF MY PROBLEMS. . . .
MY MOTHER IS ABOUT TO HAVE DINNER WITH THE MAN I HATE MOST! AND I REALLY DON'T KNOW WHAT TO DO!
WILL! ARE YOU BACK?
CAN YOU COME DOWN HERE FOR A MINUTE?

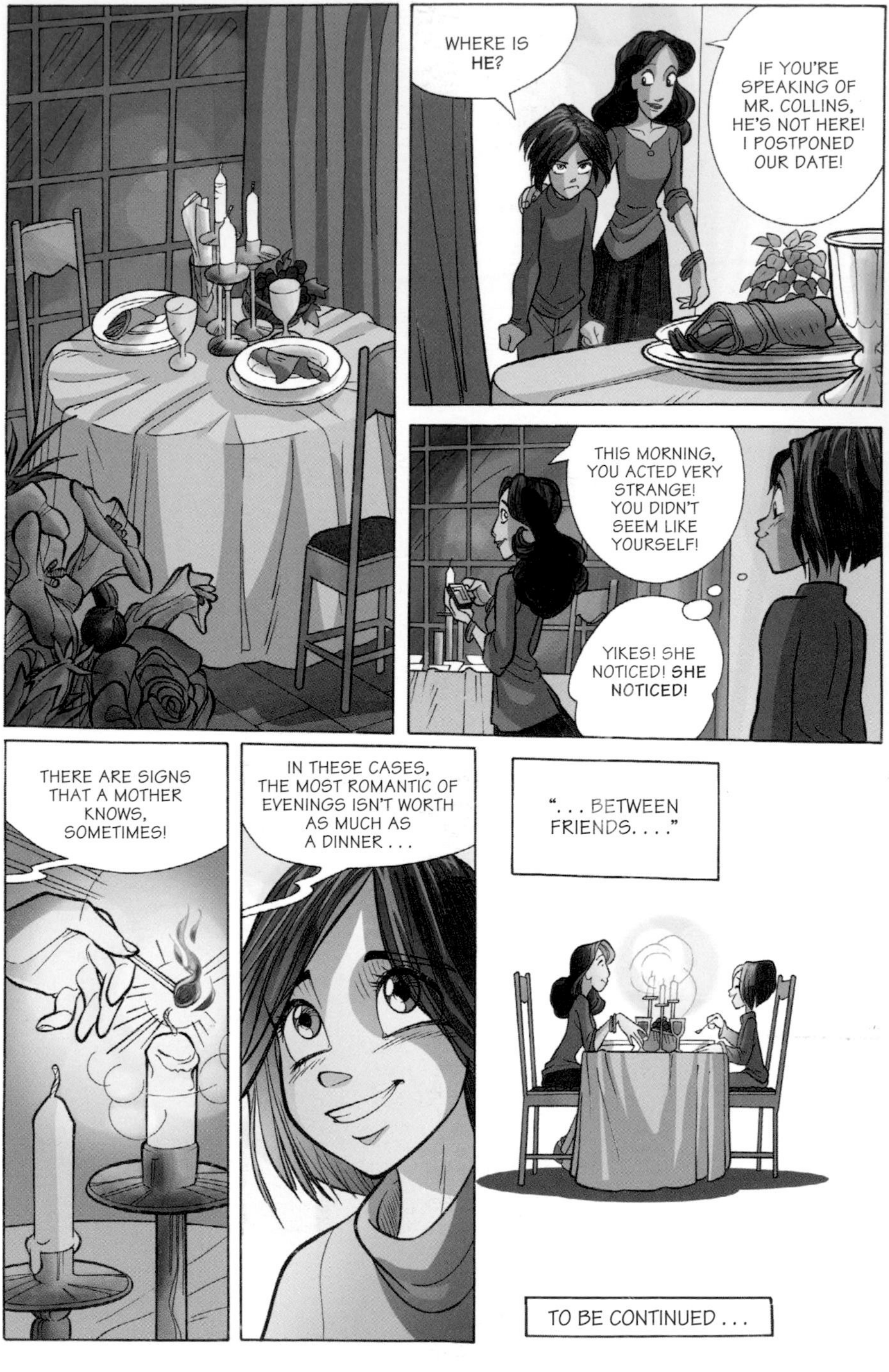
WHERE IS HE?
IF YOU'RE SPEAKING OF MR. COLLINS, HE'S NOT HERE! I POSTPONED OUR DATE!
THIS MORNING, YOU ACTED VERY STRANGE! YOU DIDN'T SEEM LIKE YOURSELF!
YIKES! SHE NOTICED! SHE NOTICED!
THERE ARE SIGNS THAT A MOTHER KNOWS, SOMETIMES!
IN THESE CASES, THE MOST ROMANTIC OF EVENINGS ISN'T WORTH AS MUCH AS A DINNER . . .
". . . BETWEEN FRIENDS. . . ."
TO BE CONTINUED . . .